a nest egg

POACHED

By

S.C. STRANGE

Cover art by Sue C. Hughey

Published by:
Associated Arts Publisher
536 Tiara Drive
Grand Junction, CO 81507
970-241-8024
AssociatedArtsPublisher@optimum.net

First Edition
Printed in the United States of America

ISBN-10: 0984035809
ISBN-13: 9780984035809
Library of Congress Control Number: 2011939343
Associated Arts Publisher, Grand Junction, CO

Dedicated to Hager,
my steadfast traveling companion
on the road of life

Chapter One

Rose examined her reflection in the motel room mirror. There were a few more strands of gray in her dark-brown hair, and the laugh lines emanating from the corners of her green eyes had deepened, but all in all, she was pleased with her appearance. *Not bad for a 56-year-old broad,* she thought.

She picked the newspaper from off the bureau and sat down on the edge of the bed to once more study the picture of her handsome husband, he in his best suit and tie, and she in her favorite cocktail gown, clinging to his arm as they smiled for the camera. The article beneath it read, ***Retiring Veterinarian feted.*** *Friends and colleagues gathered at the Salina Country Club to honor longtime local veterinarian, Dr. Daniel Good, who retired earlier this month. He and his...*

Rose heard Dan fumbling with his key at the motel room door. She tossed the paper aside and jumped up from the bed to greet him. "What took you so... The look on her husband's face stopped her. "What's wrong?"

Without looking her in the eyes, he shook his head and gently pushed her aside to close the door. He sat down on the bed, lowered his head, and as he had always done when words couldn't express what he was feeling, ran his fingers through his thick crop of silver hair. She sat down and put her arm around him. "Dan, what's wrong?"

A sob came from deep down inside, and he turned to engulf her in his arms.

She had seen him in tears before, but not like this. "Dan, what is it?"

He abruptly stood, and covering his mouth, stumbled to the bathroom. The door slammed, and the lock clicked.

She put her ear against the door and could hear him retching on the other side. "Dan, you're scaring me! Are you sick? Tell me what's wrong."

He coughed and said, "I will. I will. Just give me a few minutes. I'm going to take a quick shower."

Recalling his heart attack two years earlier, she said, "For Pete's sake, at least unlock the door. I won't come in unless I have to, but unlock the door."

After she heard the lock click, she pulled a chair up to the door and sat down. She called, "I'll be right here if you need me."

Leaning against the door and listening to the sounds on the other side, she tried to think of what terrible thing had caused her husband to act so out of character. They had been through tragedies before in their thirty-five years together, but she had never seen him so distraught. *Larry! It must have something to do with Larry. He must have been in an accident, or maybe even died. That must be it. Larry never would have missed last night otherwise. That must be why we haven't been able to reach him.*

She ran through the events of the night before. What a wonderful time it was...all their friends were there to wish them well on their retirement and bon voyage on their great adventure. All their friends that is, except Larry. He had organized the going-away-party at the country club and was supposed to have been the Master of Ceremonies. Everyone experienced an awkward moment waiting for him to make an appearance. Finally, another friend stepped in to take over that job.

Wondering what might have happened to him, Dan had slipped away from the party several times during the evening to call Larry's home. On the first call, there was no answer. Dan just assumed Larry was on his way to the club. An hour later, Charlotte had answered, but Dan said she was so incoherent that, after a while, he had to hang up on her. She had sobered up somewhat when he called the third time. She said Larry was asleep, and that she didn't want to be bothered by Dan's calling again.

Larry may have been dead then, instead of asleep. Charlotte lives in such an alcoholic stupor, he could be dead for a week before she'd notice. Poor Larry. And poor Dan. Larry's the closest thing Dan ever had to a brother. They've known each other since they were both in diapers. They went to the same schools, played on the same teams, joined the Navy together, were in the same fraternity... they even proposed to the same girl. I've always felt a little guilty that Larry might have married Charlotte on the rebound. Their courtship was so short.

The door jerked open and she nearly fell off the chair into Dan. As steam poured out of the bathroom, he helped her to her feet and pulled the chair away from the doorway.

She stood on her tiptoes and wrapped her arms around his neck. "Feel better, Hon?" He nodded.

"It's Larry, Isn't it?" she asked.

"Yes."

"Is he dead?"

"No," Dan growled, "not yet. But he will be if I ever catch up to him."

She jerked her arms down and stepped back. "What on earth would make you say such a thing?"

"Before I tell you, Rose, sit down. It's bad."

She searched her husband's face for clues as he sank down on the edge of the bed. She slipped back into the chair.

"Our dream is dead, Rose. Everything we had is gone. Everything we've worked for all our lives…all the things we had planned for the future." He waved his hand in a sweeping gesture. "It's gone…kaput!"

She sat silent for a moment, letting the words sink in. "But how can that be? I didn't think we had any investments left in the stock market. Besides …"

"He stole it, Rose. He cleaned us out. He took it all."

"LARRY? You mean LARRY?"

"Yeah, Larry. The guy I trusted with my life. He managed to gain complete control over all our finances. He had power of attorney over all our affairs."

"What is that?"

"It's a piece of paper that says he can legally do anything in my name that I could do myself, such as sign checks or withdraw money from our accounts." Dan picked up a shoe and threw it against the wall. "And that's just what the son of a bitch did!"

Rose jumped up from the chair and crossed the room to retrieve the shoe. "Dan! Look at this mark you put on the wall! And there may be people next door. Now settle down or you're going to give yourself another heart attack."

"I must say you're taking this well, Rose. Have you fully understood what I've been telling you? That we're broke? That we don't own a damn thing anymore?"

She dropped the shoe and sat back down. "Of course I understand what you're saying. What I want to know is how he got that piece of paper in the first place, that thing that allowed him to steal from us."

"It happened when I had my heart attack. Remember, besides you and the boys, he was the only one allowed to visit me in Intensive Care? Well, I hadn't been in there any time at all when he brought in some papers he said I needed to sign. I was really out of it, and barely remember the conversation, but he said it was for you...that if I didn't make it, he'd be able to take care of things for you. Until today, I had completely forgotten about it." Dan shook his head. "I really screwed up, Rose."

She reached over and took her husband's hand. "How can you blame yourself? Being our financial advisor all these years, Larry would have been the logical one to take care of things. I remember him telling me then that 'all I had to worry about was you.' My God, he's been like one of the family for years. Why wouldn't we trust him?"

Dan clasped both of his hands around hers. "But I should have paid closer attention myself to what was going on. I turned everything over to him: our books, our taxes, every one of our investments...everything. I didn't want to be bothered with all the paper work. All I cared about were the results. And through the years he made us some good money, enough to let us live the retirement we've always dreamed."

"Why would he do this to us?" she asked.

Dan's squeezed his eyes shut and reached up to pinch the bridge of his nose. He choked out the words, "That's the hardest pill to swallow, the betrayal by someone so close. It really hurts."

"Did you get the cashier's check at the bank this morning?"

Dan shook his head. "That's how I found out about all this. Wanda at the bank said Larry was in late yesterday afternoon. Larry said you and I had a lot to do before we left town and that we had asked him to pick up the cash so we could finalize payment on the RoadAbode, plus some other incidentals we needed to pay off."

"Did he completely clean out our bank account?"

"Not quite. He was very generous. Of the five hundred thousand or so we had in there, he left us exactly one thousand dollars."

"How did you find out about our investments?"

Just then the phone rang and Dan grabbed it up. "Yes. Hi, Bill. Yeah, I'm late. Sorry about that, but something very unexpected has come up. Listen, Bill, the wife and I need to have a little powwow with you. It's pretty close to lunchtime right now, and this may take some time. How Does your schedule look for getting together, say about one o'clock? Good. See you then."

Dan hung up the phone and sat glumly staring into space.

Speaking of lunchtime," said Rose, "I'm starved."

Dan came out of his stupor. "Well, we can forget about having brunch at the club like we'd planned. Lets go down to the lobby and see if there's anything left from their complimentary breakfast."

• • •

A uniformed girl was busily putting away paper plates and napkins when they entered the serving niche off the motel lobby. She picked up a tray that still held several donuts.

"Uhhh, miss?" said Dan as he held out his hand for the tray. "We'll take those off your hands for you. We really slept in late this morning. Any coffee left?"

"I'm sorry, sir, but I've already emptied and cleaned the pot."

"That's okay," said Dan. "I see there's still some orange juice."

He handed the donut tray to Rose.

The girl seemed rather flustered. "I've put all the cups away and …"

"I saw right where you put them." Dan opened a cupboard door and removed two paper cups. "You don't need to bother. We can help ourselves." He emptied the juice pitcher. "What do we have to complement the donuts?"

"Breakfast is available from six until ten, sir, and it's way after that. I'm supposed to have everything put away and this area cleaned up by eleven o'clock."

"Oh, we're sorry. I guess we're interfering with that." He opened the cupboard again, quickly extracted a paper plate, and placed the donuts on it. Handing the girl back the tray, he said, "We'll get out of your way right now." He spied a lonely pair of boiled eggs and popped them onto the plate. Pocketing a lone banana, he turned to the girl and said, "Don't worry, miss, we won't mess up a table. We'll just take this back to our room."

Looking relieved, she sighed and continued her work.

Back in their room, Rose took some tissues from the vanity and placed them on the small table. Dan had already stuffed a boiled egg into his mouth. She sat down and looked at the contents of the paper plate. "This is the brunch I looked forward to all morning?"

Dan wiped his hands on a tissue and reached over to lay a hand on her shoulder. "I'm sorry, sweetie. That little bit of money in the bank isn't going to go very far. We're going to have to hang on to every penny until we find that son of a bitch and try to get our money back. Eat up, now. We have to check out of this place by noon and have the rental car back by five o'clock. We have a lot to do between then and now."

Chapter Two

As Dan drove, Rose checked over the motel bill before putting it in her purse. "Almost seven-hundred dollars, nearly all of what we have left in the bank. How in the world are we going to pay it and still have money to live on?"

"Like a lot of folks do, Rose. We'll just pay the minimum every month and pay interest on the balance. We've always paid our charge cards in full, and I hate to have to pay the interest, but that's what we'll have to do until we get our savings back."

She shook her head. "I guess we should've taken the Bennington's offer to let us stay with them until we were ready to leave town."

"It was nice of her to offer, Rose, but that woman could talk the ears off an elephant. You notice Benny has his hearing aid off most of the time when she's around."

Rose gazed out the car window as the town she had known all her life passed by. "I guess we won't be leaving here after all. This town's been good to us, but I was so longing to get away from it. Your clinic has always kept us from doing much traveling. But where are we ..."

"Don't worry, we'll get to travel, Rose," he interrupted. "It may be clean to hell and back, but I'm going to track down that black-hearted snake in the grass and get whatever's left of our money if it takes the rest of my life." He glanced over at her. "It may be a long, hard road, Rosie. Are you willing to lead the gypsy life for a while? Maybe for a long while?"

Rose turned toward her husband. "You know I'm a hippie at heart. I wouldn't miss it for the world. Besides, I don't want to stick around here and endure the pity of all of our friends."

He reached over and patted her on the knee. "It might have been fun to find out just who our real friends are, though."

There was little traffic downtown, and they had no trouble finding curbside parking. Dan opened the car door for Rose, and as she stepped out she asked, "What are we doing here in front of Larry's office building? I thought you said he had skipped town."

"He has. I called his office from the bank this morning as soon as I got the bad news. Thelma said he hadn't shown up for any of his appointments. I asked her to check our file. I could hear her shuffling through papers, and when she came back on she said, rather snippily, "Well, I'm surprised to see you've closed out all your accounts. Have you taken your business elsewhere?"

"What did you tell her?"

"Nothing. I just told her we'd drop over in a little while. She said Larry had a full schedule, but when he came in, she'd tell him to expect us."

They took the elevator to the second floor of the office building, and walked a short distance down the hall. The brass placard on the door they entered was engraved with the words Larry Near Financial Services. Thelma, a graying spinster with the demeanor of a stern librarian, was on the phone and acknowledged their arrival with a curt nod of her head. "If you hear from him, please have him call his office right away. Thank you." She hung up the phone and stood to greet Dan and Rose, "Hello, Dr. and Mrs. Good."

After all these years, she still won't call us by our first names thought Rose. *Her manner is as stiff as her 1960s hairdo.*

"It's very unlike Mr. Near to be late," Thelma continued, "but I'm sure he'll be here any minute. May I offer you some ..."

"Better sit back down, Thelma," Dan interrupted. "We have some disturbing things to discuss."

Dan pulled up two chairs in front of Thelma's desk, and he and Rose seated themselves across from her. He looked down at the folder on her desk, labeled Good and picked it up. "I see you left our file out after my call."

"Yes," she answered. "I assumed the reason for your visit was to discuss it with Mr. Near."

Without answering, Dan opened the folder and began thumbing through it. Thelma quickly reached across the desk and snatched it from him. "These are private files, and Mr. Near would not approve of your viewing them without his being present."

Dan, just as quickly, snatched the folder back. "BY GOD, THESE PAPERS HAVE TO DO WITH ME AND ROSE! I'LL VIEW THEM IF I, BY GOD, WANT TO! And for your information, Mr. Near won't be present today, next week, or anytime soon!

Rose laid her hand on her husband's arm. "Dan, take it easy. You're getting all red. Don't take this out on Thelma. She's just doing her job."

Thelma bristled with indignation. "What do you mean, he won't be present any time soon? He would have told me if…"

"Here's the ugly truth, Thelma," interrupted Dan. "He closed out all our accounts, including our bank account, took the money for himself, and then evidently blew town."

Thelma sat stupefied for a few seconds. "That just isn't so. After you called, I went through your file again myself. Everything was in order, including your specific written instructions to Mr. Near to close out all your accounts, including your IRAs and 401(k) plan with penalties."

"Tell me, Thelma," said Dan, "in all the years you've worked for Larry, have you ever known a client to close all of his retirement accounts at once, knowing the penalties he'd have to pay?"

Thelma thought for a moment. "Well, I do remember one who cashed in his IRA early. But that was because …"

Dan interrupted, "Whatever the "because" was, is immaterial, Thelma. I gave no written or oral instructions. Larry must have included those instructions in our file for your benefit so that if you or the other girl, Mitzy, ever had the occasion to check it before he finished the job of cleaning us out, you wouldn't be suspicious."

"Mitzy didn't show up today either," said Thelma. "But then she does that a lot. Come to think about it, her trashy cupie doll collection and all the framed photographs she had all over her office are gone."

Behind her thick glasses, Thelma's eyes widened with comprehension. "That must be it! That shameless hussy has been after him ever since she started working here. I can't believe he would . . ." Thelma fell across her desk, beating it with her fists and screaming like a banshee. "He loves ME! I KNOW he does. WHY, Larry, WHY, WHY, WHY have you done this to me?"

Dan's eyes met Rose's. "Muddy waters really do run deep," he whispered.

"Still," corrected Rose.

"Okay, I'll be still. But see if you can calm this woman down. I've got some questions I need to ask her. I'm going into Larry's office to call the police and do some snooping in there."

Thelma sobbed uncontrollably while Rose got behind her and, with effort, pulled the woman's ample upper body off the desk and back upright in her chair. Rose noticed a box of tissues on Thelma's desk and pushed it over to her. She then gently straightened Thelma's glasses, which were hanging by one ear, and tried to pat down her disheveled hairdo. She pulled her chair up next to Thelma's and wrapped an arm around her quaking shoulders. "Do you feel like talking about it, Thelma?"

"I . . . I just can't believe he would run off with that hussy," she sobbed, "after all we've meant to each other. That witch must have put some sort of spell over him."

"You said he loved you. Were you and Larry having an affair?"

Thelma stiffened at the question. "Oh, my, no! Larry was much too much of a gentleman to ever take advantage of me like that. I know he was miserable in his marriage.

He often confided in me. It was just a matter of time before he left her, or she drank herself to death. He only stayed with her out of pity."

"Has Larry actually told you he loves you?"

Thelma dabbed at her eyes under her glasses and loudly blew her nose. "Not in so many words. He didn't have to. His actions made it so obvious."

Rose was having difficulty picturing the exceedingly handsome, worldly Larry making passes at the pathetic creature sitting beside her.

"What sort of actions?"

Thelma's voice softened, and she spoke as if she were in a trance. "For one thing, there were all the flowers."

"Larry sent you flowers?"

"Yes. He never missed a single Secretary's Day. Not once in the thirteen years I've worked for him. And he always included a sweet note, like, 'Thelma, Dear, you're the best!'"

Rose grabbed a tissue out of the box and snorted into it, hoping Thelma would think she was blowing her nose instead of stifling an involuntary laugh.

It worked. Thelma smiled sweetly at the perceived empathy. She continued, "And there were the tender touches. Once in a while he would hand me a piece of paper or something and purposely brush his hand against mine."

This poor woman is delusional, thought Rose.

Dan returned and looked shocked at Thelma's appearance. A smile played around his lips as he asked, "Do you feel up to answering a few questions, Thelma?"

"I suppose so."

"Are you the one who runs the computer?"

"No. That's why Mr. Near hired that flaming-haired hussy, Mitzy. I've had very little experience with computers. However, I am currently taking a night class and was hoping to become proficient so that I...we could get rid of her. Mitzy supposedly was a computer expert. At least that's what she put down on her job application."

"I need to see that application. Could you please get it and make a couple of copies for me?

Thelma arose from her desk and waddled to the file room, blowing her nose on the way.

"My God," said Dan, "that melted black mascara and hair standing on end reminded me of a frightened pet raccoon I once operated on."

"Shhhh!" said Rose. "She'll hear you. The poor woman's been through enough as it is."

Thelma's hosiery made swishing noises as she returned with the requested copies. She laid them on her desk, extracted her purse from a drawer, and excusing herself, left the office.

"What do you hope to learn from Mitzy's application?" asked Rose.

Dan put on his reading glasses and began studying the copy. "Whatever I can. For instance, I need her address to see if she's also left town. And if she and Larry are together, and it appears they are, they may show up at her relatives. Yes, here it is. It lists her next of kin, her parents, in some little town in Kentucky."

"Why do you need two copies?"

"One's for the police. They're not going to go chasing off to Kentucky, but they'll probably want to contact the authorities there. However, I'm going to ask them to hold off until we can do some checking there ourselves on the sly. Small-town law has a tendency to protect its own."

"Us? In Kentucky? That's a long way from Kansas. Why don't we just hire a private detective who knows how to handle these things?"

Dan gave her a look that said 'Duh.'

"Oh," she said, "I forgot."

Thelma slipped back into the office. She had washed her face, repaired her hairdo, and reapplied lipstick and mascara.

"Feeling better?" asked Rose.

"Much better, thank you." Through clenched teeth, Thelma asked, "Now, what do we need to do to get those two criminals behind bars? I will help in any way I can."

Hell hath no fury, thought Rose.

Dan hugged her around the shoulders and said, "That's the spirit, Thelma. You can start by copying everything in our file. The police will likely want the originals for evidence, as well as the office computer."

"I'll get right to it," said Thelma, "but first I've got to make some calls and cancel appointments."

Thelma was on the phone when there was a tapping on the front door. She put her hand over the mouthpiece and said, "I locked the door. Would you mind getting that, Dan, and tell whoever it is that we're closed for business for the day?"

Dan? thought Rose. *Not Dr. Good? It must have been that hug. Better watch out, Dan.*

Dan let the two detectives in and led them to Larry's office. While he was explaining the case to them, Rose assisted Thelma at the copier. Glancing over, she noticed new streaks of mascara starting down Thelma's cheeks. Thelma whined, "What's to become of me? No one's going to hire a woman my age, no matter how much experience I have."

"Do you think you could run this business?" asked Rose.

"I DO run this business. Mr...Larry couldn't have managed without me. All he ever did was schmooze the clients. I did all the real work"

"Then why not just continue here? I bet if you got yourself a good lawyer, this business could be yours."

Before she could answer, Dan appeared at the copier. "Thelma, the detectives need to speak with you now. By the way, I found this in Larry's top desk drawer. I think it will be of interest to you."

Thelma unfolded the document and quickly read it. "Is this for REAL? He turned the business over to ME? Is this a legal document?"

Dan nodded. "But have an accountant go over the books before you accept it, Thelma, and make sure Larry didn't leave you with a pile of debts."

Thelma threw her arms around Dan and loudly bawled into his chest. The two detectives hurried out of Larry's office to see what the commotion was. Thelma turned loose of Dan and excused herself to go to the restroom.

"It's okay, officers," said Dan." This whole thing has been pretty upsetting for her." Following their stare, Dan looked down at his chest. His white shirt was covered with wet, black streaks and red smudges.

Chapter Three

"We can just leave the car and walk from here," said Dan as he and Rose exited the office building. "Mitzy's place is in that fancy apartment building around the corner and down the street a couple of blocks."

"You mean the Golden Arms?" asked Rose. "How in the world can a girl with just an office job, even a computer expert, afford to pay that kind of rent?"

"From the looks of things so far, I doubt that she was the one paying the rent," Dan answered. "It was probably coming out of our investments, compliments of Larry."

"What are you going to do about that shirt?" asked Rose.

Dan opened the trunk of the car and dug around in his suitcase. He pulled out a sweater vest, pulled it over his head, and slammed down the trunk lid. "How's that for a quick fix?"

Inside the apartment building's foyer, Dan found the name, 'Mitzy McCoy,' and dialed her number on the apartment phone. After several rings without an answer, Dan dialed the manager.

A singsong male voice came over the speaker. "This is the manager speaking. How may I help you?"

"I need to speak with you concerning one of your tenants, a Miss Mitzy McCoy."

"May I ask what this is about?"

"She seems to be missing," Dan answered.

"MISSING? Have you tried her place of employment?"

"Yes, sir. I just came from there after talking with the police."

"The POLICE? I'm buzzing you in."

A slight little man in his-mid fifties met them just inside the door and ushered them into his office. After introductions, he said, "Before I allow you to check Miss McCoy's apartment, I need to know what your relationship is with her."

Uncharacteristically, Dan was at a loss for words.

"I'm her sister, from Kentucky," Rose lied.

"Oh, yes, I remember her saying she was from Kentucky. She certainly has a distinct southern drawl."

"Ye-us, suh, it's a hawd thang to git rid of," said Rose.

Dan stared wide-eyed at Rose while the manager unlocked a cabinet and retrieved a key to Mitzy's apartment.

"Follow me," said the manager.

They stepped off the elevator on the top floor, and the manager led them down the wide hallway where he stopped and knocked on an apartment door flanked by potted palms. Dan asked, "She has a penthouse apartment?"

"Yes, it's one of our nicest." After several more knocks, the manager unlocked the door.

It opened into a spacious, beautifully furnished apartment with a bird's-eye view from the balcony of the city park across the street. "Hellooo," he called. "Is anyone home?"

"My . . . Mah goodness," said Rose, "Ah had no ideah mah sistah was doin' so weall." Rose marched directly into the bedroom, which reeked of cheap perfume. Empty coat hangers littered the king-sized bed and the floor around it. She opened the large, walk-in closet, where only two garments remained hanging. By the time she had pulled out several empty dresser drawers, the two men had entered the room.

"Well, Rose," said Dan, "wherever your sister went, it appears she went voluntarily, and in somewhat of a hurry."

After quickly surveying the bedroom, the manager stepped into the adjoining bathroom and flipped on the light. "Oh, dear. This is *most* unacceptable!"

"What is it? Asked Dan as he and Rose tried to see around him.

"Candles! There must be a hundred candles in various stages of meltdown. How will we *ever* get all the wax off of this beautiful jet tub? Wax has even run down the sides of the tub and into this lovely plush carpeting." The manager stood with his hands on his hips, shaking his head. "The worst part of it is, this sort of thing is definitely against the building's fire code."

Rose made note of the empty champagne bottle lying next to the trash receptacle and the two glasses on the edge of the tub.

"Was her rent paid up?" Dan asked.

"As I recall, her six-month lease expired a couple of weeks ago. When I contacted the owner of the building about it, he told me not to worry. Evidently, he does a lot of business with her employer, who assured him that a new lease would be signed and the rent paid by Monday." The manager slapped his hand to his cheek. "Monday. That's today."

"Well, I assume she paid first and last month's rent when she moved in," said Dan, "so the owner won't be out anything. And the damage deposit ought to take care of the bathtub and carpet."

"I'm afraid not. Her employer, Mr. Near, co-signed the lease for her since she didn't have any references. Out of courtesy to Mr. Near, the owner allowed them to forego those payments." The manager turned to Rose. "Do you have any idea why your sister left so suddenly and where she might have gone?"

Rose shook her head.

"Since Miss McCoy left without notice," he continued, "I suppose poor Mr. Near will be expected to pick up the tab."

"Yes, poor Mr. Near," said Dan.

They thanked the manager for his trouble and quickly left the building, stepping into a light rain. "Stay here under the awning, Rose, and I'll go get the car."

"It's not raining that hard. I could use the exercise. We'll just walk fast."

By the time they reached the car, they were in a downpour, soaked to the skin. "Just look at me!" wailed Rose as Dan opened the car door for her. "And I just had my hair done!"

"You should have taken me up on my offer," scolded Dan.

He looked at his watch as he turned on the ignition. "It's almost two o'clock and I told Bill we'd be at his sales lot by one."

As they drove, Rose looked in the mirror attached to the back of the sunshade. She tried to fluff up her limp, wet hair, but to no avail. "Well, if I'm going to be a hippy, I may as well get used to looking like one."

Dan glanced over at her. "You girls all worry too damned much about your hair. Rosie, you're so gol-darned pretty you don't even need hair to look good."

"Sure," she mumbled.

"And another thing. You're pretty dammed sly, too, telling Mr. What's-his-name that you're Mitzy's sister. That was fast thinking."

"I hate to lie, but it was apparent he wasn't going to let just anyone in her apartment."

The rain was just a drizzle by the time they pulled into Dewey's R.V. Sales and Service.

A balding, pudgy little man in a suit and tie hurried out to greet them. He removed the cigar from his mouth and said, "Looks like you got caught in the rain. We've got the RoadAbode all detailed and gassed up." He turned toward the building and waved with his cigar for them to follow. "Come on in. We just need to get paid up, finish the paper work, and you can be on your merry way.

He was smiling broadly as he pulled two chairs up to his desk. He plopped down in his swivel chair, grabbed up a stack of papers, and laid a set in front of Dan and Rose.

Dan said, "Bill, remember I said we needed to discuss some things? That our circumstances have changed?"

After Dan explained what had happened to their finances, and that they couldn't pay what was still owed on the RoadAbode, Bill ceremoniously snuffed out his cigar and was no longer smiling. "Why that dirty, low-down son of a bitch! I've known Larry for years, and he's the last man in the world I would have thought would do something like that."

Bill suddenly pushed his chair back. "Say! I'VE got money invested with him. Did anyone else get taken?"

"Who knows?" Dan answered. "I'm sure the law will have an accountant go over the books with a fine-toothed comb. A good number of folks in this town were invested with him, but I doubt if any of them made it as easy for him as I did."

"So I guess you'll be wanting the money back that you've already put down for the RoadAbode," said Bill dejectedly as he gathered up the papers from his desk.

"Not so fast," said Dan. "What do you have out there that the down payment on the RoadAbode would buy, with maybe a little left over?"

Bill perked up. He twisted his stubby neck around and looked out the window. "The rain has stopped. What do you say we just get on out there and see what we can do."

After showing them several small, used, older RVs, Bill seemed exasperated. "That RoadAbode you folks picked out is one of the slickest models made, and I know anything less has got to feel like a big come-down. But what I've just shown you are the ones you can afford."

"Yes, I know," said Dan, "and I know you'll give us a good deal on any of them. But whatever we get is going to be our home, so we need to be a bit particular. And we can't take the chance that those older vehicles you showed us may need a lot of repairs down the road."

"I understand." said Bill. "But the only kind of new vehicle you're going to get with that kind of money is a converted van with few extras. We have a couple on the back lot."

The three solemnly walked along, stepping around puddles made by the rain. *I suppose we can sleep in a van,* thought Rose, *but how am I supposed to cook? And what are we supposed to do about a john?*

Bill stopped to answer his cell phone. "It just came in? What kind of shape is she in and how many miles does she have on her? Really? Is that a fact? Sounds great. I'll be right there."

Bill slapped his cell phone shut. "A converted long-bed van just came in, and it's loaded. It's a ninety-seven, but it's got real low mileage, and Joe says it looks brand new. He says a little widow lady had just been keeping it for sentimental reasons after her husband died in ninety-eight, but she's remarried now and her new husband wants to get rid of it. Want to check it out?"

"That story sounds too good to be true," answered Dan, "but sure, what do we have to lose?"

Bill removed a cigar from his vest pocket and offered it to Dan, who declined. Bill stuck the cigar in his mouth and lit it. "I tell you what. I know you nice folks have had a terrible setback and I'd like to help. I'll try to get the best deal out of her I can, and if you'll agree to forgo our usual ninety-day or five-thousand-mile warranty, I won't tack a cent of profit on her."

"Being a retired businessman myself," said Dan, "I know just what a generous offer that is."

"Oh, there'd be a catch to it," said Bill. "Whenever you latch on to that no-good and get your money back, and want another pretty like the RoadAbode, you'll come right back here and buy it from me."

"That's a deal," said Dan as he offered his hand.

"I'm going to have to ask you two to stay out of sight till the dealing's done. Otherwise if the sellers know I've got potential buyers waiting, they're going to want top dollar."

"Is it okay if we just wait over there in the RoadAbode?" asked Rose.

"Sure," Bill answered, "but you *will* leave your shoes at the door, won't you? We don't want mud on that fancy carpeting. And please don't use the toilet. Make yourselves at home and I'll get back with you as quickly as possible."

While Dan sat in the plush captain's chair, fiddling with the various controls on the dashboard, Rose slowly walked through the luxurious parlor with its lavish furniture and entertainment center. She ran her hands over the faux-granite kitchen countertop and stopped to once again admire the state-of-the-art range, oven and microwave, and refrigerator with freezer. She opened the cherry-wood cabinets that were so perfectly designed for traveling dishes and cookware. She walked past the stacked washer and dryer, past the bathroom with a lovely vanity and glassed-in shower, and into the bedroom with its queen-sized bed, ample closets and storage. She saw a strange woman across the room, looking back at her from the mirrored wall. The woman had a drawn face, rumpled clothes and stringy hair. She was much different from the woman who had stared back at her from the motel vanity mirror this morning.

Rose flopped down on the bed and lay staring up at the ornate glass light fixture overhead. Prismatic colors danced around it on the ceiling. *How appropriate. A shattered rainbow.*

Chapter Four

Dan drove their newly acquired van to the car rental agency, with Rose following in the rental car. In the parking lot, Dan helped her out of the car saying, "If we'd gotten here ten minutes later, we'd have to pay for another day."

He got their bags out of the trunk, and Rose followed him to their van. She thought, *well, it does look brand new – not a scratch on it. And the tires look good. That shade of blue isn't the color I would have chosen, but it's something I can live with.*

As Dan put the bags in the side door, he said to Rose, "I can't believe the good luck we had at Bill's. Settle in our new home here while I return the rental car keys and get checked out."

She climbed into the passenger seat and studied the RV's interior. She swiveled her seat around and then stood up. *It's really just a customized, long-bed van that you can stand up in.*

Once again, she checked out the miniature sink, two-burner stove, and tiny refrigerator. She then opened the door of the compartment enclosing the portable toilet. *Dan is a big man. He could get stuck in this little cubbyhole.*

Rose seated herself on the padded bench that they would later fold out to make a double bed. Looking around, she thought, *There's hardly any room in here for our things. We can't possibly take everything we have in storage.* The day had been so eventful; she hardly had time to think. Now that she was alone, the enormity of their situation came crashing down on her. She fell sideways onto the bench and cried.

"Sorry I took so long, Rose."

At the sound of Dan's voice, she sat up quickly and wiped her eyes. Before he could climb in, she snatched up her sunglasses and put them on. *He doesn't need to see that I've been crying. He feels bad enough already.* "What now?" she asked.

"We'd better get over to the storage place and get our stuff out while we still have some daylight."

"Dan, we can't possibly take everything. There just isn't room."

"We'll have to sort then and take just the bare essentials."

Rose nodded. "The Salvation Army was glad to get all the leftovers from our estate sale. I'm sure they'd be happy to get more."

"Considering our present state of affairs, Rosie, maybe we'd just better take the stuff to a secondhand store and see what we can get out of it."

It was almost dark by the time they finished sorting out their essentials and stowing them in the van. "We'll come back in the morning and box up the rest of it," said Dan. "We won't have room to open out the bed if we try to take it all now. I'm hungry. Let's go find something to eat."

Rose remembered seeing a two-for-one special at the fast-food restaurant they had passed earlier. They got two burgers to go and, instead of soft drinks, ordered two waters. "What you're buying is mostly ice anyway," said Dan.

"Shall we go to the park to eat these?" asked Rose.

"I hope you don't mind that we eat on the run," Dan answered as he pulled into the street. "We still have some business to take care of at Larry's place."

In an upper-class neighborhood, they slowly drove past the house that, until just ten days before, had been their home for twenty-eight years. The well-placed yard lights lit up the home's exterior, and the lighting inside revealed the new owners' family seated around the dining room table. Rose felt a pang of regret. "It looks just like a Thomas Kinkaid painting," said Rose. "Do you think we'll miss it?"

"I won't miss the yard. Even with the riding lawnmower, it was a heck of a lot of work, especially after the boys went off to college and I lost my help."

"And I won't miss the housework. If we'd stayed much longer, I would have wanted to get a maid service. Life's just too short at this stage to spend what precious time there is left keeping up a big house."

They drove two more blocks before pulling into the driveway of a large, but rather plain two-story Cape Cod. "Larry said he was going to get this place painted this summer. He never got around to it. And now, he never will."

Dan got out of the van and leaned in the window to say, "The lights are on inside, so it looks like she's home. Why don't you wait here till I see for sure."

Dan soon returned to the van and climbed in. "I laid on that doorbell for at least five minutes. I *know* she's in there. The TV *and* the stereo are both going full blast. She must be passed out. We'll have to try again in the morning."

Dan turned on the ignition. Rose asked, "Where are we going to spend the night?"

Dan turned off the ignition. "What's wrong with right here?" He mistakenly turned on the windshield wipers before finding the switch for the interior lights.

While Dan pulled out the double bed, Rose pulled the curtains over the side and back windows. "Dan, people can still see in the windshield. Do we have anything to cover it?"

"We don't have to worry about it tonight, Rose. The van is facing the garage door, so no one can see in. We should have thought to get a windshield shade at Dewey's. We'll pick one up tomorrow on our way out of town. We'll get some netting, too. We can hang it around the van to use for extra storage."

"What do you mean, *extra*? Storage room in here is non-existent."

Dan watched her dig around in her suitcase and pull out a pair of flannel pajamas. "Dan, would you please douse the lights while I get dressed for bed?"

He opened the windows slightly for air, and after turning off the lights, sat in the driver's seat while Rose undressed. "I sure am going to miss that black negligee set you look so good in. And that red frilly nightie."

"Like you suggested, we took only the essentials," said Rose. "I'm down to the bare basics."

"You are? *Fantastic!* I'll be right there."

Chapter Five

"**W**ake up! Wake up in there!" A shrill female voice demanded. "Who do you kids think you are?" Rose peeked over her pillow, and in the gray light of dawn, saw Larry's wife, Charlotte, hanging on to the van's aerial with one hand and banging on the windshield with the other. "You kids get this van out of my driveway right now or I'm calling the police!"

Dan wrapped the blanket around himself, pulling it off Rose in the process, and stumbled toward the front of the van. Rose grabbed Dan's shirt off the floor and quickly slipped it on over her naked body.

Dan rolled down the passenger-side window. "Shhhhh! Be quiet, Charlotte, or you'll wake up the whole neighborhood!"

"YOU! What the hell are you doing in my driveway at this time of day? And who's the slut you've got in there with you?"

"I'll have you know that slut is my wife. I mean that's no slut, that's my *wife*, Rose."

Charlotte knows darned well it's me in here, thought Rose. *She's always been jealous of me. She's always hated me.*

"Charlotte," said Dan, "Would you please turn loose of my aerial? Look at that. You've bent the hell out of it."

Still hanging onto the aerial for support, she stepped down, barefooted, from the bumper.

She pulled the scraggly, mouse-brown hair back from her bleary, sunken eyes. "You tell me where that no-good husband of mine is. I know he's been keeping company with some whore, and you better tell me who she is. He doesn't keep anything from *you*, his old bosom buddy!"

A door slammed at the house next door, and an angry-looking man in his robe and pajamas glared at them while snappily retrieving a newspaper from his front yard.

"Charlotte, we can't talk here. Can we go inside?"

She glanced over her shoulder at the neighbor. "I suppose so, before old News Nose over there can spread anymore gossip around the neighborhood."

"We've got to get dressed. Leave the front door unlocked and we'll just let ourselves in. We'll just be a few minutes."

"Suit yourself." Charlotte gathered up the hem of her pink chenille robe and sashayed into the house.

"You go on," said Rose. "I'll make up the bed and get some things organized."

"No way!" said Dan. "I can't deal with that female on my own. I've got to have some backup."

"Chicken."

A few minutes later, Rose and Dan let themselves in the house and found Charlotte seated at the dinette table, a mug of coffee in one hand and a cigarette in the other. She was still in her chenille robe. Rose noticed a half-empty bottle of bourbon sitting on the cluttered kitchen counter. *I'll bet that's not all coffee in her cup.*

"Say, that coffee smells awfully good," said Dan. "Got any to spare?"

Halfheartedly, Charlotte motioned toward the coffee maker. "Help yourselves. The mugs are to the right of the sink. There may be some sugar there too, but you're out of luck if you use cream or milk."

Dan opened the cupboard and retrieved two mugs. "That's okay, we'll take it black." After setting the filled mugs on the table, Dan asked, "Aren't you going to sit down, Rose?"

"I haven't been invited."

"Oh, for crap's sake, sit down, Rose," Charlotte sneered. "Do you always have to be so damned proper?" She looked across the table at Dan. "Now tell me what you two were doing out there, spending the night in my driveway."

"We tried to see you yesterday evening, Charlotte, but you evidently didn't hear the doorbell. I rang a number of times."

Charlotte took a drag off her cigarette. "That doorbell's another damn thing that needs fixing around here."

Dan and Rose exchanged knowing glances.

Charlotte pushed back in her chair and crossed her arms. "Now for the big question. Where's Larry and who's he with?"

After Dan finished relating yesterday's events, Charlotte remained silent. She got up from the table, poured herself a half-cup of coffee and topped it off with a big slug of bourbon. She took a sip and then turned around to face Dan. "How long have you known about that young slut?"

I can see she's really concerned about what Larry did to us, thought Rose.

"Less than twenty-four hours," answered Dan with obvious irritation. "Aren't you the least bit concerned that he might have left you financially high and dry too?"

A worried look came over Charlotte's haggard face. "I've got some money in my own personal checking account. And this house is paid for. It ought to bring plenty."

"Are you sure about that?" asked Dan. "Larry may have refinanced it, pocketed the money, and left you with some hefty mortgage payments." Charlotte plopped into her chair, holding onto her mug with two shaking hands. "How would I know? Larry handled all our finances."

"If you don't mind my rummaging around in Larry's desk, maybe I can find out."

"Be my guest. I wouldn't even know what to look for. While you're doing that, I think I'll take a shower and get dressed."

Less than an hour later, Charlotte joined Dan and Rose in the library. Her hair was pulled back in a French roll, and she was wearing black stretch pants and a white pullover. *It's amazing what a bath and a little grooming can do*, thought Rose.

Dan looked up from the piles of paper on the desk. "Better have a seat, Charlotte." He pulled a chair over to the desk for her. "Rose and I have pretty much gone through everything in Larry's files. We have some good news and some bad news."

Charlotte seated herself. "Lay it on me. What's the bad news?"

"I'm afraid my suspicions about the house were correct. Larry refinanced it two months ago. There's a thirty-year mortgage on it."

Charlotte buried her face in her hands.

Dan continued, "The good news is, the house is now fully in your name, and Larry's paid the first six month's payments. See? Here's the payment book. There's not one due for another four months."

Charlotte studied the book. "That's the *good* news? What I have in my bank account wouldn't cover even one payment. What the hell am I supposed to do?"

"These figures show that the down payment on the new loan was equity left in the house, about twenty percent of its worth, which is a pretty sizable amount. If I were you," said Dan, "I'd get an appraiser and a broker out here, and then get this place on the market as soon as possible."

"How much is the equity?"

"Right at a hundred grand. That should support you comfortably until you can find a job."

"A *job*? At *my* age? I haven't worked since before we were married."

"You're forgetting about Social Security, Charlotte," said Dan. "How old *are* you, anyway?"

"Fifty-nine," she mumbled.

"Well, you'll be eligible for Social Security when you're sixty-two. If you're careful with the equity money, it should last until then."

"How much will I get from Social Security?"

"Half of whatever Larry is eligible for. It certainly won't be enough to afford you the living you're accustomed to, but it will keep you from starving."

Charlotte clenched her teeth and banged her fist on the desk. "I'm not willing to settle for just enough to stay alive! I have needs!"

"Hey, don't take it out on the messenger. At least you're left with some. Right now, Rose and I have *nothing*, and I won't be eligible for Social Security for four more years."

Charlotte sat quietly for a few seconds, trying to process everything she had been told. Finally she said, "You two are homeless now. Why don't you stay here with me? You could help me do all this house-selling and paperwork business and you'd have a roof over your heads for a while."

My, isn't she thoughtful, thought Rose. *Right now homeless doesn't sound so bad.*

"Thanks, Charlotte," said Dan, "but we've got to get on the road as soon as possible before Larry's trail gets cold."

"But aren't the police taking care of that?"

"There's an APB out on them, but the police can only do so much. We plan on doing all we can ourselves to find them. I'd like to keep a couple of these documents for Larry's handwriting samples, and give one to the police. They're obsolete, and nothing you'll be needing."

Dan picked up a brochure and showed it to Charlotte. "Here's a picture of a Mercedes with a big red circle around it. Did Larry buy a new Mercedes recently?"

"Yeah," answered Charlotte. "He's had it a couple of months. I'm surprised he didn't tell you about it. I don't know why he bought it. He wouldn't let me drive it and . . ."

"Isn't your license suspended?" asked Dan.

"What of it!" snapped Charlotte. "Does he have to blab to you about everything?"

"Sorry I pointed that out," said Dan.

"Anyway, I don't think he's had it out of the garage since he drove it home. He even keeps a cover over it like he's afraid a little dust might settle on it."

"Is it in the garage now?"

"Well, yeah. At least it was when I put the trash out there day before yesterday."

"Let's go have a look," said Dan.

Charlotte and Rose followed as he headed for the garage and stood in the doorway as Dan made his way past Charlotte's car to Larry's.

Rose glanced down at the trash bins sitting next to the door. *I hope she at least does the environment some good by recycling that mountain of liquor bottles.*

Charlotte cried out as Dan pulled the cover off the car. "That's his old Buick! He must have the Mercedes."

"It would appear so," said Dan. "What color is it?"

"Kind of a silvery color."

They returned to the house and to the kitchen for another cup of coffee.

"I hate to ask," said Dan, "but do you have anything to eat? Rose and I are starving."

"I never eat before noon," answered Charlotte. "Check the refrigerator and see what you can find."

Dan set a block of cheese, three pre-cooked wieners, and a jar of dill pickles on the table. "Got any crackers?"

While Rose and Dan ate their breakfast off paper plates, Charlotte gave her coffee another slug of bourbon. When he finished eating, Dan asked, "Charlotte, have you noticed anything else of Larry's that is missing?"

"No. I never thought he'd get the guts to actually leave me, so I haven't even checked."

"Isn't the master suite just down the hall from the library?" asked Dan as he got up from the table.

"That's my room. Larry's room is upstairs."

• • •

Once upstairs, Dan excused himself to use Larry's bathroom and Rose sat on the bed while Charlotte checked the walk-in closet. She called out, "I don't see his silk suit, and his best shirts and slacks are gone. So are his best shoes."

Dan stepped out of the bathroom. "Girls, come look at this." Dark brown stains covered the sink and were splattered about. Several stained towels lay on the shower floor. "See what I fished out of the trash? A bottle of Clever Girl Hair Coloring."

"Well," said Rose, "I guess we'd better tell the police they're looking for a man with dark brown hair, rather than light gray."

"Yes, I need to tell them about the Mercedes, too. They should be able to trace the tags."

When they stepped back into the bedroom, Charlotte was standing at Larry's chest-of-drawers, staring at something she was holding, and quietly crying.

Rose crossed the room to her. "What is it?"

Charlotte held a man's wedding ring and a small piece of paper. "I didn't know he hated me this much."

Rose took the note from Charlotte's shaking hand and read, "This ring symbolizes thirty-six years of living hell. I hope I left you with the means to drink yourself to death. Your loathing husband, Larry."

The doorbell rang. "Dan, would you see who that is?" sniffed Charlotte.

Within a few seconds they heard Dan say, "Hello, detectives. Glad to see you're on the job. You saved me a trip downtown."

"Yes, and by answering the door, you saved us from having to break it down. We couldn't raise anyone here yesterday afternoon and just now got the warrant we needed to search the place. Is Mrs. Near home?"

Chapter Six

After the detectives left carrying two boxes of documents and Larry's home computer, Rose and Dan left to scout for empty cardboard boxes. They found all they needed in the alley behind a liquor store and drove back to the storage facility.

"There are so many things here that just tear my heart out to give up," said Rose.

Dave crammed the last of the boxes into the van. "Yes, there are some nice things here. We should be able to get quite a bit for them."

Rose picked up her guitar and strummed her fingers across the strings. "I will especially miss this."

Dan studied her for a moment. "Rose, I said we'd have to get rid of all the nonessentials. That certainly can't include your guitar."

"Really, Dan? But it'll take up so much room."

"It's light. We can hang it in the netting."

He slammed the side door shut and opened the passenger door for Rose and her guitar. There's not much room left for you two, but hop in, Hon. We're ready to roll."

• • •

Rose hummed to herself and strummed her guitar in the van, while inside the secondhand store, Dan dickered with the owner. She looked up to see him storm out of the store. She could tell things had not gone well by the color of his face and the set of his jaw.

He climbed into the van, cursing under his breath. "What we brought here would take several thousand dollars to replace, yet that lousy cheapskate only gave us one hundred and eighty dollars for the whole lot!" Dan opened up his fist to reveal a wad of bills. "Why, my putter alone is worth that much!"

"Dan, you didn't sell your lucky golf clubs! I know how much they mean to you."

"Well, yeah, but they're hardly essential. Heck, we can just about eat for a week for what one game of golf usually costs. I may never play again."

"That's not positive thinking, Dan. You've won so many tournaments that most of the guys at the club won't even bet with you anymore."

Dan thought for a moment. "By, God, you're right, Rose! I might be able to do some hustling with those babies."

He jumped out of the van and disappeared into the store. He soon returned, slid open the van's side door, quickly climbed in with the clubs, slammed the door shut, and plopped into the driver's seat.

"My goodness, what's the big rush," asked Rose. "Did you steal them?"

Dan turned on the ignition and peeled out of the parking space. "*He* thinks I did. That bastard tried to charge me two-hundred and fifty bucks for my own clubs. I tried to reason with him, but he wouldn't settle for less."

"So what did you do?"

"I threw the hundred and eighty bucks in his face and took back my damned clubs."

"Gee, I guess you really showed him. We could have avoided all the trouble if we had only taken the things to the Salvation Army, like I suggested."

"Yeah, we would have been better off. It wouldn't surprise me if the jerk calls the cops on me. We'd better get the rest of our business done and get out of town quick."

It was late afternoon by the time they had picked up supplies and a few groceries, gassed up the van and were headed out of town. "I can't believe we're finally on our way," said Rose. "How far do you think we'll get tonight?"

"We'll make pretty good time on I-70. We should be able to find a good place to camp just east of Kansas City"

"Are we going to stay in one of those RV parks?"

"We can't afford to stay in *those* places, or the state parks either for that matter. We'll just have to make our own camp spots."

Dan had been driving a little under the speed limit, following the same cars for quite a distance, when he suddenly stomped down on the gas, pulled into the passing lane, and sped past them.

"Dan! What are you doing?" cried Rose. "You're going way over the speed limit!"

"Rose! See that silver car that just passed us? When I get close enough, read that license tag to me."

"You think that might be Larry?"

"It could be."

After a chase of several miles, they were finally close enough for Rose to make out the car's tags. She read the first two letters before Dan interrupted her. "Never mind. Hell, that car's not even a Mercedes."

"I certainly hope you're not going to risk our necks every time a silver car passes us!" Rose scolded. "Remember, we don't have enough money to get buried."

"Sorry, Hon. I'll try not to get too paranoid. But we *do* need to keep on the lookout. The police gave me Larry's tag number before we left. It's burned into my brain. You got a pencil and something to write on? I want you to write it down and help me check out every silver Mercedes we see."

Daylight was fading fast by the time they pulled into a rest stop. When Rose came out of the ladies' room, she saw Dan sitting at a picnic table, staring off into space. *Poor Dan.* She walked over to him and laid her hand on his shoulder. "What a beautiful sunset. Come help me bring out the dishes, and we'll have us a picnic right here."

While they were eating, Rose glanced around the area. "Why don't we just stay here for the night? That corner way over there looks like a good place."

"I suppose we could. I didn't see any signs that said we couldn't."

"Look, Dan, the evening star." She put her arm around him. "When was the last time we watched the stars come out together?"

Dan leaned over and kissed her cheek. "It *has* been a while, hasn't it, sweetie." A big eighteen wheeler pulled into a parking space and hissed to a stop, blocking their view. Dan stood up and began clearing the table. "So much for star gazing. We'd better get the van moved over before someone else gets there first."

They awoke early the next morning and, since it was still chilly outdoors, drank their instant coffee and ate their instant oatmeal inside the van. Afterward, Dan slung a towel over his shoulder, grabbed his shaving kit, and left for the men's room.

To save propane by heating dishwater, Rose took the plastic dishpan into the ladies room and filled it with hot water. She carried the steaming pan back to the van, sloshing much of the water down her slacks. Dan had not returned by the time she put the dishes away. She changed her slacks and underwear, and walked back to the ladies' room to wash her face and comb her hair. He was still not back when she returned to the van.

After sitting in the van for some time, wondering what was keeping Dan, Rose decided to find out. *I've read about bad things happening at these rest stops . . . rapes, robberies, and who knows what else.* She was at the door of the men's room, with her hand raised to knock, when the door suddenly flew open, and a huge burly man bumped into her on his way out. "Hey, Lady! The women's is on the other side of the building!"

"Sorry."

Rose watched the man get into his truck and drive off. She then yelled up at the vent above the door. "Dan! Are you still in there?"

"Yes, Rose. I'll be out in a minute."

Rose seated herself on a bench a short distance away. She leaned her head back and closed her eyes. *Take your time, Dan, now that I know you're okay. This sun feels wonderful.*

Her quietude was soon interrupted. "Sorry I took so long, Hon, there were truckers shaving at both sinks when I went in there, and as soon as one left, here would come another."

"You mean they just barged in front of you?"

"No, I told them to go ahead of me. Time is money to them, and I knew they were all eager to get on the road. Speaking of which, we'd better get on the road ourselves."

As they climbed into the van, Dan glanced back at Rose's slacks and panties, hanging from a line she had stretched across the interior. "How'd you happen to wet your pants, Rose?"

• • •

In between watching cars that passed them on the interstate, Rose enjoyed the scenery. "Too bad we're in such a hurry. It would be nice to stop once in a while to explore the places we're rushing through."

"Yes, it would. And someday we can take our time and do just that. But we've got to at least *try* to get the jump on Larry."

"So did the detectives give you any clue as to what we can expect when we get to that place in Kentucky that Mitzy's from? What was the name of that place?"

"Jericho. It's in Cedar County. The detectives told me they had contacted the county sheriff, and he didn't have much to offer. He said that it wasn't really a town, just a wide spot in the road. He said there wasn't much there but a gas station and a general store with a post office where all the hill people picked up their mail once in a while."

"Hill people?" asked Rose.

"Yes. Jericho happens to be right in the middle of one of the poorest and most backward places in Appalachia. The sheriff said the law hardly ever gets called into those hills. The folks around there pretty much handle their own affairs, so there's not much information on any of them."

"Well, is the sheriff going to help us find Mitzy's family?"

"We're going to Cedarville, the county seat, and talk to him. But according to the detectives back home, we shouldn't expect to get much help from him."

Rose was silent for a long time, trying to imagine what fate had in store.

Finally, Dan broke the silence. "Whatcha thinkin' about, Rose?"

"A lot of things. For instance, what are we going to tell the boys? They were so excited when we called them from the motel. They want us to call whenever we can, so they can keep up with us and all our adventures."

"I don't want them to know about any of this, Rose, at least not just yet. I don't want to worry them. And if we can catch Larry right away, the news won't be so bad."

West of St. Louis, they encountered several miles of stop-and-go road construction. Rose took the opportunity to fix sandwiches, and they ate in the van while waiting for the traffic to move. It was midafternoon by the time they reached town.

Rush-hour traffic was already beginning to build on the interstate as they continued through the city. Dan said,

"Look over there, Rose, that's the Mighty Missouri River. Big Muddy is what they called it when this was the gateway to the frontier."

"I remember that from history class," said Rose. "Wasn't it Mark Twain who said the river was too thick to drink and too thin to plow?"

Dan chuckled. "Sounds like something he'd say."

"Oh, look!" Rose exclaimed. "It's the famous Gateway Arch. Isn't it a sight to see! Look how the sunlight plays on it and how it seems to change colors as we move toward it."

The arch remained visible for several miles as they followed the Missouri River south to the bridge into Illinois.

They left I-70 and took up I-64 to cross Illinois. In Indiana, they stopped at a rest stop where Rose heated a can of chili for supper. They drove until dusk and stopped for the night at another rest stop.

Rose lay in the dark, listening to serenading frogs in a nearby pond and looking out the window at the starlit sky. "Dan?"

"Huh?"

"We're kind of like those early settlers who went through St. Louis on their way west, only we're going east. But we're taking off across the great unknown too, with not much more than the clothes on our backs. It's scary, but then it's exciting too, don't you think?"

"I guess," Dan mumbled sleepily. "It's a good thing we have a guitar and a set of golf clubs in case we run into any hostile Indians."

Chapter Seven

The farmland and rolling hills of southern Indiana and eastern Kentucky gave way to rugged, thickly wooded mountains as Dan and Rose neared the Appalachians. Tightly gripping the armrests, Rose was petrified as Dan maneuvered the winding mountain highway that dangerously narrowed to two lanes.

The van made a sudden, sharp turn; Rose shrieked and braced herself against the dashboard as the van headed toward the highway's outer edge.

Dan jerked the van to a stop and applied the emergency brake. "What the hell was that all about? You scared the liver out of me and almost made me go over the edge!"

"I scared *YOU*? I thought we *were* going over the edge! Why did you pull over like that?"

"I need to check the map again," said Dan. "I don't want to miss that turnoff to Cedarville."

"Well, for Pete's sake, let me know ahead of time when you're going to do something like that!" Rose peered over the edge of the highway shoulder to the valley far below. "I'll never get used to mountain driving."

"Rose, why don't you drive."

"ME drive? Are you nuts?"

"Believe me, you'll feel much better about mountain driving if you have control of the wheel. Just give it a try."

"Well, okay. But I'm not stepping out on this side. Move back so I can just slide over there."

Rose adjusted the driver's seat, and then slowly pulled the van back onto the narrow highway. After several miles she remarked, "You're right. This is better. I *do* feel more secure when I'm driving."

They made the turnoff to a secondary highway and soon found the sign "Welcome to Cedarville, Population 3,386."

"The sheriff's office is in the court house," said Dan, "so it should be easy to find."

They drove slowly through the small town. It appeared to be all but deserted, with many of the storefronts along Main Street boarded up. "Well, we've gone clear through the town," said Rose. "I didn't see anything that looked like a court house in this poor little place. Are you sure Cedarville is the county seat?"

"Yes. It says so right here on the map. Turn around and drag Main again."

Rose turned right and circled the block through a residential area. "Just look at this," she said. "These houses must be over a hundred years old. And it looks like they haven't seen a coat of paint since they were built; and most have *clotheslines*; and *outhouses*! Can you believe it, in this day and age?"

Turning back toward Main Street, they came upon what appeared to be the city square, vacant, except for unkempt grass, weeds, and tall trees. "Pull over, Rose. There's some kind of monument. I want to see what it says."

"I'm coming too," said Rose. "I really need to stretch my legs."

At the edge of the square, Dan pulled away some bindweed that had draped itself over the front of the monument. "Well, I'll be damned. It says Cedar County Courthouse."

They followed a walk that ran from the monument toward the center of the square, to a blackened stone foundation, partially hidden in the surrounding tall grass and weeds. "No wonder we couldn't find the court house." said Dan. "Looks like it burned down. But the county must still be in business. I wonder where . . ."

"Over there," said Rose. "The sign on the old two-story building across the street reads Cedar County Courthouse."

The building's front door screeched when they opened it, and they were met with the musty smell of mold. The wood floor squeaked and gave under their feet as they walked across the main parlor to a door that had Sheriff's Office crudely painted on its hobnail-glass pane.

Dan knocked lightly before opening the door. "Sheriff?"

There was a scraping of boots as they swept down from the desktop. Taken by surprise, the slender man behind the desk clumsily got to his feet and said, "Come in." He studied Dan intently as he entered the room. When he saw Rose, the wrinkles on his face folded into a grin. "You must be the Goods."

"How did you know?" answered Dan, extending his hand.

The sheriff gave Dan a hearty handshake. "I'm Sheriff Banks. I've been expecting you. We don't get many strangers comin' through these parts, so I figured it *had* to be you. And I've sure been on the lookout fer strangers since that detective fella called. I ain't seen that pair he described, and I sure ain't seen no Mercedes around these parts." He motioned to two antique oak chairs. "Have a seat, and I'll tell you what I know."

Sheriff Banks sat down, opened a drawer, and pulled out a sheet of paper. "Ever since that detective called, I've done some askin' around. They don't get their mail delivered, but accordin' to the post office, they's only four families named McCoy livin' in Cedar County, and they all live within a few miles of one another. So if one of 'em ain't the right McCoy, you won't have far to go to get the one your a lookin' fer."

"Aren't you going to come with us, Sheriff?" asked Rose.

"Sorry, ma'am, my deputy's laid up, and I cain't afford to go off on some wild goose chase."

"But what if they're up there?" she asked. "Are we supposed to bring them in all by ourselves?"

Sheriff Banks picked a business card off his desk and handed it to Dan. "If you find 'em, just call the number on that card."

He handed the paper to Dan. "Now, the McCoy's all live way off from the county roads, so they's gonna be a little hard to find. The hill folks just kinda make their own roads through them backwoods, so they ain't marked down nowheres." He reached over the paper Dan was studying and poked it with his scrawny finger. "So I sorta scratched out that thar map from what different folks has told me. I hope it helps some."

"Thank you," said Dan. "We really appreciate the information. Is there anything else you can tell us about the McCoys?"

"If they ever was any kinda papers on 'em, they ain't none now. The old courthouse burnt down a few years back, and ever blamed thing in it went up in smoke."

"That's a shame," said Rose. "Wasn't there anything they could do to save it?"

"No, ma'am, I'm afeared not. The whole danged volunteer fire department was over in the next county at a big turkey shoot. They *did* manage to save the granite blocks, though. Granite don't burn, ya understand. Them blocks cleaned up right nice and the county managed to get some good money fer 'em, enough to buy this nice building, anyway."

Rose asked, "How did the fire . . ."

Dan laid his hand on hers and interrupted, "About the McCoys . . . do you know anything at all about what kind of people they are?"

"Well, I can tell ya they ain't none of 'em been in no trouble with the law. At least not in the time I've been sheriffin' here. The folks at the general store say people by that name show up once in a while and fill up a wagon with goods. None of 'em has much to say. Like I told that detective fella, them hill people pretty much sticks to themselves. We never even hear when any of 'em gets borned or when any of 'em gets buried."

Dan stood up and reached across the desk to shake the sheriff's hand. "Thanks again, Sheriff. Say, could you tell us where there's a good restaurant? We didn't see one when we came through town."

"That's cause there ain't none. A real good cook used to have one just down the street, but some city feller run off with her. Everybody sure does miss her. The folks at the general store over in Jericho make real good sandwiches, though."

After driving the twelve miles to the small settlement, Dan and Rose ate their lunch, all to themselves, at a small, round table in a corner of Jericho's general store. "Just look around this place," said Rose. "It's like a set for an old-time movie."

"The whole town looks like a movie set," said Dan. "I feel like we're in some kind of time warp."

"If this is the civilized part of the county," said Rose, "What in the world can we expect up in those hills?"

"Rose, maybe you'd better stay here in town at that boarding house we passed, while I go talk to the McCoys. As you say, it's hard to know what to expect. It could be dangerous."

"And miss all the fun? Not on your life! I find all of this utterly fascinating!"

A middle-aged, heavy-set woman ambled over, while wiping her hands on her greasy apron. "Did y'all like the sandwiches?"

"Yes," answered Dan. "They were delicious."

"The hog that ham come offa was out of our very own stock."

"You don't say," said Dan.

"You folks wantin' anything else?"

"Yes," said Rose. "I need to pick up a few groceries and my husband's going to fill up our van with gas. Why don't you make us two more of those delicious sandwiches to go. May we put it all on a credit card?"

"I'm sorry, ma'am, but we ain't set up for no credit cards. And we don't take checks. It's cash on the barrelhead."

The woman excused herself to wait on a customer, and Rose leaned across the table to whisper. "Dan, we don't have much cash left. What are we going to do about groceries?"

"We won't need much," he answered. "Just get enough for breakfast and maybe lunch tomorrow. We should be back in civilization by tomorrow evening where we can charge stuff."

Later, Dan studied the sheriff's map, while Rose drove the ever-winding highway.

"According to this map, we turn left on the third road past the old Jenkin's place."

"The old Jenkin's place?" asked Rose. "How the heck are we to know where that is?"

"Well, let me see . . . he made an X here. I can hardly read this, but I think it says big fallen' down barn."

After a few more twists of the highway, Rose said, "There's an old deserted place. Could that big pile of lumber out back be a fallen down barn?"

"It's possible. Now be on the lookout for roads off the highway. It's indicated here that none of them are marked and are hard to see because of brush."

They turned left at what they hoped was the third road. They had gone several miles when Rose asked, "How do we know for sure we're on the right road?"

"We'll know as soon as we see an old, one-eared mule in a treeless pasture on the right."

"Golly, Dan, that sheriff has sure left a lot to chance with his directions. What if that mule has been sold or died since he drew up that map?"

"The trees are so thick along here, a treeless pasture should be easy to spot, mule or no mule," he answered.

A few miles farther, Dan exclaimed, "Well, I'll be damned! Look at that. That old mule's just standing by the fence like he was expecting us. And sure enough, he's missing one ear."

"The poor thing," lamented Rose. "How do you suppose that happened?"

My guess is that some hunter mistook him for a deer, and it got shot off. You'd be amazed at how many farm animals are mistakenly shot by hunters every year. I've had to dig bullets out of more than one of them."

"This is kind of like a treasure hunt," said Rose. "What's our next clue?"

"Well, let's see. Next, we'll pass an old abandoned pickup truck on our left, and in a few miles, we'll come to a place where this road branches off into three. It just says here, "pick one."

"Pick one? That's not being very explicit."

They passed the rusted hulk of an abandoned pickup truck, and when they came to the place where the one road forked three ways, Rose stopped. A sign was posted "No county maintenance beyond this point. Use at your own risk."

"I don't like the looks of this, Dan. None of these even look like roads. See how narrow they are?"

"Yeah, they do look a little rough, all right. It's a good thing this van sets up high. I'll do the driving from here on if you'd like. Since you claim to be somewhat psychic, Rose, you pick the road we should take. Which one will lead us to the McCoys?"

Rose opened the van door and stepped out. She walked back and forth a few times before opening the passenger door and climbing back in the van. "The one in the middle."

"Did you use your psychic powers to come to that decision?"

"No, I did it scientifically. I used eeny, meeny, miney, moe."

"Is that how you make all your decisions?"

"Of course. That's how I decided to marry you."

Dan chuckled and, turning on the ignition, headed down the bumpy middle road. The farther they went, the more narrow and deeply rutted the road became, winding its way through dense, dark stands of tall pines. All afternoon, the van rocked and bounced along at a snail's pace as Dan maneuvered the ruts. "We could walk faster than this," he grumbled.

At length, the fading sun was able to break through an opening in the pines up ahead, where the rutted roadbed became solid rock, and the road began curving around the side of a mountain.

"Oh, Dan!" cried Rose. "Look how narrow the road is here. It's single lane. And it's a sheer drop-off on this side! What if someone's coming around the bend?"

"I'd sure be surprised," said Dan. "We haven't seen a soul on this road all day. But just in case, I'll honk to let anyone know we're coming."

Dan honked, slowly made the sharp turn, and then stopped, staring ahead in disbelief.

Rose's heart began pounding wildly. The road ahead was seemingly no wider than the van itself, and merely a ledge on a sheer rock wall. "Dan, we can't possibly go any farther. We'll *have* to go back."

"Which would you rather I do, Rose, turn around or back up?"

"Oh, God!" cried Rose. "What are we going to do?"

"It's going to be tight, but it's only several hundred feet across to the woods over there, and evidently others navigate this road, so we should be able to."

"The sheriff said they came to town in *wagons*, Dan. They must not be as wide as this van."

"We don't have any choice, Rose, we've got to get across here. There's no use in both of us taking chances. You get out and either follow, or walk ahead."

"Oh, Dan. I don't know when I've been so scared. Please don't try it. *Please!*"

Dan opened his door as far as he could and squeezed out. "Come on, Rose, get out on this side."

Rose shakily unbuckled her seat belt and crawled over the driver's seat, tears streaming down her face. She threw her arms around Dan and sobbed into his chest.

"Come on, now, Rosie, I wouldn't do this if I didn't think I could make it."

She looked up at him. "I know I'm always nagging you to fasten your seat belt, but please don't do it this time. I want you to be able to bail out of there in a second if it starts to go over."

"Don't worry, Sweetie. I'll be careful and go very slowly. Just follow."

"No, I'm going to walk ahead. If it gets any worse, we need to know in advance."

Walking ahead of the creeping van, Rose heard a screech of metal against rock. Quickly turning her head, she watched the driver's side-view mirror fold up between the rock wall and the van. The outside wheels were right on the edge. She gasped.

Dan put the van in park and disappeared into the van's interior. He reappeared on the passenger side and threw Rose's clothesline over the van's hood and onto the road. He yelled, "Rose, measure the width of the road where we are now with that cord. If you see anywhere up ahead that looks iffy, use the cord to measure it." He then tossed a pen onto the road. "You can mark it with that."

Rose stretched the cord out in front of the van. She placed one end against the rock wall and anchored it with a rock. She then marked where the other end met the edge of the road. She peered over the edge and caught her breath. *My god! There's a rusted wreck of a truck way down there. Lord, save us.*

Rose measured the road in many places as the van crept along, scraping its way across the cliff but finally into the dark woods safely on the other side.

When they were across, Rose stood waiting as Dan climbed out of the van. They silently embraced for several minutes. Rose finally choked out the words, "Thank you, God."

A strong wind seemed to come from out of nowhere, putting the pine branches overhead into a frenzy. Dan looked up. "I'm sure glad that wind waited until we were across."

They scrambled back into the van and continued on the narrow, rutted trail. The van's headlights panned the forest up and down and back and forth as they bumped along. Rose finally said, "Now that I'm over my fright, I'm starving."

"Me, too," said Dan. "I've been looking for a place where we could pull off this trail and make camp, but it looks like we'll just have to settle for a wide place in the road."

A few miles farther along, the road widened for a short stretch. Dan pulled over, straddling the van's wheels on either side of a shallow gully running alongside the trail. After they had washed up, Dan turned off the interior lights and they sat in the dark, eating their ham sandwiches and listening to the howling wind. They shared an apple before falling, exhausted, into bed.

Sometime in the wee hours of the night, Rose awoke to the deafening sound of rain pounding the van's roof and what sounded like a river running nearby. "Dan! Dan, wake up! It's raining! It's raining really hard and we're going to be stuck here!"

When Dan didn't move, Rose held her hand to his nose to make sure he was breathing. *He's really out of it. I guess there's no use trying to wake him. That would just make two of us lying here worrying all night. He couldn't do anything tonight in that downpour anyway. We're already stuck.*

Chapter Eight

Rose and Dan sat at their table, cradling their coffee mugs in their hands and glumly staring out at the rain. "I don't know what the hell we're going to do, Rose. We're in mud up to the middle of the hubcaps, and my shovel is at the damned secondhand store."

Rose reached into a drawer and retrieved a small paper sack. "Well, we might as well have breakfast." She laid out two napkins and placed a sweet roll on each. "These home-made rolls we got at the general store look pretty good."

"Yes, they do. But why don't you put one of them away for later. They're pretty big; we can share one."

Rose returned a roll to the sack while Dan cut the other one in two. "You're right. We don't have much food, and there's no telling when we might get out of here."

Dan's half roll disappeared in a couple of swallows and he washed it down with the last of his coffee. Once again, he picked the cell phone off the dash and dialed 911.

Rose sipped her coffee. "Dear, we haven't moved since the last time you dialed."

"I know; we're still out of range. But I feel so damned helpless, just sitting here doing nothing."

At lunchtime, they shared the second roll and their one remaining apple. Rose strummed on her guitar and softly sang some ballads while Dan took an afternoon nap. It was still raining at dinnertime when they shared their only can of soup. After dinner, and until sundown, they played several games of dominos. Occasionally, they felt the van shift slightly from the force of the water eroding the earth from around its wheels. Dan didn't want to run the battery down by turning on the lights, so Rose played and sang some of his favorite Marty Robbins' songs before they turned in for the night.

They awoke the next morning to the sound of several raucous blue jays in the branches overhead. Rose sat up and peered out the window. "Look, Dan! The sun is shining. The rain has stopped."

Rose made coffee while Dan dressed. "It looks like a mug or two of coffee will have to do us for breakfast," she said, "but we at least have that."

Dan sat down and picked up his steaming mug. "Maybe a few sips of this brew will stimulate my brain enough to help me figure a way to get us out of here."

Rose nodded to a couple of trash bags and a roll of duct tape Dan was clutching. "What are you going to do with those?"

"That mud looks pretty deep, and my waders are at the secondhand store, along with my shovel."

Rose watched as Dan put his leg in a bag, wrapped it around, and then taped the opening around his thigh. He tore off one strip of tape after another and applied several layers to the bottom of the bags as soles for his trash-bag boots. He gulped down the last swallow of coffee, zipped up his windbreaker, and opened the van's side door. Ferocious snarling erupted just outside, and Rose jumped from her seat. "Dan! What in the world is that?"

"It's a poor old hound dog. I must have startled him."

Rose stepped into the doorway, next to Dan. "The poor thing; he's hurt. Just look at him. He's got gashes all over him and he's covered with blood."

In a low voice, Dan said, "Something chewed him up, that's for sure."

The dog backed away and, although he was shivering, barked ferociously.

Rose squatted down and extended her hand toward the dog. "Here, boy. It's all right. Come here, fella."

The dog quit barking, his pain-filled eyes fixed on Rose.

She continued talking to the dog in soothing tones while Dan disappeared into the back of the van. "Keep talking to him, Rosie. See if you can get him settled down. I'll get my bag and see if I have a tranquilizer. Now where did I stash it?"

By the time Dan found his bag, the dog had come to Rose. She cooed and gently stroked his head. She looked up at Dan and said, "He's so weak he can hardly stand."

Dan laid several plastic trash sacks on the floor, then slowly stepped out of the van while talking to the dog. "You know we're trying to help you, don't you, boy?"

Dan jabbed a hypodermic needle into the dog's flank. The dog yelped, snapped at Dan, and then turned to run away. He covered only a few feet before dropping to the muddy ground. By the time Dan reached down to pick him up, the dog was limp. Dan gently lifted him and carried him to the van. "Step back, Rose, and I'll lay him out on those plastic bags. Heat up some water. We'll have to clean him up the best we can."

Kneeling, Rose washed and then shaved the hair from around the dog's gaping wounds.

Leaning in the wide side-door, Dan applied disinfectant and stitched up one ugly gash after another. "I'm so glad you kept the tools of your trade," said Rose. "What do you suppose happened to him?"

"The way he's torn up, it looks like either a bear or a mountain lion got hold of him. It's a good thing I still had some tranquilizer syringes left in my bag."

"Do you think he's going to be okay?"

"It's hard to tell. He's lost an awful lot of blood. If we were at the clinic, I'd have an IV in him right now. He's going to need nourishment soon. Hell, *we're* going to need nourishment soon. I'm starving. We might wind up having to barbeque *him*."

"Dan!" scolded Rose.

Dan tied off a stitch, snipped free of it, and then carefully reexamined the dog's body. "I think we're done on this side. I'll turn him over so we can do the other side." Dan carefully picked up the dog. "Easy does it. He may have a broken rib or two."

"Okay, you son of a bitch! I gotcha covered!" barked a man's voice.

Dan turned his head to look behind him as Rose stood up to peer over his shoulder. She stared into the eyes of a scruffy looking, bearded, older man who was pointing a rifle at Dan's back. A younger man and a boy of about fifteen stood on either side of him, their rifles held at ready. Two hound dogs, resembling the one injured, were at their sides.

"What are you doin' with my dog?" growled the older man.

"Put that gun down right now!" snapped Rose. "How *dare* you!"

The man looked somewhat perplexed, like a scolded child might, as he lowered his rifle.

"Your dog showed up here half dead," said Dan as he turned to face them. "We're just trying to patch him up."

The three came closer to get a better look at the limp form in Dan's arms. The dogs came too, vigorously sniffing at their counterpart, and Dan, as well.

"That's ole Skeeter all right," said the older man. "Looks like he's dead already."

"He still has some life left in him," said Dan. "If you care about this dog, you better let me finish sewing him up before he comes to."

"How do you know to do that?" asked the man.

"My husband's a veterinarian," Rose said sternly.

"Well, I got a cousin that's a Presbyterian, but that don't mean . . ."

"Grandpa?" interrupted the boy. "He's one of those animal doctors."

"Oh," the man said sheepishly. "Go to it, then, mister."

Dan laid the dog down and Rose kneeled to clean the next wound. When Dan began stitching, the men, boy, and dogs crowded around, pressing against him, and craning their necks to watch. Dan straightened up, pushing them back in the process. "Look, guys, I can't do this with you breathing down my neck. You'll have to stay back."

As if they were the only offenders, the younger man bellowed at the two dogs, "Git over thar and lay down!"

While Rose and Dan worked, the men and boy bided their time by walking around, studying the van and peering in its windows. "You sure got yourself stuck here, mister!" yelled one.

"Sure do," Dan yelled back.

Rose whispered to Dan, "Do you think those men mean us any harm?"

"No, I don't think so; but let's hope this dog makes it."

"You sure got your nice vehicle all scraped up on Buzzard Pass, didn't ya?" barked another.

"Sure did," yelled Dan.

"I see you got Kansas tags. That's way out yonder in the west somewheres, ain't it?"

"Sure is," answered Dan.

"We see ya got a nice geetar in thar. Are ya any good with it?"

"It belongs to my wife here; and yes, she's pretty good with it."

The dog whined and began squirming just as Dan finished the last stitch. Dan straightened up and pulled off his surgical gloves. "That does it."

Rose got to her feet and retrieved a bath towel to lay over the patient for warmth. She then plopped onto a seat to rub the life back into her cramped legs. Dan stepped back to let the two men and boy crowd around the door.

The dog groggily raised his head to look at them, and then laid it down again, his tail thumping against the van's floor.

"Can we take him home now, Doc?" asked the boy.

"He's hurt pretty bad. I recommend not moving him for at least twenty-four hours. It looks like we won't be leaving here before then. We'll keep an eye on him and you can come pick him up tomorrow."

The two men stepped toward the front of the van to talk, leaving Dan and the boy with the dog. Rose slipped into the passenger seat and quietly rolled the window down a notch, straining to hear their conversation. "I ain't leavin' no valuable animal like Skeeter to perfect strangers," the old man argued.

"But, Pa, Skeeter's pretty bad hurt. How you figure they can run off with him when they's stuck in the mud like they is? They ain't goin' nowheres soon. I say we leave him fer now."

The older man grudgingly agreed, and the two returned to where Dan and the boy were talking. Dan said, "I was just telling the boy here that Skeeter's going to need something to eat pretty soon. We'd feed him, but we don't even have food for ourselves."

The younger man dug into the pocket of his overalls, drug out a package of jerky, and offered it to Dan. The two dogs immediately appeared, expectantly wagging their tails and licking their chops. The man ordered, "Git," and the dogs stepped back.

Dan took the package, and extended his free hand. "My name's Daniel Good. What did you say your names were?"

"I don't recollect say'in." He looked at his right hand, wiped it on his overalls, and then shook Dan's hand. "We-uns is the McCoys." At the mention of the name, Rose rolled the window all the way down in order to hear better as the man continued. "My name's Burl." He reached over to touch the older man's shoulder. "This here's my pa, Seth." Pulling the boy over by his shirt, he added, "And this here's my boy, Clyde."

"You say your name is McCoy?" Dan asked excitedly.

"Yes, suh."

"Do you know a Mitzi McCoy?" Dan continued.

"Used to."

"Used to?"

"Yes, suh."

"She don't come around here no more," Seth offered.

Turning to the older man, Dan asked, "Is she your daughter?"

"Cousin's."

"She's your cousin?"

"Cousin's daughter."

"Does your cousin live around here close?"

"Yep."

"Would it be possible for me to speak with your cousin?"

"Maybe."

Sensing an animosity building in Seth's answers, Dan changed the subject. "Do you happen to have a tractor to pull us out of here?"

"Nope. Don't need no gas-guzzlin', smoke-belchin' ma-chine. We got prize mules that kin do the job better 'n quicker."

"That's great!" said Dan. "Can we do it right away?"

"Nope."

"No? When, then? The wife and I don't have a bit of food and we haven't eaten since yesterday."

"We can try it in a day or two if it don't rain no more. That gumbo ain't a gonna turn loose of yore tars lessen it dries out some. No use even tryin' till then."

Burl, the younger man, spoke up, "If'in yore hungry, come on up to the house with us and I'll have the Mrs. whup you up some vittles."

Dan looked over at Rose.

I'm starving, but I'm not sure I trust these guys, she thought. Rose shrugged her shoulders.

"That's very kind of you," said Dan. "But we'd better not go off and leave Skeeter here all alone."

"The boy can stay here with him till you git back." Burl motioned to the boy. "Clyde, jist crawl in thar and watch over ole Skeeter while these folks gits a bite to eat."

Looks like they're not giving us much choice, thought Rose.

As he lifted a muddy foot to climb into the van, Rose said, "Wait just a minute, Clyde, would you please slip out of those boots and leave them outside? Just think of this as a hospital room that must be kept clean."

"I've never been in a hospital room before, ma'am. But you sound just like Ada Lou. She doesn't let me come in the house with my boots on either."

Well, that makes me feel somewhat better about being invited there for lunch, thought Rose.

The boy sat in the doorway and pulled his feet out of his rubber boots, leaving them standing outside in the mud. Rose noticed that his stockings had been darned a number of times but appeared reasonably clean.

"Dan?" called Rose out the window. "Do we have any more of those trash bags?"

"No, dear, I used the last ones to lay the dog on."

Burl looked over at the plastic bags around Dan's legs. "ma'am? Why don't cha jist stick yore feet in Clyde's boots thar? He won't be a-needin' em till you git back."

Clyde sat on the floor of the van next to Skeeter. "You're more than welcome to them, ma'am. They're a mite big for you, but if you just leave your shoes on inside them, they might fit you fine."

Rose put on a jacket, sat down in the doorway to slip her feet into the boots, and then took a few steps to try them out. She turned around and smiled at the boy. "Thanks, Clyde. I think these will work just fine."

Dan approached the van and handed the jerky to Clyde. He pointed to a water-filled pan Rose had set next to the dog. "Soften up some pieces of this in that water and see if you can get Skeeter to eat some. And let him drink as much water as he wants. He should be okay till we get back."

"I sure will, Doc. Thanks a lot for patching him up. He's a good old dog, and we sure would hate to lose him."

"You're welcome, son. I'm going to slide this door shut now to keep the draft off him."

Rose looked over at the two men who had walked ahead a ways, but stopped to wait for her and Dan. The older man, Seth, gestured to them by making a wide arc with his rifle. "Let's git a move on it!" he yelled.

"Dan, I feel very uneasy about this," Rose said under her breath.

Chapter Nine

The four spoke very little as they trudged up the mountain single file. The two dogs ran ahead in the woods, loping back and forth, and periodically stopping to sniff trees and under bushes. Seth led the way, with Burl, then Rose, then Dan, following Seth's zigzagging footsteps, which took advantage of rocks and clumps of grass to avoid the mud. After they had gone several hundred feet uphill, Rose was breathless and could hear Dan breathing heavily behind her. "Excuse me," she panted, "could we stop for a minute to catch our breath?"

Seth and Burl stopped and turned toward her. "Scuse us, ma'am," said Burl. "We forgit you flatlanders have a time with these little hills."

The dogs bounded back down the mountain to see why the procession had stopped. The smaller of the two, the female, came to Rose, wagging her tail. Rose bent down to pat the smooth, sleek body and scratch behind the velvety floppy ears. Rose looked up at Burl and asked, "Do you breed hunting dogs? These two are exceptionally fine."

"You got a good eye, ma'am; they's the best huntin' dogs in the whole county, specially ole Skeeter. Folks come from miles around to bring their bitches for him to . . . to . . . you know . . . romance."

"Looks like ole Skeeter's gonna be outa the romancin' business fer a spell," said Seth. A sudden thought struck him and visibly jolted his body. "Say, Doc! He ain't plumb *outta* business is he?"

"No, there's no problem there. His business is still intact. Do you have any idea what tore him up like that?

"Shore do," answered Seth. "The biggest, dangdest wildcat you ever seen was in the midst of clearin' out the hen house last night when ole Skeeter took off after him."

Burl added, "We spent half the night searchin' the woods and yellin' fer him. We taken the dogs with us, but they couldn't do no good in that pourin' rain. They couldn't sniff out nothin'."

"Skeeter can be hard-headed as a mule when he's after somethin'," added Seth. "He jist don't give up the chase. That's what makes him sich a good huntin' dog; but it shore fetched him a peck a trouble this time."

"He shore proved how smart he was though," said Burl. "He knew to go to an animal doctor fer help when he needed it."

Seth chuckled and gave an almost toothless grin. "You flatlanders got yore wind back yet?"

"For now," answered Rose. "Do we have much farther to go?"

"Nah. It's just a couple a hundred paces past that little rise up yonder."

His pace or mine, wondered Rose.

They trudged on until they came to what seemed like the top of a ridge where the ground became more level. Rose could see a structure beyond a stand of trees and smoke rising above the treetops. They left the roadway and, following a well-worn path, approached the unpainted, humble dwelling and outbuildings. The dogs rushed ahead to the house, barking to announce their arrival. Rose sighted an outhouse, off on a side path. "Burl, do you mind if I use your bathroom?"

"We ain't got what you might call a bathroom, ma'am. But yore welcome to use the privy there if'in yore a mind to."

When Rose later left the outhouse, she blew the air out of her lungs that she'd been holding for several minutes. *Oh, my, I don't know how they stand it.* Up ahead, she saw that the men were gathered around a washbasin atop a narrow table on the covered porch of the house. The house was built of rough-cut lumber and had a corrugated-tin roof. A downspout led from the roof's gutters, down to a large, wooden barrel set against the house. Morning glory vines encircling the porch's support posts, and drooping down along the roof's edge, overcame the drabness of the place. Rose of Sharon bloomed on either side of the stone porch steps where the men's boots and Dan's trash bags were lined up.

While Seth and Dan dried their hands on a shared towel, Burl tossed water from the washbasin out into the yard, causing the chickens pecking there to squawk and flap away. "After ya git them boots off, ma'am, I'll have ya some fresh water poured to wash up with."

"Thank you, Burl." Rose sat down on a step to remove the boots.

The men gathered at the door, talking, and while Rose was washing her hands, she looked up to see a small face peering at her through the window. As soon as their eyes met, the face disappeared.

The men stepped away from the door, and Burl motioned Rose to enter. The room was a kitchen and dining area combined, with a large round oak table and chairs in the center. A young woman turned from a big cast-iron pot atop a wood-burning stove, set two steaming bowls on the table, and then hurried around it to greet Rose, wiping her hands on her apron as she came. "Howdy, ma'am," she said, dropping her apron to extend her hand. "I'm Burl's wife, Ada Lou."

As Rose took her hand, she noticed that the petite woman was very young, probably still in her teens, and very pregnant. Her hand felt rough and calloused. Her light brown hair was pulled back from her pleasant, tanned face in a long, single braid down her back. "I'm pleased to meet you. My name is Rosemary . . . Rosemary Good, and this is my husband Daniel."

Why, she's not much older than Burl's son, Clyde, thought Rose.

The young woman's small hand disappeared into Dan's large one. "Burl says yore an animal doctor and ya patched up ole Skeeter."

"Yes, I did."

"Is he gonna be all right?"

"I think so. From what I hear, he's got a lot of spunk. The spunky ones always heal better."

"I'm mighty glad to hear that. Well, here I am, jist jawin' away, when I hear you folks is a starvin'." She hurried back around to the stove, talking over her shoulder. "Burl, see that they get seated. Cassie Jean! Git over here and help me git these here vittles on the table!"

A small form dashed across the room from a corner where she'd been hiding behind an afghan draped over a rocking chair. Ada Lou handed her a steaming bowl, and the girl carried it to the table where she struggled to lift, and then set it there. She then shyly turned away to fetch another. Rose guessed her to be four or five years old. *My goodness. Ada Lou couldn't have been more than thirteen or fourteen when she had this one.*

Rose turned to Burl. "Is that pretty little girl yours, Burl?"

"Yes, ma'am. Me and my first wife's, Clyde's ma. That there's Cassie Jean. We don't git many strangers up here, so she's a little on the shy side. But she's a good little gal. She minds Ada Lou real good, doncha, Cassie Jean?" The little girl smiled, showing the space where a front tooth was missing, and scampered back to retrieve another bowl.

Rose peered into the bowl in front of her and sniffed: *Butter beans and big chunks of ham. It looks and smells delicious.*

When all were seated, Burl asked, "Pa, would ya like to say a blessin'?" All bowed their heads.

"Dear Father up thar in heaven, bless this food we're about to eat. And thanks for havin' these good folks show up when they did so's they could help out ole Skeeter. And Lord, please help Skeeter get well real quick. Amen."

Ada Lou passed a plate of cornbread to Dan, who was seated next to her. "I done baked this yesterday and it's a mite hard, but if'in you jist drop it in yore bowl and let it soak a little in the bean juice, it'll soften up to whar it won't be so tough to chew."

"Thank you," said Dan as he took a piece and then passed the plate to Rose. "I'll try that."

Ada Lou then passed a pitcher of iced tea. "Sorry we don't got no milk. Our milk cow, Daisy June, is in a family way and due to calve any day now."

Everyone was hungry, and the meal went quickly and silently, except for the slurping, most notably from Seth and Burl. Rose glanced up from her bowl, and her eyes met the little girl's, staring at her from across the table. Rose winked, and the girl quickly dropped her eyes.

Seth signaled the meal's end by standing up and announcing, "You folks better git back and see how Skeeter's gettin' along. Think you can find the way back by yoreselves? We got a peck a chores to get done."

"No problem," said Dan. "We'll just follow the path to the road, and the road downhill to the van."

Thank God, it's all downhill, thought Rose.

Ada Lou asked, "Kin ya come back fer supper? I'll kill some chickens and whip ya up a *real* meal this time."

"Thank you very much," said Rose, "but we had better stay with Skeeter." *I think I climbed enough mountains for one day, thank you,* she thought. "This was a delicious and filling meal. It should last us."

Dan asked, "Do you folks have a few eggs to spare? Eggs are really good to feed an ailing dog."

"Shore do," answered Burl. "Cassie Jean, did you gather up the eggs this mornin' like you's supposed to?" The girl nodded. "Then go on out to the spring house and fill yore little basket up with eggs fer the doctor here." The girl was out of the room in a flash. He continued, "Ada Lou, is thar any beans left in the pot over thar?"

"Yes. I'll dump em out in a little pail for these folks ta take back with 'em fer supper. And here's a little cornbread left I can throw in too."

Burl emerged from a back room and handed Dan a pair of old rubber boots. "Here, you kin borrow these fer a spell."

As they were walking back down the path, Rose said, "Ada Lou and the little girl seemed genuinely sad to see us go."

"I think they were sad to see *you* go, Rose. They probably don't have much outside female companionship."

"That may be. I wonder if little Cassie Jean even gets any schooling. I thought maybe she couldn't speak until she said 'bye' as we were leaving."

Dan stopped to help Rose around a large puddle where the path met the roadway. "It's hard to believe people still live that way in this day and age. I guess they just prefer their total independence to life in our so-called civilized world."

"Dan, did you have a chance to ask Burl or Seth any more about Mitzy?"

"No, I didn't bring up her name again. I got the distinct impression she's a subject they'd just as soon not discuss. I think they're beginning to have some trust in us though, and I'm hoping they'll tell us how to find her parents."

"Do you think Mitzy and Larry could be in this area?"

"The more I see here, the less inclined I am to think so. I know one thing. If Mitzy warned Larry about Buzzard's Pass back there, he sure wouldn't take a new Mercedes over it. And I just can't picture Larry in these backwoods.

He enjoys his comforts too much. But if we can learn more about Mitzy, it might help us figure out where they might have gone."

"Hold up a minute," said Rose. "These boots are getting heavy!" They stopped, found a tree to lean on, and with a stick, scraped the mud off their boots.

"You know, Dan, I'll bet Ada Lou knows some things about Mitzy. I'd be very surprised if she didn't. If I get a chance to be alone with her, I'll see if I can find out anything."

"That's a good idea, Rosie. She does seem to like to talk."

Rose discovered that going downhill could be more treacherous than going uphill, as she slipped in the mud and then saved herself from a fall by grabbing a nearby sapling. "Whoa!" she cried. "I nearly spilled the beans . . . literally! It's a good thing you're carrying the eggs!"

Clyde was sitting in the van's passenger seat, shielding his eyes from the sun with one hand as he watched their approach. When they got near, he stuck his head out of the window and excitedly said, "I'm sure glad you're back, Doc. Skeeter doesn't look good at all. I think he's dying." Rose noticed tears had streaked the dirt on Clyde's freckled face.

Dan slid the side door open while inside Clyde left his seat and fell to his knees beside the dog. Dan leaned in the door. "Here, Clyde, put these eggs over there on the cabinet for me, will you?" Clyde took the basket, and Dan pulled the towel from the seemingly lifeless dog.

Returning to his knees, Clyde said, "See there, Doc? I got one sip of water down him right after you left, and he hasn't had anything since. I keep talking to him and whistling, but he won't even open an eye at me."

Dan pulled over his black bag, opened it, and pulled out a stethoscope.

"What is that, Doc? What are you going do to him?"

Dan slipped in the ear tubes and placed the scope on the dog's chest. "I'm just going to listen to his heartbeat and his breathing." Dan moved the device several times to different areas of the dog's body, and then pulled the tubes from his ears. "Everything sounds just fine in there." He held the stethoscope toward the worried looking Clyde and asked, "Would you like to hear?" The boy nodded, and then stuck the pieces in his ears while Dan placed the other end over Skeeter's heart.

"Well, I'll be danged! It's going thumpity, thumpity, thump in there."

While Clyde was being enthralled with the stethoscope, Dan lifted the dog's tail and inserted a thermometer. Clyde pulled the tubes from his ears and looked wide-eyed at the process. "If old Skeeter was himself, he sure wouldn't lie still for that! Why are you doing that?"

Dan didn't answer, but in a few minutes, retrieved the thermometer, and turned to hold it up to the light. "He's got a little fever, but no more than would be expected. He's doing just fine."

Feeling relieved at the news, Rose opened the van's front door and sat on the edge of the floorboard to pull her feet out of Clyde's boots.

"Then how come we can't get a rise out of him?" Clyde questioned.

"He's just in a very deep sleep. When animals are badly hurt, they will go into a deep sleep like that, almost as if they're in hibernation, so that all of their energy goes into the healing process. And he probably still has some of that tranquilizer left in his system." Dan laid the towel back over the dog and sat down in the doorway to remove the boots. "Don't worry about him, Clyde. I think he's going to be all right."

"Come on up here in the passenger seat, Clyde," said Rose. "Your boots are right outside the door." She moved over into the driver's seat and watched him as he slid his feet into the boots.

"We enjoyed meeting Ada Lou and your little sister, Clyde. They seem really nice."

"Yes, ma'am."

"How long have Ada Lou and your father been married?"

"Right at a year, I reckon. I thought some day, she'd be *my* gal until Pa up and married her."

"What happened to your mother?"

"She died right after Cassie Jean was born."

"I'm sorry to hear that, Clyde. You must miss her very much."

"I sure do, ma'am. She's buried under that big blackjack tree out back of the house. I go out and talk to her every day and tell her all the news. She'll be glad to know old Skeeter's going to be all right. She raised him up from a pup." Clyde stood up, reached in to grab his hat off the dash and pushed the door closed. Dan had entered the van and was struggling to reach across the dog to close the side door. "Let me get that for you," said Clyde as he slid the door shut. He stuck his head back in the window. "I'd better be getting on home and get my chores done. Guess I'll see you folks tomorrow. Goodbye."

"Goodbye, Clyde," they said in unison.

Rose stayed in the driver's seat, watching Clyde trudge up the hill until he was out of sight.

In a little while, Dan plopped down in the passenger seat and looked over at her. "You're awfully quiet up here. Why, Rose, are you crying?" He got down on his knees and wrapped his arms around her. "What's wrong, Sweetie?"

"That poor, motherless boy," Rose choked out. "It's so hard being a teenager, especially with one parent gone. And then the girl he has a crush on marries his *father*, for Pete's sake." Rose suddenly burst into a crying jag that lasted several minutes. Dan held her close without saying a word. She finally stopped and pushed him away so that she could blow her nose. "I think I know why it's affected me so deeply," she said. "He's such a sweet boy. He reminds me of our boys when they were his age. Sometimes, I get so lonesome for them." She began crying and Dan held her close again.

"I guess motherhood is just something you never get over," said Dan. "And you were a good mother, Rose. You raised two fine young men. We'll give them a call just as soon as we get out of here." He kissed her softly and gave her a squeeze. "I'm going to pull out the bed and take a nap. That hill climb about did me in. Why don't you come join me."

• • •

Rose was awakened a little later by the wind buffeting the van. She looked out of the window at the swaying trees. *Oh please, Lord! Don't let it rain!* She got up carefully so as not to awaken Dan and turned the fire on under the kettle for tea. She heard a whimper and looked down at Skeeter. He lay still, but his visible eye was fixed on her. She knelt down beside him and gently laid her hand on his head. "How are you feeling, boy?" she whispered. The towel covering him rose up and down where his tail thumped the floor. "Good boy. That's a good sign."

She got to her feet and retrieved a couple of eggs from the icebox. Dan rose up on one elbow. "If you're fixing water for tea, I'll have a cup too. Wow! Hear that wind?"

"I'm busy with my other patient right now," said Rose. "He's awake, and I'll bet he's hungry. I was just about to crack a couple of eggs to feed him."

Dan leaned over to look at Skeeter. "Hi, ya, Skeeter! Would you like something to eat?"

Rose beat the eggs in a small bowl and then knelt down to join Dan beside Skeeter. Dan gently lifted, and then supported, the dog's upper body while squeezing his jaws open. "Pour just a little at a time down his throat, Rose. We don't want to choke him."

The dog swallowed the eggs willingly and licked his chops. Rose then held a bowl of water up to his muzzle and he lapped it up greedily.

"Good boy!" said Dan. He stood up and then offered to help Rose to her feet. "We'll turn him over again and do this about every hour or so until bedtime."

"I'm just going to stay down here with him for a little while," said Rose, gently petting the dog. "At least until you make us some tea."

They played dominos in between caring for the dog, ate the rest of the beans and cornbread, and then Rose played her guitar and sang until bedtime. Skeeter seemed to enjoy the music, for every once in a while, he would lift his head to look at Rose and then wag his tail. Before turning in for the night, Dan stuffed a large sponge between Skeeter's hind legs. "Doggie diaper," he explained.

As she lay in the dark, tears came once again to Rose, and she cried as silently as possible to keep from waking Dan. Somber thoughts swirled in her head, keeping her from sleep. *The McCoys have so little, yet are wealthy compared to Dan and me. How in the world are we going to get by? I think I'd rather be dead than to be a burden on our sons.*

Chapter Ten

The strong wind continued through the night and was still blowing hard when they awoke the next morning. Rose looked over at Skeeter. "He seems to be breathing normally." She got out of bed and stepped in wetness. *"Oops!* I think Skeeter's diaper leaked." At the sound of his name, the dog lifted his head to look at her and wagged his tail.

"That's a good sign," said Dan. "That means we're getting plenty of liquids down him and his kidneys are functioning normally."

Dan and Rose spent the next hour mopping the floor, washing the dog, applying disinfectant salve to his wounds, and feeding him. He seemed grateful for the attention, except when he yelped in pain at being turned over.

At last, the dog was clean and comfortable again and snoring peacefully. Rose poured some warm water into the washbasin and proceeded to give herself a sponge bath. "Dan, the McCoys gave us more than a dozen eggs for Skeeter.

Do you suppose there would be enough left for him if we had a couple of them for *our* breakfast?"

"Seeing as we don't have anything else to eat, and seeing as I'm starving, and I'm sure you are too, it's my professional opinion that, yes, we can have some for breakfast. Besides, there's plenty of that dried meat left for him."

After breakfast, in between caring for the dog, Dan and Rose sat in the van's front seats, reading. They waited until well past noon to boil a couple of eggs for their lunch, which they had with herbal tea. They were on their knees, feeding Skeeter the last two eggs, when above the sound of the incessant wind, they heard a strange, clanking noise. While they were giving the dog water and settling him back down, the sound got progressively louder. Rose got up and returned to her seat to look out the windshield. "It's the mules! Here come the McCoys with two mules!"

Dan slid open the side door and sat in the doorway to quickly put on his boots. He stood up to face the approaching procession. "I sure didn't think they'd be able to pull us out of here today."

"Afternoon!" yelled Seth.

"Good afternoon! You and those mules are a sight for sore eyes!"

Burl barked, "Whoa," and dropped the reins to join the others at the van's door. Skeeter's tail wagged wildly as he struggled to get to his feet. The other two hounds danced around, whining and yelping a happy greeting.

"Jist look at ole Skeeter thar," said Seth. "He's a standin' up already!"

"That's about all the excitement he should have for a while," said Dan. "Better order him to lie back down, Seth."

There was a quiver in Seth's voice as he laid his hand on the dog's head. "Down, Skeeter. Lay back down, you ole scallywag."

Rose kneeled beside the trembling dog and helped him down. Seth turned to Dan, his eyes glistening. "He *is* gonna be all right, ain't he, Doc?"

Dan pushed the other two dogs out of the way and slid the van door shut. "Sure looks that way."

Burl motioned to the van. "You ready to git this thing outa here?

"You bet! You think the mud has dried out enough?"

"Yep. You can thank the wind fer hurryin' it up. I see yer vehicle has a trailer hitch."

"It does?"

Visibly surprised by Dan's response, Burl continued. "It'll make hitchin' up the chains a danged sight easier. And pullin' downhill will be a danged sight easier on the mules."

Burl's yelling to the mules and the violent jerking of the van excited Skeeter, and he tried to get up again. Rose sat beside him and gently held him down. "It's okay, Skeeter, all this commotion just means you get to go home."

In one, long, final pull, the van was freed from the mud. Rose heard the clanging of the chain as it was disconnected from the hitch. She watched out the window, as the men and boy used sticks and shovels to clean the mud off the van and its tires as best they could. Finally, Dan slid open the side door. "Rose, grab hold of Skeeter's towel and pull him out of the way to make some room. Seth and Burl can sit here in the doorway and ride up the hill with us."

Clyde rode on the back of one of the yoked mules. Sitting in the passenger seat, Rose watched them in the rear view mirror until a turn in the road left them out of sight.

The van rocked back and forth as Dan manhandled the steering wheel, struggling to avoid the many deep puddles. Seth and Burl clung to whatever they could reach, their feet and lower legs dangling out of the open door. Dan yelled over his shoulder. "Hang on, boys, it's going to get even rougher up ahead!" Skeeter occasionally let out a yelp as the van bounced and slid its way up the hill.

As they rolled toward the house, Burl hopped out of the van. Seth followed, saying "This dadburned thang bucks more'n a mule on loco weed!"

Dan parked close to the front porch with the side door facing the house. Seth trudged over and leaned in. As he started to pick up Skeeter, Dan cautioned "Wait! Don't pick him up like that. You two get on either side of that towel he's lying on and use it like a stretcher to carry him."

They laid Skeeter on the porch while they all removed their muddy boots. Rose sniffed the air as she followed the men and dog into the house. "Mmmm, somebody's cooking!"

"Yes, ma'am! Supper's almost ready," said Ada Lou as she wiped her hands on her apron and turned her attention to the men and dog.

Skeeter was gently lowered onto a pallet made from an old quilt, placed in a corner near the warm stove. Ada Lou set a bowl next to the dog's head. "Lookey here, Skeeter. I done fixed you up somthin' special: chicken'n dumplins' with the livers and gizzards."

While they all watched the dog eagerly lapping at the bowl's contents, the sound of small feet ran the length of the porch. Cassie Jean burst through the door. "Is Skeeter here? Kin I see him?"

The men stepped aside and the child dropped to the floor to pet the dog. "Oh, Skeeter, I've been so lonesome fer you. I was worried sick." She looked him over and began crying. "I'll take care of you, and pretty soon you'll be yer ole self agin; you'll see."

"That's enough, Cassie Jean," said Burl. "Let Skeeter eat his supper. You get washed up and help Ada Lou get *our* supper on the table."

Rose couldn't remember when she'd had such a delicious meal, or when she appreciated one as much; chicken and dumplings, fluffy biscuits, home-canned green beans cooked in salt pork, and a dish she had never heard of before: creamed poke. Cassie Jean made a point of telling everyone that she had gathered the pokeweed all by herself in the woods near the house.

Ada Lou set two warm apple pies on the table. "I shore wished we had us some whipped cream to go with these. After Daisy June has her calf, we'll have us plenty."

The men went out on the front porch to sit and talk while Rose helped Ada Lou and Cassie Jean clear the table. "Ada Lou, that meal was simply delicious. You're an exceptional cook to be so young. Did you learn from your mother?"

Ada Lou poured a kettle of hot water into the large enameled dishpan. "Thank you, ma'am. Yep, I learned from my ma. She brings home ribbons every year from different things she enters at the county fair. I won a couple of ribbons there myself."

Holding a dishtowel, Cassie Jean stepped up on an overturned bucket and reached to pick up a dish from the drain pan.

"I'll take that towel, Cassie Jean," said Rose. "Why don't you go keep Skeeter company?"

The little girl smiled and stepped off the bucket. "Kin I Ada Lou? Kin I?"

"Yes, but just don't wear him out none. Make sure his water dish keeps filled up."

Rose and Ada Lou chatted about cooking and their families as they did the dishes. Finally Rose asked, "Did Seth or Burl mention what we were doing here?"

"We don't hardly never git no flatlanders up in these parts, and any we do git is usually lost. Burl said you two come here a'purpose. He said you wanted to talk to Mitzy's folks. I was a'wonderin' how you come to know 'em."

"How well do you know Mitzy?"

"Not hardy a'tall. I was jist a little sprite when she left these parts, and she ain't been back since. I hear tell she was a wild one, though. I do remember she was real purty. She had curly, red hair and all the fellers follered her around like sick puppies."

"Do you know why she left?"

"She got herself in a family way and run off somewheres. She stole all the money her mama had hid away and even took her mama's genu-wine gold locket. She rode off in the night on one of her daddy's mules, with the other one tethered behind. She left her folks in one heck of a fix; they had three little ones to feed, and no money to buy seed, and no mules to do the plowin'. If'n it hadn't been fer my folks and others, they'd a starved to death, I reckon."

"Oh, my," said Rose. "Did they ever find out where she went? Or what happened to her baby?"

"As fer as I know, no one never heard from her again. But then her folks jist might be too ashamed to tell anyone if they ever did. They's proud people. They try real hard to pay back all the kindness they was showed after what that girl done to 'em."

When the last dish was put away, Ada Lou took off her apron and plopped down into a rocking chair. Kicking off her shoes, she put her feet on a footstool. "'Scuse me, Rosemary, but I've been on these poor feet all day." She pulled off her stockings and lifted one foot in the air. "Jist look at how my feet and ankles is all swoll up."

Rose sat down in a chair next to her. "Mine did that too, when I was pregnant."

The women sat talking about things female, hardly noticing the fading light.

In time, the screen door creaked, and the men and Clyde filed back into the room, along with Cassie Jean with a jar of lightning bugs. "Skeeter's startin' ta come out," said Seth. The dog lifted his head and ears to look at Seth. "Not you, boy. Them danged bugs yore named after."

"How come he's named Skeeter, Grandpa?" asked Cassie Jean.

"Cuz when he was little, he kept a dartin' here and there, stickin' his nose where it didn't belong, jist like a dadburned skeeter."

"Come here, Cassie Jean, and let me see your lightning bugs," said Rose. "I used to catch them when I was a little girl, too; but I haven't seen one in years."

"We calls 'em far flies. How come you don't see em 'no more?"

"We lived in Kansas farm country. The pesticides the farmers use must have killed them, along with the bad bugs.

Every year, there were just fewer and fewer lightning bugs, until there just weren't any at all."

"Well, ain't that a shame," said Ada Lou.

"Yes, it is," said Rose, peering into the jar. "These bring back memories of so many pleasant times spent outdoors on summer evenings."

Cassie Jean took the jar from Rose. "I'm gonna go back out and turn these loose."

Burl lit the room's two coal-oil lamps and then went into an adjoining room, returning with a fiddle and bow. "Time fer a little music."

Seth picked a banjo off the wall where it was hanging.

"I was wondering who played that," said Rose.

Clyde sat down on a stool and lifted a large, earthen jug to his lap.

Burl looked down at Ada Lou. "What would you like to sing, Darlin'?

"I don't feel like singin' tonight. I jist don't have the wind fer it. But why don't you play somthin' purty fer Daniel and Rosemary? How 'bout, 'The Old Rooster Cain't Crow No More'?"

Burl stomped his foot three times and the room erupted into a fast-paced ditty. He looked over and winked at his son, Clyde, who was carrying bass by puffing hard and fast into the jug. Cassie Jean danced into the center of the room and, holding her skirt hem, bounced and swirled around the room. "Lookey how big my shadow is, Pa!" she cried.

Ada Lou rocked in her chair in time to the music. Rose clapped her hands and noticed that even her musically challenged husband was tapping his foot to the rhythm.

The piece ended with a big "whoop" from both the musicians and audience, and Cassie Jean dropped to the floor, laughing and breathing hard.

"That was great!" exclaimed Dan. "Encore! Encore!"

Seth and Burl stared quizzically at Dan.

"He wants us to play some more," said Clyde.

"Why, shore," said Seth. "Is there anything special you'd like to hear?"

"No," said Dan. "Just something lively, like that last one."

"Here's one that'll loosen up yore joints," said Burl as he started up the fiddle.

Cassie Jean was up in a flash, whirling around the room. Dan came to Rose and, taking her hands, pulled her out of her chair and to her feet. "Dan! I can't dance to that!"

"Just close off your mind, Rosie, and let your feet take over," Dan said as he began whirling her around the room. Rose was soon enraptured by the music, and they danced as energetically as a couple of teenagers, with Ada Lou clapping loudly throughout.

When the music stopped, Rose and Dan just held one another, trying to catch their breath.

"Say, I jist recollected somthin'," said Seth. "You've got that geetar out thar in yore vehicle, jist a goin' to waste. How about you givin' us fellers a rest and do some playin' fer us?"

"Rose would love to," said Dan as he headed for the door.

"I'll have to catch my breath first," said Rose. "You boys play so well; you're going to be a tough act to follow."

Dan returned, handed Rose her guitar, and pulled her chair into the center of the room. She sat down and took a few seconds to tune up. "What kind of song would you like to hear?"

"Somethin' slow and purty," said Ada Lou.

Cassie Jean sat down at Rose's feet, with her elbows on her knees and her chin in her hands, peering up at her. Rose strummed her guitar, and in a clear, sweet voice, sang a most heartfelt rendition of "Danny Boy". Being mindful of her own dear boys, her throat constricted and she nearly choked on the last few words, "I love you so."

The room was completely silent when the song ended. Rose opened her eyes to see Cassie Jean hugging her knees, her face buried in them. Rose looked around the room at saddened faces and tear-filled eyes. "Well, I guess I really know how to liven up a party."

"Ma'am," choked out Seth, "that was the most beautifullest thang I ever did hear."

Cassie Jean got up to hug Rose around the neck while the others showered her with praise.

Rose glanced at Dan, who winked at her and smiled broadly.

"Well, thank you, everyone," she said. "Here's one that's not quite so sad." After a few strains of Rose's singing "Tennessee Waltz," Burl helped the barefoot Ada Lou out of her rocking chair and, holding her as close as her condition would allow, waltzed her around the room. Clyde got up from his seat and, with his back to the couple, squatted down in the corner to pet Skeeter.

Ada Lou suddenly stopped short and looked down at the floor. Rose stopped singing and watched the water pouring onto the floor from underneath Ada Lou's dress. "My God!" cried Ada Lou. "What's happening to me?"

Rose stood up, laid her guitar in her chair, and reached out to put her arm around Ada Lou. "Your water just broke, sweetie. That means your baby's coming, and soon." Rose looked up at Burl, who seemed incapable of speech or movement. "Burl. It's time to call for the doctor."

Rose led Ada Lou to the rocker, and then turned back to look at Burl, who stood motionless, staring at the puddle of water at his feet. "Burl! The baby's coming! Get the doctor, quick!"

"There ain't no doctor," said Ada Lou. "Burl's first wife's sister, Clementine, does the mid-wifein' in these parts. She's real good, an she'll come a'runnin' soon as she hears."

Burl finally snapped to and crossed the room to grab up his hat. "I'll saddle up the mules and go fetch her right away."

"Burl, you ain't a'goin' nowhere!" Ada Lou cried. "I want you here while this child gets borned. Clyde can go fetch her."

Clyde had been nervously pacing back and forth and seemed relieved at the suggestion. Seth followed him out the door saying, "I'll go help get the mules hitched up."

Cassie Jean called out, "Skeeter's actin' like he needs to go out agin'. Since Clyde and Grandpa ain't here, who's gonna take him out?"

"I will," answered Dan as he crossed the room to the dog.

"Don't you think you'd better git in bed, Ada Lou?" asked Burl. "Kin I carry you in thar?"

"No. I'm doin' fine right here. I'm jist a little achy. I feel like settin' up a spell."

For more than an hour, Seth, Rose, and Dan sat talking quietly in the flickering lamplight. Burl sat close to Ada Lou, trying to comfort her as her contractions became closer and more intense. With each one, she emitted a small cry, gritted her teeth, and tightly squeezed Burl's hand. Cassie Jean slept soundly on the floor beside Skeeter, where she had spread out her quilt and pillow.

Seth became silent. Dan's head drooped to his chest, but snapped back when Seth erupted with thunderous snoring. Rose got up from her chair, poured a glass of water from the pitcher sitting on the table, and handed it to Ada Lou. "You're a brave girl, Ada Lou, especially since this is you're first. Next time you feel a pain coming on, pant like a dog. It really helps."

Ada Lou drank the water and handed the glass back to Rose. "Thanks, Rosemary, I'll try that. I think I'll go lay down now. Why don't you folks go on to bed too? It's gittin' late and there's no tellin' when this youngin's goin' to git here."

"I wouldn't feel right about leaving you," said Rose.

"I'll be jist fine. Clyde should be back with Clementine real soon now."

"I suppose you're right. Can I get you anything first?"

Ada Lou started to answer, but her face became contorted with pain from another contraction. "We'll be just fine," said Burl. "I'll watch after her."

"Please come out to the van and get us if we can be of any help at all," said Rose.

Before they left, Dan checked on the sleeping dog, and Rose pulled the quilt up around Cassie Jean. They tiptoed across the room and then opened the squeaking door to let themselves out.

Chapter Eleven

"**D**octor Good! Doctor Good! Wake up! We need yore help!" Seth's frantic cries were accompanied by his banging on the van's door.

"I'll be right there," Dan called. He and Rose quickly slipped into their clothes and stepped out into the bright moonlight.

Seth was on the front porch, waiting for them, and wringing his hands. "Doctor Good, thank the good Lord yore here. Clyde jist got back home and Clementine weren't with him. Ada Lou's in a bad way and she needs you right away."

"Needs *ME*?" Dan asked incredulously.

"Yore a doctor ain't cha?"

"Well, yes; but I treat animals, not people."

"Well, there cain't be that much difference. Now quit yore jawin' and git in thar."

Dan stood with his hands on his hips, shaking his head. He was about to protest further, when Rose laid her hand on his shoulder. "Dan, you've got to see what you can do. These people don't have anyone else; and there's no one here right now more qualified than you."

Dan looked down at Rose. "Okay, but the AMA better never get wind of this. Get my black bag while I get washed up. Seth, pour me out some clean water."

"We cain't thank you enough, Doc," said Seth as he watched Dan vigorously scrubbing his hands and forearms. "Burl's quivering in thar like a hunk a hog-bone jelly, and I shore don't know nuthin' about sich thangs. Clyde's out thar in the barn puttin' the mules up and cryin' like some dadburned little baby."

Ada Lou's loud moaning could be heard from the front porch. Rose dampened a washcloth and rushed into the bedroom to lay it on her forehead. Ada Lou thrashed back and forth, seemingly oblivious to anything but her pain. Rose looked over at Burl, who was bug-eyed and shaking. "Go on out there and stay with Cassie Jean," ordered Rose. "She looks scared to death with all this commotion going on."

As Burl got up to leave, Ada Lou let out a piercing scream. In the next room, Skeeter let out a mournful howl, and the two dogs outside joined in the chorus. Burl stopped short and looked at Rose. "Go on," said Rose. "We're going to be busy in here, and you'll just be in the way."

Dan passed Burl on his way out the door and ordered Rose to open his bag, which she had set on the dresser. "Seth, set that lamp over here on this table. That's good. Now bring in that clean basin of water and set it on that chair by the bed. Rose, get those surgical gloves out of my bag and open the package. Be careful not to contaminate them."

As Dan pulled on the gloves, he said to Seth, "Go out there and see if you can quiet those dogs. And you and everybody else stay out of here and out of the way."

"You bet, Doc. If'n you need anything, jist holler."

"Rose, pull up Ada Lou's dress. The lye soap in the washbasin ought to be a good disinfectant. Use that washcloth, and wash her privates as good as you can so I can examine her."

Ada Lou screamed again. "Dan, can't you give her something for the pain?" pleaded Rose.

"I wouldn't *dare* give her anything," said Dan, as he examined the squirming Ada Lou. "I have no idea how the medication I have would affect a human. Rose, you're going to have to hold her down while I get this baby turned. No wonder she's having a hard time of it. This kid's all twisted up in here."

Rose held on to the screaming Ada Lou and watched the sweat pop out on Dan's forehead as he worked. The love and pride she felt for him at that moment brought tears to her eyes.

Another contraction began.

"Okay, Ada Lou, push," said Dan. "Push, girl, push."

Rose pulled away from her as Ada Lou rose up on her elbows, gritted her teeth, and pushed with all her might.

"That's a good, girl. It's almost here," said Dan. "At the next contraction, take a deep breath, and push again."

Ada Lou screamed at the top of her lungs as the ultimate contractions shoved the baby, and then the afterbirth, out of her. She limply fell back on the bed.

"Oh, my God!" said Dan. Rose looked over at the nondescript bundle of flesh Dan was holding. "The umbilical cord is wrapped all around it and choking it."

He quickly unwound the cord from around the baby. Rose gasped when she saw that the child was blue and not breathing.

Ada Lou weakly raised her head and mumbled, "What's wrong? What's wrong with my baby?"

Rose mopped Ada Lou's sweat-soaked hair back off her face. "Shush, Ada Lou. Everything's going to be all right. Just lay back and take it easy."

Rose turned her attention back to Dan as he cleaned out the baby's mouth with his forefinger. He lifted the tiny body up to his face, and gently sent puffs of air into its lungs.

Oh, God, please don't make a liar out of me. Please let that baby live, thought Rose.

Suddenly, the child sucked in a lungful of air and let it back out with a yowl. Rose both laughed and cried. "Hear that, Ada Lou? That's your baby boy making all that noise. He's going to be just fine." Upon hearing the baby's crying, the dogs added to the racket by resuming their howling.

Burl stood in the doorway, his hand to his mouth and tears streaming from his eyes.

Dan deftly tied off and then cut the baby's umbilical cord. "This kid's a big one. He must weigh eight or nine pounds."

"Kin I come in now?" asked Burl.

"Could you wait just a few minutes until I get things cleaned up in here?" said Rose.

Burl disappeared from the doorway.

Rose bathed Ada Lou, put a clean nightgown on her, and then changed the bed linens. Dan bathed the baby, diapered him, and wrapped him in a baby blanket. The entire time, a crying Ada Lou never took her eyes off her baby.

Rose propped up the pillows behind Ada Lou, and Dan gently lowered the baby into her arms. He called out, "Okay, you guys can come in now."

Burl and Cassie Jean rushed to the bedside. Seth patted Dan on the back. "You done good, Doc." His voice cracked. "You done real good."

"I'm just glad I could be of service," said Dan. "This is *my* first baby, too, you know."

Burl fell on his knees beside the bed and kissed Ada Lou. Cassie Jean leaned over to intently study the baby. "Pa says he's a boy. I wanted a girl so we could play dolls together, but I guess he'll have to do. What's his name?"

"This here's Daniel," said Ada Lou. "This is our little Danny Boy."

"Like in the song?" asked Cassie Jean.

"Like in Daniel, the good doctor what saved him . . . *and* me. Reckon we wouldn't be here no more if'n it weren't fer him."

Rose looked at Dan. His head was lowered, and he appeared to be blushing.

"That's right," said Burl. "I seen the whole thang. You two woulda been goners, that's fer sure if'n it weren't fer the doc here." He looked up at Dan. "How can we ever repay you, Doc?"

"You already have," said Dan. "Say, where's Clyde? Shouldn't he be here for this momentous occasion?"

"I went out to the barn a little bit ago to tell him he had a new baby brother," said Seth, "but he was sound asleep in the hay. I figured mornin' was soon enough fer him to find out."

Ada Lou said, "Why don't you folks go on out and try to get some rest now. You look plum tuckered out."

"Are you sure?" asked Rose. "You're the one who should be tuckered out."

"I am. I'll rest too. Burl's here if'n I need anything."

They returned to the van and wearily climbed back into bed. Rose scooted next to Dan and gave him a big hug. "You were wonderful tonight, dear. Burl's right. That girl and her baby would surely have died if it hadn't been for you."

"You were pretty wonderful yourself, Rosie. If I had known you were such a good assistant, I would have hired you to work in the clinic years ago."

"I think I would have liked it, too. I've always loved animals."

Dan was silent for a long while. Rose thought he was asleep until he said, "You know, Rose, what happened tonight was one of the most gratifying things I've ever experienced. I don't even know how to express what I felt."

"I felt it too, Dan. It must just be the miracle of birth. It's witnessing the hand of God at work, creating a new life."

"I think you're right."

Wrapped in each other's arms, they drifted off to sleep.

Once again, Seth's yelling and banging on the van door awakened them. "Doctor Good! Wake up! We need yore help!"

Chapter Twelve

Dan jumped out of bed and slid the door open. "What is it, Seth? Is something wrong with Ada Lou or the baby?"

"No. It's Daisy June. She's havin' her calf and she's a havin' a hard time of it."

Dan let out a big sigh. "It must be the full moon. I'll be there as soon as I get dressed."

Dan stepped into his pants. "Rose, there's no telling how long this is going to take. You stay here and try to get some sleep."

"Not on your life. I'm you're new assistant, remember?"

"Not this time, Sweetie, this is a whole lot different. There's nothing you can do to help. This could take some time, and Ada Lou's going to need your help tomorrow. Hell, it's already tomorrow. Just lie back down and try to get some rest, okay?"

"You're sure I can't help?"

Dan leaned down and kissed her. "Thanks, Hon, I'm sure."

A short time later, the crowing of a rooster awakened Rose. She peered out the window at a pink-streaked sky. *Morning already? It seems like I just got to sleep.* She sat up and stretched. *Up and at 'em, Rose. This is going to be a busy day.*

Rose dressed, and then tiptoed across the McCoy's front porch. Not wanting to open the squeaky screen door, she peeked in through the bedroom window. Burl was asleep in a chair in the corner of the room. Ada Lou was sleeping peacefully and the baby was asleep in its cradle beside her bed. Rose quietly stepped down from the porch. The two hound dogs crawled out from under the van to follow her across the yard to the barn, scattering the clucking chickens in their path. As she struggled to pull back the large door, the dogs tried to wriggle inside. Remembering Burl's previous command, she said, "Git!" The dogs reluctantly backed off.

The sun, pouring in between the vertical boards of the barn's wall, made bright stripes on the hay-strewn, dirt floor. Dan, Seth, and Clyde were at the far end of the large structure, sitting on the top rail of an enclosure, and staring down into it as they talked. "Good morning," said Rose.

Dan jumped down from the railing. "Good morning, Rosie. Come see what we have here."

Rose peered over the railing. "Two! There are two of them?"

"Yup," beamed Seth. "Purty little Daisy June done herself real proud."

Rose studied the cow as it licked one wobbly calf and then the other. "Is Daisy June okay? You said last night that she was having trouble."

"With twin births, sometimes one of them is breech," said Dan.

"The Doc got that first un turned around and out, slick as a whistle, though," said Seth.

"And right after that, out pops little Mary there. We never spected thar'd be two of em."

"Mary?" asked Rose

"Yup. They's two little heifers. If'n they's anythin' like their mama, we got us two good milk cows comin' up."

"The first one's name is Rose," offered Clyde. "Granpa named them after you, Mrs. Good; Rose and Mary."

Dan grinned at Rose. "Don't you feel honored, dear?"

"Well, uh . . . I guess. I've never had a cow named after me before, much less two cows."

"If'n you think Daisy June can do without us now, Doc," said Seth, "let's head on up to the house fer some breakfast."

"She seems to be pretty much in control of the situation now," said Dan. "I could sure use a cup of coffee."

As they walked back to the house, Cassie Jean came bounding down the porch steps, crying, "Skeeter's gone! Papa said for me to come tell you, Grandpa. We gotta find Skeeter!"

"I think I know where he might be," said Rose. She walked to the van and leaned down to look under it. "Here he is."

Seth bent down to have a look. "Skeeter! What in the tarnation are you a doin' under thar?"

Looking somewhat sheepish, the dog crawled out from under the van, wagging his tail.

"Looks like we're going to have to clean him up before we can wash up ourselves," said Dan. "Look how the dirt is stuck to all the salve I put on him."

While the men busied themselves with cleaning the dog, Rose entered the house to find Burl stoking the kitchen stove. "Good morning, Burl. The men will be in as soon as they get Skeeter cleaned up."

Burl set the large enameled coffee pot on the stove. "They found him already?"

Rose answered, "He hadn't gone far."

"I guess I didn't git the door shut good after I come in last night from the privy. He musta nosed his way out."

Rose glanced over at the closed bedroom door. "How are Ada Lou and little Danny this morning?"

"Why don't cha jist slip in thar and see fer yerself. That little bugger woke up a squallin' fer his breakfast jist a little bit ago. Ada Lou's feedin' him right now."

Rose opened the door and peeked in to see Ada Lou in her rocking chair, the baby suckling at her breast. "Good morning, Ada Lou. How is everything this morning?"

"Mornin', Rosemary. Everythin's fine ceptin' I'm hongry enough to eat a horse."

"I've never cooked on a wood stove before," said Rose, "but if Burl will show me where everything is, I'll see what I can do."

Rose set out all the ingredients to make biscuits. *It's been years since I made biscuits from scratch. I hope I can remember how.* Burl fried the bacon, and Cassie Jean set the table. While the biscuits were in the oven, Rose cooked a big batch of scrambled eggs. Burl helped Ada Lou put the sleeping baby back in his cradle and then helped her to the table.

After Seth said grace, Burl helped himself to the biscuits and passed them around. "That shore was a stroke of luck,

Daisy June a havin' twins," he said. "What's the chance of that happenin', Doc?"

"More often than you might think. Depending on the breed, two or three out of a hundred."

"I sure would like to be an animal doctor like you," said Clyde. "Could you teach me?"

Dan passed the butter to Seth. "After the way you helped with the calving last night, Clyde, I think you'd make a good one. But becoming a veterinarian takes a long time. After you get out of college, you have to go to veterinary school for four years."

"Four years? And I'm never going to get to go to any college. How come it takes so long, anyhow?"

"Quit askin' sich silly questions, Clyde," said Burl. "Larnin' sometin' like that takes time. Everone knows animal doctors got to know a whole lot more than people doctors."

"Oh?" said Dan. "How do you figure?"

"It just stands to reason," answered Burl. "Animals cain't tell you whar it hurts like people can."

Ada Lou slammed her fork down on the table. "I don't wanna hear no more about animals! You'd think Daisy June was the only one around here who done somethin' special last night!"

Burl leaned over and took her pouting face in one hand and turned it to him. "Darlin' Ada Lou, nobody could a done nothin' more special than whut you done last night, even if'n you didn't have twins."

Smiling, Rose got up from the table and soon returned with the coffee pot.

"Anyone need a refill?" As she filled Seth's cup, she said, "Sorry about the biscuits. They sure can't hold a candle to yours, Ada Lou. I must have forgotten how much baking soda to use."

"Don't worry about it none," said Seth. "I've had a whole lot worse in my lifetime."

Sitting back down, Rose asked, "Burl, whatever happened to your cousin who was supposed to deliver the baby?"

"Clementine? She was over in Piney Haller deliverin' a baby. But her old man said he'd ride over to Ada Lou's folk's place and tell em Ada Lou was a havin' hers."

"Ma ought to be here any time," said Ada Lou. "She'll be a bringin' some things fer the baby, and she'll stay as long as I need her to help out around here."

"If'n I didn't have all them weeds to hoe, and if'n she warn't such a good cook, I'd go off in the woods and stay while she was here," said Seth.

"Grandpa, you got no call to talk that a way about my mama!" Ada Lou scolded.

"Seth," interrupted Dan, "Rosemary and I plan to stay as long as Ada Lou needs help, but with her mother coming, we'll be leaving as soon as she gets here."

"Yore plannin' on leavin right away? What about Skeeter? "

"Skeeter's healing fast and doing just fine. He proved that this morning." said Dan.

At the sound of his name, Skeeter wobbled over to Seth, wagging his tail. Seth dropped a large piece of bacon, and Skeeter snapped it up in mid-air. "But what about all them stitches?"

"They'll need to come out in four more days. You can do it; I'll show you how," said Dan.

"*I* can do it," said Clyde. "Show *me* how."

"I'm sure you can, Clyde. I'll give you both a lesson right after breakfast. I'll also leave the rest of that salve for you to use on him."

"There ain't no way we can thank you fer all you done fer us," said Seth.

"I can think of a way," said Dan. "You can tell us where we can find Mitzy McCoy's folks."

Skeeter had curled up at Seth's feet, and Seth reached down to fondle his long floppy ears. "I don't know how come you won't say why yore so set on findin' em, but after seein' the kind of folks you and yer misses is, I know you don't mean 'em no harm. They don't take kindly to strangers a comin' round. None of us does. But you folks ain't no strangers no more. Not to us, anyhow."

Seth shoved back his plate. "Clyde, I got some words I want you to put down on a scrap of paper fer the doc to take to them McCoy cousins. I'll put my X on it. That, and some of Ada Lou's blackberry jam oughta make 'em a mite more friendly. Hell, fer the doc here, I'll even throw in a smoked ham."

"That would be very kind of you, Seth," said Dan. "Before you give me directions, let me ask; will we have to go back over Buzzard's Pass to get back to a main highway?"

Rosemary's heart leapt to her throat at the thought.

"Nope, you'll be a goin' in the opposite dee-rection. You jist have a couple of little cricks to cross over till you git to the Cannonball Highway. The McCoy place is about four miles from here as the crow flies, and the highway is another twenty or so."

Ada Lou slowly rose from her chair. "I shore do thank you fer fixin' breakfast, Rosemary.

"I had a lot of help," she answered.

"I reckon I better git back in bed now. I'm feelin' mighty peek-ed."

Burl swept Ada Lou up in his arms and carried her back to the bedroom. Rose began clearing the table, and Cassie Jean joined in without being asked. "You're a good girl to help," said Rose. "With a new baby to care for, Ada Lou's going to need a lot of help. She's lucky she has you."

"Yes, maam," said Cassie Jean.

Dan excused himself and went out to the van to take a much-needed nap.

Burl came out of the bedroom and quietly closed the door behind him. "Thank you, Mrs. Good, fer cleanin' up. We men have a passel of work to do. That rainstorm done put us way behind. Pa and Clyde probably have the mules hitched up by now, so if'n you'll excuse me . . .

"Of course," said Rose. "We'll take care of things around here. Go on to work and don't you worry about a thing."

Burl slapped on his hat and headed out the door. "Thank you, maam."

Rose washed the dishes, while Cassie Jean stood on the overturned bucket to dry them.

"Cassie Jean, do you go to school?"

"No, maam. I heered about school, but I ain't never been thar. I got me some picture books though what Clementine give me. Wanna see em? I kin read some of the words. Wanna hear me read?"

"Yes, I'd like that, as soon as we finish the dishes and sweep in here. Is Ada Lou teaching you to read?"

"No, maam, Clementine is. She's a teachin' Ada Lou too. Ada Lou says any child of hers is gonna know how to read and write."

"What about Clyde? Did Clementine teach him too?"

"Clyde knew how to read before I was borned. He reads a lot. Our mama done taught him. He kin write real good too."

The morning passed quickly for Rose. She tidied up the house, helped Cassie Jean with her reading, and when Ada Lou awoke from her nap, showed her how to bathe the baby. She was diapering him, when the dogs began barking. Cassie Jean ran to peek out the door, and then scampered back to the bedroom. "It's Aunt Clementine! Clementine's here!"

The dogs quit barking, and then there were sounds of footsteps on the porch. "Hello! Anyone home?"

Cassie Jean was already at the door. Rose looked out of the bedroom to see her hugging a tall, wispy woman around the waist. "You sweet, little thing," the woman said. "I'm glad to see you too. Is Ada Lou . . ." Looking toward the bedroom, she stopped short when she saw Rose standing in the doorway.

"That thar's Rosemary," said Cassie Jean. "She's real nice. She helped take care of Ada Lou, and little Danny, and Skeeter, and . . ."

"Cassie Jean, hush!" said the woman. With a defiant look on her face, she walked toward Rose.

"Hello," said Rose, smiling.

The woman hesitated, wordlessly glowering at Rose before stepping past her to enter the bedroom.

Gee, thought Rose. *She doesn't seem too friendly.*

"Hi, Clementine," said Ada Lou. "It's good to see you. Come see little Danny."

"I'm so sorry I didn't get here in time, Ada Lou," said Clementine as she leaned over the bed to look at the baby.

"My, but he's a big one. I hope you didn't have any trouble with the delivery."

"As a matter of fact, I did. If'n Doctor Good hadn't been here, I reckon Danny and I wouldn't be here neither."

"The *doctor*? *What* doctor?"

"Dr. Daniel Good. He's really an animal doctor, but a people doctor couldn't have done no better. Rosemary over there is his wife. They's real good folks."

The baby began to cry, and Ada Lou cuddled him to her breast.

Clementine spun around to face Rose. "Real good folks?" she snarled. "We'll just see."

Chapter Thirteen

Feeling extremely unwelcome in Clementine's presence, Rose brushed past Cassie Jean and left the house. She climbed into the van and shut the door as quietly as possible. Dan rolled over. "You don't have to be quiet, I'm getting up."

"Good," said Rose. "It's time we left."

"I thought I heard a horse and buggy pull up," said Dan. "Are Ada Lou's parents here?"

"No. It's Burl's sister-in-law, Clementine. She can take care of things now, and I don't want to stay here another minute with her here."

Dan stood up and reached for his pants. "She must have made quite an impression on you."

"Yes, she did. If she'd had a knife, I think she would have slit my throat."

Dan pulled a T-shirt over his head. "My goodness, what did you say to her?"

"That's just it! I smiled when I first saw her, and said 'hello,' but I never had a chance to say anything else. I have no idea why she was so hostile toward me."

They heard the men's voices approaching, and then Clyde yelled, "Aunt Clementine's here! There's her buggy."

"Oh, my," said Rose. "It must be lunchtime, and I don't have a meal ready for them."

Rose stepped out of the van as Burl was saying, "Take Clementine's things on in the house, Clyde, and then come right back out and take care of her mule and buggy."

Rose hurried into the kitchen area and began stoking the stove while the men were busy washing up on the front porch. She didn't hear Clementine come up behind her.

"That won't be necessary," said Clementine coolly. "I brought plenty of food the relatives sent, already cooked."

"How nice," said Rose. "I'll set the table then."

Clementine turned and began emptying the food basket Clyde had set on the table. "Ada Lou told me all the good things you and your husband have done here. But she didn't explain, at least not to my satisfaction, *why* you're here."

Seth burst noisily into the room. "Clementine, gal, yer a sight fer sore eyes!" He picked her up by her slender waist and twirled her around.

She can actually laugh, thought Rose.

After all had finished eating and the chatter at the table had died down, Dan announced that he and Rose would be leaving right away. "We'd like to get to your cousin's place this afternoon, Seth. May we have that note Clyde wrote out for you with the directions?

Clementine stood up. "There are some things I need to say about that. Cassie Jean, why don't you go on out and play."

"But I want to . . ."

"Do as your aunt says," said Burl. "You go on out and play."

Clementine followed Cassie Jean to the door and closed it after her.

"Now, what is it you got to say, Clementine?" asked Seth.

Clementine stood at the head of the table, her arms folded over her chest. Her glowering eyes darted back and forth between Dan and Rose. "I want to know what interest these people have in Jesse and Sarah."

"Why, they just want to talk to 'em. Somethin' about Mitzy."

"You really don't know anything about these two, do you? Clementine flung her hand toward Dan and Rose. "Where they come from, who they're working for, or why they're way back here in these hills."

Seth scratched his beard. "I know theys from way out west. Kansas I think it was. And I know theys real nice folks."

"Just who, or what, do you think we are?" asked Dan.

"I think you're a pair of those sneaky, State Social Services do-gooders."

Suddenly, all eyes turned to Dan and Rose, filled with suspicion.

Finally losing patience with Clementine and her attitude, Rose snapped, "That's absolutely absurd! I assumed you came here to help, but it seems to me you're just here causing trouble!"

Clementine started to respond, but Seth held up his hand, signaling her to be quiet. He turned to Dan. "You seem like a good man, Doc. But jist in case Clementine's right, you ain't gittin' nothin' from me lessen you tell us *why* you come up here lookin' fer Mitzy's folks."

Dan took a deep sigh, and then narrated the entire story of Larry and Mitzy's thievery.

With downcast eyes, Seth sat silent for a minute, shaking his head. He finally looked up. "That's a real sad story. After whut that girl done to her own folks, I ain't surprised one bit. How come you was so set on not tellin' us before?

"I guess I had an issue with trust, too," answered Dan. "I was afraid if you knew we were after Mitzy, one of you would try to warn her or her folks."

Burl looked up at Clementine. "Well, how about it, Clem. Does that answer yer questions?"

During Dan's recitation, Rose had kept her eyes on Clementine. She watched as the hardness in the woman's demeanor softened, and the hate left her eyes.

As she spoke, Clementine looked at Dan, and then at Rosemary. "Yes, it does. Please accept my apology. I was so certain . . ."

"Your apology is accepted," said Rose, "but what if we *were* social workers. What are you so afraid of?"

Clementine pulled out her chair and sat back down. "My sister, Ida Mae, Clyde and Cassie Jean's mama, was two years younger than me. We had an older brother, and one just a baby, when our family got torn apart. I was just about six years old then. Our daddy accidentally got shot when he was out hunting . . ."

"I ain't so shore about that accidental part," interrupted Seth.

"That's another story, Pa," said Burl. "Let Clem finish."

"Anyway, Daddy was hurt real bad and they brought up a doctor from Cedarville to take out the bullet. He was real citified, fresh out of some medical outfit back east. He took word back to the authorities that our family was too poor for us children to be properly cared for. So a couple of social workers from the state showed up with some papers and just took us children away." Clementine dropped her head. "We never saw our mama and daddy again. Sometimes at night I still wake up hearing my mama screaming after us."

Rose reached over and laid her hand on Clementine's. "How terrible. What happened to you children?"

"Ida Mae and I got to stay together with a foster family in Lexington. He was a preacher, and they were nice enough folks, but they weren't family. We never did learn what happened to our brothers. Someone said they thought it was our older brother who was seen around our folk's place some years later, but the folks were dead by then, and he just disappeared."

"Your mother and father were dead?"

"They say Daddy never did heal right, and he died soon after Mama did. They say Mama died of a broken heart."

Burl spoke up. "When Clementine's husband and I were jist young bucks, we were in Cedarville pickin' up supplies, and jist happened to meet up with Ida Mae and Clementine at the drug store soda fountain. It had been at least ten years since we'd seen 'em last, but we knew right away who they was. They was the two purtiest gals in the whole county."

Burl caught himself and glanced over at a pouting Ada Lou. "They was purt'near as purty as Ada Lou there."

"Our foster parents were conducting a revival in Cedarville," interjected Clementine, "and they always had Ida Mae and I sing and collect donations at the different revivals. We were in Cedarville for a week that summer, and Ida Mae and I would sneak out whenever we could and meet the boys somewhere."

Burl continued, "Billy Jack and I courted those girls by mail for the next two years. We couldn't write too good, and they'd always mark corrections on our letters and send 'em back with the ones they wrote us."

"They came to Lexington one time to see us," laughed Clementine, "but the preacher wouldn't let us out of his sight. The boys spent the entire afternoon in the parlor with us and the preacher and his wife."

"It was a whole lot different when we come back the next time, though," said Burl. "We come askin' fer the girl's hands, and we wouldn't take no fer an answer."

"Ida Mae and I had something to do with the outcome," said Clementine. "We had told Parson Jones and Millie, his wife, that we were going to run off anyway if they said no. They were getting old, they're both dead now, and I think they weren't too unhappy about it. The Parson gave us a double wedding before we left."

"How did you learn to be a midwife?" asked Rose.

"After I graduated from high school in Lexington, I worked in the maternity ward at the hospital. I got to see a lot of births, and even delivered one myself when the doctors had their hands full during an emergency. It was such a gratifying experience, I did the training to get my certification."

"I know what you mean about a gratifying experience," said Dan. He pushed his chair back and stood up. "I hate to have to say goodbye to all you good people, but I'm afraid we must. I'll go out to the barn and check Daisy June and her calves one more time, and then we really must be off." Sensing his savior was about to leave, Skeeter followed Dan out the door.

When Dan returned, there were handshakes and hugs all around. Seth and Skeeter followed Dan and Rose to the van while the rest stood in the shade of the porch to wave and see them off. Seth hugged Dan. "Whenever I look at little Danny, I'll think of you, Dr. Good." He then turned to hug Rose. "And whenever I look at them two little heifers, I'll think of you, Rosemary." Seth opened the door for Rose to climb in. "Do you folks think you'll ever git this way agin'?"

"It's doubtful," said Dan, "but you never know."

"You know you're always welcome."

"We know," said Rose.

Skeeter howled pitifully as they backed out of the long drive and turned onto the road. Rose looked back to see the dog and Seth still standing where they had left them. "Dan, did you see the tears in Seth's eyes when we left?"

"Yes, that old codger's a lot tougher on the outside than he is on the inside. I kind of hate to leave right now. I actually think I'm going to miss them all. But we can't afford to let Larry and Mitzy's trail get any colder than it already is."

Chapter Fourteen

The weather had been sunny and hot during their stay with the McCoys. The muddy road had dried, but was deeply rutted. The van bumped and swayed, as it made its way to the home of Mitzy McCoy's parents. "I thought Seth said it was only four miles to their place," said Rose.

"As the crow flies," said Dan. "According to the trip meter, we've already come seven."

They finally came to the turnoff Clyde had indicated on the map he had drawn for them. The van rolled to a stop in a farmyard and was met by three snarling, yapping hounds. "Looks like some of Skeeter's relatives," said Dan.

The slight figure of a man, rifle in hand, appeared in the doorway of the barn. Rose glanced at the dilapidated house to see the front door close and faces appear at the window.

Dan started to open his door, but the dogs leapt up, snapping at him through the open window. While the dogs were fixed on Dan, Rose yelled to the man. "Hello! We're friends of Seth and Burl. We've just come from their place."

The man lowered his rifle and whistled for the dogs. They ran to him immediately, and he motioned them into the barn. Without leaving his place in the doorway, he called out, "Ya'all can step outta there now."

Dan walked around the van and extended his hand. "Hi! Fine looking hounds you have there. You must be Jesse McCoy."

"That's right. And jist who might you be?"

After introductions, Jesse said, "You say you jist come from Seth and Burl's place?"

"That's right," said Rose. "And they sent some things for you."

Jesse snapped his fingers and the dogs filed out of the barn. Rose felt uneasy, but stood still as the dogs sniffed her and Dan thoroughly. One licked her hand and, in unison, the three began wagging their tails. "Yep," said Jesse, "you jist come from their place all right."

Jesse carried the ham Seth had sent, and Rose and Dan followed with the jars of Ada Lou's preserves. When they got to the home's front door, it opened, and a thin, red-headed woman extended her arms to take the jars from Rose. *How striking she is,* thought Rose. *She must have been a beautiful woman at one time.*

"This here's Dan and Rosemary Good," said Jesse. "They jist come from Seth and Burl's place." The woman nodded.

"You must be Sarah," said Rose.

Jesse invited Dan and Rose to sit at the large kitchen table. "I'm ready for a little snack, how 'bout you folks?"

While Sarah sliced a loaf of freshly baked bread, Rose glanced around the room. In one dark corner stood a boy of twelve or thirteen. She smiled, saying, "Hello, there."

As the boy emerged from the shadows, Rose saw that he was a child with Down Syndrome. Without a word, he came to Rose, threw his arms around her neck and hugged her tightly.

"Eugene! Turn her loose!" scolded Jesse. "Whut's got inta ya, boy?" Laughing, Rose pulled his arms from their grip around her neck and held his hands in hers.

She looked into his distinctly-slanted eyes. "It's nice to meet you, Eugene. Thank you for the hug."

"Sorry about that," said Sarah. She took the boy by his shoulder and led him to a chair at the table. "I ain't never seen him do that before. He don't usual cotton to strangers"

"That's perfectly all right," said Rose. "Everyone can use a hug now and then."

As they ate bread and butter slathered with Ada Lou's preserves, Dan and Rose related all the recent happenings at the other McCoy household.

"So Ada Lou had a little boy," said Sarah. "Ain't that nice. I'll have to hurry up and finish the lil' quilt I'm a makin' fer it."

Jesse turned to Dan. "You delivered the baby *and* the calves?"

"Yes, I did," answered Dan. "All in one busy night."

"Say, Doc, would you mind takin' a look at one a my shoats? She's been a ailin'."

"I haven't had much experience with swine," said Dan, "but I'll take a look at her."

Dan was wondering how he was going to be able to snoop around the grounds, thought Rose. *This is his opportunity.*

The men left the house, and Eugene shuffled after them.

As she helped clear the table, Rose said, "I understand you have a daughter."

"I have two daughters. One's married and livin' over in Stovepipe holler and the younger one's off visitin' a friend. She ought to be back directly."

"Don't you have a third daughter?" asked Rose. "Mitzy?"

Sarah dropped the plate she was carrying and it shattered on the floor. "It's a good thing you didn't mention that name while Jesse was here. He don't allow that name spoke . . . ever."

Rose reached down to pick up pieces of the plate.

"Never mind that," said Sarah. "I'll get the broom and dustpan."

When Sarah returned, Rose saw that she was crying.

"How do you know about, Mitzy?" Sarah choked out. "Do you know where she's at?"

"No," said Rose. "We were hoping you could tell *us* that."

Sarah bent down and quickly swept up the broken plate. "I ain't had no word of that child since she left here seven long years ago."

Sarah stood up and looked piercingly at Rose. "Why are you askin' about her?"

She doesn't know Mitzy's whereabouts, thought Rose. *Nobody could put on such a good act.*

"I know what she did to you," said Rose. "Together, she and a person we thought was a friend did the same thing to Dan and me. They stole everything we had."

Sarah dumped the contents of the dustpan into the trash and sat back down at the table. "Sit down and tell me whut happened. If the men folk come back, don't dare let on whut we've been talkin' about, okay?"

While Rose related the story, Sarah sat with her head in her hands, sobbing. When Rose finished, Sarah pulled a handkerchief out of her apron pocket and blew her nose. "She was such a purty li'l thang. She looked like one of God's angels, but turns out she was one of the devil's disciples. She done really bad things from the time she could walk. She weren't like my other children at all."

Rose reached over and patted the woman's hand. "I'm so sorry to burden you with this."

"Don't be sorry. There ain't been a day goes by, what I don't wonder where she's at and how's she's a doin'. Bad news is better'n none at all. Jesse won't claim her, but no matter whut she's done, she's our flesh and blood. At least now I know she's alive. Tell me, do you know if she had a child with her?"

Rose shook her head. "No, I'm almost sure she didn't."

Sarah got a faraway look in her eyes, and Rose knew she was thinking about the baby Mitzy carried in her womb the night she disappeared. "Jesse blames me fer her bein' the way she is. He says she was a bad seed, and I guess he's right. He said if he'd a knowed I had Hatfield blood, he never would a married up with me."

"Hatfield?" asked Rose. "You mean like in the Hatfield-McCoy feud?

"Yes, ma'am. My Great Grandaddy was a Hatfield."

"But I thought that story was something out of Hollywood. Are you telling me there really was such a feud?"

"Yes, ma'am. It was real, fer sure. It started up right after the Civil War and carried on fer nigh thirty years. More'n two hundred from both sides died from murders and all-out warfare. Great Grandaddy said he had to carry a gun jist to go out to the privy."

"Jesse shouldn't put the blame on you for how Mitzy turned out. She's as much a part of him as she is of you. She's a Hatfield *and* a McCoy."

"Thank you fer that," said Sarah. "Seems like nothin' we ever did could satisfy that girl. One time when she was jist a tadpole, we was in Cedarville a pickin' up supplies, and she spied a tely-vision they had goin' there in the store. She never had seed one before and couldn't take her eyes off'n it. All the way home, and from then on, all she could talk about was how poor we was. She was always goin' on about how someday she was goin' to be rich and have fancy thangs like whut she saw on that tely-vision."

Sarah continued on about Mitzy's grandiose plans for the future. "I jist took all her ramb'lins to be a young girl's pipe dreams." Sarah dabbed her eyes with the handkerchief.

"You're a very handsome woman, Sarah," said Rose. "Do all your girls favor you?"

"Mitzy is the only one. When she got older, and of course I was much younger, everyone used to say she and I could pass for twins."

Never having seen a picture of Mitzy, Rose made a mental note of the information.

"I wonder how she learned to become a computer expert," said Rose.

"You say she's some kind of an expert? That girl was as smart as she was purty. She was as sly as a fox, too. One time she . . ."

"We're baaack," yelled Eugene. He barged through the front door, followed by the men.

"Doc here says that shoat's gonna be jist fine," said Jesse. "He jist et somethin' he shouldn't of. Doc even took care of ol' Buster. I hadn't never noticed his back leg was festered."

Dan said, "I had a pretty good tour of the place." He made eye contact with Rose and subtly shook his head as if to say, "they're not here." He continued, "Well, as much as I regret having to do so, I guess we'd better tell you folks why we're here and ask for your help in finding . . ."

Rose abruptly got out of her chair and reached out to take Dan's arm. She squeezed it hard and whispered, "Don't dare mention Mitzy." She turned around to face Jesse. "Yes, we need help in finding our way to the highway." She looked up into Dan's befuddled face and winked. "Dear, didn't Seth call it the Cannonball Highway?"

"Shucks, that's an easy one," said Jesse. "Once you git back on the road goin' south, jist stay on it to the highway. There ain't no way you could git lost."

Apparently relieved that Mitzy's name would not be brought up again, Sarah asked, "Why don't you folks stay fer supper? I can boil up some taters and string beans to go with that big ham."

"Thank you very much," said Dan. "But we'd like to be well on down the road before nightfall."

"Well, then, at least let me make you some ham sandwiches to take with you," said Sarah.

"That's very kind of you," said Rose. "But Seth gave *us* a big ham too."

"Well, then, let me slice you off some fresh bread to take with you for sandwiches."

While Sarah sliced the bread, she said under her breath, "Thanks fer see'n to it that Mitzy's name weren't mentioned, specially after whut you told me she done. Jesse goes plumb loco at jist the mention of her."

"I understand," said Rose.

"Would you do me a favor? If'n you do ever find her, could you some way git word to me without Jesse knowin' about it? I don't know whut good it would do, 'cept for my peace of mind. I'd like to hear how she is."

"I'll certainly try. How would it be if I get word to Ada Lou and then she could tell you."

"That would be jist fine."

When Dan and Rose were ready to leave, Jesse walked out the door with them, and then headed back to the barn. With her hands clasped over her heart, and a wistful look on her face, Sarah stood leaning against a post of the porch as the van backed down to the road.

While bouncing along the twenty-mile stretch of bad road to the highway, Rose told Dan of her conversation with Sarah. "I felt so sorry for that woman. It's hard to believe someone could be as heartless as Mitzy, yet I think Sarah would forgive her in a minute."

"After what you just told me," said Dan. "I'm glad I didn't bring up the subject to Jesse. He seemed pretty high-strung. But I guess we came all this way to Kentucky for nothing."

"It couldn't have been for nothing, Dan. There are two people alive in this world that wouldn't be if we hadn't come. To me, it just seems like . . . well, like providence."

"Maybe so," said Dan, "but we've sure lost a lot of time. We need to call the detectives as soon as we get in range and see if they have any new leads. Did Sarah tell you anything at all that would give a clue as to where Mitzy might have gone?"

"She did say that Mitzi used to talk about living in Miami some day, where she was going to have a big house with servants and a swimming pool where she could lay around all day in a bikini."

"The girl certainly had ambitions, didn't she?" said Dan. "And Miami sounds like a place Larry would like. He always said that when he retired he was going to leave Kansas and head some place south where there was plenty of action."

"He may get more action than he can handle," said Rose. "He's fifty-nine years old, and I just learned Mitzy's only twenty-five."

"Wow," said Dan. "She's young enough to be his daughter."

"And he's old enough to know better," said Rose.

Once back on a highway, Dan made up for lost time. As much as the mountainous terrain would allow, he sped through the western tip of Virginia and stopped to gas up before crossing the crest of the Appalachian Mountains, where it marked the boundary between the eastern tip of Tennessee and the state of North Carolina.

It was nearly dark when they stopped at a rest stop somewhere in South Carolina and ate their ham sandwiches at a picnic table. "Have you noticed how little traffic has gone by while we were sitting here?" asked Rose. "And we're the only ones in the rest area."

Dan looked around. "Yes. This looks like a good, quiet place to spend the night. And if we're still not within the calling area, I can use the telephone booth over there in the morning."

It began raining as they prepared for bed. "Darn!" said Rose. "I'm not getting out in that rain to go to the ladies' room. Guess I'll have to use the potty in here before I turn in."

"Don't worry about it," said Dan. "We'll find a dump station down the road pretty soon."

Rose opened the little door to the potty chamber . . . and let out a piercing scream. She slammed the door shut and pushed hard against it.

Dan banged his head jumping out of bed, but was beside her in an instant. "My God, Rose, what is it?"

"There's someone in there!" she choked.

Chapter Fifteen

Dan pushed Rose away from the door. He grabbed her nearby guitar and held it over his head. "Whoever you are, come out of there with your hands up."

Rose quickly pulled a club out of Dan's golf bag and held it out to him. "Take this! She whispered. Don't you *dare* hit anyone with my guitar!"

"Don't shoot," came a voice from within. "I'm coming out."

The door slowly opened. Dan squinted his eyes and peered into the dark cubbyhole. "CLYDE! What the HELL are you doing in there!"

Rose swung the door aside. "Clyde?"

An incredulous Dan stepped back to let Clyde slowly emerge from the cramped space. Clyde stood up and kicked out one leg, and then the other, while stretching. "That sure is a little bitty privy. It feels really good to stand up again."

Dan put his hands on his hips and, through his teeth, said, "Do you want to explain what the *hell* you think you're doing young man?"

Clyde looked down at his feet.

Rose put her hand on his shoulder. "Clyde, have you run away from your home?"

Clyde looked at Rose. His eyes filled with tears, and his lower lip began to tremble. "I just couldn't stand it anymore, Mrs. Good. I just had to get away from there. I don't mean to cause you folks any trouble. You were just my best chance of leaving."

"But *why,* Clyde? Were they mean to you?"

"I never saw any evidence of that," growled Dan.

"No, ma'am. My Pa and Grandpa are the greatest. I know I'll miss them. And I'll sure miss little Cassie Jean and the dogs. I just couldn't take being around Ada Lou anymore."

"Oh, *she* was the mean one," said Dan, sarcastically.

"No, sir, that's just the trouble. She's the sweetest gal I've ever known. I wish she *were* mean. Then I could hate her instead of . . . instead of . . ."

"Instead of loving her?" offered Rose.

Clyde put his hands to his face and sobbed. "Yes, ma'am."

Dan stood, shaking his head while waiting for Clyde to regain his composure. Finally he said, "Well, young man, you've made a big mistake. You can't come with us. Even if we had room for you in here, which you can see we don't, we can't afford you. Hell, we're going to have trouble just feeding ourselves. We have no choice but to take you back home in the morning. And that makes me mad, because it's going to cost us time, and money for gasoline, neither of which we can afford!"

Clyde set his jaw, and with determination in his voice, said, "No, sir. I'm not going back. Like I said, I didn't mean to cause you any trouble. You can drop me off in the next town you come to, and be on your way. Or if that doesn't suit you, I'll gather up my things and leave right now. But I'm not going back. No sir!"

Rose hung up her guitar and took the golf club from Dan's hand. "You're not going anywhere tonight, Clyde, certainly not in this rain. We'll talk about all of this in the morning."

She brushed the hair back off his forehead. "Things always look better in the morning. Why don't you wash up and I'll try to find you something to eat."

"No need for that, ma'am. I brought plenty of food with me." He reached into the potty chamber and retrieved a large pack. And there wasn't much else to do in there but eat."

Dan disgustedly plopped down on the bed. "Where do you propose we put our guest for the night, Rose?"

Rose walked to the front of the van and adjusted the passenger seat into a reclining position. "You can sleep here, Clyde. Is there anything you need? A blanket perhaps?"

"Thank you, Mrs. Good. If I get chilly, I've got my jacket here."

While Clyde was settling down in the seat, Rose crawled over Dan, into bed. "Goodnight, Clyde," she called.

"Goodnight. And thank you. This is right comfy."

"Just don't get too used to it," snarled Dan as he turned off the light.

The rain intensified during the night, and by morning, the wind was gale force. The cell phone was still out of range. Dan dug through his belongings for his raincoat, and then dashed through the downpour to the telephone booth.

Rose poured herself another cup of coffee before sitting down to chat with Clyde. "I hope you've had second thoughts about leaving home. Will you let us take you back?"

"No, ma'am, I've been planning to leave ever since Pa and Ada Lou got hitched. The feelings and thoughts I have for her just aren't right. I think about her day and night. I make myself sick thinking about her, and I just can't keep from it. It just ain't . . . isn't right. If Pa knew the thoughts I have, he'd run me off anyhow."

"I doubt that," said Rose. "But I can understand what an uncomfortable situation it must be for you. Nevertheless, your disappearing is going to cause them an awful lot of worry."

"I left a note. Clementine can read it to them. Grandpa and Pa know I can take care of myself. Both of them left home when they weren't any older than I am now."

Rose wiped the condensation off the window to peer out at Dan. He was making another call. "How old are you, anyway, Clyde?"

"I'll be seventeen in just five more months."

"That's awfully young to be thinking about being on your own."

"I'll be just fine. I can do all kinds of things. I can read and write, and I've done a lot of studying. I'll find some kind of a job."

Rose thought about how little cash she and Dan had left. "What did you plan to do for money until you found a job?"

"Pa gives me money once in a while. And I've done some odd jobs in Cedarville and around that I got paid for." Clyde reached into his back pocket and pulled out an old, worn leather wallet. "I've been saving up for this for a long time." He dramatically slapped his palm with the wallet. "Why, I've got close to ninety dollars in here."

That boy thinks he's rich, thought Rose. *He has no idea what it takes to get along in the outside world.*

Dan climbed into the van and shook his umbrella out the door. He handed it back to Clyde, saying, "Here. Open this up and lay it on the floor back there. And sit down and snap on that seat belt. We're ready to roll."

With its windshield wipers flapping, Dan pulled the van out onto the highway. They had gone but a short distance when Clyde yelled, "Hey! That sign said thirty miles to Charlotte, NORTH Carolina! You're headed the wrong direction!"

"No, we're headed right," said Dan. "You're going home."

"NO, I'M NOT!" yelled Clyde. Rose turned to see him rip off his seat belt, stand up and grab his knapsack, and then reach for the side door handle.

"DAN!" yelled Rose. "Pull over *immediately*! He's going to jump!"

"SIT DOWN, YOU CRAZY KID!" yelled Dan. "I'll pull over the first chance I get, but SIT BACK DOWN!"

Dan pulled onto the first side road he came to. Carefully avoiding the deep puddles on either side of the road, he turned the van around to face back toward the highway. He switched off the motor, unbuckled his seat belt, and then turned to face Clyde. "I thought we discussed this last night. I told you, you can't come with us! Do you remember my telling you that?"

"My remembering is better than your hearing," answered Clyde. "I told you I wasn't going back." He stood up and pulled his jacket over his head as he reached for the door handle. "Thanks for the ride."

Clyde slid open the door and the van filled with cold, blowing rain.

"SHUT THAT DAMNED DOOR AND SIT DOWN!" yelled Dan, as he grabbed the back of Clyde's jacket.

Clyde slammed the door shut and plopped back into his seat. "You can yell all you want, Dr. Good. But you can't make me go back. No, sir!"

Dan looked down at the floor and shook his head. "So, you think you're man enough to strike out on your own." He looked up at Clyde. "Boy, you have no idea what you're getting into."

"That boy has more sense than a lot of grown men I've known," said Rose. "And I don't see that his future would be all that bright if he did go back."

Clyde reached over to lay his hand on Rose's shoulder. "Thank you for that, Mrs. Good."

Dan threw his hands in the air and then turned around to start the van back up. "Looks like I'm outnumbered here," he grumbled. "I don't know what the hell we're going to do with you, Clyde."

"I told you, Dr. Good. Let me out at the first town you come to."

The miles rolled away in relative silence, except for the flapping of the windshield wipers.

Rose looked over her shoulder. Clyde was using his rolled-up jacket as a pillow, and leaning against the window fast asleep. She looked over at Dan. "Well, what did you find out? Were you able to reach either of the detectives?"

"Yes. If it's them, they're heading south all right."

"If it's them?"

"A couple closely matching their descriptions and driving a silver Mercedes checked out of a motel in Little Rock day before yesterday. He said the police there didn't follow it up though, because the car license they gave at the motel check-in didn't match Larry's, and the credit card they used didn't have Larry or Mitzy's name on it."

"Well, how often do you suppose the motel clerk actually checks license plates?" asked Rose. "And how hard is it to get a credit card?"

"That's just it," said Dan. "What really makes me think it's them is the fact the clerk told the Little Rock Police that the woman was a real looker, a redhead, and young enough to be the guy's daughter."

"I saw you making at least two calls," said Rose. "Who else did you call?"

"The detectives have stayed in touch with Thelma. By the way, she *is* taking over Larry's business."

"Good!"

"So, I didn't bother calling her," Dan continued. "According to the detective, Larry hasn't tried to reach her. But I did call Charlotte. She said Larry called the day after we left to ask about Flip."

"His dog?"

"Yeah. He thought a lot of that dog. It must have killed him to have to leave him behind. I wonder why he did."

"Maybe Mitzy doesn't like dogs. I wonder why he'd jeopardize his whereabouts by calling."

"Who knows? Maybe he just felt guilty about abandoning Flip and wanted to make sure Charlotte would take good care of him."

"What did Charlotte have to say to him?"

"She told Larry that since *he* wasn't available, she'd had to settle for shooting the dog."

"Charlotte shot Larry's dog?"

"No, but she said by the way Larry cussed her out, *he* believes she did. The detectives said the call was made from a pay phone in Oklahoma City. I remembered Larry had some kind of property there, but I didn't know enough to help the detectives any. And evidently Charlotte knew nothing about it."

Rose was lost in thought for a few minutes before speaking, "How long have we been gone? A week, maybe? And if that *was* Larry and Mitzy, they left Little Rock about two days ago. So they may have spent several days before in Oklahoma City. Larry liquidated everything he owned back home . . ."

"Yeah," interrupted Dan, "including everything *we* owned."

"So I'm wondering," continued Rose, "if there's some way we could check out recent business sales or commercial real estate sales in Oklahoma City."

"That's something to think about," said Dan. "It's probably worth having the detectives check it out. You never know what they might uncover. I'll give them a call the next time we stop."

Rose picked up the cell phone. "Speaking of calling, I'm going to see if we're in range to call the boys."

"Why don't you wait until we can call on a land line. We can't afford the roaming charges. Besides, with the weather the way it is, you might not be able to hear for the static."

"You're right. It really hasn't been that long ago that we talked to them anyway. I'd just like to hear their voices." Rose put the cell phone back on the dashboard. "So where are we heading now?"

Dan squinted his eyes against the rain blanketing the windshield. "For now, I just hope we can stay on the highway. I can hardly see a thing out there. And we sure aren't making good gas mileage, beating against this wind."

"Remember the weather report we heard yesterday?" said Rose. "There was a hurricane somewhere off the eastern seaboard."

"Yeah," said Dan, "It wasn't supposed to hit land. But it sure is causing a blow."

Suddenly a dark form loomed in front of them, and Dan jerked the wheel sharply to the right, sideswiping a barricade. He laid on the horn while yelling, "TURN ON YOUR LIGHTS, YOU DAMNED FOOL!"

"What good did all that hollering do?" asked Rose.

"It made me feel better," snarled Dan.

"Well, you can do something to make *me* feel better. You can get off this highway the first chance you get. It's suicide to drive in this storm."

"I agree," said Dan. "I've been hoping we'd find a gas station. We're going to need gas soon."

The sudden jerking of the van had awakened Clyde, who now sat with his face pressed up against the window. "Golleeee! How can you see anything out there, Dr. Good?"

"I can't. Help me watch for anyplace I can pull off."

A few minutes later, Rose said, "Look! Over there. Is that a filling station?"

"I believe it is," answered Dan.

"You'd think they'd have their lights on so people could see them through the rain."

"Maybe their power's off," answered Dan as he cautiously pulled off the highway and under the canopy next to a pump.

"I don't want to get out in that wind and rain just yet." said Dan. "We're going to just sit right here until someone asks us to move."

"That may be a while," said Clyde. "The place is boarded up and there's a For Sale sign in the window."

"Great!" grumbled Dan. "At least we're safe. No telling how long we'll be here." He reached across to the glove compartment and retrieved a deck of cards. "Rosie, do you know any card games that three can play?"

• • •

As the day wore on, they tried to occupy their minds by playing cards, while the storm increased in intensity. At five o'clock in the afternoon, it became dark as night. Suddenly, hail thundered down on the canopy above them and drowned out the possibility of any conversation. It seemed as though they were under attack with hailstones bouncing against the sides and windows of the van. With a deafening screech, the canopy above them peeled away and disappeared into the darkness. A huge tree limb blew toward them and landed upright, as if it grew there, pressing against the front of the van with its branches spread out over the van's roof.

Thank God, thought Rose. *Maybe that tree will protect the windshield.*

Clyde helped Dan string blankets and sheets in front of the windows to deflect any possible broken window glass. They had eaten very little during the day, but now the violent rocking of the van suppressed any appetite they might have had for dinner. Dan pulled out the bed and he and Rose lay huddled together. Clyde rolled into a fetal position on the floor beside them, with his knapsack as a pillow and his arms protecting his head.

After what seemed forever, the wind suddenly stopped, and the rain let up somewhat. Clyde sat up. "Wow! That was some storm! I've never seen anything like it."

"I was in a tornado when I was a boy back in Kansas," said Dan, "but that storm was over in a few minutes."

"I don't know about you two," said Rose, "but I'm starving. Fold this bed up, Dan, and let me see if I can rustle us up something to eat."

"You don't need to bother, Mrs. Good," said Clyde. "I've got enough food in my knapsack here to last a week."

Clyde plopped down in the passenger seat, dug into his pack, and began laying packages of jerky, bread, and dried fruit on the dashboard.

Dan sat in the driver's seat and munched on a hard biscuit while gazing out of the windshield. "We can't do much now in that rain, but first thing in the morning, Clyde, you and I are going to have to move that big tree out there before we can go anywhere."

"Yes, sir."

After they had eaten, although it was still misting slightly, the three walked around the grounds of the gas station to stretch their legs. The night sky had an eerie glow that enabled them to see well enough to step over and around the windblown debris.

Back in the van, Rose brewed some herbal tea and poured each a cup. When Dan finished his, he kicked off his shoes and stretched out on the bed. Rose picked up her guitar and began strumming. Soon she and Clyde were harmonizing in song.

"I'm amazed that you know so many of the old songs, Clyde."

"The old ones are all Grandpa and Pa played at home," he answered. "Besides, there's not too many of the new ones that fit a fiddle and a banjo."

"That's so true," laughed Rose. "Or *your* instrument of choice, the jug."

She reached over and tousled his hair. "You do a great job of singing. Doesn't he have a wonderful voice, Dan? Dan?"

Dan responded with a loud snore, and Rose and Clyde erupted into giggles.

Rose showed Clyde how to adjust the passenger seat into a reclining position. When he was all settled in for the night, she brushed the hair back off his forehead, where she planted a kiss.

"Gollee, Mrs. Good. It sure has been a long time since anyone tucked me into bed."

"It's been a long time since I did any tucking," answered Rose. "Sweet dreams, sweet boy."

"Thanks, Mrs. Good. Sweet dreams to you too."

Some time in the night, while the three were soundly sleeping, the wind and rain returned with a vengeance. There was a sudden explosion of force that flipped the van over on its side.

Chapter Sixteen

A barrage of debris pummeled the van's underside as Rose, Dan, and Clyde worked to free themselves from their bedding and from one another. "Are you two all right?" yelled Dan above the screaming wind.

"I will be, as soon as you two big lugs get off of me," answered Rose.

"I got a pretty good knock on my noggin," yelled Clyde. "What's happening?"

"It's got to be that hurricane that wasn't supposed to hit land," said Dan.

The three huddled together in the pitch darkness, wrapped in bedding and backed up against the bed's mattress, now standing on its side. Rose clutched Dan's arm and prayed, *Dear Lord, please spare us, and please let it be over soon.*

In time, the wind diminished, and the faint light of dawn peeked through the side window, now overhead. Dan tossed the pillow off his head. "That was some blow. Thank God it's over, and we're still in one piece."

"That was every bit as bad as the storm last night," said Clyde. "How do you know it's over?"

"That was all one big storm, Clyde. A hurricane has a hole in the middle, sort of like a big donut. When we got out to walk around last night, the hole, called an eye, was passing through."

"Golleee," said Clyde.

Rose glanced around the van's jumbled interior. Pots and pans, dishes and silverware, clothing and bedding were all scrambled together. "Look at this mess! I'm glad the dishes are plastic."

Dan threw off his blanket and struggled to stand up. "Oh, my God, the potty!"

"I don't know why I locked the lid down last night," said Rose, "force of habit, I guess, but I'm sure glad I did."

"Me too. But to be on the safe side, don't anyone open that door till we get this baby back on its feet."

Dan slipped into his jeans and a jacket, and then reached up to slide the van's door open. Standing on a suitcase, he was able to pull himself out onto the van's side. Clyde followed after him.

Rose dressed and then stuck her head out into the light mist. "My, Lord, have you ever seen such destruction?"

The roof of the gas station had disappeared, and just a few of the cement blocks making up its walls were left in place. Two of the gasoline pumps had been knocked down, and the few trees left standing were filled with debris. Rose saw Clyde poking around in the refuse left inside the building's ruins. *At least we don't have to worry about moving that tree off the van. I wonder where it went.*

After creating stairs by adding another suitcase and a box, she managed to climb up and then pull herself out of the door. "Dan? Where are you? I need help getting down from here."

"On this side, Rosie." She scooted over and looked down at him.

"Just slide over the side," he said, "and I'll catch you."

"My hero," said Rose as Dan lowered her to the ground. She kissed his cheek, and then turned to look at the van. "How in the world are we ever going to upright this thing?"

"I'm still contemplating that. I know one thing, though. It's fortunate that it flipped over. The underside acted as a shield and probably saved us. And it's amazing that only one window was broken."

Clyde walked back from the ruins, dragging what appeared to be a large chain. "Look what I found, Dr. Good."

"What is that?"

"It's an old engine pull. See that pole next to the van, where the roof used to be? See how it's all bent over? I could shinny up there and attach this pulley."

Dan squinted up at the pole leaning across the van. "Clyde, you're a genius! I think it just might work!"

While Dan and Clyde rummaged around in the ruins looking for more parts they could use, Rose walked over to inspect a pile of old rubber tires that the storm had deposited against an embankment. She stopped short. *What was that noise?* She took a few more steps. A pitiful "meeeow" emanated from behind the tires. *A cat!* "Here, kitty kitty."

When the cat failed to appear, Rose peeked around the pile. A huge, buff-colored cat lay on its side, obviously dead. A wet, shivering kitten sat next to it, looking up at Rose with huge yellow eyes. "Oh, you poor thing." When she extended a hand toward it, it spit at her and crouched back against its mother.

Not wanting to scare the kitten away, Rose quickly walked back to the van, where Dan and Clyde were preparing to rig the pulley. "Dan! I found a poor little kitten behind that pile of tires. It's mother is there too, but she's dead. I need to . . ."

"For God's sake, not now, Rose. We've got some problems of our own to take care of."

"Can I go see it?" asked Clyde.

"Now? We've almost got this thing put together."

"I'll just be a minute," said Clyde, as he bounded off toward the tires.

"Thanks a lot, Rose!" snapped Dan. "How good are *you* at shinnying up a pole?"

"Well, excuse me!" Rose turned to go back to the kitten.

Dan squatted back down to continue working. "Tell that boy to get back over here, pronto!"

Rose found Clyde, leaning over and peering into a stack he had made of three rubber tires. "I got him, Mrs. Good, He ought to be safe in here till we have some time to take care of him."

Rose looked down at the kitten. It hissed and then turned to press itself into the inside of a tire. "Oh, look, Clyde. The poor thing has lost part of its tail."

"It never had much of a tail, Mrs. Good. That's why they call it a bobcat."

"A bobcat? I don't believe I've ever seen one before. No wonder it's so big. How did you manage to capture it, Clyde? It seemed pretty fierce to me."

"I just grabbed him up by the nape of the neck. All cats get sort of paralyzed when they're held that way."

"Clyde!" yelled Dan. "Will you get back over here and give me a hand?"

Quickly picking up some boards and placing them on top of the stack, Clyde said, "That's so he can't climb out."

He then grabbed two tires and began rolling them toward the van. Following alongside, Rose asked, "What are those for?"

"I'm going to make me a stairway. There's enough tires to make a pretty good one, and I can work up there a whole lot better when I don't have to worry about hanging onto a pole too."

Dan disapprovingly watched their approach. "Are you through playing, Clyde? And maybe ready to do a little work?"

"He *has* been working!" shot Rose. "He's been working that genius brain of his!"

While Rose explained Clyde's plan to Dan, Clyde trotted back to get more tires. Dan and Rose soon followed to help. "I don't know what's got into you, Dan," scolded Rose. "Why are you being so nasty? Why are you being so hard on him?"

"To begin with, we already had enough problems before he added to them by tagging along. I resent the extra burden of having to worry about him too. And I hate to admit it, but I can't make heads or tails of that pulley thing. You know how I am with machinery. Clyde seems to know what he's doing, and I just wish he'd get it done."

"Then quit barking orders at him, and show him some respect. You'll get a lot more out of him."

With the three of them rolling tires, they soon had enough for a makeshift stairway against the pole. "This is a good idea, Clyde," said Dan. "I can climb up there too, and give you a hand setting all this up."

"I got me another idea, too," said Clyde. "If you think you can handle it, Mrs. Good, every time we pull the van up a ways, you can cram some tires under it so we don't lose her."

"A piece of cake," said Rose. "I'll go get some more tires while you two rig that thing."

"Excellent, Clyde!" said Dan. "Another excellent idea."

Work began, and with every movement of the van upwards, Rose gritted her teeth at the crashing and banging going on inside. After much grunting, pulling, and shouting, the van was finally upright. Clyde let out a "whoopee," as he and Dan turned loose of the pulley rope.

The tires were rolled out of the way, and the three walked around the vehicle, examining the damage. The entire van was badly dented and scraped, first from the Buzzards Pass crossing, next from sideswiping the highway barricade, and then from its being knocked over in the storm. One rear door window was smashed, as well as one side-mirror. The other side mirror, which Dan had duct-taped back in place while at the McCoy's, had held up pretty well. "Oh, Dan," said Rose, "I can't believe what has happened to our beautiful van."

"It is a shame, but it could be worse. Let's just hope it'll still run."

After Dan and Rose finished putting the van's interior back in order, Dan stuck his head out the window. "Hey, Clyde! If you're bent on going with us, you'd better get aboard."

"Coming, Doctor Good!"

The side door rolled back, and Clyde set a crudely-constructed wooden crate inside.

"Oh, no!" said Dan. "You're surely not thinking of taking that thing with us!"

"Well, you wouldn't want me to just leave the poor little thing back there with its dead mother, would you, Doctor Good?"

Dan threw up his hands in exasperation. "Oh, what the hell! What's one more problem on top of all we've got already?" He turned on the ignition. "Shut the damned door and get buckled up!"

The engine turned over several times before it coughed and then ran roughly for a few seconds. "Come on, Baby, you can do it . . . pleeese," said Dan. He shifted into drive as soon as the engine ran normally.

They drove for miles over the debris-strewn highway without seeing any other vehicles. Several times, they stopped while Dan and Clyde moved tree branches so they could continue.

At last, they came to a small gas station and attached café. Signs were either down or askew, but otherwise the building was intact, and the pavement had been swept clear of debris. "There's no cars around," said Dan. "I sure hope they're open. The gas gauge is on empty."

Dan found the pump as well as the station door locked, so went next door to the café. Rose saw him try the door, peer in the window, and then rap on it. In a short time, the door opened, and he went inside. He soon reappeared, followed by an older man wearing overalls. While the man was unlocking the gas pump, a slightly built woman, her gray hair pulled up in a bun, motioned to Rose from the café's doorway. Rose grabbed her purse. "Come on, Clyde. Let's see if she's got anything hot to drink."

The smiling woman held the door open for them. "We sure weren't expecting any business today." Chairs were still upended on the café's four tables, so Rose and Clyde seated themselves at the counter. The woman set two water glasses down in front of them. "My name's Joan, and I'll be your waitress." She and Rose chuckled, but the humor of the comment was lost to Clyde.

"Which way did you folks come from? I didn't think anyone was gettin' through."

"Why is that?" asked Rose. "Are things that bad?"

"The bridge over Piney Creek, just north of here, is clean washed out, and the highway south is under water for miles." She pointed to the menu on the wall behind her. "See anything you'd like?"

"Excuse me," said Rose as she opened her purse and dabbed at her nose while discreetly checking the money in her billfold. She glanced at Clyde, who was intently staring up at the menu. *Poor boy. I wish I had more. He looks like he's going to start drooling any minute.*

"Yes, ma'am," said Clyde. "We'll have the two-egg special. And one for Doctor Good, too. He'll be back in directly. Does that sound good to you, Mrs. Good?"

The look on Rosemary's face must have prompted Clyde to say, "Don't worry about a thing, Mrs. Good. This one's on me. How do you and Doctor Good like your eggs?"

"Clyde, you . . . " began Rose.

"It says up there that the special comes with coffee," Clyde interrupted. "I'll have mine with cream, please."

The bell over the door jingled, and Dan and the man in overalls entered while Joan set out cups. She smiled up at Dan. "Does the doctor use cream in his coffee?"

"He's not just any old doctor," boasted Clyde. "He's an animal doctor, and a darned good one at that."

Joan locked eyes with her husband's. "Did you hear that, Willy? He's an *animal* doctor." She poured their coffee, including a cup for her husband, and then disappeared into the small kitchen. Willy sat down at the counter next to Dan.

After she had served their large plates loaded with eggs, sausage, country fries, and biscuits, Joan leaned against the counter and joined in the lively conversation they were all having about the storm. Clyde said very little as he wolfed down the meal.

When Rose had eaten all she could, she pushed her plate toward Clyde. "That was delicious, but I can't eat another bite. Can you finish this up for me, Clyde?"

"If you're sure you don't want any more, I'd be glad to, Mrs. Good."

Rose asked Joan, "May I use your restroom?"

"Sure, honey. Here's the key. It's around back."

While there, Rose took the opportunity to remove her tee shirt and bra and wash herself as best she could, and then pulled her hair back into a pony tail.

As she was leaving the restroom, she heard voices nearby. Dan, Clyde, and Willy were squatted down around something under a nearby tree. When she approached them, she saw a large dog lying between them. She stopped to hear what they were saying.

"How old is he?" asked Dan.

"He's at least eighteen. He showed up here about that long ago, a starvin' little pup." The man affectionately ran his hand over the dog's body. "Old Stoney here has been my best buddy ever since. When he was up to it, his job was keepin' all the critters away from the trash bin."

"He's in pretty bad shape," said Dan.

"The Missus says I should have put him out of his misery a long time ago, but I just don't have the heart for it."

"Would you like for me to do it for you?" asked Dan.

"That's why I asked you to take a look at him, Doc. I was hopin' you'd have somethin' you could give him. I can't bear the thought of just shootin' him."

"Clyde, would you please get my black bag from the van? Do you know the one I mean?"

"Sure, Dr. Good. I'll be right back."

"How will this work, Doc?" asked Willy.

"Why don't you just sit down and lean up against that tree, and sort of cradle him."

As Willy pulled him onto his lap, the big shaggy dog opened his eyes and slowly wagged his tail. Even from where she stood, Rose could hear the dog's labored breathing.

Clyde set the black bag down next to Dan. "Here you go, Dr. Good." He squatted down and watched intently as Dan prepared the hypodermic syringe.

Joan appeared next to Rose. "I saw the boy fetch that black bag. The doctor's going to put old Stoney down, isn't he?"

"Yes. It's a painless procedure."

She started to say something else, but instead, Joan stopped short and, with her face in her hands, nodded. Rose put an arm around her.

The drug worked so swiftly, it was difficult to tell when the old dog stopped breathing. Dan listened with his stethoscope. "He's gone."

Willy hugged the dog, burying his face in the deep coat. Clyde wrapped an arm around the old man's shaking shoulders. "Mister, I'm sorry for your loss. I know how it feels to lose something you love. Can I bury Stoney for you?"

Willy looked up long enough to say, "Thanks, son. I'd rather do it myself."

Dan stiffly got to his feet and came to where Rose and Joan were standing. Joan held out her hand to him. "We can't thank you enough, Doctor. We'd been praying Stoney would go peacefully. I guess you were the answer to our prayers. What do we owe you?"

Dan looked back at Willy. "Not a thing. But I do need to give you a warning. A big, shaggy dog like that is bound to have a lot of fleas. The minute they figure out the dog is dead, they'll hop to their nearest victim. That would be Willy. Dan motioned toward the small house at the back of the property. If you don't want your house infested, have Willy leave all his clothes outside, and have him take a good shower.

"I'll do that. Thank you again, Doctor."

As Joan turned to go back inside, Clyde trotted up to her. "I almost forgot to pay for breakfast. How much do I owe you?"

"Don't be silly. Breakfast is on us. It's the least we could do."

"Well, golleee. Thank you." He turned to Dan and Rosemary. "You hear that?"

Rose said, "That's wonderful. But Clyde, you'd better see if she could sell you some milk for your furry friend."

"I almost forgot."

Dan and Rose were sitting in the van discussing the highway closures, when Clyde returned, all smiles. "Look what she gave me." He held up a milk-filled baby bottle. "When I told her all about the bobcat kitten, she even warmed up the bottle."

Clyde got in the van and started undoing the rope he had tied around the cat's crate. "That ain't . . . isn't all. She said there's a place just a few miles back the way we came from that takes in all kinds of wild critters that have been hurt. Can we take him there?"

"I'll say we can," said Dan as he started up the van. "Just tell us how to get there."

Rose traded places with Clyde and took over the job of bottle-feeding the kitten in the back of the van, while Clyde sat up front, giving directions to Dan. "There's a sign ahead, Dr. Good. Yep, that's it. Ark of the Woods. Turn in right there."

They traveled the winding road for at least a mile, stopping often to clear the way of storm debris. The road led to a circular driveway and a large beautiful log building. Rose could see several large outbuildings beyond this one and large enclosures. A bronze statue of a mother bear and two cubs stood in the center of the circular driveway. A small sign at the drive's edge read, "Please take animals to Building A, Deliveries to Building C." There was a young man nearby, piling broken branches into a stack.

Rose said, "My goodness. Even with all the storm devastation, this place looks more like a posh resort than a wildlife rehabilitation facility."

"It does at that," said Dan. "These big log structures can evidently take a hell of a beating. I see some roof damage, and a few broken windows, but no major damage."

"Looks like that drive will take us to Building A," said Clyde, pointing. He craned his neck as he watched a pretty, young girl raking debris near an enclosure. She stopped to wave at them.

Dan pulled up in front of Building A, which was a smaller version of the main building. A sign next to the door read, please ring. "You two wait in the van until I see what the procedure is."

In the back of the van, Rose was looking over the grounds from the side window, when she heard Clyde gasp.

She leaned forward to peer in the direction of the building. "What is it, Clyde?"

Dan was in the doorway, engaged in a passionate kiss with some strange woman.

"This sure is a friendly place," said Clyde.

Chapter Seventeen

They were so entwined in one another, they seemed not to hear the van door slam, nor Rose's approaching footsteps. Dan's body blocked Rose's view of the woman, but she could see her hands still locked around his neck. *No wedding ring.*

She heard the woman say, "I can't believe it's really you. You don't know how often I have fantasized about this very moment. How on earth did you find me?"

"Find . . . *Find* you?"

Rose cleared her throat. "Ahem."

The woman stepped sideways to peer around Dan. "Good morning. May I help you?"

A flustered Dan turned around. "Rose, dear, you won't believe who this is."

"Try me."

A combined look of shock and utter disappointment came over the woman's face as she glanced back and forth between Dan and Rose.

"This is Monica Millikin, an old school chum from K-State," said Dan. "You remember my telling you about Monica."

Your old school chum seems a bit too chummy. "Yes, I think I remember your mentioning the name. It's a melodious name, easy to remember."

"Well, uh . . . thank you," Monica stammered.

Rose looked Monica up and down. *No woman her age has a right to look that good, or to plant her lips on my husband.*

"'Scuse me," came a voice from behind them. Rose turned to see Clyde holding the cat's crate at arms's length. "He kind of made a big mess in here and it was stinking up the van. What should I do with him?"

That ought to break the spell.

Obviously grateful for the interruption of an extremely awkward situation, Monica turned her attention to Clyde. "Just set that crate down over there in the grass. We'll leave it out here. I'll be right back with my gloves to get the cat."

"No need for that, ma'am," said Clyde as he threw back the lid and withdrew the kitten by the nape of its neck. "Just show me where you want him."

Monica opened the door. "In here. All of you."

The acrid odor of disinfectant assailed Rose's nostrils, as the procession followed Monica down a hallway to an examination room. *It smells just like Dan's clinic.*

Monica retrieved long leather gloves from a drawer while studying Clyde. "Are you going to introduce me to your son, Dan? Or is he your grandson?"

"Neither," said Dan. "This is Clyde. Clyde McCoy. He's just with us for the time being."

Monica felt the cat's legs and body, while Clyde still held it by its nape. "I assume this animal is a victim of the storm. Have you examined him thoroughly, Dan?"

"I haven't so much as touched him."

Monica donned her gloves and then took the kitten from Clyde. Once released from the nape hold, the cat yowled and clawed at her gloves. "Calm down, Tiger! He's pretty feisty. That's a good sign. I'll put him in this cage over here, where we can observe him for a few days."

Monica quickly pulled off her gloves and tossed them back into the drawer. She turned to face Dan. "I heard you had your own clinic back in Kansas."

"Yes, Salina. I retired and sold the business a couple of months ago."

"I *thought* it was Salina, but my letters were all returned, stamped address unknown."

Dan nervously glanced at Rose. "Really?"

"Dan, I don't know how else to ask you, except to just come out with it. I desperately need help right now. This is an incredible coincidence that brought you . . . " A cell phone in her lab coat pocket rang, interrupting her. "Ark of the Woods. Dr. Millikin speaking. Oh my. Thanks for the heads up, Monty. We've got a skeleton crew here today, so be prepared to give us a hand when you bring them in. Okay. Bye."

Monica put a hand to her forehead and closed her eyes in concentration for a moment before looking up. "Dan, we already have several animals that need immediate attention. I should be over in the stables right now, stitching up a seriously lacerated horse. That call was the third today from the Division of Wildlife, and I can expect more. Not only are they bringing in injured wildlife, but lost and hurt domestic animals as well. Because the bridge is out and the highway flooded, there's nowhere else for them to go but here. I honestly don't know what I'm going to do without your help. The only staff I have today besides the nutritionist, are two volunteers who were stranded here during the storm. They're high school kids, who mainly do the feeding and cage cleaning, and have no veterinary medical training whatsoever. I'm begging you. Please say you'll stay and help."

"Under the circumstances, I don't know how I could refuse."

"Oh, thank God. We have no time to lose. You'll be pretty much on your own. The two O.R.s are just down the hall. They're laid out well and fully equipped, so you won't need any indoctrination from me." Monica fished a key out of her pocket and held it out to Dan. "This is to the drug and medicine cabinet, which is in the first O.R. There are two rooms directly across the hall from the O.R.s; one holds incoming patients, and there are four in there right now. Just start on the one that needs care the most. The other room is the recovery room, and there are two in there that I just finished up with. You'll need to keep an eye on them."

Monica pulled a clean lab coat out of a drawer, looked at the size, and then tossed it to Dan. "Now go, and I'll check in with you whenever I get a chance."

Dan kissed Rose on the cheek. "I hope you don't mind. Are you going be all right?"

"Of course. You heard her. Get going."

Dan hurried out of the room, and Monica turned to Rose. "Are you a vet too? Please say yes."

Rose shook her head. "I'm afraid not."

"Do you have any veterinary assistant training at all?"

"I'm sorry to say that I don't."

"Ma'am," interrupted Clyde, "I know a lot about taking care of animals. I'd like to help."

"You'll do." Monica grabbed another lab coat out of the drawer. "See that bag on the table next to you? Pick it up and follow me."

"Wait!" said Rose. "I'm not completely helpless. Surely there's something I can do."

Monica stopped and studied Rose for a moment. "As a matter of fact, there is." She reached into her pocket to retrieve the cell phone. "The telephone lines are down, so this will have to do. Just park yourself up there at the big desk by the entryway and field incoming calls. That would be a huge help to me."

"What should I tell people when they call?"

"The procedures are on that yellow sheet under the see-through desk mat. Just follow that. When they show up at the door, direct anything larger than a dog over to the stables. That's the building right next door, where I'll be. All other animals will go down this hall to Incoming for Dan to take care of. Got all that?"

"Got it."

Rose seated herself at the big desk. After she had memorized the procedure instructions, she studied the photographs, also under the transparent desk mat. There were pictures of Monica with all kinds of birds and other animals, large and small. *My goodness. Here she is with an elephant . . . and clowns. She must make circus calls.* Rose then studied the walls of the room. They were covered with framed pictures, some evidently of award ceremonies featuring Monica. Among the pictures were at least a half a dozen award plaques for her work with wildlife, as well as work with troubled teens.

The phone rang, and Rose answered the first of many calls that would come in this day. Besides people arriving with domestic animals and pets, Wildlife Service employees brought in two small bear cubs, an injured raccoon, and a hawk with a broken wing. All but six of the animals, three cows, two goats and a donkey, went down the hall, where Dan worked feverishly. Rose had the others delivered to the stables next door.

Rose retrieved Monica's leather gloves from the drawer, and a lab coat for herself, and spent what extra time she had helping Dan. The front door bell was wired to also ring at the opposite end of the hall, so it could be heard from anywhere in the building. When she wasn't running to answer the door, Rose used a gurney to transport caged, injured animals to Dan from the Incoming Room. She cleaned and sanitized each cage before she took the animals to the Recovery Room after their operations.

The busy day sped by, and at dusk, Monica stopped by to see how things were going. "I was concerned because you didn't have an assistant, Dan, but I see I needn't have worried. You two are doing a great job."

Dan looked up from setting a bear cub's broken leg. "Rose has been a tremendous help. I couldn't have managed without her."

"Nor I without Clyde," said Monica. "He is a real jewel. He's even been doing some stitching. It's like he's an old hand at it."

"The boy's a quick learner, that's for sure," said Dan.

"How many patients do you have left in Incoming?" Monica asked.

"Just one." answered Rose. "It's a poor old cat that's lost an eye. But she seems to be okay otherwise."

"Then it appears the crisis is almost over. When you finish up in here, you two head on over to the main house. James will show you to your room and you can get freshened up for dinner."

"Our room?" said Rose.

"Of course. Surely, you don't think I'd just send you off into the night, after all you've done." Before Rose could answer, Monica said, "Gotta get back. I'll check your post-op patients before I head to the main house. See you at dinner."

Moths were buzzing around the porch lights of the main house when Rose and Dan arrived at the massive, hand-carved front door. As they wondered whether to ring the doorbell, or just let themselves in, the door swung open, and a smiling young man greeted them. "Come in. You must be Dr. and Mrs. Good. I'm James. Let me have your bag there, and I'll show you up to your room."

They followed him up the wide, rustic staircase that led to a balcony overlooking the spacious great room and fireplace below. There were large oil portraits on the wall between the several doors they passed. James stopped at a door and pulled a big key ring out of his pocket.

"You keep the bedroom doors locked?" asked Rose.

"Yes, ma'am. A lot of our help are teenaged wards of the court, working off community service sentences. None of them have been in any really bad trouble, just misde-meanors, but Dr. Millikin thinks it's a good idea to avoid any temptations." He opened the door, set the bag down inside the room, and then handed Dan the key.

"So they stay here?" asked Rose.

"Yes, ma'am. There are seven bedrooms here in the main house, where the girls stay, and the boys stay across the way in the bunkhouse."

"How many are here at any one time?" asked Dan.

"It varies. There's room for eight in the bunkhouse, plus Josh's private room. Then there are three rooms in this house that can hold up to three girls each. But there's usually just one or two in them."

"Who's Josh?" asked Rose.

"He's our nutritionist. Not only does he prepare the food for all the animals, but he's also the cook. He's pretty good, too." James looked at the clock on the dresser. "You'll get to sample some of his cooking in just about an hour."

"Does he ever get the menus mixed up?" asked Rose.

James laughed. "If he does, it's not too noticeable. See you folks at eight."

After James left, Rose looked around the rustic, but expensively furnished room. "How can a nonprofit organization afford a place like this?"

"They can't." said Dan. "All this used to be the vacation home of Monica's family."

"So, you've been here before?"

"No, but she used to talk about it a lot. You've heard of the Millikin Oil Company?"

"Yes, based in Wichita. Don't tell me! She's *that* Millikin?"

"The same."

Rose took her change of clothes out of their shared bag and laid them out on one of the two queen beds. "Dan, it's so obvious that after all these years, she still has a thing for you. Not only is she beautiful and highly intelligent, but she's also loaded! You two have so much in common, too, like the same profession. How in heaven's name did you let her slip by?"

Dan dumped the rest of the bag's contents onto the other bed. "It's all your fault, Rose. I kind of remembered you when you were a scrawny, freckled-faced teenybopper, but never took much notice of you until I saw your picture on Larry's desk in our room at the frat house. Remember when you and I first officially met?"

"It's forever seared into my brain . . . and into my heart, I might add."

"You and Larry, and my date and I double-dated at some big function at the Blue Moon."

"Yes. You asked me to dance when Larry went after drinks, and your date went to the ladies room. I remember that after several dances in a row, Larry cut in on us, somewhat annoyed."

"I knew that night that it was over between Monica and me," said Dan.

"That was Monica? Your date was Monica? I barely noticed her. Or anyone else that night. Anyone else but you, that is. That's the night I gave Larry back his ring. I knew that if I could feel that way about someone else, I wasn't ready for marriage."

"Yes, that was Monica," said Dan. "She's much thinner than she was, and her brown hair is white now. I certainly didn't recognize her when I first saw her this morning."

"Were you serious about her?"

"I suppose so, at one time. But I never proposed to her. She just assumed we'd get married. As you might have noticed, she's a take-charge kind of gal."

"That she is," said Rose. "Admirably so."

"Yes, she's a fine person," said Dan. "And we might have had a good life together."

Dan playfully grabbed Rose and threw her to the bed. "If it hadn't been for you, you little vixen!"

It had been days since they'd had the privacy to make passionate love.

Afterward, Rose insisted that Dan shower first, so that he could lie down and rest a few minutes before dinner. "Check the time, Rose. You'd better get in here with me if we're to get to the dinner table on time. Besides, I need a good back scrub."

They hurried down to the dining room, which was an extension of the great room. A huge chandelier, made from antlers, was suspended from the ceiling of the second story by a heavy chain and hung over the large round oak dining table. *This table could seat twenty people*, thought Rose. After introducing himself, Josh, a stooped little man seated Rose and Dan, and then poured them each a glass of wine.

A smiling Clyde, fairly glowing with cleanliness, clomped across the highly polished, plank floor from a nearby French door. He drug out a chair and sat down at the large table. "Good evening, Dr. and Mrs. Good. This has been some day, hasn't it? I'm hungry enough to eat a horse. Know what? There's a room over there in the bunkhouse full of shower-heads. I pointed them all at me and turned them on full force. If I wasn't so hungry, I could have stayed in there all night."

"Yes, a hot shower did feel good," said Dan, "Especially after a day like this. We heard you did really well today, Clyde. Do you still think you'd like to be a veterinarian?"

"More than ever. Guess what! Dr. Millikin says . . ." Clyde looked toward the stairway. "Here she comes now. Golleee, don't . . . doesn't she look pretty!"

Slowly swaying down the stairs, Monica wore a low-cut, skin-tight, tiger-striped lounge outfit. Her long white hair, which she had earlier worn in a ponytail, was fashioned into an upsweep, and gold hoop earrings dangled from her ears.

Now there's a predator on the prowl, thought Rose. *And here I am with my scraggly, damp hair, dressed in my cleanest, dirty T-shirt and jeans. I wonder if she dresses like this for the teenaged delinquents.*

"Sorry I'm late," Monica said, as she seated herself next to Dan. "We hardly ever eat this late." Josh entered the dining room with the wine decanter. Following him and carrying a soup tureen was the pretty young girl, who had waved at them upon their arrival that morning. Clyde straightened up in his seat and brushed back his hair.

Monica turned to Josh as he poured her wine. "What's on the menu this evening?"

"Nothing fancy. I've had too many mouths to feed today. Just some defrosted leftovers, I'm afraid."

"We understand," said Monica. "I'm sure whatever you've conjured up will be just fine."

Clyde looked at the wine decanter. "Do I get some of that?"

"That would depend on how old you are," answered Josh.

"Really? How old do you have to be?"

"Twenty one here in South Carolina," Josh answered.

Clyde looked over at the girl who was serving the soup. She looked to be in her mid teens, about his age. "I guess I'll have to wait a couple of years."

Rose poked Dan in the ribs with her elbow, and he smiled back at her.

James joined the girl and Josh in delivering the food to the table before the three of them seated themselves. Clyde grinned as the girl bypassed several other chairs to sit next to him.

"You've already met James and Josh," said Monica. "May I introduce Sherry? Sherry and James are two of our volunteers-on-call whenever we're shorthanded. And as you know, we were especially shorthanded today of all days. The county hasn't sent us any community service workers for some time."

"In a way, you could say that was a good thing," said Rose.

"I suppose so," said Monica. "But even if our volunteers weren't so busy with their own problems from the storm, most wouldn't be able to get here because of the road and bridge closures. I'm still thanking my lucky stars that the three of you showed up. I can't believe my good fortune."

Dan passed the bread plate. "Speaking of road closures, has anyone heard anything about Route 278 south being reopened?"

"Sure did," answered Josh. "They said on the news that the water's down, and they have crews out right now clearing off the mud and debris. They said it should be open by mid-morning tomorrow."

"That's great news," said Dan.

Monica turned to Dan. "Surely you're not thinking of leaving tomorrow."

"Well, yes, Monica. With the highway opened up, most of the domestic animals can start getting moved out. We'll be around all morning to help, and by noon, things should be manageable around here, shouldn't they?"

"Let's discuss that after dinner." She turned her attention to Josh, seated across the table. "Josh, leftover or not, this beef stew is delicious."

They had sherbet for dessert, and afterward, everyone carried their own dishes to the large kitchen. "James and Sherry will take it from here." said Monica. "I see Josh has made a pot of decaf. Pour yourselves a cup, and let's go into the great room and relax a bit before bedtime."

"I'll be heading over to the bunkhouse," said Josh. "It's been a long day. You coming, Clyde?"

"I'll be along later, if it's okay." He looked across the room at Sherry. "I'll stay here a while and help with the dishes."

"Suit yourself. You know where your bunk is. I'll leave the light on for you."

Monica, Rose, and Dan went into the great room and seated themselves in posh leather chairs grouped around a beautiful cherry wood table with hand-carved legs.

"How did you wind up in the business of caring for wild-life?" Rose asked.

"That's a long story. As Dan already knows, this place was my family's vacation home, where Daddy also raised racehorses. He had some of the best breeders and trainers in the business here full time. All of the outbuildings you see were part of the operation. I've always loved animals, all animals, and Daddy was thrilled to death that I wanted to study veterinary medicine. He was grooming my brother to take over the company some day, and me to take over the horse operation."

Monica took a sip of coffee. "But things happen. Bad things, as you well know. To put it all in a nutshell, Daddy died unexpectedly, the oil business collapsed, and my brother committed suicide."

"That's terrible," said Rose. "And what about your mother?"

"My real mother died when I was thirteen. Daddy had three wives after that, all of them no good. All were after him for his money. Not only did they all get big alimony settlements, they made several lawyers wealthy by claiming rights to Daddy's estate. I was able to hang on to this place, because Daddy deeded it to me when I turned eighteen. After the business collapsed, I had no income. So I was forced to sell the horses."

Rose had forgotten she still had Monica's cell phone in her pocket, and when it rang, she nearly jumped out of her chair. She handed the phone to Monica, who got up and distanced herself from them for a few minutes. Returning, she said, "That was a bit of good news. We'll be getting three young men and a young lady tomorrow."

"How do you handle these young delinquents, Monica?" asked Dan. "Aren't you afraid they'll do something bad while they're here?"

"The ones who come here have been carefully screened. I've been taking them in for nearly fifteen years now, and any troubles I've had in all that time are hardly worth mentioning. This isn't detention, you know. It's more like camp, but with a purpose. Almost all of the kids genuinely enjoy taking care of the animals, and many sign up as volunteers after they've completed their service. They also do house-work and some maintenance. They learn a lot while they're here and are better people when they leave."

"So what about the wildlife?" asked Rose.

"Well, this was my base for my veterinary practice, which was mainly large animals. I didn't keep many here, just an occasional horse or cow that needed surgery. The rest of the time I was on the road to some farm or ranch. When the bottom fell out of the beef market, there weren't that many cows around to care for. I get some income from investments, but it takes a lot to keep up a big estate like this."

"I noticed your driveway is more than a mile long," said Dan. "How much land do you have here, anyway?"

"Roughly sixteen-hundred acres. It's all zoned Conservation now, so the taxes are minimal.

"Getting back to my story," Monica continued, "I was broken-hearted at the thought of selling the place, but I was preparing to do just that and join a practice in Columbia, the state capital. Five people on the payroll and the taxes here were killing me. Every once in a while, someone from the Fish and Wildlife Service would ask me to care for some hurt or sick animal. One day, I told Monty, one of their chiefs, that I was putting the place up for sale. He's the one who gave me the idea to establish the Foundation. Now funds come in from several wildlife preservation organizations, as well as from private donations and various government grants."

"Do you have to pay for any of the help now?" asked Dan.

"Just Josh. He used to work for the Barnum and Bailey Circus, doing pretty much what he does now. He was tired of traveling and was happy to settle down here. One of my former patrons, District Judge Vince Weaver, who lives over in Barnwell, had a hand in providing the rest of my help. He thought taking care of animals and doing other work around here was a good community service. Some kids commute, but if they live too far away, they stay here."

"Well, I'm glad that it all worked out well for you, Monica," said Dan. "And, well, for a lot of others, too." Dan stood up. "Guess we'd better head on up, Rose. We have a busy morning ahead."

Monica took his hand. "Please wait, Dan. There's more I need to discuss with you. Clyde explained his problems at home to me. Do you think it would be all right for him to stay here?"

Dan sat back down. "Of course. It would be a wonderful opportunity for him. You'll need to clear it with his father, but I know he'd want the best for Clyde."

Monica kept her grip on Dan's hand. "Clyde also told me all about your misfortune. I'm so sorry."

Boy, is she ever giving Dan the goo-goo eyes. I think I'm going to be sick, thought Rose.

"I would never have expected a thing like that from Larry," Monica continued. "Weren't you and he roommates at the frat house?"

"Not just my roommate, but my lifetime best friend."

Monica looked at Rose. "Weren't you engaged to Larry at one time?"

"Yes, I was."

"What he did is a hard thing to forgive," said Monica.

"There are some things that don't deserve forgiveness," said Dan. "What he did is one of them."

"But I forgave you," Monica said.

Dan pulled his hand from her grip. "I beg your pardon?"

"I have a proposition for you."

Why doesn't that surprise me? thought Rose.

"You two have nothing," Monica continued. "You're practically destitute. You could stay here and help me run the Foundation. Heaven knows I can use the help. Your salaries wouldn't be much, but living here, you wouldn't need much."

Rose's response was immediate. "I don't think so, Monica."

Monica turned to Dan. "Dan? Please say yes."

Dan's thoughtful silence caused a sickening feeling in Rose's stomach. She stood up. "It's just been a little over a week since all that happened. We're not destitute until all hope of finding Larry is lost. Come on, Dan, it's late."

As Dan arose from his chair, Monica did also. "What do *you* say, Dan?"

The nerve of that woman! I already said no!

"It's definitely something to think about," said Dan. "We'll have to sleep on it."

Back in their room, Rose exploded as quietly as possible. "I can't believe you would actually entertain the idea of staying here. Can't you see how she's making a play for you?"

"Come on, Rose, you know I've always been faithful to you."

"Yes, so far. But for the same reason she keeps these doors locked to keep the teenagers honest, there's no need to invite temptation. And I've been wondering about those letters she said she wrote. Did she write to you after we were married?"

"Well . . . yes. She mailed them to the clinic. After the first few, I had that "address unknown stamp made."

"You mean to say you didn't read any of them?"

Dan plopped down on the bed, jerked off his shoes, and tossed them aside. "What is this, Rose, the third degree? I read the first one. That's all. After that, I threw some away, and when they kept coming, I started stamping them and sending them back. They finally quit coming."

"And why did you stop reading them after the one?"

"Well, because. It was inappropriate."

"You mean the content of the letter was inappropriate?"

"Well, yes. And just her writing like that to a married man at all was inappropriate."

"Well, I'm proud of you for that," Rose said as she pulled her nightgown down over her head. "I hope you will be just as honest when I ask my next question. "Did you know about Monica and this place when Jean suggested we bring the cat here?"

"Absolutely not! She was living in South Carolina the last I knew, but I didn't know where. Do you think I *arranged* this? How the hell could I have done that? Rose, I never knew you to be paranoid before."

"Well, you have to admit, our just happening upon this place and her set up is pretty coincidental."

"And that's all it was, Rose, coincidence! Or, as you say, maybe it was providence.

"Well, whatever, I'll be glad to leave here tomorrow."

"Rose, just give it some thought. Chances are, we may never see our money again. All we have right now is a beat up van we call home. Staying here would be a sure thing. This is a beautiful place to live, and I would have a respectable job again. I'm too old, and don't have the means to try to start over on my own, and I sure don't ever want to be a burden on Chess and Brad."

The thought they might be a burden on their sons was the last straw. Rose began to cry.

Dan threw back the covers of one of the queen beds. "Come on, sweetie, crawl in here. As you always say, things will look better in the morning."

Rose flipped back the covers of the other bed. "I'll sleep over here, thank you."

Chapter Eighteen

The bellowing of an animal in one of the large pens outside awakened Rose. In the faint light of dawn, she turned over to look at her husband, snoring softly in the other bed. She quietly dressed, pulled her hair back into a ponytail, and then gently closed the door behind her.

Rose tiptoed down the staircase and saw a path of light across the floor of the great room, coming from the kitchen. *I wonder if I would be so lucky as to find a fresh pot of coffee in there.* At the bottom of the stairs, the delicious aroma wafting across the room answered her question.

There was no one in the kitchen. Rose looked through the cabinets until she found a mug. She filled it from the large coffee urn and then looked around in the refrigerator until she found some cream. She opened and shut several drawers and jumped when a voice behind her said, "The spoons are in the drawer to the right of the dishwasher."

"Monica! You startled me. Excuse me for rummaging around in your kitchen."

Monica was in a very short, dark red, sateen dressing gown, and leaning against the door to the veranda with a coffee mug in her hand. "I'm pretty much a stranger in here myself. The kitchen is Josh's domain." She studied Rose as she took a sip from her mug. "You're up early."

"Yes," said Rose. "Some animal out there woke me up."

"You'll get used to that."

When Rose started to speak, Monica opened the screen door and motioned with her coffee mug. "Come on out on the veranda, and we'll talk."

Rose seated herself in a wicker chair, while Monica settled in the porch swing and set it into motion. Rose couldn't help but notice how the gap in Monica's dressing gown revealed her ample bosom, and the sateen fabric accentuated her nipples. After a few moments of silence, except for the chirping of crickets, Monica said, "Just look at that sky . . . and listen to all the birds. This is my favorite time of day."

"It is beautiful," said Rose. "Do you usually get up this early?"

"Pretty much. There's a lot to do around this place. One has to start early to see that it all gets done. Dan's taking part of the responsibility will lift a big burden off of me, though."

Rose felt her hackles rise. "Monica, I thought I made it pretty clear last night that we would *not* be staying."

Monica nonchalantly continued swinging, "I didn't get that impression from Dan at all. I'd like to hear what *he* has to say on the matter. I'm betting he'll stay."

Rose stood up and angrily tossed the rest of her coffee over the banister. "You're deluding yourself on that point, Monica."

Rose spun around to leave and was startled to find Dan standing on the other side of the screen door. "What point is that?" he asked.

Rose looked down at Monica, who had brought the porch swing to a halt. "She's got the rest of our lives planned out for us, Dan. *Yours* anyway." Rose opened the door and pushed Dan aside to enter the house. "It's your choice, Dan, but I will not live under the same roof with that woman. I'll be in our room. Let me know what you decide."

Rose ran up the stairs, slammed the door after her, and then threw herself on the bed. The sobs would not stop, and she felt that her heart would break. When no more tears would come, she got up and straightened the bed covers. *What on earth is taking him so long?*

She washed her face and applied a cold washcloth to her eyes to reduce the puffiness crying had caused. While applying her makeup, she listened to muffled voices and the clatter downstairs. She then plopped down in a chair, wondering what she should do next.

What am I going to do if Dan decides to stay? I've given him an ultimatum that I will keep, come hell or high water. Rose glanced at the clock on the dresser. *I've been waiting up here for nearly two hours. Why hasn't he come yet? He's had plenty of time, unless . . .*

There was a knock on the door. "Mrs. Good? Are you in there?"

Rose opened the door a crack. It was James.

"Good morning, ma'am. Breakfast is ready. Better come on down while it's hot."

I'm not hungry, but if I'm going to strike out on my own, I'd better eat while I can.

Rose opened the door. "Thank you, James. I'll walk down with you."

As they entered the dining area, Josh stood up from the table for a moment, wiping his mouth with a napkin. "Good morning. Breakfast is buffet style. Just grab a plate and help yourself."

"Morning, Mrs. Good," Clyde said. "You've gotta try those biscuits. I didn't think anyone could make them better than Ada Lou, but I think Josh has her beat."

Rose noticed that Sherry was, once again, seated next to Clyde. "Good morning, everyone. Where are Dan and Monica?"

"I saw them heading out to the barn earlier," said Clyde. "They must have been in a big hurry about something, cause Miss Milikin wasn't even dressed yet."

He means hardly dressed, with her in that skimpy outfit.

Rose filled her plate with scrambled eggs, sausage patties, and two biscuits, and then sat down next to Clyde. "Did they say why they were going to the barn?"

"I hollered and asked them if they needed me for anything, but they just waved and said to tell Josh not to wait breakfast on them."

Josh got up from the table. "Excuse me, folks. I've got a whole bunch more mouths to feed yet. Soon as you get done there, Clyde, come on in the kitchen and give me a hand."

"Sure thing, Josh."

Clyde and Sherry chatted away while Rose picked at her food. Her mind's eye saw Monica in her revealing attire, and Rose imagined what might be taking place in the barn. She found it hard to swallow her food. She made biscuit sandwiches with the sausage and eggs, and then wrapped them in paper napkins. She scooted her chair back and stood up to leave. Clyde looked up at her. "Why, Mrs. Good, are you done already?"

"Yes, I have to get going."

"I guess I'd better get going soon too," said Clyde. "Right after I have another biscuit and jelly." He respectfully got up from his chair. "We've all got a real busy day ahead, don't we?"

Rose grabbed Clyde in a bear hug, tears welling up in her eyes. "Clyde, I'm going to miss you." She stepped back and looked into his eyes, saying, "I wish you all the success and happiness in the world."

When Rose turned to go, Clyde caught her arm. "What do you mean you'll miss me? Miss Millikin said we were all going to live here and work together."

"Not me, Clyde. Not me." Rose stepped away and hurried toward the stairs. Over her shoulder, she said, "Say goodbye to everyone, will you?"

Back in their room, Rose gathered up all of her things and stuffed them into the small bag that had contained both her and Dan's belongings. *He won't be needing this bag.* She picked up his billfold from off the dresser and looked inside. *Thirteen dollars. He won't be needing these either. She'll take good care of him.*

Anger burned away the tears as Rose hurriedly made her way down the stairs. She gathered up all of Dan's things in the van and dumped them into a pile on the front porch. The last item was his golf bag, which she tossed on top of the pile. *Maybe Monica will turn part of her sizable estate into Dan's own private golf course.*

Rose crawled back into the van and peeled out of the circular drive, onto the one-lane road leading back to the highway.

After about a mile, a large truck appeared on the narrow road, headed in her direction. Seeing that they could not pass one another, Rose stopped. A man got out of the truck, and as he approached, Rose recognized him as being the Fish and Wildlife ranger she had met yesterday. He touched the brim of his hat. "Good morning, Mrs. Good. Are you taking a break?"

"You could say that. Are you bringing in more animals?"

"Yep. We're fully loaded. And I also brought Dr. Millikin some help." He pointed toward a passenger in the truck. "That's our staff veterinarian. He normally just does inspections but has offered to stay around and help out here for as long as he's needed."

"Well, I'm sure the good doctor will be pleased."

"Mrs. Good, would you mind backing up? There's a treeless spot over there off the road that I think you'll fit into. I'll get back there and direct you."

Rose had driven the van very little and had never backed it up. In spite of the ranger's frantic gestures, she slammed into a tree. On the second try, her foot slipped off the gas pedal, and a tree raked the van along its entire length. *Oh, no! That was the van's least damaged side.*

The ranger appeared at her window. "I'm sorry about that, ma'am. I guess I should have been the one to back up, but I hated to run that big old truck backward, out onto the highway."

"Don't worry about it. What's one or two more scars on this poor vehicle?"

"Thanks, Mrs. Good." The ranger turned back toward his truck. "See you around."

Probably not in this lifetime, fella.

As the ranger's truck slowly rolled past, Rose saw there was a passenger van that had stopped behind the truck, also waiting to pass. The driver waved as the van slowly drove by, and Rose noted the words on the its side, "Allendale County Services." *There goes more help for Madam Monica, and they don't look too happy about it.* Rose waved at the four sullen-faced teenagers peering out at her, but only the girl waved back.

Driving down the highway, Rose was on an emotional roller coaster. She felt anger, sadness, and apprehension, but also a strange feeling of exhilaration. She was free. Free as a bird, having to answer to no one. She could do exactly as she pleased. She punched the button to turn on the radio, then the scan button. *Don't they listen to anything but country around here? Oh, there we are.* Rod Stewart was singing an oldie, "It Had to be You," and Rose accompanied him at the top of her lungs. *I know what I'll do to get by. I'll find some nice, respectable bars along the way where I can sing for a living. I've always dreamed of a singing career, and now's my chance.*

The next Rod Stewart oldie was, "We'll be Together Again." Rose joined in for just a few words, before they began to stick in her throat as she thought of Dan.

With tears streaming down her face, Rose's reverie was interrupted by lights flashing over her left shoulder. An angry looking motorcycle cop motioned her to pull over.

Shaking, Rose steered off the highway, wiped her eyes, and then rolled down the window. Through the side mirror, she watched the patrolman dismount and then saunter toward her. *Why is he stopping me? I wasn't speeding. I never speed.*

"Lady, why didn't you pull over way back there when you heard my siren?"

"Your siren? I'm sorry, I didn't hear it. I had the radio on."

"Step out of the vehicle, please."

Step out of the vehicle? He didn't even ask for my driver's license. I've read about this sort of thing. He may be one of those rapists, with a phony badge and disguised as a policeman.

Rose quickly turned the ignition back on and started to roll the window up. The policeman reached in, and had the door unlocked and her keys in his hand before she even knew what happened. "I said step out here!" he growled.

"I will not! Not until you tell me why you stopped me. And I demand to see your identification."

The officer pulled a plastic card from his shirt pocket and held it up to Rose's face. She studied it for a minute, and then said, "Well, it looks real enough, but you tell me why you stopped me."

"Okay, lady," the officer said as he stuck the card back in his pocket, "I'm through playing games. Are you going to step out of there, or do I have to use force?"

The minute Rose climbed down from the van, the officer twirled her around, pulled her arms behind her back, and snapped on handcuffs.

"What do you think you're doing?" she screamed. "What have I done to deserve this?"

He pushed Rose against the van, and while he was patting her down, he said, "Don't play innocent with me. You're being arrested for grand theft auto.

"What? But this is *my* auto. Let me get my purse. I can prove it."

The officer calmly walked Rose back to his motorcycle while reading her her rights. "You have the right to remain silent, you have the right to . . ." Rose's mind was in a fog as his voice droned on.

"Do you expect me to ride on the back of this thing? With handcuffs on?" she asked.

He reached into the motorcycle to retrieve a radio mike. "No, lady. I've got to call for a prisoner pick-up unit."

An approaching car slowed to a stop, and a man stuck his head out of the driver's window. "Wha'd she do, officer?" His wife leaned across him to stare at Rose.

"Keep moving," yelled the officer.

He and Rose watched the car slowly drive away, the man staring into his side-view mirror and his three kids staring out the back window.

It was then that the patrolman noticed a figure speeding down the highway toward them on an all-terrain vehicle. "That crazy fool! I told him to stay put!"

The ATV pulled up behind the motorcycle, and a disheveled Dan jumped off. "Rose, what the hell do you think you're doing?"

"And what do you think *you're* doing?" asked the officer. "I told you, you can't drive that thing on the highway. You're just begging for a ticket, aren't you?"

Dan grabbed Rose and held her tightly. "Rose, I can't believe you'd leave me. What were you thinking?"

The officer tapped Dan on the shoulder. "You didn't tell me you and the perpetrator were acquainted."

Dan turned to face him. "I'm sorry, officer. I just didn't know what else to do. I was afraid I'd never see my wife again."

"So you're telling me this vehicle wasn't stolen after all?"

"That's right, officer. I'm sorry if I've caused you any trouble."

Without a word, the patrolman reached over to take the keys out of the ATV. He then picked up his radio mike and spoke into it. "This is officer Kelly on Highway 278, about six miles south of the Ark. I need a pick up for two prisoners. Roger. Out."

Chapter Nineteen

"**W**hat are you doing?" asked Dan. "Are you *arresting* us?"

"You have the right to remain silent, you have the right . . ."

"Wait just a minute. This is ridiculous. My wife has done nothing wrong. Just give me the damned ticket for driving an unlicensed vehicle on the highway, and we'll be on our way."

"You don't get off that easy, mister. Filing a false complaint is a serious offense."

Dan raised his voice several octaves. "I just explained all that to you. I demand you take those cuffs off my wife right now or . . ."

The patrolman put his hand on his holster. "Turn around. Now!"

Dan started to protest, and the patrolman pulled his gun halfway out of its holster.

"Dan!" cried Rose, "For Pete's sake, do as you're told. We can straighten this out later."

Mumbling through his teeth, Dan turned around and the patrolman cuffed him. After reading him his rights, the patrolman ordered Dan and Rose to sit on the ground. As Dan tried to make himself comfortable, he glanced up at the van. "My God, Rose, what happened to the side of the van?"

The patrolman said, "Remember the part about your right to remain silent? I suggest you take advantage of that. Anything you say can, *and will,* be used against you."

"The cocky bastard," Dan snarled under his breath.

The patrolman strutted back to his motorcycle, and Rose heard him radio for a tow truck to pick up the van and the ATV. She then heard him radio again, asking for a search warrant to be processed.

Rose and Dan sat quietly fuming until a large passenger van pulled up, and the patrolman ordered Dan and Rose to their feet. The side of the van read, Allendale County Services. Rose recognized the driver, who got out to talk to the patrolman. "Hi, there, Officer Kelly. Since we were in the area makin' a delivery, the state asked us to do this pick up. Hey! I recognize that van. And that's the gal who was driving it. I thought she acted awful nervous, the way she banged that thing into those trees comin' out from the Ark. Did she steal drugs or somethin'?

"Well, Pete, we'll find out soon enough. They're getting a search warrant for the van as we speak."

The patrolman ordered them to stand up, and then motioned Dan and Rose toward the van. He pulled the step down from the high vehicle and steadied Rose's elbow as she climbed in. A steel mesh grating separated the cab from the back of the van. As Dan climbed in beside her, he made one more attempt to reason with the patrolman. "You're making a big mistake, officer. Why don't you just call . . ."

"Tell it to the judge," he shot back.

"I'll do that," snapped Dan. "And I'll give him your regards. What was your name again, officer? Barney, wasn't it? Barney Fife?"

The patrolman slammed the van door and stalked off.

"That kind of talk won't help your case none," said the driver as he pulled out onto the highway.

"Why did you leave, Rose?" asked Dan. "Look at all the trouble you've caused."

"I told you I wouldn't live under the same roof with that woman. It was pretty clear to me that you had made the choice to stay."

"For your information, right after you left us on the veranda this morning, I informed Monica we were *not* staying, and we'd be on our way by noon."

"Then why didn't you come tell me that? I waited for over three hours before I left. When you didn't show up, what was I supposed to think?"

"I'm not in charge of what you think, Rose, but I would have thought you'd have more faith in me than what you exhibited this morning."

"Oh? The word I got was that you were traipsing out to the barn with Monica. And she was still in that skimpy, provocative dressing gown. It seemed evident you were up to something much more important than having breakfast, or informing your wife of your decision to leave the place. How long after you got to the barn did her dressing gown stay on?"

"Oh, for God's sake, Rose, you've let your imagination run away with you. When I asked her if she could replenish my medical supplies, you know I've used up a good deal of them just since we left home, she took me out to her vault in the barn and filled up my bag. While we were out there, we checked on some of the animals she operated on yesterday, and one of the horses was in trouble. That's when she put on her coveralls. And I do mean *cover alls*. After working on the poor animal for more than an hour, we both determined it was futile, and had to put him down.

"We were walking back to the main house for breakfast, when several llamas, goats, and antelope ran past us. Monica knew immediately that their pen had been compromised. So we ran back to the machinery shed and each grabbed an ATV. We scouted the perimeter of one of the large pens until we found the break, and then spent at least half an hour repairing it. After that, we charged all over the entire estate, rounding up the animals that had gotten out. When we got back to the house, Clyde was beside himself and told me that you had left. I jumped right back on the ATV and took out after you. About a mile down the highway, Barney Fife back there pulled me over and gave me the riot act about riding the ATV on the highway. I guess I shouldn't have told him that someone had just stolen my van, but I was afraid if I didn't sound urgent, he wouldn't go after you, and by that time, I sure wouldn't be able catch up to you."

Dan nudged her shoulder. "And that's the important thing, Rose. He stopped you. How would I ever have found you otherwise?"

"You could have called me on the cell phone. Wouldn't that have been easier?"

"Rose, I took the phone out of the van last night. It's been in my pocket all morning."

Oh, my God. If that policeman hadn't stopped me . . .

Rose dropped her head. "I'm sorry, Dan. I guess I really played the fool. You know jealousy is not in my nature. But in Monica's case . . . well, she's an exception, for darned sure. It was like . . . she wanted you, and by God, she was going to have you. It was like I was a mere impediment that she could just brush aside."

Dan leaned over and kissed Rose on the cheek. "That's all over now, Sweetie. We just have to concentrate on how the hell we're going to get out of this mess." She turned her face, and their lips locked in a lingering kiss.

When their lips parted, Rose's eyes met the driver's in the rear-view mirror. His focus quickly darted back to the highway. He cleared his throat. "You seem like decent folks."

"Well, we are decent folks," said Dan.

"I'm supposed to take you to the jailhouse in Barnwell so's they can book you and stick you in the pokey till a trial date can be set. What do you say we cut through all that bullshit and go right to the judge? I understand he and Dr. Millikin are thick as fleas."

"You can do that?" asked Dan.

"I think so. Judge Weaver usually has Fridays off. He should be home. We'll just see."

Rose and Dan chatted with the driver for the time it took to get to just outside of Barnwell. He pulled off the highway and stopped at a wrought iron gate, where he got out and talked for quite a few minutes into a talk box. The gate swung open. They followed a tree-lined drive to an impressive, colonial-style, country estate. The driver got out of the van to climb the wide porch stairs and ring the doorbell. A handsome, distinguished-looking man about Dan's age and size answered the door with a drink in his hand. Dressed in a casual, short-sleeved shirt and shorts, he set his drink on the porch banister and then followed the driver down the stairs to the van. He leaned down to look in at Dan and Rose. He turned and said to the driver, "Would you lower the window please, Pete?"

The man rested one arm on the window opening. Rose got a whiff of a pleasant aftershave cologne. "Hello, I'm District Judge Vincent Weaver," he said in a soft southern drawl. "So you're Daniel and Rosemary Good."

"Why, yes," answered Dan, "how did you know our names?"

"I just spoke with Dr. Millikin. She speaks highly of you both."

Both? thought Rose.

"Pete here tells me you had a run-in with Officer Kelly." The judge opened the van's door. "Why don't the both of you come up here on the veranda and tell me all about it."

Dan scooted over to the door, and then slid out.

"My goodness," said the judge. "You're handcuffed?"

"I'm afraid so."

Rose scooted over to the door. "Would you mind helping my wife out? She's got on cuffs, too."

"How terribly unfortunate for you both," drawled the judge. He looked at Pete. "I assume you have the key?"

Pete lowered the step for Rose. "No, sir, I don't carry them." He held her elbow as she stepped down. "As you know, I usually don't transport prisoners, just the juvies."

"Well, we'll see what we can do," said the judge. He took Rose's arm to help her up the porch stairs to a cushioned wicker settee. Dan followed and sat down beside Rose.

"Make yourselves as comfortable as possible. I'll be right back."

The judge entered the house, and returned in a few minutes with an older, white-haired black man. "This is Dr. and Mrs. Good, Eli." The man nodded his head. "And this is Eli, who runs my household. He's going to see about removing those damnable handcuffs."

"Boy, are we glad to meet you," said Dan.

Eli chuckled and said, "Okay, who's first?"

"Ladies first," Dan answered.

As she stood up, Rose noticed Eli pull something from his pocket that looked like a crochet needle. "Is this going to hurt?"

"Oh, no, ma'am. Just turn around and we'll have those ole cuffs off in a jiffy."

Rose heard a "click" and felt the irritating cuffs fall away. She turned to Eli, while vigorously rubbing her wrists. "Oh, thank you so much. What a relief!"

Eli handed the cuffs to Judge Weaver, and then proceeded to remove Dan's cuffs.

"You're my man!" said Dan as he hugged Eli's shoulders. "How in the world did you learn to do that? And so quickly!"

Eli smiled and looked at the judge. "That's a rather long story, ain't it, Judge?"

"Yes, it is, but one with a happy ending. Would you mind bringing out that big pitcher of lemonade you just made, and some glasses for these folks?"

"Yes, sir. Be right back."

The judge then addressed the driver. "Pete, while you're waiting for the lemonade, would you get on your radio and see if you can run down that tow truck? Tell him I said to deliver the Good's van, and that other vehicle back to the Ark. Will you do that for me, please?"

"Sure thing, Judge. What about the search warrant?"

"Oh, yes. Would you also call Jane and tell her it won't be necessary to process one."

After they resumed their seats, the judge asked Dan to explain what had happened.

"Well, to put it in a nutshell, Rose and I had a misunderstanding, and she left me at the Ark this morning in our van. I took out after her on one of Monica's ATVs. When Barney, I mean Officer Kelly, pulled me over, I told him someone had just stolen my van. I *had* to do something drastic. That van is our only home, and I didn't know how I would ever reach Rose otherwise and get her back. Even if I had known my lying about the van's theft was a serious offense, I still would have done it."

A large orange tabby cat that had been sunning itself suddenly jumped down from the porch railing and hopped onto Rose's lap.

"I hope you'll excuse Boswell, ma'am," said the judge. "He's an extremely discriminating animal when it comes to socializing. You should feel honored."

"Oh, I do," said Rose as she stroked the tabby's fur.

The judge studied Rose. "Do you want to go back to your husband, little lady? Has he mistreated you in any way?"

"Oh, my no. I mean no, he's never mistreated me, and yes, I want to go back to him. As Dan said, it was just some silly misunderstanding. I take the blame for everything that's happened."

"Case closed, then. I'm sorry you both were inconvenienced. Officer Kelly is new on the force, and perhaps a mite overzealous, but he is a fine young officer just doing his job."

"With exuberance, I might add," said Dan, sarcastically. "He obviously loves his work."

Eli returned with a tray of iced glasses, and poured a round of lemonade.

"Pete?" said the judge, "Would your duties allow you to return Dr. and Mrs. Good back to the Ark?"

"No problem, Judge. My next pick up is in Barton, so it's right on the way."

They chatted while drinking their lemonade, and the conversation eventually turned to Rose and Dan's plight. Judge Weaver seemed intently interested in their story. "You say you think these two, Larry and Mitzi, may be heading to Miami?"

"Yes," said Dan, "at least from the information we've been able to gather so far. But I can't even imagine how we're going to track them down in such a large city."

The judge swirled the ice cubes around in his glass. "I have influential friends in Miami. Let me take down all your information, including your cell phone number. I'll make a few calls and get back with you."

"Oh, Judge Weaver, you would do that for us? How kind of you," said Rose.

"You are most welcome. You see, not only is it my profession, but my obsession, to see to it that bad people do not get by with doing bad things."

The judge ushered Dan and Rose into the library, where he wrote down everything they could think to tell him. After a while, Pete stuck his head in the door. "Sorry to interrupt, but if we don't get a move on, my day's schedule is going to be shot."

The judge pushed his leather armchair back from his desk and stood up. "I think we have everything we need at this point. Thank you for your patience, Pete. And thank you for having the good sense to bring the Goods here to me like you did."

As they were leaving the library, Dan hugged Pete's shoulders. "We thank you, too, Pete. Looks like getting arrested was the best thing that could have happened to us."

As they were all going down the porch steps, a large peacock, his colorful tail feathers fully extended, strutted by on the lawn, accompanied by three peahens. "Oh, look at that one," said Rose, pointing to a hen whose neck was grotesquely bent. "What on earth happened to her?"

"The poor things were blown out of their tree during the storm the other night," said Judge Weaver. "You'll notice NBC has some of his tail feathers missing, too."

Without saying a word, Dan hurried over to the surprised peahen and scooped her up in his arms. He deftly popped her neck vertebrae back into place, and then bent over to set her down. Dan cried out in pain as the peacock came from behind to give him a hard peck in the rear end. Grabbing his behind and quickly turning, Dan lifted the hostile bird with one foot, tossing him several yards away. "How would you like to lose *all* of your tail feathers, Mr. Fancy-Pants?"

Dan and the bird stood their ground, glowering at one another while Rose, the judge, Eli, and Pete howled with laughter. Holding his side from laughing so much, the judge finally said, "Thank you, Dan, and I'm sure peahen thanks you, too. I'm sorry you were so painfully repaid for your good deed. You've just discovered how protective NBC is of his little harem."

As they started down the long driveway, Rose looked back. The judge and Eli stood on the lawn, waving, with huge grins still on their faces.

Once again on the highway, Rose's thoughts turned to Monica. *I thought I had seen the last of her. I'm certainly not looking forward to our next meeting.*

Chapter Twenty

P ete let Rose and Dan out in front of the Ark's main building. Dan's belongings were still in a pile on the porch. "After I get these things loaded in the van, we've got to find Monica and say our goodbyes," said Dan.

"I'll help you load this stuff, and then I'm going upstairs to use the bathroom before we leave. You can go find Monica if you like, but I'll be happy if I never see her again. I'll be waiting for you in the van."

"Just to be on the safe side, may I please have your car keys?" kidded Dan.

"Not on your life. You've got thirty minutes, then I, and your precious golf clubs, are gone." The look on Dan's face made Rose think he believed her.

After the van was loaded, Dan headed for the clinic. Rose went inside the lodge, up the stairs to their room of the night before, and into the adjoining bathroom. Before leaving, she washed her face and re-did her pony tail. When Rose opened the bathroom door, she was startled to find Monica sitting on the edge of one of the beds. Monica looked up. "I heard your footsteps on the stairs."

"You must have thought it was Dan," Rose said sarcastically.

"Definitely not. What I heard was pitter pat on the stairs, not clompity clomp."

"Then you're here to see *me*?" asked Rose, incredulously.

Monica patted the seat of a nearby chair. "Yes. Please have a seat."

Rose seated herself as Monica continued. "I want to apologize for whatever part I may have had in today's fiasco. You must have had some pretty strong feelings to take off the way you did."

"Yes, Monica, I've had strong feelings since the moment I saw you kissing my husband."

"I can imagine you would. Maybe you can forgive me if you could just put yourself in my shoes. Just think of what an incredible twist of fate it was that brought Dan to my doorstep. When I opened the door to find him standing there, of course my first thought was that he was here to see me. And I was overcome with happiness to see him."

"You'll have to admit, Monica, that your happiness was not at seeing a long lost friend, but at finding a long lost lover."

Monica lowered her head. "To me, he was both." She covered her face with her hands, but couldn't hide the tears starting down her cheeks.

"You would take Dan back in a second if I were not in the picture, wouldn't you, Monica?"

Monica grabbed a tissue from a box on the nightstand and blew her nose. "Yes, damn you. You bet your sweet life

I would. He broke my heart, but I've never gotten over him. I'm a one-man woman and doomed to love him until the day I die." She grabbed another tissue and sobbed into it.

I hate her, but I can't help feeling sorry for her. Rose sat down on the bed and put an arm around Monica's shaking shoulder. "Under the circumstances, you know we can't stay. I have to admit, Monica, that the big reason I feel such jealousy is that you'd be such a great catch. Other women have made advances to Dan throughout the years, but I've never felt threatened before now."

Monica dabbed at her eyes. "Thank you for that."

"Surely, Monica, in all these years, there have been other men. I don't understand this fixation you have on Dan."

"Well, I don't understand it either. Sure, I've had other men. The Judge and I even had a little fling. But when I am with a man, all I can do is compare him to Dan. None of my affairs have ever held a candle to what I felt for him. Seeing Dan again has just intensified my longing for him. Loving him is like having a disease that there's just no cure for." She stood up. "Come, I want to show you something."

Rose followed her down the hall and into Monica's personal quarters. Monica motioned toward a chair beside a table. "Have a seat."

Monica disappeared into her cavernous walk-in closet. Rose looked around the large, beautifully furnished room. Unlike the rustic features of the rest of the lodge, the room's delicately carved furniture was gilded and upholstered in rich brocade. The paper on the walls was a flower design of gold and shades of red. An elegant, fringed canopy hung over the large four-poster bed. Rose's eyes found their way to Monica's dressing table and hesitated at a portrait displayed there.

She got up and walked toward it to make sure it was who she thought it was. *My God, it is Dan.* She picked up the picture for a closer look. It was signed, "With all my love, Danny." *He couldn't have been much older than twenty in this picture.*

"Isn't that a great picture of him?"

Startled, Rose set the picture back down and turned to face Monica, who was holding what appeared to be a large scrapbook. "How long have you kept this picture on your dresser?"

"Why, ever since he gave it to me. It seems like yesterday. Come back to the table so I can show you my scrapbook."

Rose sat down, and Monica placed the scrapbook in front of her. Leaning over Rose, Monica began turning the pages, while giving a running dissertation about each old photograph. They were all of either Dan or Monica, or Dan and Monica together on sailboats, on horses, at parties, dancing, cuddling, and on and on. Some pages had pressed flowers or flattened corsages between them. Halfway through the book, Rose put up her hands to shield herself from the sight of it. "Monica, what on earth is your purpose for showing this to me?"

"I'll tell you, but first, I want to show you one more picture. I saved the best for last." She turned the book to the last page.

Rose gasped. There was an eight-by-ten photograph of Monica in a wedding dress, hanging onto the arm of a tuxedo-clad Dan, who was looking lovingly into her face. "What on *earth* do we have here?" asked Rose. "I think Dan would have told me if he had been married before."

Monica gave a little giggle. "It does look authentic, doesn't it? The photo shop did a great job. That's the dress I had all picked out for when Dan proposed."

Rose lowered her head to study the picture. "This shot of Dan. Where did you get it?"

"I'm surprised you don't recognize it, Rose, seeing as how it was taken at your wedding."

"At our wedding? How did you get it?"

"From the photographer who took your wedding pictures. He's also the one who made the pictures of Dan and me into one."

Rose felt queasy. "Monica, you're a very disturbed woman. I . . . "

Monica sat down in the chair across the table and took Rose's hands in hers. "I can understand how you might think that, Rose. But I assure you, I'm perfectly sane and have both your and Dan's best interests at heart. I'm really very fond of you, too, Rose, and feel we could be like sisters. I showed you these pictures, especially the last one, to steer your thinking in a certain direction."

Rose wriggled her hands from Monica's grasp. "Oh, like what?"

"How do you feel about polygamy? I've been studying about it, and there are some definite advantages . . . "

Rose stood up so fast that her chair fell over backward. "My God, Monica, you're serious, aren't you?"

"Hell, yes, I'm serious. I have a lot to offer you both. Just hear me out."

"Monica, I can't believe you'd propose such a thing to me after all that's happened this morning. You're out of your mind!"

"It was *because* of what happened to you this morning that I thought you might listen to reason. Can't you see how vulnerable you both are? Without money, you're just hopeless, hapless vagabonds. If I hadn't had influence with the judge, you two would be in the pokey right now, and who knows for how long."

"Well, thank you for that, but . . ."

"What will you do if one or both of you gets sick?" Monica interrupted. She smiled broadly and gestured a wide embrace. "We can all live here in comfort, like one, big, happy family."

"And you want me to agree to your marrying my husband. That's insanity!"

"Well, it's more honest than sneaking around behind your back."

"And has that been happening?"

"Not yet. In many world societies, polygamy is a normal thing. In fact, it's biblical. If you find the idea of sharing your husband so disagreeable, we can always join one of those fundamentalist Mormon sects."

"You never give up, do you?" Rose turned and headed for the door. "That does it. We're out of here."

Monica followed Rose down the stairs. "Well, surely you two can have lunch before you go, and we can discuss it further."

"No, thank you! End of discussion!"

Rose raced toward the front door, but Monica got there first and backed up against it blocking Rose's way. "Please don't be angry, Rose. I truly mean well. I may have lost Dan, but I have you both to thank for Clyde, and I want you to know how grateful I am for your bringing me that dear boy. I already feel like he's the son I never had."

"After just getting a preview of the way your mind works, Monica, I don't think we should leave him. I'm going to go find him and tell him to get his things together."

"Don't be absurd, Rose. I'm not totally paranoid . . . just when it comes to Dan. What on earth do you have to offer Clyde? You and Dan are going to have a tough enough time just taking care of yourselves. Clyde has a future here. And do you intend for that smashmobile out there to be a home for three?"

Rose mulled over Monica's words. *I hate to admit it, but she's right. We certainly can't keep him with us. And Clyde does seem to love it here. Except when it comes to Dan, Monica seems rational enough. I just hope Clyde's mature enough to not let her control his life too much.*

"You win, Monica, but keep in mind that he isn't yours. He's his own person. Take my advice. Don't smother him, and don't try to manipulate him the way you do everyone else. He's a good boy, and he's smart, and I know him well enough to know he won't abide that."

The door latch clicked, and the door pushed against Monica. Dan stuck his head inside. "There you are, Monica. I've been looking everywhere for you."

Monica whispered to Rose, "May I give him one last kiss?"

"Over my dead body." Rose shot back.

"What about your body?" asked Dan.

"Never mind." Rose opened the door to step outside. "Let's get going."

As Rose descended the porch steps, she saw that Clyde was standing beside the van. "Hi, Clyde, I'm so glad you're here. I would hate to leave without giving you a proper goodbye."

"I'm sure glad Dr. Good caught up with you, ma'am. He was awful upset about you taking off the way you did. So was I, for that matter. Are you going to behave yourself from now on?"

Rose laughed. "I'll try. And how about you, Clyde? Are you going to be all right here?"

"You bet I will. I really like it here. I especially like learning how to be a veterinarian. Dr. Millikin is real nice, and she's a good teacher. But I sure will miss you and Dr. Good. I wish you'd stay."

Rose hugged Clyde. "We'll miss you too, Clyde. We'll give you a call once in a while to see how you're doing."

Clyde opened the van door for Rose. "That would be real nice. I'll be wondering about you too."

Rose climbed into the van, and glanced up at the porch to see Monica wrapped around Dan, and puckering up for a kiss. Rose leaned hard on the horn and spooked a herd of deer in a nearby pen, causing them to crash into the fence. Monica pulled away from Dan to yell, "For God's sake, Rose, what do you think you're doing?"

"You know perfectly well what I'm doing," yelled Rose. "Come on, Dan, get a move on!"

Clyde reached down to retrieve a small box he had dropped during the ruckus. Dan approached the van, scowling at Rose. He held out his hand to shake Clyde's. "I guess this is so long, partner. Keep your nose clean, and you'll go far."

Self consciously, Clyde reached up to feel his nose. "That's just an expression, Clyde," said Rose. "It means stay out of trouble."

"Oh." He looked at the small, taped-up package in his hand, and then held it out to Rose. "I almost forgot to give this to you. But promise not to open it till you get to Georgia."

"My goodness, what can be in here? Why do we have to wait until we get to Georgia?"

"You'll see. Do you promise?"

"Sure. And thank you for whatever it is."

As Dan turned the van toward the road leading out, he waved at a tearful Monica still standing on the porch, while Rose blew kisses to Clyde.

After a few minutes of silence, Dan said, "I swear, Rose, the way you acted just now . . . I feel like I don't even know you anymore."

"Well, maybe you'll understand me better when you hear Monica's latest proposal. Did you know she still keeps your picture on her dresser?"

"What picture?"

"The With all my love from Danny Boy picture."

"What? Why, that picture's more than forty years old. What the hell is she hanging on to that for?"

"Oooh, that's just the beginning. Wait till you hear what she keeps in her closet."

By the time Rose finished telling Dan about the scrapbook, they were on the highway. Dan appeared stupefied. "Good Lord. I realized she was trying like hell to seduce me, but I didn't think she was crazy. The woman is absolutely deranged."

"You think *that's* deranged; she proposed that you and she get married."

"Get *married*? She knows I would never leave you."

"Oh, she didn't suggest you leave me. What she had in mind was bigamy."

Dan was strangely silent for several minutes.

Rose looked over at him. "Well? What are you thinking?"

"What am I thinking? I'm thinking that really would be big of me, wouldn't it?"

Rose picked her handbag up off the floor and swatted Dan with it. "You smart alec."

"I suppose you turned Monica down without even consulting me." Dan turned toward Rose with a feigned expression of disappointment on his face. "It seems like I should have had a say in the matter."

Rose laughed. "Be serious, Dan. Do you remember the movie *Fatal Attraction*? Monica could be a danger to you . . . and me, too."

"She does seem to have a screw loose, but don't let it worry you. *We* don't even know where we'll be from one day to the next, so she won't either."

"But she certainly can afford a private detective." Rose turned around to study the car behind them. "From now on, I'm going to be very watchful for anyone who may be following us."

• • •

It was mid afternoon when they reached Savannah, Georgia. "What are we going to do about eating?" asked Rose. "We only have thirteen dollars cash to our name."

"I know," answered Dan, "and we need to save every penny. Josh was fixing bratwurst sandwiches and sauerkraut for lunch, and he gave me some to take with us. I put it in our little fridge."

Rose stared out the window at the beautiful old city. "What I read in a travel magazine a while back is certainly correct. Savannah has got to be one of the loveliest cities in the U.S. Just look at those beautiful old buildings."

"It's a pretty place, all right. Next time we pass one of those little parks, we'll pull in there and have our bratwurst."

They found another of the many city parks and ate their lunch at a picnic table under a large tree draped with Spanish moss. Rose gazed around at the old Southern mansions lining the park. "This city is so delightful. That article I read said there's a walk downtown some place along the Savannah River that passes a lot of historical old warehouses. I think it's called Factory Walk . . . or something like that. Do you suppose we could spare the time to take a little walk?"

Dan gathered the wrappings off the table, stuffed them into the sack, and then wadded it up. He made a perfect toss into the trash can some twenty feet away. "Sure, Hon, we can spare a few minutes. Lord knows I can use the exercise. Josh feeds too good."

As they were getting into their van, a patrol car drove slowly by. Dan waved at the officer to stop. Walking over to him, Dan said, "Excuse me, can you tell us where we can find a place called Factory Walk?"

"You mean Factor's Walk. You're close." The officer reached down to get something off the seat and opened a brochure. "This has a little map of the downtown area." He opened the brochure and pointed. "See, you're here, and here's Factor's Walk along the river."

"Thanks," said Dan. "Did you mean for me to keep this?"

"Sure. I get a lot of people asking directions, so I just carry those brochures around with me. It saves a lot of time for all of us."

They had to drive around a while before finding a parking place. Dan put a quarter in the meter. "That will give us half an hour."

"That's not nearly enough time," protested Rose. "Can't we spare a whole hour?"

Dan fished around in his pocket for another quarter. "It's the money I'm thinking about. I never thought I'd begrudge money spent on a parking meter."

They walked briskly along the sparkling river until they came to an information pedestal and stopped to read it. "So that's why the funny name," said Dan. "This area was big in the selling and shipping of cotton, and the cotton dealers were called Factors."

They were enjoying the walk and sights so much that they lost track of time. Dan finally looked at his watch. "Oh, my God. We've been gone over an hour.. We should have started back five minutes ago. We literally can *not* afford to get a parking ticket. Come on, Rose, we're going to have to speed walk to get there in time."

They arrived back at the van, huffing and puffing. The time on the meter had expired. As Dan was pulling out of the parking place, Rose looked back to see a meter maid rounding the corner. "That was too close for comfort. But that walk felt wonderful. Do you know what else would feel wonderful?"

"Yes, I do. But we'll have to wait till I find a more private parking spot."

"Dan! What I was thinking about is a barefoot walk on a sandy beach. I haven't seen the ocean since I was a kid, and we're so close."

"Rose, we've already lost so much time."

"Puleeeeese? Look, that sign says it's just a few miles to Tybee Island."

• • •

They spent the rest of the afternoon enjoying the beach and watching the boats along the Savannah River Delta. It was dusk by the time they were back on Interstate 95. To conserve gas, Dan kept his speed down to sixty. "We had a good lunch," he said, "and it was a really late lunch. So do you think we could forgo dinner?"

"Certainly. There are still some snacks in the back if we do get hungry."

"Good. I figure we're about two hours from the Florida state line. We'll start looking for a place to stay the night as soon as we cross over."

Rose dozed off, and when she awoke, it was dark. She yawned and stretched.

"Have a nice nap?"

"Yes. Do you want me to drive for a while?"

"Sure. There ought to be a rest stop coming up pretty soon."

Suddenly, headlights bounced up and down in the median and then headed straight for them. Dan slammed on the brakes and tried to avoid the oncoming vehicle. Rose screamed.

Chapter Twenty-One

The flash of oncoming headlights was blinding. With its brakes squealing, the van skidded sideways, missing a head-on collision by mere feet. The out-of-control car scraped the van's left rear fender and then careened over a guardrail. Dan quickly pulled the van off the highway and yelled, "Rose, call 911. Tell them we're southbound on highway 17 coming into Brunswick."

Rose placed her hands over her thumping heart, as if to keep it within her chest. "Do you think anyone's hurt?"

Dan jumped out of the van. "We'll know in a minute."

Rose frantically searched for the phone among the broken dishes, bedding, and much of the van's contents scattered about on the floor. She noticed a flashlight and grabbed it up. Finally the phone was in her shaking hands. She dialed.

A woman's voice answered, "911."

Rose quickly described what had happened.

"Are there injuries?"

"My husband went to check."

"A patrol car is on the way, but we'll need to confirm injuries before an ambulance is dispatched."

Rose opened the van door and stepped out. "Hold on. I'm going to check right now."

The runaway car was upright, its headlights defining a furrowed field. The two front doors were open, and the interior lights silhouetted Dan, leaning into the driver's door. As she made her way through the tall grass on the steep embankment, Rose turned the flashlight on the car. She noticed that its sides were deeply dented and scratched, and the cargo basket attached to the car's roof was missing its lid. *Wow, it rolled. I just hope the occupants were wearing their seat belts.*

"Dan, I have 911 on the phone. The dispatcher needs to know if there are any injuries."

When Dan turned to take the phone from her, Rose saw that the driver, a slender and balding older man, was the car's only occupant. His head was lying against the headrest, his face covered in blood.

Dan stepped back from the car. "Dr. Daniel Good here. Yes, ma'am, the sole occupant is going to need an ambulance. He has a bad gash on his forehead, but any life-threatening injuries are not apparent. Yes, I'm a doctor. I'm a veterinarian. I beg your pardon? Well, he's moaning, but he's unresponsive. Yes, of course. We'll stay with him until help arrives. Thanks."

Dan slipped the phone into his pocket. "Stay with him, Rose. I'm going to move the van farther off the shoulder and turn on the flashers. We don't want to cause another accident, and the emergency responders will be better able to find us."

Rose handed him the flashlight. "Take this."

Almost as soon as Dan left, the man moaned and raised a hand toward his head. Rose took his hand in hers. "You have a bad cut. You mustn't touch it."

The man's eyes blinked open, and he rolled his head in her direction. "Who are you?"

"My name is Rose. What's your name?"

The man appeared puzzled, and then answered, "Arrrr . . . Arrr . . . Arr . . . nold."

"You've been in an accident, Arnold." Rose patted the hand she held. "But things are going to be just fine. Help is on the way."

Arnold's head rolled back and his eyes closed. A few seconds later, Rose felt his hand tense. His eyes opened wide, and he cried, "Mother! Is Mother all right?"

"Your mother? Was your mother with you?"

Pleading eyes looked up at Rose. "Yes . . . please . . . see if she's . . . all . . . right."

"We will, Arnold. Just close your eyes and relax."

Rose heard Dan trudging back through the grass. She gently laid Arnold's hand on his chest, and then stepped away from the car to meet Dan. She spoke to him in lowered tones. "Dan! His mother was with him in the car. There's an injured, or maybe even dead, old woman out here somewhere."

"Oh, my God," said Dan. "*He's* got to be seventy or older. I'll start looking for her, but it's doubtful anyone his mother's age would survive being thrown from a car." Dan began scanning the area with the flashlight beam. "Stay with him, Rose. See if you can find out her name."

Rose again took Arnold's hand. It was limp. "Arnold?" No response. "Arnold?" His eyes fluttered open. "Arnold, it's me, Rose. Can you tell me your mother's name?

"Mother . . . is she all right?"

"Her name, Arnold. What's your mother's name?"

Rose leaned in closer in order to hear him above the wail of approaching sirens.

His voiced faded as he murmered, "A . . . bi . . . gail," and his eyes closed once again.

Rose turned and saw Dan trudging through dense brush, sweeping it with the flashlight beam as he went. She called out, "Dan! Her name is Abigail."

As lights from the approaching patrol car swept the area, Rose caught a glimpse of what appeared to be a head of white hair, near the top of a short tree. "Dan! Back this way! Check out that tree to your right."

Two paramedics, a man and a woman, arrived at the car, carrying medical equipment on a stretcher. "How's he doing?" the heavy-set woman asked.

"He's in and out. But you need to see to his mother. She was thrown out of the car and I think she's in that tree over there where my husband's aiming his flashlight."

They set the stretcher down, and the young man, accompanied by a highway patrolman who had just approached, raced toward Dan.

"His name is Arnold," said Rose as she stepped out of the woman's way. The paramedic leaned into the car to check Arnold's breathing and heart rate. "ARNOLD? CAN YOU HEAR ME, ARNOLD?"

Arnold opened his eyes. "Why are you yelling? You make my ears hurt."

"I'm just checking you over. I wanted to see if you were awake. That's a nasty cut on your head. We'll get that tended to." She pulled back his eyelids and shined a light into his eyes.

"Leave me alone," Arnold sputtered.

The large woman backed out of the car to speak to Rose. "He doesn't look too bad. They may need me over there. Can you stay with him while I check?"

"Of course," Rose answered. She took Arnold's hand. He gave her hand a gentle squeeze.

Rose watched the lights playing in the tree, and was able to make out the form of a woman among the branches, and see a male figure climbing up to her. *Oh, I hope she's still alive. I wish I could make out what they're saying.*

It wasn't long before the two paramedics, the patrolman and Dan, came walking back to the car. *They've all left her. That doesn't look good.*

"Please step back, ma'am," said the officer. "The paramedics need to get him loaded up."

When Rose started to take her hand from Arnold's, he held tight. "Don't go, Rose. Please don't leave me."

"They need to take you to the hospital now, Arnold. You'll have to turn me loose."

As they were loading him on the stretcher, Arnold cried out, "Mother! Did you find my mother?"

"We found her," answered the female paramedic.

Rose gave Dan a questioning look. He shook his head negatively.

Oh, poor Arnold, thought Rose. *How sad.*

"Take good care of my mother," said Arnold as the paramedics carried him away.

"We'll need to get a statement from you two," said the officer. "Would you please come join me in the patrol car?"

Rose and Dan climbed into the backseat of the car and listened while the officer called for a unit to come extricate the body from the tree. He had just finished the call when the female paramedic leaned in his window. "We're having a time with Arnold back there, and we can't give him a sedative until he gets checked out." She looked back at Rose. "Are you the Rose he keeps asking for, or is that his mother's name?"

"I'm Rose. Her name is Abigail. Why?"

"Would you be so kind as to accompany him to the hospital? He's going to pop a blood vessel if he keeps up like he is, and you may be able to calm him down."

"Well, I suppose so, if I can be of help."

"Tell you what," said the officer, "You follow them on into town, Dr. Good, and I'll catch up with you at the hospital as soon as things are taken care of here."

The woman opened the back door of the ambulance. Arnold was moaning and thrashing around on the stretcher while the male paramedic was trying to restrain him.

"It's Rose, Arnold. I'm here," said Rose as she climbed in and sat on the side bench next to him. She took his hand, and he immediately relaxed.

"Would you look at that," said the paramedic. "Janie, let's see if we can get that IV back in him now."

With its siren wailing, the ambulance sped off into the night. Janie, the female paramedic, sat next to Rose, occasionally checking Arnold's vital signs. He seemed unconscious, but each time she touched him, he jerked away. Janie whispered to Rose, "He just doesn't like me. Head patients can be contrary."

"Can you tell me about his mother?" whispered Rose.

Janie shook her head. "We have to be careful what we say around head patients. They may seem out of it, but stuff just seems to soak in."

At the hospital, Rose walked beside the gurney on the way to the emergency room, holding onto Arnold's hand. She held it until he was sedated, and then tiptoed out of the room. Dan was waiting for her just outside the door. He put his arm around her shoulder and led her down the hall to a small waiting room. They helped themselves to coffee from an urn there, and then took a seat to wait for the officer.

"It's so sad about Arnold's mother," said Rose. "I wouldn't want to be the one to break the news to him."

"About her being dead?" asked Dan. "He already knows."

"Already knows? How could he? I was with him the whole time."

Dan set his styrofoam cup down on the table next to him. "Turns out his mommy is a mummy."

"What on earth do you mean?"

"That old lady was stiff as a board and as shriveled as a prune. One of her legs had broken off and was lying under the tree. The only way we could tell her limb from the other dead limbs lying about was that hers was wearing a shoe. There's no telling how long she's been dead. She was totally mummified."

"Dear God!" said Rose. "How weird is that? I thought it was odd that when he knew she'd been found, he didn't ask how she was."

"He didn't ask because he already knew," said Dan.

"He seems so childish for a man his age," said Rose. "It seems unlikely that he might have killed her."

"Its hard to tell about people. I'd like to stick around to see what the outcome is, but we're going to have to break away from here as soon as we can and get back to our own business."

Rose looked at the clock on the wall. "It's nearly midnight. I hope that policeman shows up soon. I'm pooped. Speaking of which, where are we going to spend the night?"

"What could be safer than a hospital parking lot?" said Dan. "I checked out a nice, quiet corner out there. And we can have breakfast here in the morning. Hospital cafeterias are usually pretty inexpensive."

Rose laid her head on Dan's shoulder and closed her eyes. They soon both nodded off. The officer later awakened them. "Sorry to keep you folks up so late. We're short-staffed this week, and I had to stay with the vehicle until it got towed away and impounded."

The officer asked questions and took notes while Dan and Rose recounted the accident. When they finished, he said, "Your account is pretty much what the evidence showed. The only skid marks were yours, which is indicative of his falling asleep behind the wheel. I am puzzled about something though. You said the other car barely grazed your left rear fender. I checked your van over out there in the parking lot, and the extent of damage to it doesn't match what you're telling me. Do you want to explain that?"

Dan stood up. "I'd be glad to. There's an interesting story behind each and every dent and scratch on that otherwise fine vehicle. So that I don't forget anything, let's go out to the parking lot and we'll have show and tell."

Rose went with them, and after Dan had pointed out and explained all the van's damage, she asked the officer what she'd been dying to ask, "What has been done with the body?"

"It's right here in the hospital morgue awaiting autopsy."

"When will you know how she died?" asked Rose.

"That depends. As you see, our hospital is pretty small . . . just the basics. They will probably have to send tissue samples to a forensic lab, and that can take time. But I've pretty well figured out why she's in such a mummified state."

"How's that?" asked Dan.

"He'd been carrying her body in a cargo basket on his car's roof. The basket's top was torn off when the car rolled, and the body was catapulted out of it and into the tree. The bottom portion was still attached to the car, and it was lined with satin quilting, just like a coffin. A patch of her scalp was missing on the back of her head, and I found it, with a patch of her white hair, stuck to the satin material where her head had lain."

"I see," said Dan. "The temperatures inside that thing must have gotten pretty damned hot. But wouldn't it have just cooked her?"

"Maybe not," said the officer. "If the weather was cold when he first put her in there, the body may have just dried out slowly. It's something for the forensic guys to figure out."

Rose felt the coffee coming back up in her throat. "Dan, I don't feel well. I'm going to bed. "Goodnight, officer."

As Rose was unlocking the van's door, she heard the officer say, "She's going to bed? Are you two planning on staying overnight here in the parking lot?"

"Why, yes, is that all right?"

"Not normally, but it *is* pretty late. I guess in this case, we can make an exception. I'll let the security guard know so he won't roust you. Thanks for everything. Maybe I'll see you in the morning. Say, you might want to have breakfast in the hospital cafeteria. Their chow isn't too bad."

"Thanks for the tip. We just might do that. Goodnight, officer."

Dan undressed in the dark and then crawled in beside Rose. "Are you still awake?"

"How could I not be? I can't get the vision of that cargo basket and its contents out of my mind. It's sickening."

"Well, it's a good thing then that you didn't get an eyeful of Mommy. Not a pretty sight." Dan yawned. "You know what's funny? I've always thought those cargo baskets looked a little like streamlined caskets."

"Knock it off, Dan. I'm trying to quit thinking about it."

Within a few minutes, Dan was snoring softly, while Rose was tossing and turning and still thinking about it.

Chapter Twenty-Two

Rose awoke to the sound of car doors slamming in the hospital parking lot. She rolled over and looked at the dashboard clock. *Eight thirty!* Dan had left a note on the floor. "I'm shaving in the men's room. Meet me in the same waiting room we were in last night."

Rose brushed her hair and pulled it back into a ponytail. She dressed and with her small cosmetics bag headed for the hospital ladies' room.

She later found Dan in the small waiting room, sipping coffee from a Styrofoam cup and reading a magazine. "I didn't realize you read McCalls," she said.

"Hey, there's some pretty steamy stuff in here. I think you women aren't just liberated; you've returned to the wild."

"Well, this wild girl is hungry. Do you know the way to the cafeteria?"

Dan threw the magazine aside. "Not only do I know the way, I've checked everything out. Come with me."

"Dan, why do you have that stethoscope around your neck?"

"You didn't even hear me when I came back to the van after it, did you?" He asked.

"No, why did you?"

"I noticed that doctors get a discount."

"Dan, you're shameless!" said Rose as they entered the cafeteria.

When they brought their food trays the to the check-out, the cashier looked at Dan and said, "Good morning, Doctor. I haven't seen you here before. Are you new at the hospital?"

"No . . . I'm just here to give a second opinion."

"In case you didn't know, doctors get a twenty percent discount. Is the lady with you your assistant?"

"Uh . . . yes, she is."

"Then she gets a discount too. That all comes to $7.20 for the both of you."

Dan paid the woman and then sheepishly looked around the room while he followed Rose to an empty table. "This is good timing," he said as he set down his tray. "There are very few people in here right now, and none of them look like doctors. I'd hate for one to come over and ask who the hell I was."

"You should be ashamed for fibbing like that," said Rose as she seated herself. "Telling her I'm your assistant!"

Before he sat down, Dan pulled the stethoscope from around his neck and crammed it into his pocket. "You assisted me in picking out this table, didn't you?"

Halfway through breakfast, Dan said, "You're awfully quiet this morning. Are you still thinking about last night?"

"That too."

"Well, what else?"

"You, Dan. I've never known you to tell such bald-faced lies. I just can't believe you passed yourself off as a visiting doctor by saying you were here for a second opinion."

Dan studied his coffee cup for a moment and then asked, "How did you like the breakfast burrito?"

"I thought the eggs were a little on the rubbery side," answered Rose.

Dan set his cup down hard. "And I thought it could have used a lot more spice. There you have it, Rose, a damned second opinion."

"Well, you don't have to be so snippy. Can't you take a little chiding?"

"I don't like lying any more than you like hearing it, Rose, but what I saved will hopefully buy us a gallon of gas that will take us another sixteen miles or so closer to our goal. Do you realize how little cash we have left? Desperate times call for desperate measures."

"How much cash *do* we have left?"

"Exactly six dollars and twelve cents. We're going to have to charge the gas."

"Thank goodness we can charge it."

"Yeah, but the trouble is we had over twelve-thousand dollars worth of charges on our card when Larry cleaned us out. We've never paid interest on it because I always paid the balance in full by the payment-due date. But right now, we can only afford to make the minimum payments, which won't even cover the interest we're going to owe every month. Even if we never charged another thing, at this rate, we'll just get deeper and deeper in debt."

"Oh, Dan, what are we going to do if we never get our money back?"

"Don't worry, Rose. I'm still physically fit. I can always find work, and hopefully in my field."

"I don't really have a field, but I'm sure I could find some way to make a little money, too. But it's going to be hard for people our age to get hired."

Dan downed the last of his coffee. "Remember, this country has laws against discrimination, and that includes age discrimination."

"But age can't help but be a factor when an employer has several job applicants to choose from," countered Rose.

"Hey," said Dan, "If Larry can dye his hair, so can I."

As they were finishing their breakfast, a nice-looking, middle-aged man in gray slacks and a dark blue blazer approached their table. "Excuse me. Are you, by any chance, Dr. and Rosemary Good?"

"Why, yes, we are," said Dan.

"I'm Detective Pete Larson. I'm here on the Arnold Watson case. Patrolman Ackerly told me you might be here. I don't want to interrupt your breakfast, but do you mind if I join you?"

"Sure, we were just finishing," said Dan. "Pull up a chair."

"How *is* Arnold this morning?" asked Rose. "Do you know?"

"I stopped by his room just now. The nurses were busy with him, so I didn't go in, but I did talk to the doctor. He's doing well and could be released from the hospital in a day or two."

"That's good to hear," said Rose. "I've been worried about him."

"I've read Patrolman Ackerly's report on the accident, Mrs. Good. He mentioned that you had spent time with Mr. Watson, and that you actually had some conversation with him."

"I don't know that I would call it conversation," said Rose. "It was just a few words."

"I would like for you to tell me, Mrs. Good, exactly what he said regarding the mummified body he had in his possession."

This isn't the greatest breakfast conversation. It's a good thing I'm finished. Now if I can just keep it down.

"The body was evidently his mother's," said Rose. "There was no one else in the car with him, and he kept asking about his mother, so that *must* have been her. I asked him what his mother's name was, and he said it was Abigail. He never mentioned the fact that she was dead, but he did seem very concerned about her. He asked about her several times. Oh, and he said when they were taking him to the ambulance, 'Take good care of my mother.'"

"You seem to have established a good rapport with him," said the detective. "I understand you came to the hospital in the ambulance with him, and at his request."

"Yes. He reminded me of my children whenever they were hurt . . . like he needed his mommy to be with him. He seemed rather immature for a man his age."

"Have you found out anything about the guy?" asked Dan.

"Some. We ran a check on him . . . nothing criminal. He's from a little town in Nebraska. According to his charge card account, he'd been doing a lot of traveling. A business card in his billfold identified him as a funeral director. It's still too early out there in Nebraska to be able to talk to anyone at the mortuary named on the card."

"Do you think he might have killed her?" asked Rose.

"I hope to find that out when I interview him," answered the detective. "The doctor said he seemed to be in full control of his faculties this morning, but he's being a little cantankerous with the nurses."

Dan shoved his chair back from the table. "I think my wife has given you about all the information *she* has to offer. If you'll excuse us, we need to get on down the road. Are you ready to go, Rose?"

"Dan, would you mind if we just stop by Arnold's room for a minute to say goodbye?"

"Why on earth would you want to do that, Rose? You barely know him."

"I don't know. I just feel like we should. He's such a pathetic little man, and he seems so all alone. A little kindness might help him."

"Actually, your talking to him might help *me,*" said the detective. "Since you've established a good rapport with him, he might tell you things he wouldn't tell me."

Dan stood up. "You two go on, then. I've got to get the van straightened around before we can take off anyway." Dan extended his hand. "Glad to meet you, Detective Larson. Good luck with the case."

"Thank you, Dr. Good. I really think Mrs. Good can be of service. I promise I won't keep her long."

After leaving the cafeteria, they stopped at the nurse's station and were told that Arnold might be napping, but it was all right to wake him up to question him.

A uniformed policeman was sitting in the hallway outside Arnold's room. "Is Arnold a prisoner?" asked Rose.

"He is until he's cleared of all suspicion of wrongdoing," the detective answered.

The detective peeked into the room. "Mrs. Good, I think it's best if you go on in alone. His bed is by the window, and a curtain is pulled partially across the room. After you get him engaged in a conversation, I'll slip in behind the curtain to hear what he might have to say. See if you can get him to tell you how his mother died."

Rose quietly walked into the room and stood beside the curtain. Arnold's closed eyes were blackened, and his head and left hand were bandaged. "Arnold?" She whispered.

His eyes fluttered open. "Not again! Can't a fellow . . . oh, it's you . . . Rose. I remember you. You're the sweet lady that helped me last night."

"It's good to see you again, Arnold. How are you this morning?"

"Oh, my head hurts a little. They said I have eighteen stitches. I guess I have a slight concussion, too."

"I see your hand's bandaged."

He lifted his hand to look at it. "Oh, yeah, I've got a couple of broken fingers, too. Luckily, I'm right-handed."

"Last night you were asking about your mother, Arnold."

Arnold dropped his eyes. "They say she's downstairs in the morgue."

"That's what I understand," said Rose. "I'm so sorry. How did she die?"

He looked up at Rose. "You knew she was already dead? Before the accident?"

"Yes. My husband was one of the ones who found her."

"You're married?"

"Yes."

"I might have known . . . a pretty woman like you."

"*When* did your mother die, Arnold?"

"A year and a half ago. She had a stroke. She was just fine when I left her one morning, and dead when I came home after work that evening."

"That must have been quite a shock, finding her like that."

"Well, she *was* getting up in years. I worked in the funeral business, so I'm used to dead bodies. But it's a whole lot different when it's your own mother."

Rose laid her hand on his shoulder. "I can imagine. Tell me, Arnold, why were you carrying her body around in the cargo basket on top of your car?"

"It was a promise I made. Mother loved to travel. We used to take a little car trip every vacation, but never had time to go very far or see very much. She wanted to see the whole country, and be able to say she'd been in every state. I promised her when I retired, we'd do just that. She died just three months short of my retirement, but I'm keeping my promise."

"So you took her anyway? Is that legal?"

"Probably not. That's why I didn't ask."

"How did you manage to get off with her body?"

"I told you I worked in the funeral business. Mother was a small woman, and it was easy to sneak her out the night before the funeral. It was a closed-casket service, so nobody knew she wasn't in the casket we buried. I wrapped up some jars of mother's home-canned pickles and put them in the casket to give it some weight."

"Pickles?"

"Yes. I never had the heart to tell her, but they weren't very good."

Rose heard a snort from behind the curtain. Arnold heard it too, and turned his head.

Thinking quickly, Rose put her hand to her mouth. "Well, excuse me. I must be allergic to something."

She continued, "So, after she'd been in every state, what did you plan to do with her?"

"I've been thinking on that. I'm not sure. We've got four more states to go, Alaska and Hawaii among them. Those two are going to be a problem."

Acting as if he had just arrived in the room, the detective cleared his throat and stepped from behind the curtain. He held his badge for Arnold to see. "Good morning, Mr. Watson, I'm Detective Larson."

"You're a police detective?" said Arnold. "Am I in trouble?"

"Possibly. We're checking into what, if any, laws you might have broken in the transporting of the body. Tell me, is there a death certificate?"

"Certainly. The original is in Lincoln, and I have a copy."

"With you?"

"Yes. It's in a plastic envelope, tucked into a pocket of the lining of the cargo casket."

"We'll check that out," said the detective. "I'll be back later to talk with you." He touched Rose's arm, and then motioned with his eyes for her to meet him in the hall.

"I have to leave now, too," said Rose. "I do hope you have a speedy recovery."

"Will you be back?"

"I'm afraid not. My husband and I have urgent business in Miami."

Sadness fell over Arnold's face. "Well . . . goodbye then."

Rose waved as she left the room. "Goodbye, and good luck, Arnold."

Detective Larson was waiting in the hallway. "I can't thank you enough, Mrs. Good. That was the easiest interrogation I've never had to do."

"You're very welcome. Will he be released from custody now?"

"There'll be an inquest, but if his story can be corroborated, he should be a free man very shortly. May I see you out?"

"Thank you," said Rose. "That won't be necessary."

She shook hands with the detective and then found her way to the parking lot. Rose got into the van and quietly closed her door. Dan was in the driver's seat in the van, engaged in a conversation on the cell phone.

"Barring any more delays, we should be in Miami by late afternoon," said Dan. "Yes, of course, we'll be sure and keep you posted. We really appreciate all you've done, Judge Weaver. Rose and I can't thank you enough."

Chapter Twenty-Three

Dan slapped the cell phone closed. "That was Judge Weaver. He sure didn't waste any time contacting the Miami police. He faxed them all the information we gave him, and they already have an APB out on Larry and Mitzi."

"Miami is an awfully big place," said Rose. "It seems it would be like looking for a needle in a haystack to try and find them. And we don't even know for sure that's where they're heading."

Dan turned on the ignition. "Well, we have to use whatever leads we have, and they all point to Miami. We sure don't have anything to lose by trying. Besides, we've always wanted to see Miami."

• • •

A couple of hours later, they were just south of Jacksonville, Florida, and running low on gas. "We'd better pull off at the next exit and fill 'er up," said Dan. "They *would* have to raise the gasoline prices just when we need every dime we have."

There were three filling stations near the exit, and Dan pulled into the one offering the cheapest gas. He reluctantly paid at the pump with his credit card, and then pulled over to the air pump. "Can you believe this? They want a dollar for air. It's just *air* for Pete's sake! Are we having a shortage on *air*, along with the gasoline? Rose, dig around in the glove compartment and get the tire guage."

"What does it look like?"

"It looks like a damned tire gauge!"

"Well, *excuse me!* It's not my fault we're almost out of cash. Don't be taking your mad out on me. I've never put air in tires before. How am I supposed to know what a tire gauge looks like?"

"I'm sorry, hon," said Dan. He reached across Rose, popped open the glove compartment, and dug around inside. He pulled out a small, taped-up package. "Looks like surgical tape. What the hell *is* this?"

"Oh, for goodness sake," said Rose. "Clyde gave that to me when we were leaving the Ark and told me not to open it until we were in Georgia. I forgot all about it."

Dan handed the package to Rose and then pulled the tire gauge from the glove compartment. He held it up to Rose. "See this? In case you ever have to check a tire yourself, this is a tire gauge."

"Great," said Rose. "Does it come with instructions?"

Dan opened the van door. "Come on out here, and I'll show you how it's done."

"Some other time. I'm dying to see what's in this package."

While Dan checked the tires, Rose peeled the tape from the tightly wrapped package, which consisted of a heavy paper, folded over and over. She unwrapped the paper, and a number of bills dropped into her lap. *Oh, Clyde! You shouldn't have done this.* Rose counted the bills. There were seven five-dollar bills and forty-seven ones. *Eighty-two dollars! That's all the money he had.* Rose pressed the bills to her breast.

Dan opened the door of the van and climbed in. "Rose, what's wrong? Why are you crying?"

Rose handed Dan the crinkled paper that had held the money. He looked at it quizzically, and then began to read out loud. "Dear Dr. Good and Mrs. Good, You have been such good folks to me and my kin. I don't know what we all would have done if you hadn't showed up when you did. I won't need this money any more since I will be working for my room and eats. So I want you to have it. You need it worse than me. I did leave out three dollars just in case. I hope you catch those dirty crooks and get your money back real soon. Please write me sometime or call to let me know you are all right." Dan hesitated a moment, and then cleared his throat before continuing. "I love you like you was my own kin. Yours truly, Clyde."

Dan's voice cracked as he asked, "How much money did he give us?"

Rose held the bills out to Dan. "Eighty-two dollars . . . all he had in the world, minus three dollars. He worked months for this money. We've got to send it back to him."

"Send it back? It's a Godsend, Rose. Clyde's right. He won't need it. Monica will take care of all his needs. And he knows that we sure as hell can use it. I didn't want to have to tell you, but the credit card is almost maxed out."

"Dear God, said Rose. "But it still doesn't seem right, taking money from a baby."

Dan turned on the ignition. "Baby? Why, just a few days ago, you were bragging about how mature he is for a boy his age. And he just proved you right. We're going to accept it graciously, Rose, and with any luck, we can pay him back some day . . . with interest."

• • •

As they neared Daytona Beach, they left the interstate to take Highway One, which followed the Intracoastal Waterway. They passed signs showing the way west to Orlando and Disney World, and east to the John F. Kennedy Space Center and Cape Canaveral. "Gee, I hope I get to visit those places before I die," said Dan.

"Can't we spare just a few hours?" asked Rose. "It will probably be too late to do anything today by the time we get to Miami anyway."

"We could spend a couple of weeks seeing all there is to see in those places," answered Dan. "Even if we had the time, we don't have the money. They're not free."

"We'll just have to come back sometime, then. When we get our money back."

"Well, right now, I'm thinking more about our immediate future . . . like our next meal," said Dan. "I'm hungry."

"Me too. Let's stop at the next store we see and pick up some groceries."

• • •

They stopped in the town of Palm Shores, and then drove across a bridge spanning the Intracoastal Waterway. Dan pulled the van into a small beachside parking lot where Rose made sandwiches and packed a lunch to take out to a picnic table on the beach.

As they ate, Rose watched a small redheaded girl and her slightly older brother playing in the sand nearby. "Aren't they adorable? Do you think we'll ever have grandchildren?"

A lone seagull was circling overhead, eyeing Dan. He tossed it a breadcrumb, and it swooped down to catch it in midair. "I suppose," said Dan. "Well, sure, why wouldn't we?"

"I worry about Chess. Remember, he had the mumps when he was thirteen. I read somewhere that having mumps in puberty sometimes causes sterility. And neither one of the boys has a serious girlfriend. At the age they both are, you'd think they'd be settling down."

Dan tossed another breadcrumb, and three gulls swooped after it. "Things are a lot different with the young people nowadays. Marriage doesn't seem to be a priority."

Rose laid out two napkins, and then set a small pastry on each for their dessert. "That doesn't seem to keep them from having children, though. I want grandchildren, but I want bona fide, legal daughters-in-law first."

Dan leaned down to pick up a paper that had blown off the table, "Well, my dear, I'm afraid that's all out of our hands." Suddenly, a half a dozen gulls were overhead, fighting over the pastry one had snatched off the table. "Did you see that? That damned bird got my dessert!"

"Well, what did you expect? You shouldn't have been feeding them." Rose quickly gathered up their trash. "We're being bombarded by those darned birds. Let's get out of here!"

• • •

Since it was Friday evening, most of the traffic was leaving the downtown area as they approached Miami proper. Dan pulled a note from his shirt pocket and handed it to Rose. "Here's the address of the Miami Police Department. Read it to me."

"400 Northwest 2nd Avenue. But why are we looking for it now? It's after five. Won't it be closed?"

Dan slowed down to look at the street signs they were passing. "We're in luck. They have numbered streets going in both directions. That should make it easy. To answer your question, no, the police department won't be closed, but the detective we're supposed to see might be gone for the day. Let's hope he's still on duty."

They found a parking place just a block from the police station, and were soon standing before a pleasant dark-haired young woman in uniform, seated at the front desk. "You're here to see Detective Cortez? He's supposed to be off duty at five o'clock, but I think he's still back there. Is he expecting you?"

"Yes, but he didn't know when we'd be here. We're the Goods and friends of Judge Weaver in South Carolina."

The woman picked up the receiver. "Ed, the Goods are here from South Carolina. They said they're friends of a Judge Weaver and that you're expecting them . . . de nada." She looked at Dan. "He'll see you. He'll be right out."

A smiling, forty-something man with a five-o'clock shadow, wearing faded jeans and a T-shirt, walked toward them down the hall. "Hello, Dr. and Mrs. Good. I see you made it."

Dan extended his hand. "Thank you for seeing us, detective. I understand you're staying late for us."

"No problem." The detective extended his hand to Rose. While shaking her hand, he must have noticed her studying his clothes. He flashed a smile full of beautiful, gleaming-white teeth. "Please forgive my attire. One of the cases I'm currently working on goes better if I don't wear a suit and tie." He spun around to head back down the hall. "I have some very good news for you. Come on back to my office."

Rose and Dan seated themselves in front of the detective's desk. "You have good news for us?" Dan excitedly asked.

"We caught your man not more than two hours ago."

"You got Larry? And what about Mitzy? Do you know where our money is?"

"We grilled him for over an hour, but he won't tell us anything. Like they all do, he claims we got the wrong man. Maybe he'll change his tune when he sees you two face-to-face."

"Where is he?" asked Dan. "When can we see him?"

The detective looked at his watch. "In about eight minutes. Regulations say we have to give them a full half an hour for their meals. We're lucky we don't have to burp them, too. If you'll excuse me, I'll go tell the guard to take Mr. Near to the interrogation room as soon as he's finished eating."

When the detective returned, Rose asked, "How did you catch him?"

"One of our officers pulled him over for running a red light just a few miles from here. The new Mercedes, the license tag, and his description all matched." The detective pulled a large, manila envelope from a drawer and tossed it onto the desk. "It's a good thing we caught him when we did. From what we found in the glove compartment, looks like he was planning on leaving town on a cruise ship." The detective dumped the envelope's contents on the desk. "Here's the car's registration, registered to a Sherman Findley, the same name the tags are in. But you say his name is Larry?"

"Yes, Larry Near. Sherman Findley must be his new name."

"We found several I.D.s here in his billfold, but not that one. He'd have to have a passport if he was leaving on a cruise, but fake ones are easy enough to come by, if you know someone and have the money."

Dan picked up a cruise ship brochure. "Oh, he has the money, all right." Dan opened the brochure. "The Ocean Lady. Holds 1,918 passengers and a crew of 288. That's a damned floating hotel." He flipped the page. "Fourteen islands in twenty-one days." He turned another page. "Departs from Miami on May 5th, May 26th, June 9th, June . . . hey! June 9th is circled. What's today?"

Detective Cortez again looked at his watch. "June 7th. Like I said, it's a good thing we caught him when we did. He should be in the interrogation room by now. He's even had time to brush his teeth."

Rose thought her heart would pound out of her chest as they walked down the hall to the room. *This is going to be terrible. What can he possibly say to us to defend himself for almost wrecking our lives? I feel like scratching his thieving eyes out.*

They entered a small room where a uniformed guard stood over a man seated with his elbows on the table and head down, his fingers dug into his dark hair.

Cortez nodded to the guard. "Thanks, Ed. Sherman Findley I presume?"

"The same."

"Sherman?" said Cortez, "The Goods are here to see you."

That dirty bastard. He doesn't have the guts to look us in the eye, thought Rose.

Dan leaned over the table. "Hey, Larry! Aren't you going to say hello to your old friends? Your old bosom buddies? You cowardly son of a bitch."

He looked up at Dan and said, "Tell them they got the wrong man."

Dan's hands dropped to his side, and he dejectedly looked over at the detective. "You've got the wrong man."

Cortez appeared both disappointed and embarrassed. "Well, I'll be damned. He sure fit the description, right down to the dyed hair."

"I can see how you'd think it was him," said Dan. "I thought so too, until I saw his face."

"So who *are* you?" Cortez growled.

"Like I've been tellin' ya. Floyd Snow."

"So how did you get the car?"

"Like I been tellin' ya. I wasn't stealin' it. I borrowed it from the Hotel Del Mar parking lot. I was gonna return it. Honest."

• • •

As they walked back down the hall, Dan asked, "What now? If Larry and Mitzi are taking that cruise ship, we've got to act fast."

"I know. The best thing we can hope for is that your friend reports his car stolen. In the meantime, first thing in the morning, I'll check on some of the notes and phone numbers that were scribbled on papers we found in the glove compartment."

"We really appreciate all your efforts, detective." Dan shook his hand again. "What time would be good for us to be here in the morning?"

"I doubt if I'll be able to have any information much before ten o'clock. Why don't you check with me about then?"

• • •

With the van still parked on the street, Rose fixed a dinner of red beans and rice, with a small salad. As they were eating, she asked, "Where are we going to spend the night?"

"What's wrong with right here?"

"Right here? Is that legal?"

"I didn't see any No Camping signs out there. And parking's free after 6:00 p.m. and on the weekends. It should be safe, being this close to the police station."

• • •

In the wee hours of the morning, some noise awakened Rose from a deep slumber. She listened and heard muffled voices close by and sounds of metal against metal. She poked Dan.

He raised his head. "What?"

"Shhhhh. There's something going on out there."

Chapter Twenty-Four

Dan quietly got up and peeked through the curtains behind the two front seats. He reached through them to retrieve something from the dashboard, and then made his way to the back of the van. When he began rummaging through a drawer in the dark, Rose whispered, "Dan, what are you doing?"

"Looking for the flashlight."

"Why? What's going on out there?"

Dan leaned over her and whispered, "There's a gang of hoodlums out there, stripping that car parked in front of us. I'm going to call the police before they get away. I've got the phone, and the number, right here."

"Dan, they could be dangerous. We can't let them know we're in here. Don't turn on the flashlight. They'd be able to see the light through the curtains."

"Well, I'm not going to just sit here and do nothing."

"Get in the potty chamber and shut the door. You can use the little light in there."

"You're right. They shouldn't be able to hear me in there, either."

"And be careful not to rock the van. They could see that too."

Rose could barely hear Dan's muffled voice as he made the call. When he finished, he silently slipped back to Rose, where she was sitting on the edge of the bed. "There's only two officers there at the station right now. They've called for backup, but one is going to try to nab the thieves in the act."

"How many hoodlums are out there?"

"I saw three, but there could be more. They have a car parked in front of the one they're working on, and a cargo van parked next to it. They're probably using it to put their loot in."

"It sounds awfully dangerous for one man to take on."

Just then, Rose and Dan felt something under the van, and heard a metallic sound. The left, front side of the van began to rise.

"That does it!" said Dan under his breath. "Those tires are almost new. They're not going to get those."

Dan rose to his feet, and Rose grabbed the shirttail of his pajamas. "Dan, sit down! What do you think you're going to do?"

Dan pulled away from her, and opened the back door to climb out. Rose was afraid that the movement might have drawn the hoodlum's attention, but they were still busily engaged with jacking up the van. She pulled back the curtains on the street side, looking to see where Dan was. *That impetuous fool! He's going to get himself killed!*

He was standing in the shadow made by the hoodlum's van, and pointing what looked like a gun at the three hoodlums. *I didn't know we had a gun.*

"Okay," he said in his gruffest voice, "stand up, and get your hands up!"

Rose grabbed the large flashlight lying beside her and quickly climbed out of the open back door. She backed up against the side of the van, and slid along it, stopping near the front. She could see one of them, with his hands in the air, facing Dan. A voice from one out of sight said, "Hey, look, he don't got no shoes on. And what kind of a uniform is that? He ain't no cop."

The hoodlum in Rose's view relaxed his arms, and a smile worked its way up his ugly face.

"Put your hands back up," Dan shouted. "Do as I say or I'll call!"

"Or you'll call?" cackled one. "Hey, watch out, guys, that cell phone he's pointing at us is liable to ring any minute."

The smiling hoodlum Rose had in sight pulled a gun from where he had it stuck in the back of his jeans. Before he could raise it toward Dan, Rose raced toward him screaming, "Run, Dan, run!" She came down hard with the flashlight on the hoodlum's arm, and heard the gun fire before it fell to the ground. Someone yelled in pain. Before the hoodlum could react, Rose whacked him in the face with the flashlight. The blow must have broken his nose, and he staggered backward, holding his bleeding face. "You're dead, you bitch!"

Fearing the worst, Rose looked for Dan. He was standing, unmoved, with a blank expression on his face, staring wide-eyed at Rose. There at his feet, one hoodlum lay on his stomach, moaning and clutching his bleeding behind. The third had his hands in the air and was staring at a point somewhere behind Rose. She heard a click and turned to see a police officer putting handcuffs on the hoodlum she had just attacked. A second officer, his gun drawn, stood beside him. "Well, lady," he said, "looks like you pretty well have things wrapped up here."

With their lights flashing, a patrol car and police van were soon on the scene and loading up the three hoodlums. A small group of people from a nearby all-night café had gathered and were yelling insults at the hoodlums while applauding the police.

One of the officers walked over to them. "Thanks for your support, folks. Now break it up. You heard me . . . get a move on it. We've got work to do here, and you're in the way."

Feeling faint, Rose backed up to the van and slumped to the sidewalk where she began crying uncontrollably. Dan was soon on his knees beside her and grabbed her up in his arms. "You silly little fool. You could have gotten killed."

Rose pushed him back and slapped him hard. "Yes, I could have been killed. And so could have you. Would some stupid tires have been worth our lives?"

Blinking, Dan held the side of his face. "Why, Rose, in all our years together, I believe that's the first time you've ever laid a hand on me. You pack quite a wallop."

"And you'll get more of the same if you ever try an idiotic stunt like that again."

"All right, break it up you two," said an officer standing over them. "Are you all right, ma'am?"

Rose nodded, and he helped her to her feet. He said to Dan, "She's right, you know. You used extremely poor judgment, trying to take on those thugs . . . especially when you knew help was on the way."

Dan lowered his head. "I know that now. I did a very stupid thing." He looked down at Rose and then pulled her close to him wrapping himself around her. "Rose," he whispered, "you can see everything you've got under that thin nightgown."

"You never complained before."

The officer stared at them for a moment. "What are you two doing out here in your night clothes, anyway? Where did you come from?"

"Right here, officer. This is our van."

"You mean you were spending the night here?"

"Yes, sir."

"We have an ordinance against that in this city. I'm going to have to write you up."

While the officer took down their names and vehicle information, two tow trucks arrived and began hooking up the vehicles belonging to the hoodlums.

After walking around the van and looking it over, the officer said, "Is this thing in running condition? Or do we need to call another tow truck?"

"Of course it runs," Dan answered. "Please don't make us move. It's been a long night, and we're to meet with Detective Cortez here at the station tomorrow morning."

"Oh, yeah? What other kind of trouble are you in?"

"None. Come on, officer, give us a break."

The officer finished writing in his notebook, and then tore off a carbon copy and handed it to Dan. "For the little lady's sake, you can stay. It's nearly daylight anyway. See if you can keep out of trouble for the rest of the night."

Dan helped Rose back in the van and then shut the back doors and locked them. Without turning on a light, and before climbing back in bed, he tossed the paper the officer had given him up on the dashboard. "The damned, ungrateful bastard. We catch a passel of crooks for them, and *we* wind up with a ticket. I wonder what *that's* going to cost us."

Dan crawled into bed and cuddled up to Rose. "That was such a brave thing you did, Rosie. You were like a mama tiger, the way you pounced on that guy. You probably saved my life."

"Probably."

"Come on, Rose. Don't be mad at me. You must like me just a little bit to do what you did."

Rose started laughing. She laughed till tears ran down her face and her stomach hurt.

Dan backed away. "What's this? Are you having a hysterical reaction from all the adrenalin?"

"No . . . ha ha ha. From you. Ha ha ha . . . 'Put your hands up' . . . ha ha ha . . . 'or I'll call'."

"I was nervous. I had them fooled for a while."

A banging on the side of the van interrupted Rose's laughter. A drunken, male voice called out, "Hey, you in there. You got a five spot for a cup a coffee?"

"Get outta here," yelled Dan. "Or I'll turn my tiger loose on you."

They lay still and heard him mumbling as he shuffled away. "Damned, no-good, circus tramps oughta be run outa town."

Because they had trouble getting back to sleep after all the excitement, it was after nine when Dan and Rose awoke. Dan quickly dressed and put his toothbrush and shaver in his pocket. "I'm going to shave in the men's room at the station. Will you be all right if I go on? We can't be late."

"Of course, but what about breakfast?"

"That will have to wait." Dan started to open the door. "I almost forgot." He retrieved the copy from the dashboard and stuck it in his pocket. "Maybe Detective Cortez can help us out with this."

It was nine fifty-seven when Rose walked into the police station. There was a different officer at the front desk for the morning shift. "Good morning. May I help you?" she asked.

"Good morning. I'm Mrs. Good. My husband and I are meeting with Detective Cortez at ten o'clock."

The tall, stockily-built woman got up and came around her desk to take Rose's hand in hers. Pumping it up and down, she said, "What an honor it is to meet you, Mrs. Good."

"It is?"

"Absolutely! You're the talk of the whole town this morning."

"I am?"

"Aren't you the modest one. Those punks you helped capture last night are part of a ring we've been after for months. The one whose nose you broke, we suspect him of being responsible for several murders. He's an ex-con, a real bad dude."

"What about the one who was shot? Was he hurt very badly?"

"The bullet went through both buttocks. They fixed him up at the hospital, but he won't be sitting down for a while."

Several other police officers had gathered around Rose, waiting to shake her hand. One said, "The arresting officers told us all about it this morning, but we'd like to hear it again . . . from you."

"Thank you all," said Rose. "I just did what any wife would do when her husband was in danger."

"Not just any wife," said one.

"I really don't think I can add anything, and besides, my husband and I have an appointment with Detective Cortez, and I don't want to keep him waiting."

The female officer said, "Detective Cortez is still on the phone. He's been on the phone all morning. He may be a while yet."

Rose looked around the station room. "Where's my husband, Dr. Good?"

"He's in the break room. Would you like to join him for coffee and donuts?"

"That would be wonderful."

"By the way, I'm Officer Dolores Dean. But you can just call me Dee."

Rose politely extricated herself from her fans, and Dee escorted her to the nearby break room. Dan was alone, sitting at a table with his back to the door and staring out the window. "I'm here," said Rose.

"I heard."

Rose helped herself to coffee, put a couple of donuts on a paper plate, and then joined Dan at the table. "You seem awfully glum. Aren't you feeling well?"

"I was until I got here. I seem to be the main source of amusement around this place."

"What do you mean?"

"About last night and how you saved my hide."

"Oh, Dan, you shouldn't . . ."

Dan picked up a newspaper lying nearby and snapped it open. "I'd really rather not discuss it further."

Oh, my. How very fragile is the male ego. I saved his hide, but wounded his pride.

Rose had just finished eating when Detective Cortez burst into the room.

"Good morning, folks. Mrs. Good, let me congratulate you." He put the folder he was carrying under his arm and took her hand in both of his. "You did an incredibly brave thing. Did you see the news this morning?"

"No, I haven't. It made the news?"

"Sure. The TV crews weren't there for the action, of course, but they got film of the felons and the arresting officers."

"Good God," said Dan. "I hope they didn't give out our names. After all we've been through chasing Larry, we can't afford to have him hear we're in town."

"No, the news just called you an unidentified couple. You must have told the officer who wrote up the report that you were to see me. It's policy not to give out any personal information when there's an ongoing case."

"So where are we on the case?" asked Dan.

"Let me grab a cup of coffee and a donut, and I'll give you the rundown."

After a minute, he sat down at the table and opened the folder. "Sherman Findley has never called to report his car stolen. He's either unaware that it's been stolen, or he doesn't want to draw attention to himself. We checked the Hotel Del Mar, and there is neither a Sherman Findley nor a Larry Near registered there, so he's evidently registered under still another name."

"Couldn't he have left his car in that hotel parking and walked, or taken a cab, to another hotel just to cover his tracks? asked Rose.

"That's possible, but unlikely. That hotel is very remote and a good mile or more from any other."

"Hell, Larry wouldn't have even walked across the street," said Dan. "When we played golf, he always took a cart. Besides, I just don't think he'd be wily enough to take a cab to throw anyone off. He has no reason to believe anyone's looking for him in Miami."

"I agree," said the detective. "I also talked to the Salina police a few minutes ago. I'd hoped they could fax photos of the fugitives, but none were available. It seems Mr. Near's wife burned all of his shortly after he disappeared."

"What a *stupid* thing for her to do," said Dan. "She wants him caught as much as we do, and then to go and pull a stunt like that. She was probably in one of her alcoholic rages."

"Is there any chance you have a photo of either, or both, of them?"

"Unfortunately, no." said Dan.

"When we were at her parents home in Kentucky," Rose interjected, "I specifically asked her mother for a photo of Mitzi, and she said she didn't have one. But I remember her mother vividly. When she said people claimed Mitzi looked just like her when she was young, I took a mental picture of her. I feel very confident that I could identify Mitzi."

"Well, the fact that we don't have photos does complicate things," said the detective. "Apparently, you two are the only ones who can identify them."

"How can we keep them from getting on that cruise ship?" asked Dan.

"One of the things we did this morning was get a copy of the Hotel Del Mar's room reservations and went over it to see which ones are checking out today. There were 417 couples.

We also had the Ocean Lady fax over today's boarding list, so we could check names to see which hotel guests were taking the cruise. We have it narrowed down to 298 couples."

"Narrowed down?" said Dan.

"We've got a lot going on right now," said the detective. "The best we can do for you in such a short time, is to position you, along with an officer, to check passengers as they're boarding."

"Only one officer?"

"We really don't have the manpower to spare even one. But when the chief learned about how Mrs. Good was responsible for taking those three hoods off the street, he could hardly deny me. We owe you that much."

"The ship's captain has already been informed that he will likely be taking a couple of fugitives on board. He said he would cooperate with apprehending them in any way he could. I'll call and tell him you and an undercover officer will need to be stationed near the top of the boarding platform, preferably out of sight of the boarding passengers."

"That sounds like a good plan," said Dan.

"Boarding begins promptly at three o'clock and continues until half past eleven. The ship sails at midnight. I would advise you to dress as arriving tourists and disguise yourselves as much as possible in case your cover is not the best."

"Thank you so much for all your hard work, detective," said Dan. He cleared his throat, reached into his pocket and pulled out the paper the officer had given him the night before. "This is rather awkward. As you know, we're pretty much destitute, and I don't know what we're going to be able to do about this."

Cortez took the paper from Dan's hand and read it, smiling. "Have you read this?

"No. But it's a summons, isn't it?"

"Officer Rodriguez turned the original of this over to the chief this morning."

Dan looked worried. "Illegal camping is that big a deal?"

The detective's smile grew larger. "Oh, it went further than that. It went clear to the mayor's office."

"What? Said Dan. "They take their ordinances around here awfully serious, don't they?"

The detective burst out laughing. "This is a recommendation for Mrs. Good to be presented with an award at our annual Heroes Appreciation Banquet in January."

Dan grabbed the paper from the detective and studied it. "Well, I'll be damned."

Cortez winked at Rose. "Make him bring you back in here in January. You deserve it. Good luck with your undercover job."

Dan grumbled all the way to the door. "See what I mean? They're all a bunch of jokesters . . . and at my expense."

As they were leaving, Dan noticed an empty parking place almost directly in front of the station. "Rose, stand in that spot until I can drive around the block and park there."

Rose was thankful that she didn't have to wait long. She and Dan were soon going through their meager wardrobes, selecting their best travel attire. Rose chose a lightweight, pale yellow pantsuit and leather sandals. She piled her hair atop her head and then donned a yellow, wide-brimmed, cloth hat. Gold earrings and dark glasses completed the outfit. "I'm taking the camera," she said. "The zoom lens should help me get a good fix on them."

"Good idea. I'll take the binoculars, too. What do you think? Do I look like a tourist?" Dan wore navy blue slacks, a brightly flowered Hawaiian shirt, and a red sun visor.

"You look a little *too* touristy, I'm afraid. That shirt will draw much, too much, attention. And you need to cover up your hair. Larry would recognize you from that. He always envied you your thick head of hair. Don't you have a suitable hat?"

Grumbling, Dan changed into a light blue, short-sleeved dress shirt, and slapped on a tan billed cap. "Okay, is this boring enough?"

"Much better. Perhaps we should take a light jacket, too. We may be out there on that ship deck until almost midnight."

Dan grabbed his tan jacket and binoculars and looked around the van. "I guess we're ready. Let's go."

"I feel better with the van parked this close to the police station, but after what we experienced last night, I sure hate to go off and leave all our belongings unattended."

"Me too." Dan was thoughtful for a minute. "Rose, why don't you take your big travel bag, and at least put all our important papers in it. Being in the financial shape we're in, if someone stole our identity, they'd deserve it, but we brought papers we can't afford to lose."

"Good idea. We can keep our jackets in the bag, too, until we need them."

A few minutes later, Dan stepped out of the van and held the door for Rose. "You look terrific, hon."

Rose handed him her large bag while she climbed out. "I'm so excited. I've never even seen a cruise ship up close before."

Dan gave Rose a hug. "If all goes well tonight, sweetie, we'll be able to go on some cruises for real."

Chapter Twenty-Five

The female plainclothes officer was waiting for them in the lobby of the police station.

"Good afternoon," she said. "My, don't you both look nice. Are we ready to go?"

"Hi, Dee," said Rose. "You look very nice yourself."

"Yes, we're ready," said Dan. "We're supposed to meet the officer here who's going to help us with the stake-out. Do you know where we can find him?"

"I'm him," said Officer Dean.

"YOU?" said Dan.

"Why, yes, do you have a problem with that?"

"I . . . I . . . don't know," stammered Dan. "Are you going to be able to apprehend them all by yourself if we identify them? Larry's a pretty big guy."

"Don't worry, Doctor, I have my assistant right here," she said as she pulled back her jacket to reveal a holstered pistol. "Besides, if we see them, I'll be calling for backup. The only way I would approach them without another officer present is if they recognized one or both of you and made a run for it. So, it's very important that you make yourselves as inconspicuous as possible."

Another officer drove the three of them to the pier where the Ocean Lady was docked. "Unless I hear otherwise," he said, "I'll pick you all up right here at midnight by this lamppost."

"You hear that, Goods?" said Dee. "If somehow we get separated, we'll rendezvous right here at midnight. Understood?"

"Sure," said Dan, "but if all goes well, we'll have those two in the lockup well before midnight."

"By the way," said Dee, "do you have a cell phone with you?"

"Oh, no!" said Dan. "I forgot to bring it."

"That's okay. We'll just have to stay within sight of one another."

As they exited the squad car, Rose looked up at the towering ship before them and exclaimed, "Oh, isn't she magnificent?"

Rose and Dan followed Officer Dean to a big canvas tent on the pier next to the ship. In large letters on its side were the words Board Here and an arrow pointing to a doorway where an armed guard was stationed. Officer Dean approached the guard and showed him her badge. After she spoke with him, he used his cell phone and then opened the tent door for her. She motioned to Dan and Rose. "In here."

Rose laid her travel bag on the conveyor belt, and Dan had to remove his belt and put it and his keys in the basket for the X-ray machine. Before following Rose through the metal detector, he said to the attendant, "Jeeze, this is just like the airport. But at least this line is shorter."

As he was going through Rose's bag, the attendant said, "You two are the first. It'll start getting busy pretty soon."

Dan and Rose followed the arrows leading to the tent's exit, where Officer Dean was waiting.

"Hold it," said another attendant. "This is where we check IDs and collect passports. Since you're not passengers, we'll need to see some form of identification and take your photographs."

Rose dug around in her bag, looking for her billfold containing her driver's license. "I had no idea we'd have to do all this, or I would have been prepared."

"Security's gotten pretty tight since 9-11," said the attendant, "especially on these larger cruise ships."

Rose looked at her watch. *Two thirty-eight . . . almost boarding time.*

They followed Officer Dean up the long ramp and were met at the top by one of the ship's young officers.

"Officer Dean? Welcome aboard, if only temporarily," he said with a very English accent. "And this must be Dr. and Mrs. Good. I'm Security Officer Nigel Nelson. The captain has asked me to assist you in whatever you might need."

"We just need to station Dr. and Mrs. Good at the best observation point possible, without their being conspicuous to the boarding passengers."

"Might I suggest that each position himself or herself at the stanchions on either side of the boarding gate. The stanchions will keep them partially hidden from sight, yet they'll have a clear view of the passengers."

"Yes," said Officer Dean. "It would probably be best to separate them like that. They would be less noticeable and have different vantage points."

"As for you, Officer Dean, since you'll need to be close by, I suggest you don ship officer's attire. Come with me, and we'll fit you with a cap and jacket." Before leaving, he turned toward Dan and pointed. "See the deck chairs? Why don't you and your wife make yourselves comfortable until boarding time."

Rose stretched out on one of the chairs and Dan sat down in one next to her. "Doesn't this feel wonderful? It's like we're off on a cruise ourselves to see the whole wide world." Rose shut her eyes and could almost feel the roll of the ocean and the breeze on her face.

The slamming of car doors interrupted her reverie. She opened her eyes to see Dan at the railing. "People are starting to arrive," he said. "We'd better man our posts."

They reached the boarding platform at the same time as did officer Dean, decked out in a white jacket and a ship officer's cap. "Ahoy," she said. "Stations, everyone."

From behind the stanchion, Rose tried to glimpse passengers exiting taxis and hotel and airport shuttle buses, but the security tent blocked her view. After several minutes, passengers finally started up the boarding ramp, which was bedecked with colorful fluttering pennants hanging from its canopy. *Those darned pennants don't help matters. People have to be almost on the deck before I can get a really good look at them.*

As people stepped off the ramp, an attractive uniformed female greeted them. She handed each a schematic of the ship and pointed them in the direction of the dining room where snacks were being served. Their path took them past the stanchion where Rose stood at the rail, enabling her to see them up close. She noticed that the majority of passengers were near her age, senior citizens with graying, white, or thinning hair, and many were overweight. *At least they're not walking so briskly that I might miss one or two.*

The boarding went at a good pace until shortly after seven o'clock, and then trickled down to just a handful within ten or fifteen minute time spans. At a time when no passengers were boarding, Rose stepped over to where Officer Dean was leaning against the ship's side. "I never realized standing could be so tiring," said Rose.

"Yeah," said the officer. "As far as I'm concerned, stakeouts are the toughest part of this job. But this one hasn't been so bad. It's fun to watch all the people and their get ups."

"I've *got* to take a potty break," said Rose. "Do you know where the ladies room is?"

"It's not real close. Go through those doors there, down the main passageway to the right and just past the dining room. You can't miss it."

"Thanks, I'll make it as quick as I can."

"I'll go tell Dr. Good you're going, so he can be extra vigilant."

As Rose passed the dining room she peeked in to see several passengers picking over mouthwatering tidbits laid out on a long table. She hadn't eaten since breakfast and was starving. *I've got to have something before I faint. This won't take but a minute.*

She stepped to the table and stuffed a big shrimp in her mouth just as a young man in a white jacket approached her carrying a tray of drinks. "Champagne, ma'am?"

Oh, how I wish I could, she thought while shaking her head no. As soon as he stepped away, Rose began loading a napkin with goodies to eat on the way to the restroom.

Coming back from the ladies' room, Rose stopped again at the dining room to fill another napkin with a snack for Dan. When she reached the double doors leading to the deck, a uniformed ship's staff member blocked the exit. "Sorry, ma'am, we're keeping this side of the deck clear except for boarding passengers."

"But I just came through these doors a little bit ago. Someone's waiting for me out there."

"Sorry, ma'am but we have an emergency going on."

"What kind of emergency?"

"A female passenger is down. An ambulance has been called. Why don't you go back to the dining room and make yourself comfortable until all this is over?"

"How are the boarding passengers getting in?"

The young man pointed down the passageway, opposite of where Rose had just been. "The boarding ramp has been moved down there to the next set of double doors."

Rose grabbed the young man's hand and stuffed the food-filled napkin into it. "Thanks!" she said as she turned to run down the passageway.

There was another staff member at those doors, ushering the boarding passengers in either direction down the passageway. Rose waited until she could get the young man's attention. "Have many come through these doors since they moved the boarding ramp?" she asked.

"Not many in the last few minutes. There was a pretty good mob at first, though. They kinda stacked up while the ramp was being moved. Are you looking for someone?"

"Well, yes I am. Did you happen to see a couple, an attractive man about my age, with a much younger redheaded woman?"

"As a matter of fact, I did. It would be hard not to notice *her*. I thought she was some movie star whose name I should know . . . Is she?"

"Not hardly," said Rose. "I didn't see them in the dining room or passageway. Where else would they have gone?"

"To their cabin, I guess. Do you know their number?"

Rose shook her head. "No."

As the young man greeted several more passengers, Rose heard sirens approaching.

He finally turned his attention back to Rose. "Would you like for me to have them paged?"

Rose stood peering out a nearby window. "No, thanks. I appreciate your offer though."

While the young man was engaged in showing a couple where their cabin was located on the ship's schematic handout, Rose slipped out the door and onto the deck. An ambulance and three police cars were parked at the curb, lights flashing.

She saw that it was useless to try and get through all the ship personnel and medics on deck. Dan's white head popped into sight above the crowd and she furiously waved to him. But he quickly dropped from view without seeing her.

Frustrated, Rose went back through the doors and waved at the surprised attendant there as she passed him to hurry back down the passageway. *I guess I'll just have to wait until all the hubbub is over with.*

She walked back to the first double doors and stood at a nearby window to watch. The attendant there gave her a cold look but didn't say anything.

The crowd on the deck finally parted, and Rose caught a glimpse of Dan. He stood watching while paramedics lifted the stretcher and carried a prone figure down the ramp. He finally turned around and spotted Rose waving at him through the glass.

Rose met him as he came through the doors. His shirt and hands were covered in blood. "What happened?" she asked.

Chapter Twenty-Six

"**W**here's the men's room?" asked Dan. "I need to wash up."

As Rose led him down the passageway, Dan said, "I'll swear, Rose, I never realized what a tame life we had back in Kansas until we started on this trip. It's just been one damned thing after . . ."

"Okay, Dan," she interrupted. "Tell me what happened. How'd you get blood all over yourself?"

"Dee came over to tell me to be extra sharp cause you had gone for a leak. We were just shooting the breeze and watching this couple as they stepped off the boarding ramp. Wham! Down the lady went. Instead of helping her, the jerk she was with took one look at her and ran inside the ship. We didn't know what the hell was going on."

They stopped at the men's room. "To be continued," said Dan as he stepped inside.

Rose waited outside the door for what seemed like hours. Although only a handful of men came and went, she heard the hand dryer inside running continuously. While she waited, the ship's speakers announced the last boarding. She looked at her watch. *Eleven thirty.*

Dan finally emerged, wearing a rather wrinkled, but clean shirt. "I guess we'd better get out to the lamppost before they take away the boarding ramp. I sure was hoping we'd see those two, but all this has just been in vain."

"No it hasn't, Dan!" said Rose. "They're on board."

"You've seen them?"

"No, but one of the boarding attendants has."

"How would he know? What makes you so sure it was them?

"From the way he described them. Mitzi is a knockout redhead, and he thought the woman he saw was a movie star. How many redheads do you know? I bet there's not one redhead in a hundred. Besides, I can just feel it in my bones. It was them."

"I don't know what to do," said Dan. "They'll be taking the boarding ramp down any second, and we're supposed to be at that lamppost by midnight."

"Well, I'm not leaving this ship until we have those two," said Rose. "We haven't come this far just to let them slip through our fingers. Where is Dee anyway?"

"She went after the shooter. I haven't seen her since."

"The shooter?"

Rose jumped when a blast from the ship's horn split the air. She looked at her watch. *Eleven forty-five.* Loud voices came from out on the deck and the ship's engines rumbled to life.

They quickly walked down the passageway and joined the throng of passengers pouring out onto the deck to watch the crew casting off the dock lines.

Rose squeezed Dan's arm as they stood at the railing and watched the dock slowly slip away. "Oh, Dan, isn't this exciting?"

Dan pointed toward the pier. "See that policeman standing over there with his hands on his hips and staring out here at the ship? That must be his patrol car parked under the street lamp, our rendezvous spot."

"I guess you'd better call to let the police know we're staying on board," said Rose.

"Remember, I forgot to bring the phone."

"Well, then we'd better find someone to make the call for us," said Rose.

"Wait a minute," said Dan. "If we're staying on board, we don't want anyone on the ship to know until we're way out to sea. We're now officially stowaways. They would just send us back to shore in one of those little dinghies. Dee will figure out where we are."

"What about our van?"

"It's so beat up I don't think anyone would try to steal it. And thanks to you, the tires are probably safe. It should be good where it is till Monday. After that, the police will impound it and we'll start racking up a huge storage bill."

"A storage bill? Do you think they would charge us under these circumstances?"

"Probably. I just don't know, Rose."

"What shall we do now?" she asked.

"Let's go get something to eat. I'm starved."

Many more people filled the dining room than Rose had seen earlier. The food table had been replenished, and several young waiters were handing out glasses of champagne. Dan picked a plate from the table and handed another one to Rose.

"We better not stay in sight too long. That English security officer might see us. Fill up your plate, and we'll eat out there on the deck."

"I'm more worried that Larry and Mitzi will see us," said Rose, "and make a run for it."

"We're going to feel awfully foolish if it turns out they're not aboard," said Dan as he kept piling on the food.

"They're on board," Rose answered.

With a plate in one hand and a glass of champagne in the other, Rose pushed through the doors, and Dan followed. Rose found a table with chairs in a darkened spot on the deck.

They were both so hungry that conversation was at a minimum while they ate. Rose finally finished her plate and then downed the rest of her champagne. "Would you like another?" asked Dan.

"Oh, my no. That was wonderful, but I couldn't eat another bite."

"I was referring to the champagne."

"Well, why not?" said Rose. "Who knows when we'll be able to drink champagne again."

Dan picked up the empty dishes and went back inside. He returned in a few minutes with two full glasses in each hand.

"My, but you are talented," said Rose as she took two glasses from him.

"And resourceful," he said as he reached into his pants pocket and withdrew a napkin wrapped around several cookies. "Care for some dessert?"

After eating a cookie, Rose settled back and lifted her feet onto her deck chair. "Okay, Dan, now that our stomachs are full, tell me what in the world happened out here."

Dan motioned to a place on the deck. "Like I said, Dee and I were standing right over there talking when this couple came aboard and the woman just dropped like she'd been shot. As it turned out, she *had* been shot, but nobody close had heard it. Dee and I were so shocked we just stood there for a second looking down at her. Dee says to me, 'She's bleeding. You're a doctor. Do something!'

"I got down on my knees beside the woman while Dee called for an ambulance. The blood had soaked this lady's blouse pretty quickly, and when I pulled it off her shoulder, the blood spurted right up. I knew that only a bullet could have caused a wound like that, and it had pierced an artery. All I could do was apply pressure until the paramedics arrived. She lost some blood, but I got it stopped before it became critical. I think she'll be all right."

"Do they know who shot her?"

"As soon as I told Dee the woman had been shot, she yelled the information to the security guards down by the boarding tent and then pulled her gun and took off running down the boarding ramp. I don't know if they ever caught the shooter, but we think it was the woman's ex- husband."

"What made anyone suspect him?" asked Rose.

"One of the security guards right away tracked down the sniveling coward she had boarded with. He said that the woman's ex-husband had threatened them both, and there was a restraining order against him. He was sure more worried about his own skin than hers."

"That's really scary," said Rose, "to think how close that bullet came to *you*."

"Yeah, I thought about that. You never know what's going to get you . . . or when, do you? How about some more champagne to celebrate my still being alive?"

"Don't you think we've had enough?"

"I've never had enough to know how much enough is," said Dan as he got up from his chair, "but I'm willing to find out." He picked up the empty glasses. "I'll be right back."

The ship had turned and the waxing moon was now in view above the horizon, making a lighted pathway to the ship. The sight of it, along with the champagne, made Rose feel so wonderful and happy to be where she was at that moment that she almost felt like crying.

Dan reappeared, carrying an open bottle of champagne and two empty glasses.

"You brought a whole bottle? How did you manage that?"

"I just told the young man that I was trying to romance a beautiful woman out on the deck and asked if I could just take the bottle so I wouldn't have to be interrupted by having to make another trip to get more. He said he recognized me as the doctor who had come to that woman's aid earlier, and he just handed me the bottle. It's only about half full."

"You really are shameless. Dan, come sit beside me and help me watch the moon rise."

Dan looked at the moon. "Hey, where did that come from?"

They finished off the champagne and then both dozed off in their deck chairs.

A little later, Rose woke up shivering. Her head felt like a balloon about to float away. She leaned over into the moonlight to check her watch and nearly toppled out of her chair. *Almost two o'clock!*

She dug her sweater out of her bag and had trouble putting it on. *Dan's going to be wishing he had his jacket on.*

She reached over and shook Dan's shoulder. "Dan. Wake up." He snorted and rolled over in his chair. She felt dizzy, but kept shaking him until he finally woke up.

"Whasha madda, Rosie?"

"Dan, we can't stay out here all night. Where . . . where we gonna sleep?"

"I'm doin' juss fine right here. Lay down and go back to sleep."

Rose unsteadily got out of her chair. She took hold of Dan's arms and in trying to pull him out of his chair, fell over backward. Dan rolled out of his chair and it folded over both of them.

"Rose! Are you hurt?"

Rose giggled and then began laughing hysterically.

Dan shoved the chair away and got to his knees. "What the hell are you tryin' to do, Rose? And how come you've got your sweater on backward?"

Rose quit laughing and wiped her eyes on her sleeve. She put her hands on Dan's shoulders and tried to get to her feet. "It's getting cold out here," she whined. "We need to find some place else to sleep. And besides, it's gonna look awfully funny if they find out we stayed the night out here."

"Okay, Rose, you win. I don't know where we're goin', but les go." They helped each other to their feet and Rose retrieved her bag from the chair. With their arms wrapped around each other, they staggered along the deck.

"Damn, but the sea's rough," said Dan. "It's making me sea sick." He turned loose of Rose and rushed to the railing, where he retched loudly over the side. Rose felt the contents of her stomach rising, too. She threw down her bag and joined him at the railing. After a few minutes of vomiting, she felt as if she'd been turned inside out. Lights came on in a nearby cabin.

"Dan, we woke somebody up. We better get away from here."

Dan wiped his mouth on his shirttail and grabbed Rose's bag. "Come on."

Hanging onto the rail, they followed it for almost the entire length of the ship.

A short way ahead, a light came toward them, arcing back and forth on the deck.

"Dan! Here comes someone with a flashlight."

Chapter Twenty-Seven

They ducked into a door and found themselves near the familiar passageway, which was now dimly lit. "Thank God," said Rose. "The restrooms are just around the corner."

Rose held her head as close to the water faucet as possible and washed the vomit out of her hair. Splashing her face with cold water helped clear her head a little.

Dan was waiting just outside the restroom door. They made their way back down the passageway and out onto the deck. "I feel better," whispered Rose, "but I need to lie down somewhere and get some sleep."

"While I was waiting for you, I studied the ship's diagram on the wall in the passageway. Let's go up to the next deck and see if we can get in one of the covered lifeboats."

They climbed up a narrow outside stairway to the next deck. Out of breath, Rose asked, "How many stories high is this monster?"

"I counted eleven on the diagram, plus a lot of stuff up on top. There are the lifeboats," Dan said pointing.

"Those are *big*," said Rose. "I pictured something smaller, like a rowboat."

"Yeah, I bet they'd hold thirty or forty people each."

"How in the world are we going to get in one?"

"There's kind of a little platform sticking out of the stanchion next to that boat. I'll climb up there and check things out and then help you up."

"Please be careful, Dan. Remember, you're not too steady on your feet right now."

Rose thought the lifeboat's top made it look rather like a covered wagon. She could see nothing but Dan's form silhouetted against the sky, but could hear him wrestling with the canvas cover. In a few minutes, he called down to her. "Okay, come on up."

The steps up to the platform were not really steps, but horizontal supports placed almost too far apart for Rose to climb. After she handed her bag up to him, Dan laid down on the platform, and with an Indian hold on her arm, lifted her up to each of the two supports.

She finally stood on the platform, rubbing her shoulder. "I think you pulled my arm out of its socket."

Dan hopped over to the boat's canvas top, and with a firm grip on one of the roof's metal braces, held out his hand to Rose. "Jump."

When she jumped, he pulled her to him tightly to steady her. "Good girl."

"I doubt I would have done that if I were completely sober," she said.

Dan pulled back the corner flap of the canvas roof. "Crawl in there."

The moon shone through the boat's plastic windows and Rose saw that it was lined with cushioned seats. Dan followed her in and then secured the flap. "It's right cozy in here. Will this do, Madame?"

Rose looked around. She lifted up some cushions and discovered the seats were lids to storage compartments. Upon investigating, she found that they contained water bottles, canned and boxed food, first aid supplies, and blankets. She pulled out two blankets and tossed one to Dan.

"This is just perfect," she said as she stretched out on a row of seats and pulled the blanket over her.

"I have a better idea," said Dan. He tossed several cushions on the boat's deck and laid down on them. "Come on down here where we can snuggle. I promise I'll warm you up."

• • •

The morning sun pouring through the boat's windows awakened Rose. She heard voices and people walking outside on the deck. She threw off the blankets and sat up. A jolt of pain went through her head and she plopped back down with a groan.

Dan rolled over on one elbow and looked at her. "Head hurt? Me too."

"That was the second and last time I'll ever have champagne," said Rose. "The first time was at our wedding reception and it was only one glass. Our drinking that much was *stupid*."

Dan rubbed his temples. "It sure feels stupid this morning, doesn't it? Any aspirins in that first aid kit you found last night?"

"I sure hope so," she answered.

He crawled over to the seats and opened one that had a red cross painted on its side.

Rose looked around the boat and spotted a door resembling the door of the potty chamber they had in their van. "I hope that's what I think it is," she said as she shakily got to her feet.

When Rose emerged from the chamber, Dan handed her a bottle of water. After they had downed a couple of aspirins each, they ate several packages of wafers and shared a can of peaches. "I wonder what they're serving for lunch in the dining room," said Rose. "Do you think we're far enough from land that we can get out of here?"

"Why, I was thinking of just staying in here," joked Dan. "What more do we need?"

"A shower and change of clothes would be nice."

They put the cushions back in place and tidied up the boat. Rose put the empty can and packaging in her bag to discard later. Dan pulled back a corner of the canvas flap and poked his head out. "We're in luck. We're going to have to make this fast though."

He climbed out and hopped over to the platform. Just as he set Rose's bag down, an elderly couple emerged from the nearby door and looked up at him. "Good morning," said Dan. "Fine morning, isn't it?"

"Yes, it is," said the man. "How many will that boat hold, anyway?"

Dan noticed some words on the boat's top, Capacity: 50. "Fifty," Dan answered.

"How many of those lifeboats are on this ship?"

"There are enough to hold everyone on board," answered Dan.

"Well, there'd better be. Did you know the reason so many were lost on the Titanic was because there weren't enough lifeboats?"

"Yeah, I do kind of remember that."

The couple didn't show any signs of leaving.

"I came up here to adjust the riggings," said Dan. "You folks better step back. I wouldn't want this baby to slip and fall on you."

"Oh, my. No, we wouldn't want that either. So long. It's been nice talking to you."

Dan watched the couple until they had strolled out of sight. "Okay, Rose, they're gone. Come on out before someone else comes along."

• • •

Rose and Dan went immediately to the restrooms to wash and tidy up as much as possible. They again studied the ship's diagram on the passageway wall. Dan pointed to a spot marked Security Office. Let's go see if that English fellow is there. What was his name?"

"Nigel. Nigel Nelson. He seemed like a very pleasant young man."

They took the elevator back down to the main deck and quickly found the Security Office, which had large windows looking out onto the passageway. Dan tapped on the window. Nigel looked up from his desk and Dan waved.

Nigel jumped up from his desk and opened the office door. "Where in the world have you two been? We have turned this ship upside down looking for you."

"Sorry," said Dan. "I was afraid you'd send us back if we were close enough to shore."

"You were right. What you have done is highly irregular. I have orders to take you before the captain as soon as you turned up." He picked up the phone and punched a button. "Officer Nelson here. Tell the captain we've got them." There was a hesitation. "We're on our way."

Nigel escorted them into an elevator and punched number 7, the Navigation Deck.

"Any word from the Miami police?" asked Dan.

"They, too, are very concerned for your whereabouts."

"Did they happen to mention our van?"

"They said something about it's being impounded," answered Nigel.

"What did I tell you, Rose? No worry."

Dan and Rose followed Nigel out of the elevator and to the bridge where the captain was waiting. Rose was taken aback by the gruffness in the captain's voice. "In here," he said as he motioned them into a side room. Nigel followed them in and closed the door.

Smiling broadly, Dan extended his hand to the captain. "I saw your name on the ship's diagram. Captain Klein, isn't it? I'm Dr. Daniel Good, and this is my wife Rosemary."

The captain ignored Dan's hand. "I know who you are." He pointed to a couple of chairs.

"Have a seat." He then sat down behind the small desk.

The captain's demeanor made Rose feel like a child in the school principal's office.

"Do you two realize the penalty for stowing away aboard a ship?" asked the captain.

"Well, no," said Dan. "But you are aware that we are after a couple of fugitives from the law, are you not?"

"Yes, I am. I gave the Miami police permission to conduct a stakeout, which I understand was unproductive. You have no proof that your fugitives are even aboard, and you have yourselves broken the law by deliberately stowing away aboard this vessel."

Dan was quiet for a minute. He then sheepishly asked, "What are you going to do with us?"

"Since neither of you has any previous criminal record, I will leave that up to you. You can either pay for your fare to Aruba, your first opportunity to disembark, and catch a flight back to Miami, or you can pay for your entire fare and continue on the cruise."

Dan stood up and reached into his pants pocket. He pulled out some loose bills and some coins, and slapped them down on the desk. Spreading them out to count them, he said, "Looks like about fifty-four dollars and thirty-two cents. Now, which one will that buy; airfare for two from Aruba to Miami, or a luxury cruise?"

"What are you talking about?" asked the captain.

"I'm talking about the fact that Rose and I are completely busted. The couple we're trying to chase down on this boat of yours . . ."

"Ship!" the captain barked.

"They are on this *ship* of yours. They stole every dime we had, which was well over a million dollars."

"Well, that's very unfortunate," said the captain. "We will do everything in our power to apprehend them. But my first and foremost obligation is to the company. You may not stay aboard this vessel free of charge. You are under arrest and will be turned over to the authorities in Aruba. Officer Nelson, take them to detention."

"Wait!" said Dan. Surely there's a better way. Please! Put yourself in our position. Please don't put us off this ship. Isn't there someway we can pay for our board . . . like doing some kind of work?"

"We'll do anything!" pleaded Rose.

The captain looked sternly back and forth at the two of them. "The chief officer may have some job openings. If he does, I warn you . . . you will be shown no favors. You will be treated as members of the crew in all respects, and you will receive no pay."

Dan breathed a sigh of relief. "Fair enough."

The captain pushed away from the desk and stood up. "So be it. Officer Nelson will take you to the Chief Officer, who will assign you your duties and quarters. Good day."

Nigel opened the door for the captain as he brusquely left the office.

"We can't thank you enough . . ." Dan's words trailed after the captain unacknowledged. "Not very friendly, is he?"

"Actually, he treated you very well considering the circumstances," said Nigel. "The last stowaway we had on board got jail time and a big fine."

Nigel flipped open his cell phone. "Excuse me while I call the chief officer to let him know we're coming."

As they walked the passageway, Dan asked, "Will you be able to give us any help trying to find those two?"

"Since there are no photographs available, we can be of little assistance at this point."

"What about passports?" asked Rose. "When we were in the boarding tent, someone said they were supposed to collect passports there. Don't passports have their owners' pictures in them?"

"Well, of course," said Nigel. "Speaking of passports, we will need yours."

"We don't have passports," said Dan.

Nigel stopped walking and turned to them. "No passports?"

"Well, no," said Dan. "We weren't planning any trips abroad in the near future."

"Then neither of you will be allowed to leave the ship at any of our landings. You might even have difficulty trying to get back into the United States." Nigel let out a big sigh. "That means I'll have to start work with customs right away to try and get the paperwork for your reentry."

"I'm sorry we've caused so much trouble," said Rose. "But what about the passports? Can we go through them?"

"We can't just turn them over to you. One of our staff would have to show you the picture in each one, and it will be several more days before anyone will have the time to do that."

Nigel stopped in front of a door marked Chief Officer. He tapped on the door and then opened it to usher in Dan and Rose.

A balding, heavyset man sat behind a desk in the small office. The tag on his white uniform shirt read Chief Officer Malone. He stood up and asked, "Are these our stowaways?"

"Yes, sir," answered Nigel, "Dr. and Mrs. Good. I have to make some calls, but I'll be right outside the door if you need me."

"Thank you," said Officer Malone. He offered his hand to Dan. "Daniel is it?"

"Yes, sir. But you can call me Dan. And this is my wife Rosemary."

Officer Malone smiled and tipped his head. "Glad to meet you, Rosemary. Won't you both please pull up a chair, and we'll get right down to business.

"Since you're a doctor, it's a shame we can't use your expertise to better advantage, Dan, but we already have a full medical staff at present."

"Actually, I'm a veterinarian."

"Oh? I'm surprised. I heard about your saving that woman's life yesterday. Well, we'll find something for you. On every cruise, without fail, our staff is short-handed in one area or another. People get sick, or have family problems, or just plain don't show up before we set sail. We're pretty well-staffed on this cruise, though."

He studied his computer. "Too bad you're not a singer, Rosemary. The female vocalist we hired for the trip went in the hospital yesterday for an emergency appendectomy."

"Oh, but she *is* a singer," said Dan. "She has a beautiful voice."

"Really? Where have you performed, Rosemary?"

"Only at church and a few parties. Dan exaggerates, I'm afraid."

"Would you like to audition?"

"Actually, I would love to, but we can't show our faces any more than we can help it. Have you heard why we're on board?"

"Yes, I have. You're after a couple of thieves. I guess you *had* better lie low. They may try to jump ship if they see you before you see them."

"Exactly. The male thief knows us well, but the woman doesn't know us at all."

"I'll keep that in mind," he said as he studied the computer again. "Unfortunately, the only available positions suitable for you, Rosemary, are maintaining and cleaning heads or working in the ladies hair salon giving shampoos."

"What's the difference?"

Officer Malone looked at her quizzically, and then erupted into a big belly laugh. "Quite a bit, I'm afraid. What you landlubbers call a restroom, we mariner types call a 'head'."

"Oh. I think I'd rather work in the salon."

Still chuckling, he wrote something down on a card and then handed it to Rose. "Officer Nelson will take you to the salon and introduce you to Beverly. She runs the place."

He turned back to the computer. "Now, let's see what we have for you, Dan. There are two positions open in the engine room and one in the galley. They all involve cleaning and are the only ones that don't require previous experience. What'll it be, engine grease or kitchen grease?"

"I'll take the engine grease," Dan said unenthusiastically.

Officer Malone filled out a card and handed it to Dan. "The engineer you'll be working under goes by the name of Zarr. He can be a little rough on newbie's, but you'll be okay if you just pay attention to detail and do your job.

"We need to do just one more thing, and we'll be finished here." He checked his computer. "I see we have an empty bunk for you, Rosemary, in crew cabin B-4."

"What?" said Dan. "We can't have a cabin together?"

"I'm afraid not. The crew cabins are segregated by sex. Some sleep two and some sleep four. You're lucky, Rosemary, you'll have to share a head, excuse me, a restroom with just one other person."

With an agonized expression on his face, Dan reached over and took Rose's hand.

"Don't worry, Dan," she said. "It will just be for a little while."

"It's too bad you two have to be separated, but depending on your shifts, you may get to eat at least one meal a day together in the crew cafeteria," said officer Malone. "And there's a crew recreation room and a crew deck with a swimming pool and hot tub where you can get together."

"Oh, that sounds just peachy," said Dan.

"To add to your misery, Dan, I'm afraid we only have a four person cabin for you in B-38."

Officer Malone got up from his chair and opened the door. "Officer Nelson will take you now and introduce you to your supervisors. I'll be around to check on you every little bit. Please let me know if you have any problems.

"Thank you," said Rose. "You've been most kind."

Officer Malone smiled. "Good luck to you both. You're going to need it."

Chapter Twenty-Eight

Dan and Rose followed Nigel into the elevator. "I forgot to ask about clothes," said Rose. "What are we supposed to wear?"

"All employees wear uniforms while on duty. We'll furnish them to you at the supply room."

"But what about socks and underwear? And night-clothes? The only clothing Dan and I have with us is what we're wearing."

"If you'll notice on the ship diagrams, which by the way you'll find on all decks, there are a number of shops where you can buy just about anything you need".

"Aren't those shops pretty expensive?" asked Dan.

"Excuse me, I forgot. I'll introduce you to Sally, who's in charge of the ship's laundry room. I'm sure she'll be able to help you."

The first stop was in the ship's bowels, the engine room. Rose put her hands over her ears and noticed that everyone working there was wearing ear protection. Nigel waved to one of the men and he made his way toward them down a narrow passageway between machinery.

The nametag on the man's shirt read Zarr. Nigel had Dan present him the card from Officer Malone. After studying it Zarr yelled, "Daniel Good is it?"

Dan nodded yes.

"Have you ever been in a ship's engine room before?"

Dan shook his head no.

Zarr looked at Nigel. "Why the hell do they keep sending me these bums? What am I, a Goddamned nursemaid?"

Walking away, he yelled over his shoulder. "Be back here at O four hundred and not a minute later!"

Nigel motioned for them to exit the room.

Back on the elevator, Dan said, "That Zarr guy looks like bad news to me. Does he have a first name?"

"That's the only name on his papers," said Nigel. "Just Zarr. Like Officer Malone implied, his bark is worse than his bite."

Nigel then explained the naval timekeeping system to Dan and Rose.

"I was in the Navy a long time ago, but after a while you lose what you don't use. I start work at four in the morning, right?" asked Dan.

"Yes. That's the morning watch, which goes until eight o'clock. The watches are four hours on, four off. Your next watch after that will be at twelve hundred, the afternoon watch."

They got off the elevator and followed Nigel to the ladies hair salon, where he introduced Rose to Beverly, the manager. She had just finished shampooing one of several clients in the salon and seemed rather flustered. She tossed her rubber gloves into a nearby sink and studied the card Rose handed her. "Am I ever glad to have you. I wasn't looking forward to two weeks short staffed. We have appointments scheduled all afternoon. Can you start today?"

Rose looked up at Nigel.

"Rosemary will have to start tomorrow," he said. "We have a bit more orientation yet."

Beverly sighed, clearly disappointed. "Okay then, Rosie, I'll see you in the morning. We open for business at O eight hundred, but be here at O seven-thirty so I can show you the ropes."

Nigel then took them to the supply room on still another deck, where they were issued three uniforms each. The adjoining room was the ship's laundry, where they went next. Nigel had them wait just inside the door while he crossed the busy room to talk with Sally, a short heavy-set blond, who was busily folding sheets. She looked over at them and smiled. "Follow me," she called.

Sally opened the door of a large walk-in closet. Coats, dresses, and men's suits hung at the far end. On either side, shelves held plastic bins full of miscellaneous clothing, shoes, and other items.

Nigel's phone rang. He excused himself and disappeared.

"Help yourselves to whatever you need," said Sally. "Everything's used, but it's all clean. Men's things are on the left, ladies' on the right. There's a roll of plastic bags over there in the corner you can put your stuff in.

"Where did all this come from?" asked Dan.

"It's things passengers leave behind. We store them for thirty days, and if they're not claimed by then, we put them in here for the crew to go through. Then after another thirty days, we box it all up and donate it to one of the islands. Heaven knows they can use it."

"I can't believe people leave this much behind," said Rose.

"Well, they do. If we didn't move it out like we do, it would fill up the ship in no time. And you know what? Some of these bastards will wait a year to ask if we found something they left behind, and then give us hell for giving it away."

Nigel appeared at the door. "I'm going to have to leave you, now. Do you think you can find your way to your quarters on your own?"

"Sure," said Dan, extending his hand to shake Nigel's. "Thanks for everything. See you around."

"I'll leave you two alone in here," said Sally after Nigel had gone. "Just turn off the light and shut the door when you're finished."

The bins were all clearly labeled according to contents and sizes, and Dan and Rose wasted no time digging through them. They both soon had several changes of underwear, socks, sports wear, and nightclothes. They even found shorts and tank tops that they could use for swimming. Both found comfortable work shoes and floppies. Rose held up an indigo blue evening dress and looked at it longingly. "It's my size. Too bad I won't have an occasion to wear it."

She hung the dress back up, and then Dan turned off the light and closed the closet door.

Loaded with several bags each, they waved to Sally across the laundry room and called, "Thanks!"

They checked the ship's diagram and then took the midway elevator down to Deck B, the lower crew quarters.

Signs on the passageway wall pointed forward to Female Crew and aft to Male Crew.

"Can you feel the throb?" said Dan. "We're right over the engine room. Did you notice the higher echelon crewmembers and staff are on Deck A just above us? I'll bet it's not as noisy up there."

"Look" said Rose, "Here's the posted Rules and Regulations for Crewmembers."

"Maybe it tells when we get to eat," said Dan. "I'm starved."

They set their bags on the floor and studied the information, which was posted in several languages. "Let's see," said Dan, "we missed lunch, so we can eat dinner at either 1700 or 1800. If I remember right, that's five and six o'clock. I choose 1700."

"Look, Dan, names are listed under the different times. Evidently they tell *us* what time we'll eat. But I don't see our names. They probably didn't have time to list us yet."

Dan studied the list. "I've never seen so many foreign names in one place before. Aren't there any Americans in the crew?"

"Dan, all American names are foreign. Unless you happen to be an American Indian."

"Well, you'd expect to see at least one Smith or Jones on a list that long,"

Rose looked at her watch. "If you want to eat at five o'clock, we'd better find our cabins and get all our things put away. I'll meet you right back here."

She found cabin B-4 and was surprised to find the door unlocked. The room was completely dark. She felt the wall for the light switch and flipped it on. A young dark-skinned female was sprawled out on her stomach in the lower bunk, wearing only panties.

"Oh! Excuse me," The girl didn't move.

Rose looked around the cabin, wondering what to do next. Two small closets and drawers on one wall were separated by a mirror and small sink, and storage drawers were under the lower bunk. *I would wake her up if I tried to put my things away now.*

As quietly as possible, Rose set her big plastic bags on the upper bunk and then turned off the light and quietly shut the door.

She didn't have to wait long for Dan. Instead of the elevator, they took the stairs up to the next level and the crew's mess hall. It was shortly after five o'clock and the room was nearly full. They picked up a tray and utensils and got in the serving line. A middle-aged, oriental-looking man dished food out onto their plates, while nodding and grinning a toothless grin. Rose smiled and nodded back.

Dan scanned the room and spotted a half-empty table near the back. The four young men seated there had been engaged in conversation, but stopped to acknowledge Dan and Rose's arrival by nodding their heads. They immediately resumed talking in a language Rose didn't recognize.

The food was bland and uninteresting, creamed fish over biscuits with peas and carrots.

"This sure isn't the quality we experienced at the snack table in the dining room last night, is it?" said Dan. "Maybe after dark we could find a buffet up there and have some *good* food out on the deck again."

"Didn't you read the rules? Crew members are allowed in the passenger areas *only* if they're working there at the time."

"How the hell are we going to find Larry and Mitzi if we stay down here in the pits all the time?"

"Well, at least I'll be working upstairs and can be on the lookout for them. Maybe Mitzi will come to the beauty salon. And in a day or two maybe we'll be able to go through the passports."

After dinner, Dan and Rose each took an apple from the fruit bowl in the mess hall and went out on the crew deck. They met only two others there, a man asleep in a deck chair, and a pretty young woman standing at the railing, her eyes closed and her long, brown hair flowing out behind her in the breeze.

They sat down in deck chairs, and Dan leaned back, propping his feet up on the railing. He noisily bit into the apple. After a few bites he said, "While you're up there tomorrow, why don't you see if you can pick up some postcards of the ship. We told all our friends we'd send cards of our travels, and we can send a couple to the boys. Won't they be surprised we're on a cruise?"

"Y'all speak English!" The young woman at the railing had suddenly come to life. "I'll swear it's good to hear American. I signed on this cruise to find adventure and make new friends, like it said on the Internet. But now I wish I'd just stayed home. This is my second day on this ship and I can't find hardly anyone to even talk to. Not down here anyways, and they don't want us mixing with the passengers, like we're some kind of scum I guess. My name's Jolene, from Texas, good ole USA. Where y'all from?"

"Kansas. I'm Rose Good, and this is my husband, Dan."

Dan struggled out of the deck chair and extended his hand.

"Glad to meet you. Did y'all know this here's the crew deck?"

"Yes, we know," said Rose.

"I thought maybe you was passengers and got lost. Are you part of the crew?"

"Yes, we are."

"Well, I'll be. You don't *look* like crewmembers."

Seemingly starved for company, Jolene chattered on and on. At one point, she hesitated in mid-sentence and her eyes followed something. Rose turned to see what had captured Jolene's attention. A nice looking young man had appeared on deck and was leaning against the railing, looking out to sea.

"Oh, he's a daaall," whispered Jolene. "I wonder if *he* speaks English."

"Would you like to find out?"

Jolene smiled and nodded her head.

Rose stepped over to the young man. "Excuse me, sir, I was just asking this young lady if she'd seen a flowered scarf anywhere out here on the deck. Have you seen it by any chance?"

The young man turned, and his eyes locked on Jolene for a second before he answered. "Why, no, ma'am. This is the first time I've been out here. I'd be glad to help you look for it, though." His eyes strayed back to Jolene.

"No, that's all right. I'm sure it's probably in lost and found. Thank you anyway. Are you from the States?"

"Why, yes, ma'am. Fruita, Colorado."

"Colorado. Why, we're practically neighbors." Motioning toward Dan, Rose continued, "My husband and I are from Kansas. My name's Rose Good, and this is my husband, Dan, and this is Jolene. She's from Texas."

"Glad to meet all of you. My name's Casey Moore. It's sure good to meet someone from the States. I've never been on a ship's crew before and never knew so many were foreigners."

"That's what Jolene was saying, that she's had a hard time finding people who spoke much English."

Rose stepped to Dan's side and took his arm. "Well, we'd better be going. It's been nice meeting you both. I'm sure we'll see you again."

"I hope I see y'all again real soon," Jolene said. "And I sure hope you find that scarf, Rose."

As she and Dan left the deck, Rose looked back over her shoulder. Jolene and Casey were talking like long-lost friends.

"Why are we leaving?" asked Dan. "It was real nice out there. And when did you lose a flowered scarf?"

"For Pete's sake, Dan, use your imagination. There's no flowered scarf. I just thought those two youngsters could get better acquainted if we weren't there."

They got on the elevator and Rose punched the button to the top deck. "Where are we going?" asked Dan.

"How about the roof? The moon will be full and big and orange tonight when it rises. It would be fun to see it come up over the water."

"I thought we weren't supposed to mingle with the passengers."

"We haven't actually started working yet," said Rose. "I wouldn't think we'd run into very many people up there. If we do, we'll just act like we belong. Besides, most passengers will probably be going to the big party tonight anyway."

Because of the ship's stacks and other apparatus, most of the top deck was cordoned off except for a walkway skirting the ship. Dan and Rose stood at the railing watching the vast expanse of water before them. "Well, you shouldn't have long to wait for the moon," said Dan. "That sun's going to splash into the ocean at any minute."

Rose smelled something and sniffed the air. "Dan, do you smell something burning?"

Chapter Twenty-Nine

"It's just me," said a man's voice behind them. "And my cheap cigar."

They turned around to see a handsome, smiling man about their age. He held up his cigar. "It's hard to find a place to smoke. You know how annoyed people are with the smell of these things. Sorry. I'll go on back over to the other side of the ship."

"You don't need to for our sake," said Dan. "The breeze takes care of the smoke. And besides, I like the whiff of a cigar. I don't get to enjoy the smell very often these days."

The man stepped over to lean on the railing beside Dan. "Yeah, that's for sure. Just about everyone I know has quit smoking except me. I'll probably have one of these things in my hand when they nail down the coffin lid."

He shifted his cigar to his left hand to shake hands with Dan. "I'm Roger Petty."

"Glad to meet you. Dan and Rosemary Good here."

"Do you folks cruise often?"

"No, this is our very first," answered Dan. "How about you?"

"Every chance I get. I love the Caribbean. Can't get enough of it."

He looked out over the water. "The sun's almost down. If you haven't sailed before, you're in for a rare treat. Squint your eyes and watch the sun. The second it disappears, you'll see a flash of green. Get ready. Here it comes."

The big orange orb dropped out of sight on the horizon.

"I sure didn't see any green flash," said Dan. "What's the punch line?"

"It's no joke! I saw it!" said Rose. "But it was just for an instant."

"Some people don't see it the first time, and some people never see it," Roger said. "Try it again tomorrow."

"What causes it?" asked Rose.

"I don't know. It's a phenomenon that I don't have the answer to."

He flipped the ashes from his cigar. "Say, are you folks happy with your table assignment? I mean are you comfortable with the people you're going to share your meals with this whole trip?"

Dan thought for a minute. "Well, I don't know. The ones we just had dinner with don't exactly speak our language."

"Well, we don't have much in common with the couple at our table either. There's room for two more if you'd like to join us."

"That's very kind of you. We'll consider it."

Roger took a card from his pocket and handed it to Dan. "If you decide to join us, my cabin number is 6089 on the Upper Verandah Deck. I don't expect you to remember that, but one of the purser staff can tell you how to get in touch with me."

After a few minutes of friendly conversation, Roger asked, "Are you folks going to the ballroom tonight for the big Welcome Aboard party?"

Dan glanced at the card and then put it in his shirt pocket. "No, since it's our first cruise, we thought we'd just stay up here and enjoy the evening."

"That would certainly be my choice, but the missus wants to take it all in. Guess I'd better get back down there and put on my evening duds. It was sure nice meeting you both, and I hope we'll be able to get together again."

"Thanks, Roger. "Enjoy the evening's entertainment," said Dan.

"Wasn't he nice?" Rose remarked after Roger had left.

"Yeah, I sincerely wish we could take him up on his offer. I'm sure he'll be eating a lot better than we will."

"What time do you think the moon will come up?" asked Rose.

"I don't know. There's still a lot of daylight left."

Rose looked at her watch. "Oh, my. I can't believe it's nearly 8:30."

"2030," Dan corrected. "And I'm beat. Remember, I'm going to have to get up in the middle of the night to go to work."

"You're right." And I'd like to take a shower before I turn in. I guess the moon will have to rise without us."

• • •

The elevator became crowded as it stopped often to allow men in tuxedos and women in evening gowns, reeking of perfume and wearing fine jewelry to enter. All departed at once, leaving Dan and Rose alone to continue the trip to the lower deck. "From now on, we'll have to take the service elevator," said Rose. "Another one of the rules."

The passageway was empty when they got off the elevator. Dan pulled Rose to him and wrapped his arms around her. "This hug is going to have to last me till God knows when."

"I know. Two weeks is going to seem like an awfully long time, but surely we can meet up once in a while."

They kissed and then went their separate ways.

When she opened the door of her cabin, Rose was glad to see that the young woman she was sharing it with was gone. In checking to see what compartments were empty, she noticed that the woman had very few belongings. Rose put her things away, undressed, and then entered the tiny shower.

The water was timed to be intermittent and the pressure was low. Rose was exasperated when she finally got all the soap rinsed from her hair. *Apparently, timing is everything.*

Rose donned a short nightgown and then climbed into the upper bunk. She lay there listening to the hypnotic drone of the ship's engines. *I wish I had an alarm clock. I'd hate to be late my first day of work.*

Rose needn't have worried. She was startled awake by the clanging of bells. Daylight was pouring in from the porthole. She leaned over to look at the lower bunk. It was still empty. Rose quickly climbed down the ladder and opened the drawer where she had left her watch. Six o'clock. *Poor Dan has been at work for two hours already.*

Rose dressed in her uniform and attached her nametag. She pulled her hair into a bun on top of her head and applied a little lipstick. She then took the stairs up to the next level and got in the chow line for breakfast.

With her tray in hand, she looked around the room. A dark-skinned young woman with long black hair had just set her tray down on an empty table at the back of the room. *Could that be my roommate?* Rose made her way to the table. "Do you mind if I join you?"

The woman looked up at her with large, almost-black eyes and smiled. "You are welcome."

Thank goodness. She speaks English. Rose set her tray down and then seated herself. "Thank you. Do you mind if I ask what cabin you're in?"

The woman looked puzzled. "I'm in B-4, on the lower deck."

The accent is definitely East Indian. "That's my cabin, too. I came in last night while you were sleeping, and you were gone when I woke up this morning. My name is Rose. Rose Good."

The woman seemed embarrassed. "My name is Alisha. I'm sorry that I was in a state of undress when you arrived. The nights are so warm in this part of the world."

"For heaven sakes. You don't need to be sorry. I'm sure you weren't expecting company. But I was wondering why there's no lock on our door."

"None of the crew cabins have locks. There is no need, for theft carries great punishment, more from the other crew members than the ship's officers."

I needn't worry, thought Rose. *I don't have anything of value for anyone to steal anyway.* She took a sip of coffee. "Have you worked on this ship long, Alisha?"

"This is only my third cruise, and my very first job."

"Oh? And what do you do?"

"My job is a lowly one, but I don't mind. I clean and maintain heads. We are shorthanded right now and I have to work long hours, from 2400 until 1200. I have but one half hour to rest while I eat."

"Midnight till noon? That is a long time. I'll try not to wake you when I get off my shift."

"Don't worry. I am a very deep sleeper."

They spoke little as they both hurriedly finished their meals.

Rose stood and picked up her tray. "I'm so glad we got to meet. Having such different hours, we might never have had the opportunity."

"Thank you. It was nice having someone to share a meal with."

Rose waited outside the beauty salon for Beverly, who arrived at precisely seven-thirty.

"Good morning, Rosie. I'm glad you're on time." She unlocked the door and held it open for Rose to enter. "There's a lot to go over with you before we open up."

After relocking the door, Beverly turned to Rose and reached for her hands. She looked them over intently and then turned them over to study the other side. "You keep your nails short. That's good. We don't want any poked scalps. No rashes, cuts or abrasions, I see."

Beverly dropped Rose's hands and then stuck her face within inches of hers. "Blow in my face."

"What?"

"I said, blow in my face."

Rose did as she was told.

"Hold up your arms," Beverly commanded. She then sniffed Rose's armpits.

"You pass," said Beverly. "We get up close and personal with clients in this business, and besides a bad hair job, nothing runs off customers more than bad breath or stinking armpits."

Beverly talked all the while she showed Rose how to operate the shampoo equipment and the locations of the broom, towels, beauty and cleaning supplies. "After every cut, you need to sweep up the hair as soon as possible. We don't do many perms, but after we give one, you need to wash the curlers and put them away. We do quite a bit of color touch up, and that gets messy, so you need to get the stations cleaned up right away. And don't forget to check the water temperature before you start the shampoo. We don't want to scald anyone. Any questions?"

"I think I've got it."

"Good." Beverly looked through the glass door. "Here come Nadine and Shelley, the other two stylists. I'll introduce you."

It was a busy day for Rose, and lunchtime rolled around before she knew it. She took the service elevator down to the crew cafeteria and scanned the area for Dan. She saw him across the room, seated at a table with three other men, talking and gesturing with his hands. Their conversation suddenly erupted into laughter. Rose chose a tuna salad sandwich and a cup of tea for lunch, and made her way over to the table.

Engrossed in conversation, Dan didn't immediately notice her standing with her tray at the end of the table. One of the older men did notice her, however, and looked her up and down. "Hello, there, gorgeous. What can I do for you?"

Dan stood up. "Cool it, Romeo," he joked. "That one's already taken. Fellas, I'd like for you to meet my wife, Rose."

"Excuse, me," said the man who had first spoken. "I didn't . . ."

"No need to apologize," said Rose. "I feel flattered."

After introductions were over, Dan said, "If you'll excuse us, Rose and I have some things to talk over."

Dan picked up his tray and he and Rose chose an empty table across the room. "I was hoping you'd be having lunch about now."

"I'm sorry to interrupt. It looked like you and the boys were having a good time."

"We were. They're a great bunch of guys. We work hard down there, but there's a lot of kidding around that goes on, and it makes the time go pretty fast. Those three are also my cabin mates, so we're all working and sleeping at the same time. I feel sort of like I'm back at Boy Scout camp."

"So how are you and Zarr getting along?"

"Just fine. His bark really is worse than his bite. He has a lot of responsibility to keep this big tub moving, so it's understandable that he's a little high strung.

"Did you tell them about us? About why we're here?"

"Not yet. It hasn't come up, but I'm sure it will. How about you? How is *your* first day on the job going?"

"Okay, I guess. I hope I don't have to make it a career, though. The girls I work with are nice enough, but the clientele I've seen so far were pretty bitchy. One said something so degrading while I was shampooing her that I came close to pulling her hair out."

"Like what?"

"The bitch said something like how she appreciated people like me who were willing to do the mundane work so that gifted persons such as herself have more time for their accomplishments."

One of Dan's cabin mates stopped at their table on his way out of the room. "Remember, Dan, there's not much time left for a little shut eye before the next watch."

"I'll be right there," said Dan.

The man nodded to Rose as he was leaving. "Glad to make your acquaintance, ma'am."

"Same to you," said Rose.

"I'm beat," said Dan as he stood up. "I don't know if I'm going to get used to this weird time schedule or not, but I won't have any trouble sleeping *this* afternoon."

Rose got to her feet. "I've got to get back to work, too. Maybe I'll see you again this evening. If I'm not in here, check the crew deck, okay?"

Standing with their trays between them, Dan leaned over and kissed Rose. "Till we meet again, sweetheart."

Chapter Thirty

It was nearly six o'clock by the time Rose finished vacuuming and mopping the salon floor. Beverly was still working on the books when Rose stopped at her desk to say goodnight. "You did pretty well, today, Rosie, especially for someone new to the job."

"Thanks. I was wondering, how are we supposed to handle tips?"

"In the salon, we pool our tips and share them, according to job and seniority. I'm afraid you're low man on the totem pole, so your cut is only ten percent. Did you get some tips today?"

Rose withdrew three one-dollar bills from her uniform pocket and laid them on Beverly's desk.

"Pretty slim pickin's for the amount of work you did, wouldn't you say?" said Beverly. "Getting a tip at all in your job is a rarity. That's why we pool our tips and share. It's the only fair way to handle it."

"Do you mind my asking when you hand out the tips?"

"At the end of the cruise. Why do you ask?"

Embarrassed, Rose hung her head. "I just need a few toiletries . . . shampoo and stuff."

"Why don't you just use your shipboard credit card? It comes out of your salary and you don't have to worry about having cash."

"I don't get a salary."

"What do you mean you don't get a salary? *Everyone* gets a salary."

While Rose explained her situation, Beverly's eyes filled with tears. She got to her feet and hugged Rose. "You poor thing. I hope to hell you catch those two thieves. Is there anything I can do?"

"Nothing I can think of at the moment. I haven't exactly figured what to do if Mitzi shows up at the salon."

Beverly pointed to a big red button on the wall next to her desk. "See that? If she shows up here, just punch that button. It goes right to security, and they can be here in minutes."

"Gee, thanks, Beverly. I'm glad I confided in you."

"Me too."

Beverly opened a nearby cabinet, removed a box, and set it on her desk. "As for any toiletries you need, this box is full of all kinds of samples. Just help yourself."

"I really appreciate this," said Rose as she filled her pockets with shampoo, body wash, lotion, and make-up samples.

"Should I be here at the same time tomorrow?"

"Didn't anyone give you a copy of the itinerary? Most departments are off whenever the ship's at anchor. Of course, we have to take care of any appointments in the salon during that time, but we usually don't have but a few and so can take time off." Beverly scratched around in her desk and pulled out a brochure. "Here. Keep this so you'll know what's going on. We'll be anchoring off Oranjestad, Aruba, some-time during the night, and just about everyone will be going ashore tomorrow, including most of the staff and crew."

"I've never heard of that place before."

"It's just off the northern tip of Venezuela."

"Venezuela? Like in South America?"

"The same. It's a really small island belonging to the Dutch."

"Wow. I've never been this far from Kansas."

"Well, you're in for a treat. The beaches are great, and so is the snorkeling."

"I wish I could find that out first hand. Since we don't have passports, Dan and I aren't allowed to leave the ship."

"No passports? What a shame. At least you can relax on the crew deck and maybe take a swim in the crew pool."

• • •

Rose had a solitary meal in the cafeteria at a corner table where she could watch the entrance for Dan. When he hadn't shown up by eight o'clock, she decided to take the stairs up to the next level and the crew deck.

Quite a few young people were on the deck, talking excit-edly and laughing. Rose couldn't understand their language, but imagined the talk was about their upcoming shore leave.

She was unbelievably tired and her feet hurt, so Rose found a remote deck chair where she could stretch out and remove her shoes. Laying back, she watched the sky turn from pink to gold to dusky blue. The stars came out one by one. She was glad when darkness fell so no one could see her crying.

• • •

The first thing Rose noticed when she awoke the following morning was the silence. The ship's engines had stopped. Careful not to awaken her roommate, she climbed down from the upper bunk and was surprised to see that Alisha was not there. Rose peered out the porthole, expecting to see land, but saw nothing except the empty open sea. She pulled her hair back into a ponytail, put on shorts and a sleeveless T-shirt, and quietly pulled the cabin door shut behind her.

Dan sat alone at a table in the cafeteria. He stood up and waved when Rose entered, and then rushed over to give her a big hug. "Good morning, sweetheart. My, but you look cute this morning. Smell good, too. Are you wearing perfume?"

"No, it's just some fancy shampoo Beverly gave me." She squeezed his waist. "You seem awfully cheerful this morning."

"Well, why not? I don't have to be back on duty until twenty-hundred, when the ship sails. Just about everyone's going ashore, so we should almost have the ship to ourselves."

"But you just got off work. When do you intend to sleep?"

"I'll get some shut-eye after breakfast. Shall we eat out on the deck so we can see the island?"

After loading their breakfast trays, they carried them onto the service elevator and went up to the next level. The ship was anchored such that the nearly deserted crew deck had a perfect view of the island. As they ate, Dan and Rose watched the tenders buzzing back and forth from the ship to the island dock, loaded with happy, carefree passengers from the ship. Some were dressed for the beach, others for island exploring.

Dan drank the last of his coffee and then leaned over in his chair to put an arm around Rose. "*We* should be on one of those boats. I promise you, Rosie, if we ever see our money again, we'll go on a real cruise and have the time of our lives."

"It would be fun to see the island, wouldn't it? From here, it looks just like a picture postcard." Rose breathed deeply. "At least we can smell the sweet island aromas and feel the ocean breeze. We'll just have to take our enjoyment where we find it for now."

Dan kissed her check. "You are one hell of a lady," he said, his voice cracking, "You know that?"

She took his hand and looked into his misty eyes. "You look beat, Dan. And you need a shave. Go get some sleep, and then clean up. We'll find something fun to do this afternoon before you have to go to work."

After Dan left for his cabin, Rose wondered how to spend the long day. Earlier, she had noticed a shelf in the mess hall filled with dilapidated paperback books, so decided to see if she could find something good to read. Upon entering, she noticed that most of the people who had filled the place earlier were gone. Her roommate sat at a far table, eating alone.

Rose filled her coffee mug at the big urn and took it to Alisha's table. "Good morning, Alisha. Mind if I join you?"

Alisha looked up and smiled. "Good morning. Of course I don't mind. Please sit down."

"Are you going ashore today?" Rose asked.

"I'm afraid not. I will not be going ashore at anytime during this cruise. We are too short-handed. Besides, my shift has been changed. Today I work from 0800 to 2000."

Rose thought for a minute. "Is that from eight in the morning until eight in the evening?"

Alisha's mouth was full, so she nodded her head affirmatively.

"But if most of the passengers are off the ship, do you still have to clean all those restrooms?"

Alisha took a sip of water and swallowed the last bite of her lunch. "I'm afraid so. There are forty-two public heads on this ship that have to be constantly maintained, even if only a few people use them. And there are only two of us on this cruise to do the job."

"What a shame. Everyone deserves some time off."

"Yes, but what can I do? There is no one else to do the work."

Alisha stood and then picked up her tray. "I hope you will excuse me. I would like to stay and talk awhile. I get so lonely. But I really must get back to work."

Rose watched Alisha walk quickly across the room to empty her tray into the trash. Alisha turned around to wave at Rose, and then disappeared out the door.

Rose jumped up from the table and ran after her. "Wait, Alisha. Wait!"

Alisha had just stepped onto the service elevator and held the door open for Rose to enter. As the doors were closing, Rose said, "Alisha, I don't have anything to do for now. I'll do your job and you can go ashore for a few hours."

Alisha crossed her hands over her chest. "Oh, I could never ask such a thing of you. Besides, you would not . . . "

"If you're going to tell me I wouldn't know what to do, I've cleaned plenty of bathrooms in my day. I don't need training. I just need the tools to do the job."

"But I can't ask you to . . ."

"It wouldn't be for all day," Rose interrupted. "I have to meet my husband at about five o'clock . . . um, 1700 hours. That would give you almost four hours to enjoy yourself. Just show me where the supplies are and where to start."

The elevator stopped at the roof, and the two stepped out. Rose took a few steps to the railing and looked longingly at the beautiful island scene below. She turned to Alisha, who had followed her there. "Well, what about it? You're never going to get a better offer."

Alisha grinned and hugged Rose. "Yes. Yes, if you're willing."

Pulling on the string around her neck, Alisha withdrew a key from between her breasts. She unlocked a nearby cabinet and retrieved a carryall containing brushes, rags, and cleaning supplies, and handed it to Rose. She then grabbed up a bucket containing a mop with a telescoping handle.

"Every head has it's own paper supply cabinet, and this key fits all of them," she said as she handed the key to Rose. "But you can't work in what you're wearing. That would be against the rules. You must have a uniform like the one I have on."

"You and I look about the same size," said Rose. "To save time, let's go to the nearest ladies room and we'll trade clothes."

Alisha looked Rose up and down. "But I've never worn shorts before. In my village, a woman would never be seen in such clothes."

"I don't want to be a bad influence on you, Alisha. We can go back down to our cabin and you can change into something more suitable."

Alisha peered over the railing and studied the bathers on the beach. "There are women down there who have a whole lot less on. And I'm not in my village right now. Let's go to the ladies' room. The closest one is just around the corner."

After they had exchanged clothes, Rose said, "I'll be back in our cabin a little before five. If you're not back yet, I'll leave your uniform on your bunk. Get going now, and seize the day!"

Alisha looked down at herself. "Are you sure I look all right? I feel naked."

"You look beautiful. You'll fit in just fine with all the tourists. And you can swim in that outfit if you want."

Alisha hugged Rose. "What can I ever do to repay you for this?"

"I'll tell you what you can do. Have enough fun today for the both of us, okay?"

• • •

Rose was determined to clean as many restrooms for Alisha as possible, and kept track of the number. She was cleaning a toilet in number sixteen, when a woman exited the stall next door and washed her hands. Just as Rose flushed the clean toilet, she felt wet fingers tapping her shoulder.

"Miss, oh miss, you're out of paper towels."

With stool mop in hand, Rose turned to face the woman. "ROSE! Rosemary Good, is that YOU?"

Chapter Thirty-One

Startled, Rose dropped the stool mop and water splattered on the floor and on the woman, where it made tracks through the fine, encrusted sand on her feet and legs.

"Oh, my Gaaawd," the woman cried. "Where the hell are some paper towels so I can wash off this filth?"

Because she had on rubber gloves, Rose pushed the large woman aside with her elbow and rushed to open the paper supply cabinet. "Oh, calm down, Margaret. That was clean water."

"Clean my eye!" she said as she grabbed the roll of paper towels from Rose. "It came off a stool mop, didn't it?"

The woman soaped up a wad of towels and leaning over, began vigorously scrubbing her legs. Rose stifled a giggle as she watched Margaret's ponderous breasts try to escape the confinement of her bathing suit.

"I'm sorry, Margaret. You really gave me a start. I never would expect to run into you here, of all places."

Margaret straightened up and put her hands on her ample hips. "I gave *you* a start? What the hell are *you* doing on this ship? And in that uniform? Cleaning *toilets* no less! I thought you and Dan were supposed to be seeing the sights in that luxury RV you just bought."

"I would have thought the news had gotten around by now," said Rose.

"What news? We left for Miami the day after your going away party, and I haven't talked to anyone back home since. What's happened?"

"Larry stole all our money and ran off with an employee. He left us destitute."

"Larry Near? I don't believe it."

"Believe it. He and his floozy are on this ship."

"On this ship? You've seen him? Why hasn't he been arrested?"

"No, I haven't actually seen him yet. But he'll be arrested as soon as we can find them."

"How intriguing! I was going to go back to the beach on the next tender, but let's go to my cabin and have a drink, and you can fill me in on all the details."

"Margaret, I don't have time. I have work to do." Rose looked down at the floor. "And why did you have to drag in all this sand? Don't they have public toilets on the beach?"

"They're a little too public for my taste. Besides, the ship has people who . . . " Margaret stopped herself in mid sentence.

"People who clean toilets and mop floors?" asked Rose.

"Well, you don't have to be so defensive."

Margaret grabbed the large beach towel she had slung over a stall and tied it around her waist. "So when are we going to have a chance to get together? I'm dying to hear all about this."

Rose turned on the water at the sink and began filling the mop bucket. "I don't know. The crew isn't allowed to mix with the passengers. I usually work in the beauty salon, so that would be about the only place I'd be able to see you again."

"I'll make an appointment right away." As soon as Rose set the mop bucket on the floor, Margaret engulfed her in a fleshy embrace. "Have heart, Rose. I'm sure everything will turn out all right for you and Dan." She pulled away to ask, "And where is Dan? Is he on board too?"

"Yes, but you won't be seeing him. He's working in the engine room."

Margaret's eyes teared up and she put a hand to her face. "Oh, you two are such lovely, talented people. How could you have ever come to this?" She opened the door to leave, and then turned back to say, "Just wait till I tell Joe. He's not going to believe this."

Several minutes later, Rose had almost finished mopping the fine sand off the floor, when the door burst open and a breathless Margaret reentered. "My Gawd, Rose! I just remembered *we* had money invested with Larry. Could he have stolen from us too?"

"I doubt it, unless you and Joe gave him Power of Attorney also."

"What is *that*?"

"A piece of paper that I know little about. Ask Joe. I'm sure he can tell you. By the way, Margaret, I'm glad you came back. I've been thinking that you and Joe might run into Larry. If you do, *please* act like you know nothing about all this. And for Pete's sake, don't tell him Dan and I are on board. He'd make a run for it for sure."

"You can count on me, Rosie honey."

I wonder, thought Rose.

• • •

By the time Rose had cleaned two more restrooms, she had less than twenty minutes to get cleaned up and meet Dan. When she got to her cabin, Alisha was just getting out of the shower. "How did it go, Alisha?" Rose asked as she quickly stepped out of Alisha's uniform and tossed it and the key string on Alisha's bunk.

"It was wonderful. I'll tell you all about it later. Where did you leave off?"

"I just finished Veranda Deck." Rose stepped into the shower.

"That's great. I may even be able to get off a little early this evening. Maybe I'll see you on the crew deck after work."

"I'll be looking for you."

Alisha had strung a line across one end of the small shower room, where she hung the dripping tank top and shorts that Rose had loaned her.

Oh, good, thought Rose. *It looks like she got to spend some time in the sea.*

Rose dressed in a colorful flowered sundress, dabbed on a little makeup, and hurried off to meet Dan. He was waiting on the crew deck where they had agreed to meet, leaning over the railing and watching people on the beach below. She slipped up beside him and put her arm around his waist. "Hello, there, handsome."

"Mmmm. There's that sweet smell again." He pulled her to him. "And don't you look pretty, all dressed up for our date. What would you like to do, beautiful? I've got a little cash and the crew bar's open. Want something to drink?"

"After the other night, I thought I'd never touch alcohol again. But a glass of red wine sounds wonderful right now."

"Go pick us a spot, and I'll bring it to you."

After Dan handed Rose her glass of wine and had settled down with his bottle of beer, Rose told him about her meeting with Margaret. As she talked, Dan's forehead scrunched into a frown.

"Having those two aboard is worrisome, all right. Neither one of them know when to keep their mouth shut. They're liable to blab it all over the ship and send Larry into hiding. But tell me, Rose, what in hell were you doing cleaning heads on your day off?"

She told him about filling in for Alisha.

"That was an awfully kind thing for you to do, Rose, but you might have gotten Alisha into trouble if her supervisor finds out, not to mention getting yourself in trouble."

"How much more trouble could I possibly be in? Besides, I felt guilty because I decided to work in the hair salon instead of cleaning restrooms. Alisha wouldn't have to work twelve hours a day if I'd chosen differently."

"There you go again. You always think more about other people than you do yourself."

"Is there something wrong with that?"

Dan stared at her. "I guess not. That's probably one of the reasons I love you so much." He leaned over and kissed her lips.

As they kissed, she placed her hand on his chest and felt something in his pocket. "What's this?" Rose said as she reached in and pulled out a business card.

"Dan took the card and studied it."*Roger Petty, Petty Investigative Services.* What the . . . oh, this is the guy with the cigar that we met up on the roof. Investigative Services. Well, I'll be. He's a detective. I think I'll keep his card in a safe place. Who knows, we may need his services before this is all over."

After a bland but leisurely dinner in an almost-empty mess hall, they took the service elevator up to the roof and strolled around the deck, taking in the scenery as well as the human activity below. Before they knew it, it was nearly eight o'clock, time for Dan to report to work. The elevator going from the main deck to the lower levels was filled with staff and crew members returning from the island. Dan and Rose got off on Deck A. After the elevator doors closed, they kissed goodnight, and then Dan took the stairs on down to the engine room.

Rose went out on the crew deck in search of Alisha. She saw a small crowd gathered around someone playing a guitar. A faint female voice sang along, slightly off key. As she neared the group, Rose recognized the young man with the guitar. He was the one she had introduced to that girl from Texas, Jolene. The young woman singing along was draped over his shoulder, her long hair obscuring her face. When the song ended, the woman laughed and tossed her head back. *Jolene! And now I remember,* thought Rose. *The boy's name is Casey.*

The group clapped and clamored for more. "Okay, okay," said Casey. "I don't care where you're from, here's one I'll bet everyone knows."

"Y'all sing along this time, ya hear?" added Jolene.

He began strumming "Country Roads," and after Jolene began singing, people in the group started humming and chiming in, one by one. The song, by the late John Denver, was one of Rose's favorites. She closed her eyes and sang, remembering the words she had sung to herself so many times before.

When the song ended, Rose opened her eyes, unaware that for at least half the song, she had been the only one singing. Everyone in the group had turned to face her and began clapping. Jolene rushed to Rose's side and put an arm around her shoulder. "Now here's a lady who knows how to *sing*!"

Jolene took Rose by the hand and pulled her through the crowd to Casey. "Good evening, Mrs. Good," he said. "Did you ever find that scarf?"

"What scar . . . oh, no, I never did find it. You know, Casey, I play a little guitar myself, but I can't hold a candle to you. You are fantastic. I bet you can even play flamenco."

"A little. I'll play you one if you'll sing us another song. You're pretty fantastic yourself, you know." He scooted over on the bench. "Sit down right here and tell me what's your pleasure.

"Gee, I don't know."

"Do you know 'As Time Goes By'?"

"That's a real oldie. I think I can remember all the words. If I can't, I'll fake it."

Several couples danced to the music. It ended with a standing ovation with calls of, "more, more!"

Rose got up from the bench and bowed slightly. "Thank you all, but Casey promised us a flamenco number next."

While Casey strummed a few chords to warm up, Rose threaded her way to the outer ring of the crowd, where she stood listening to the rousing music. Just as it ended with an explosion of applause, someone touched her shoulder. A smiling Alisha motioned her to follow, and led Rose to a handsome young man standing at the railing who, like Alisha, was of East Indian descent.

"I would like you to meet my new friend," said Alisha. "He saved my life this afternoon."

"Really?" Rose exclaimed.

"I have never learned to swim, but the water looked so inviting, and children were having so much fun in the waves . . . I guess I went out too far. A big wave knocked me down, and when I tried to stand up, I could not find the bottom. If Saud had not seen it happen, I think I would not be here now."

Saud flashed a big smile. "It's a good thing for her that she is so pretty. From the moment I first saw her, I could not take my eyes off her. But I'm not sure I actually saved her life. I didn't even get to give her mouth-to-mouth resuscitation."

Alisha smiled and lowered her head. A slight color came to her cheeks.

Rose extended her hand to the young man. "I'm Rose, Alisha's roommate. How lucky for her that you were there."

Alisha looked up. "Excuse me, Rose, for not introducing you. This is Saud. He has a very important job on board. He is a waiter in the main dining room."

"I also serve in the ballroom," he proudly added. "You have a wonderful voice. You should be singing there."

"Thank you." After a few more minutes of conversation, Rose excused herself. "It's been awfully nice meeting you, Saud. I hope we will meet again. I'm a little tired, so I will leave you youngsters to enjoy the music and the rest of the evening."

Rose turned to leave, when she noticed a man in a white uniform standing across the deck near the hatchway, smiling at her. As she approached him, he clapped his hands and said, "Very nice, Mrs. Good. You really *can* sing, just as your husband claimed. And you seem to be getting along well with others in the crew."

"Why good evening, Officer Malone. What brings you to the crew deck?"

"I took this opportunity to see how you and your husband are doing. I was asked to deliver a message to you both from Security. You are to meet Officer Nelson in his office at 0800 tomorrow morning."

"Really?" said Rose. "Has Officer Nelson learned something about the couple we're looking for?"

Officer Malone shook his head. "I can't answer that. I got his message second hand with no details."

"You said 0800 in the morning? I'm supposed to be at work by 0800, and Dan will just be getting off work at that time."

"Don't worry. I'll contact Beverly and Zarr and let them know the circumstances." Officer Malone put his hand on Rose's arm and smiled. "You weren't leaving were you? I'd like to buy you a drink."

"How kind of you. Yes, I am leaving. I am very tired and am headed for my cabin. I really appreciate the offer, however."

His arm dropped to his side. "Perhaps some other time."

• • •

Aware that Alisha had gotten to bed quite late, Rose dressed as quietly as possible the following morning and was in the mess hall by seven-thirty. She had a lonely breakfast and then headed for the service elevator. When its door opened, Dan quickly exited and bumped into her.

"Whoops! Sorry, sweetheart. I was just coming to find you. Did you have time for breakfast?"

Rose entered the elevator and pushed the button for the Main Deck. "The Security Office *is* on the Main Deck, isn't it?"

"I think so."

"Yes, I had breakfast. When will you get to eat?"

"I'll grab a bite later. Do you know why we're being called in?"

"No, but I'm hoping it's to get to check out passports."

Chapter Thirty-Two

When they entered the security office, a uniformed young woman looked up from the desk. "Good morning. You must be Dr. and Mrs. Good." She stood up and offered her hand to each. "My name is Janet Horne. Are you ready to look at some passports?"

"I'll say we are," Dan exclaimed.

She led them into a small adjoining room and asked them to be seated at the table. She seated herself on the opposite side and in front of two boxes, one filled with passports. "I'm sorry that we haven't been able to do this sooner, but the start of a cruise is a busy time. In fact, I can only give you an hour this morning. Since we have almost nineteen hundred passengers aboard, it's unlikely we'll find who you're looking for this session."

"Thank you, Miss Horne," said Dan. "We appreciate whatever you can do for us."

"You may call me Janet. Now let's get started." She picked up a passport, opened it to the page with the passenger's portrait, and held it up for them to see.

"No," they said in unison.

Rose lost track of the number of photographs they viewed, but was disappointed in the seemingly small number. At the end of the hour, Miss Horne stood and picked up the two boxes. The one marked check completed was nearly filled. She promised Dan and Rose that she would contact them again when time allowed.

Walking to the elevator, Dan said, "At this rate, the cruise will be over before we get through all those passports. There's got to be some other way to hunt those two down."

He pushed the elevator Up button for Rose and then leaned down to kiss her. "Keep a sharp eye out for that red-headed floozy. Spotting her is probably the best hope we have."

"I have a good vantage point to watch for them both. The salon has windows along its full length, and I watch people walking past as much as possible."

The elevator door opened, and Rose stepped in.

"I get off my second watch at eight o'clock tonight," said Dan as the door was closing. "Meet me in the mess hall."

When Rose was about thirty feet from the salon door, a man emerged, glanced her way, and then hurried away in the opposite direction.

Larry! That's Larry! I'd know that face and that walk anywhere!

Her heart pounding, Rose passed the salon door and followed him, keeping a safe distance behind. *He seems in a hurry. Maybe he didn't recognize me in this uniform. But what if he did?*

He stopped at the double elevators, and Rose saw him press the button.

Now I've got him. I'll see which deck he gets off.

Just as Larry stepped into the farthest elevator, the nearer elevator door opened, and several people got off, blocking Rose's path. The last to emerge was Margaret.

"Rose! I was just coming to see you. I made an appointment for nine-thirty."

"Not now, Margaret. I'm in a hurry! Step aside."

They both stepped in the same direction and back and forth until Rose finally broke free of the dance. She lunged toward the elevator Larry had taken and looked up at the dial. It was coming back down! Rose's hands flew to her face and she let out a sob.

Margaret put an arm around her shoulder. "For heaven's sake, Rose, what just happened?"

"I had him," sobbed Rose. "And he got away."

"You mean Larry?"

As the elevator door opened, the couple inside stared at the two distraught women and hesitated to step out.

Margaret pulled Rose away from the door and guided her down the passageway toward the salon. "I'm so sorry, Rose. Did I cause him to get away?"

Rose stopped crying and her head snapped up. "He was coming out of the salon. Maybe we can get some information there."

Margaret bustled after Rose as she raced to the salon. Beverly was at the front counter and laughed, seeing Rose rush in. "My, my, Rose, I knew you'd be late. You didn't have to work up a lather to get here."

A red-faced Margaret burst through the door and joined Rose at the counter, breathing heavily.

Puzzled, Beverly looked at one, and then the other. "What's up with you two?"

Rose scanned the salon. The only patron there was an elderly lady under the hair dryer. "You know that man who was in here about ten minutes ago? He's the one we're after."

"You mean the thief?"

"Yes. Why was he here?"

"He just had a color touch-up. His white roots were showing."

"Did he give you a name? Or a cabin number?"

"He said his name was Robert."

"Robert what?"

"He didn't say. He was standing outside the door when I opened up this morning, so he didn't leave a name. Since we had an opening, we took him."

"Did he pay with a credit card?"

"No. He paid cash. Gave a big tip, too."

"He never was all that generous with his *own* money," Margaret interjected.

Rose started crying again.

Beverly came around the counter and put her arm around Rose. "Honey, why don't you take the day off. We can manage today."

Rose pulled a tissue out of a box on the counter and blew her nose. "I'll be all right. Now that I know for certain those two are on board, I *would* like to go to the security office and report this though. I won't be long."

"Sure, honey. Take your time."

"Shall I come with you?" asked Margaret.

Rose gave her a hug. "Thanks, Margaret, but that's not necessary. Have a seat and relax. I'll be right back to give you a shampoo."

• • •

The dinner dress on the ship that night was formal, and the salon appointment book for the day overflowed. It was after seven o'clock before Rose finally finished straightening up and cleaning the salon.

Beverly unlocked the door for Rose to leave. "It's a good thing you *didn't* take the day off as I suggested. We were *swamped*. I've got to hand it to you, Rosie. You really help keep things humming around here. You see for yourself what needs to be done, and I never have to ask you to do something."

"Thanks, Bev. That comes from years of raising kids and keeping house, I guess. See you in the morning."

When she got to her cabin, Rose took a quick shower, donned the flowered dress she knew Dan liked, and pulled her wet hair into a ponytail. While she stood looking for Dan at the entrance to the mess hall, he came up from behind and put his arms around her waist. "Your hair's wet. Did you have to work late?"

She turned and hugged him. "Yes, and my feet are killing me. Let's grab something to eat and take it up to the crew deck where we can talk more privately."

"Oh? Are you going to whisper sweet nothings in my ear?

• • •

There were only a few crewmembers on the deck, but Dan and Rose seated themselves in a secluded corner anyway.

Rose leaned across the small table. "I saw Larry today."

Dan's jaw fell, and it took a second for the news to sink in. "So your female instinct was right. You really saw Larry? So why isn't he in the brig in chains right now?"

Rose filled him in on all the details about losing Larry at the elevator.

"Drat! I knew Margaret was going to be trouble!"

"Dan! We can't blame her for the bad timing. How was she to know?"

"Do the authorities know? I especially hope that smarty-pants captain knows. He just the same as accused us of being on a wild goose chase."

"Officer Nelson took down all the information and said he would notify the captain. He also said he would free up more time for Miss Horne to have us view photographs."

"I just hope they give us *enough* time."

• • •

The following day was also at sea and uneventful. The ship docked at Saint George in Grenada sometime after midnight. Since the salon had only a few appointments scheduled, and those were for late afternoon, Rose slept later than usual. When she awoke, she found Alisha already gone. While she dressed in a T-shirt and shorts, Rose thought about Alisha and felt happy for her. She hardly saw her anymore, and it seemed that whenever she did, she was always in the company of her new friend, Saud.

Rose was eager to see the island, so decided to skip breakfast, and with a mug of coffee in hand, took the service elevator all the way to the roof in order to get the best view. Unlike Aruba, she could see very little beach. Colorful houses and buildings stair-stepped down to the horseshoe-shaped harbor, which was filled with a variety of moored sailboats. Far below, passengers and crew poured off the ship, down the gangways and onto the pier, eager to take in the sights.

The sun felt wonderful on her bare skin, and watching the bustle of the island was mesmerizing. Her stomach growled, reminding her to eat something.

Rose got a Danish roll and fruit juice in the mess hall and took it out to the crew deck, where she found a table near the railing with a good view of the island. She had almost finished eating when behind her she heard the familiar English accent.

"Mrs. Good! There you are!"

"Hello, Nigel. Were you looking for me?"

"Yes. Will you please come with me?"

"Well, of course. More passports to look at?

"No. A bit of unpleasantness, I'm afraid. We need you to identify a body."

Chapter Thirty-Three

"**A** body!"
    "We think it may be the man you and your husband are looking for."

The news hit Rose like an electric shock. "Does my husband know?"

"He will be joining us in the deceased's room within the hour."

Rose felt nauseated, as she and officer Nelson rode the elevator to an upper deck. She wanted Larry to pay for what he'd done, but never wanted him dead. "How did he die?" she asked.

"From natural causes, apparently. The ship's doctor is ashore right now, but we expect him back at any time. The nurse did a preliminary check on the body."

There were several cabin stewards outside the door of the cabin, straining to get a look inside. "Don't you boys have work to do?" Nigel said as he approached them. They scattered.

Larry was lying on his back on the edge of the king-sized bed, with the sheet pulled up to his neck. Security officer Janet Horne and the nurse stood solemnly at his bedside. Janet nodded when her eyes met Rose's. "Mrs. Good."

Rose nodded and tried to speak, but no sound could get past the lump in her throat.

With his white hair brown again, and gravity pulling the wrinkles from his handsome face, past memories flooded over Rose as she looked down at Larry. *This is a man I once loved and almost married . . . a man who was a huge part of our lives.* Rose leaned over and put her hand on the sheet covering Larry's chest. "Oh, Larry, what happened to you?" she sobbed.

"It must be him," said Janet.

"Brilliant deduction," said Nigel.

He gently laid a hand on Rose's shoulder. "You need to stand back, Mrs. Good. Doctor Weber is here."

She started to withdraw her hand from Larry's chest, but then stopped. She felt something. She placed her other hand over Larry's nose and felt a breath. "He's alive!" she cried.

Nigel pulled Rose aside as the stockily-built doctor reached around them to draw the sheet off Larry's chest.

Doctor Weber was busy with the examination when Dan entered the room and went to stand beside Rose. She put an arm around him and whispered, "He's still alive."

"Really? Then I still have a chance to kill that bastard?"

The doctor stood up, pulled the stethoscope from around his neck, and faced Nigel. "Have him brought to the infirmary immediately. We need to get an IV started."

Nigel turned away and spoke some orders into his cell phone.

"Did he have a heart attack?" Rose asked.

"I don't believe so," answered the doctor. "But he's had a close call. He has all the signs of a drug overdose."

"Drug overdose? You mean like a prescription drug?"

"Are you his wife?"

"Heavens no."

"Are you traveling with him?"

"No."

When Nigel snapped his cell phone shut, Rose asked him, "Where is that woman he came aboard with? The redhead."

"We've been searching for her ever since the steward discovered Mr. Harmon here."

"Huh!" huffed Dan. "Mr. Harmon, is it? His real name is Near. Larry son-of-a-bitch Near."

"The couple is registered as Howard and Elaine Harmon," said Nigel, "the same as the names on their passports."

"Yeah," said Dan. "I understand you can buy just about any kind of document you want in Miami. It's a big industry."

"She may have gone ashore," said Nigel.

"Sir?" said Janet from across the room. "I've finished searching the cabin. No sign of a prescription bottle anywhere. Did Mr. and Mrs. Harmon have separate cabins?"

"No. Why do you ask?"

"Because there's no sign of a female occupying this cabin. I looked in all the drawers, closets, and the bath. You'd never know a woman was here."

Nigel's brow furrowed. "Check with the deckhands. Ask if a redheaded woman went ashore with luggage this morning."

"Stand back," ordered Dr. Weber. "Give the boys room."

After the two crewmembers loaded Larry onto a stretcher, Doctor Weber motioned to Rose. "Come with me, please, and hurry."

Rose looked at Dan and shrugged her shoulders.

"Where she goes, I go," said Dan.

Nigel called after them as they quickly followed the doctor and nurse out the door, "Meet me in the Security Office when you're finished at the infirmary."

The nurse accompanied Larry onto the service elevator while the others took the passenger elevator.

On their way down to a lower deck, Dr. Weber said to Dan, "I see you're wearing a crew uniform. How are you associated with the patient?"

"We were once friends," said Dan.

Dr. Weber looked at Rose. "And how about you?"

"Let me introduce you," interrupted Dan. "I'm Dr. Daniel Good and this is my wife, Rosemary."

"You're a doctor?"

"Yes. My patients were mainly of the four-legged variety."

"I see. What is a veterinarian doing in that uniform?"

"That's quite a story," said Dan as he held the elevator door open.

Inside the small but efficiently furnished infirmary, the crew members lifted Larry onto a hospital bed. Dr. Weber ushered Dan and Rose into his nearby office and had them take a seat. "I'll be back as soon as the patient is stabilized and hooked up to monitors."

Rose strained to watch from her seat next to the door. Dr. Weber and a nurse worked together to attach an array of tubes and wires to Larry and place an oxygen mask over his face. She heard the doctor give the nurse more instructions before he returned to the cramped office.

Dr. Weber sat down and pulled some papers out of a drawer. He slapped them on the desk, picked up a pen, and then turned to Dan. "May I have the full name and address of the patient, please."

"Larry Near, and right now this ship is his only address."

"You mean he has no permanent address?

"That's right. He hasn't been convicted or sentenced yet."

The doctor looked puzzled. "Is the woman they are looking for his wife?"

"No."

"Then who is his next of kin?"

"His wife."

The doctor was becoming exasperated. "And does *she* have a permanent address?"

"Her name is Charlotte Near," offered Rose, "and her address is 519 North Bayberry, Salina Kansas. I don't recall the zip code."

"And a telephone number?"

The doctor quickly scribbled it on the form.

"Thank you, Mrs. Good. She will need to be notified."

"I don't think she'll be too interested," said Dan. "Unless he dies and she's kept up his life insurance."

The doctor slammed his pencil down. "I am very surprised by your cavalier attitude, sir. That friend of yours in there is critically ill."

"Sorry," said Dan.

The doctor continued writing. "The patient's approximate age?"

Dan thought for a minute. "He's seven months older than I am, which would make him 59."

"Any serious illnesses, accidents or operations that you're aware of? And the dates?"

"Hell, Doc, I don't even keep track of my own," said Dan.

"Remember the hernia operation he had two or three years ago?" asked Rose. "When he helped you move the big TV set?"

"Oh, yeah."

"Did the patient use recreational drugs?"

"Absolutely not," answered Rose. "He wouldn't touch alcohol and never even smoked."

"Now, do either of you know whether or not Mr. Near took out trip insurance? It should cover his medical expenses here in the infirmary."

"Haven't a clue," said Dan.

Rose shook her head.

The doctor picked up another form, laid it in front of him, and spoke as he wrote. "Dr. and Mrs. Daniel Good . . ."

He looked at Rose. "Address and phone number please?"

"We don't have an address, but our cell phone number is 785-930-9874."

"No permanent address for you either?"

"That's correct."

The doctor shook his head, finished filling out the form, and shoved it across the desk to Dan. "Now, if you'll just sign beside the x, you two can be on your way."

"What's this?" Dan glanced over the paper and tossed it back at the doctor. "You want *me* to be the responsible party if there's no insurance? I wouldn't sign that even if I had the *means* to pay."

"But *someone* has to be responsible. I thought you said you were close friends."

"*Were,*" said Dan as he stood up. "Past tense. Officer Nelson is waiting for us in Security, so if you'll excuse us."

"Do you think Larry will be okay?" asked Rose.

"It's nice to see *someone* has concern," said the doctor. "I have several tests to perform before we know. I *can* tell you, however, that he was very close to death and may still be."

On their way out of the infirmary, they stopped at Larry's bedside. Rose touched his arm and felt hot tears roll down her cheeks. Dan stood silently for a moment looking down at him, and then took Rose's hand. "I have mixed emotions, too, Rosie," he whispered. "It's pretty hard to erase all those good memories of him. Come on, let's get out of here."

Officer Nelson was filling out paperwork when they entered his office. "Any word yet on the redhead?" asked Dan.

Nigel stood up and offered them a chair. "Yes. She left the ship at 0700 with three pieces of luggage. I've pretty much finished the report. All that's left is for you two to look it over and then sign it."

"What are you doing about finding the redhead?" asked Dan.

"I'm afraid we have done all we can, Dr. Good. We have no authority or duty outside of this ship. What did you think we would do?"

"Well, you won't let *us* leave the ship. *Somebody* has to go find her before we sail."

"I fully understand your predicament, but as I said, we can do nothing."

"Well, if that's not a crock of shit!" yelled Dan. "We're supposed to just let her slip through our fingers? She needs to be in jail!"

"Dr. Good, that kind of ungentlemanly conduct will get you nothing. You and your problems have already caused this ship quite a bit in extra man hours expended. If I were you, I would be thankful for the latitude already shown to you and Mrs. Good. It is your good fortune that *you* are not in jail. I suggest you get some rest. You can read and sign the report when you're in a more favorable state of mind." Nigel jumped up from his desk and held the door open for them.

"Wait," said Rose. "What about that detective we met, Dan? Maybe he can help."

"Yes! I forgot about him. I don't have his card with me. Do you remember his name?"

"Roger something. His last name started with a 'P'."

Nigel sat back down and opened his computer. "I'll go through the 'Ps' on the passenger list and see if we can find a Roger." After a few minutes he said, "Here's a Roger Petty. Could that be him?"

"Yes!" said Dan. "That's him. How do I get a hold of him?"

"He's in cabin 6089 on the Upper Veranda Deck. Would you like me to ring him?"

"Yes, please do."

Nigel dialed the number and when he heard it ringing, handed the receiver to Dan.

"Hello, Mrs. Petty? Is your husband there? Dan Good. Tell him we met up on the top deck our first night at sea. Thank you."

After a few minutes talking with Roger, Dan put his hand over the receiver and asked Nigel, "He wants to know if I can come to his cabin so we can talk about this. Is that okay?"

"Since these are extraordinary circumstances, I think we can bend the rules. Just be sure you take the service elevator, all right?"

"The wife and I will be right up, Roger."

Dan handed the receiver back to Nigel. "Thanks, Nigel, and I apologize about the outburst. These four-hours-on, four-hours-off watches are playing havoc with my sleep. I'm a bit grumpy, I'm afraid."

• • •

Mrs. Petty answered the door. She was an attractive woman, with dyed black hair pulled into a bun atop her head. She wore large dangly gold earrings and was impeccably dressed in a light-yellow silk pants suit. She smiled radiantly until she noticed Dan's uniform. "Yes, what is it?"

"We're the Goods, Dan and Rosemary."

She looked them up and down. "*You're* Mr. and Mrs. Good?"

"Yes," said Dan. "Roger is expecting us."

Mrs. Petty left them standing in the doorway while she crossed the room and said through the balcony screen door. "Those people are here."

Roger entered the room from the balcony, a drink in one hand and a cigar in the other.

"Hello, again. Come in, come in. Good to see you again. Have a seat and tell me what's on your mind."

They seated themselves together on the small sofa. Rose couldn't help but notice the look of disdain on Mrs. Petty's face as she stood there studying the grease on Dan's shirt and knees of his pants.

Roger seated himself across from them. "What's with the uniform? Are we having one of those silly costume parties tonight? Which reminds me, I haven't seen you two at any of the functions. Where have you been hiding out?"

"As a matter of fact, Roger," said Dan, "the uniform is real. Rose and I are crewmembers. That's part of what we have to talk to you about. We could really use your help if you're willing."

Mrs. Petty picked up a purse from a nearby end table and stuck it under one arm. "I'm sorry, but Mr. Petty and I have plans for the day. We're to meet someone in just a few minutes."

"Sylvia, honey," said Roger, "why don't you and Mrs. what's-her-name go on? You two don't need me to tag along while you go shopping." He stood up to pull his billfold out of his back pocket. "Here are a few c-notes in case they don't take credit cards."

"Very well," she said as she snatched the bills from his hand and gave him a cold piercing stare. "Will you be joining us for lunch at that quaint little restaurant we talked about?"

He leaned over and gave her a peck on the cheek. "I'll try."

"Good day, Mr. and Mrs. Good." Her words dropped like ice cubes as she went out the door.

"I hate to spoil your plans," said Dan. "But this really is important."

"Spoil my plans? I can't think of anything I'd rather *not* do than follow two women around while they shop." Roger picked up his glass. "Can I fix you two a drink?"

"No thanks," they said in unison.

"So let's hear it. What's so important?"

As Dan told the short version of their story, Roger interrupted a few times to ask questions. When Dan had finished, he asked, "Will you help us?"

"Of course I'll help. I could use some action. This trip was starting to get boring." Roger set his empty glass on the end table and stood up. "If that female left the ship at seven this morning, I'd better high-tail it to shore and start asking around. The ship sails at midnight. How can I get back to you two?"

"We'll wait for you on the crew deck. Do you know how to get there?"

"I'll find it. That's one of the things we detectives do best."

• • •

Rose was glad the last salon appointment of the day was a no-show and she was able to leave before six o'clock. Without changing her uniform, she hurried to the crew deck where Dan was waiting. He was seated at a table looking out over the railing when she approached him. "I take it Roger isn't back yet."

Dan turned around in his chair. "Hi, sweetie. I'm glad you got off earlier than you expected. I've been watching for Roger, but haven't seen him yet. I saw that wife of his come aboard a couple of hours ago. She and the old gal she was with were loaded. With packages, that is. Have a seat, and I'll run down to the mess hall and grab us something to eat while we're waiting."

When Dan left, Rose took his place at the railing and watched people funneling back through the town, onto the dock and into the ship. Dan was back in a short time with a couple of hamburgers, potato chips, and soft drinks. They had just finished eating when Roger made his appearance. He plopped into a chair and let out a sigh. "Well, good people, I'm afraid I've got some bad news."

Chapter Thirty-Four

et's hear it," said Dan.

Roger looked around the deck. "Where's the waiter? I could sure use a drink."

Dan stood and reached into his pocket. "The crew deck is do-it-yourself. What'll it be?"

"I'll have a double scotch with water. You better get something for yourself and the missus, too."

While Dan ordered drinks at the bar, Roger sat with his chin in his hand, studying Rose. Finally, he broke the uncomfortable silence. "How old are you and Dan?"

"Why do you ask?"

"I was just wondering how close you were to receiving Social Security."

Before she could respond, Dan set a drink on the table in front of Roger and handed Rose a glass of red wine.

"Aren't you having anything?" asked Roger.

"Better not. I'm working the midnight watch." Dan sat down and leaned toward Roger. "Come on, lay it on us. What did you find out?"

Roger took a long swig before answering. "She's gone, folks, and I'm afraid so is your fortune."

"Well, *where* is she gone? If we can find *her*, we can find our money," said Dan.

Roger took another swig, nearly emptying his glass. "Here's the story. She left the ship just before the first call to breakfast. A taxi waited for her while she paid two deck hands to lower the gangplank. She slipped two cabin stewards a c-note each to cart three bags from her cabin to the taxi. The deckhands said that, from the trouble the stewards had lifting two of the bags, they appeared to be unusually heavy.

"When I got back to the ship, I tracked down the stewards and asked them what was in the bags. They said it had to be coins, since the load shifted around inside and two of the bags weighed at least seventy pounds each."

"It sounds like she and Larry turned our investments into gold coins," said Dan.

"That was my thinking, too."

"But if she's carrying around a load like that, shouldn't it just make it easier to track her down?"

Roger finished off his drink and slowly lowered his glass to the table. "I haven't finished the story. I took a cab to the airport and got there a little after eleven. A plane chartered out of Rio de Janeiro by a Mr. and Mrs. Harmon had taken off just eighteen minutes earlier, minus Mr. Harmon. It was supposed to depart at eight this morning, but had suffered engine problems on the way in, so needed some maintenance before it could head back to Rio. There wasn't much else I could do at that point except report to you folks, so I went in to town, had lunch with the ladies, and then took in some of the sights.

"We detectives like to follow our hunches. You see, something kept eating at me, so I took a cab back to the airport. The air controllers had lost contact with the Harmon's plane about three hours after takeoff. It just disappeared from the radar. They figured it went down somewhere in the dense jungle south of the Guyana-Brazil border."

Rose put her hands to her face. "Oh, no! Her poor mother!"

"You beat all, Rose!" snapped Dan. "How about poor *us*?"

He turned back to Roger. "Have they started a search for the plane yet?"

"No. And if left up to the Brazilian government, that won't happen. Even if the plane was spotted, the chances of getting a party to go into that jungle are nil, and if anyone survived the crash, they probably won't survive the natives. The guys at the airport said planes and outsiders go missing in that jungle all the time. Said the natives don't tolerate intruders."

"Are you saying there's nothing we can do?" asked Dan.

"I honestly don't know. I'm way out of my league here. Let's just say I wouldn't give much hope to ever seeing your money again. Even if you *did* find the crash site, it'd cost more to recover the gold than it's worth."

Roger rested a hand on Dan's shoulder. "I'm truly sorry, Dan. But it's pretty hopeless."

Rose turned toward Dan. "But we don't know for sure if they turned *all* our investments into gold coins. We don't even know those *were* gold coins in Mitzy's bags."

"I can dig some more when I return to the states," said Roger, "but I can pretty much guarantee you that your investments are scattered in that jungle."

"Is that why you questioned me about Social Security?" asked Rose.

Roger nodded. "You both are too young for retirement anyway. Attractive, intelligent people like you will do just fine. In fact, I can loan you several grand to make a new start. You can repay me whenever you get back on your feet. Whadda ya say?"

"That's more than generous of you," said Dan, "but no thanks. Like you said, we'll make out just fine. We already owe you for what you did for us today. We thank you for that."

"I started to say, my pleasure, but in this case, it was no pleasure to be the bearer of such bad news."

Roger stood. "I'd better get back to the wife. She's got big plans for the evening. Do you still have my card?"

Dan patted his shirt pocket. "Right here."

"If you folks need anything at all from me on this trip, please don't hesitate to get in touch. Give me a call at my home in a month or so to see if I've learned anything new. Okay?"

Dan stood to take Roger's hand. "You can count on it. You've been a good friend to us, Roger. We won't forget it."

After Roger left, Dan looked over at Rose, who sat staring at her glass. "Why, you haven't even touched your wine."

Rose picked up the glass and drained it, set it back down and then wiped her mouth with the back of her hand. "You know, Dan, we saved our money so that we could travel and have some adventure before we got too old. We've had more adventure, met more people, and seen more sights these past three weeks than we ever did living in Salina. I've enjoyed our gypsy lifestyle. As long as we have our health, and each another, each day can be just another adventure. I only regret that we won't be able to leave anything to our boys and grandchildren, should we ever have any grandchildren."

Dan scooted next to Rose and put his arm around her. "You are quite a philosopher, Rose, but life without an income is more adventure than I care to have. We have good credit, so maybe I can borrow enough to start another practice. Or maybe work myself into a partnership in one already established. We can choose anywhere different to live, maybe Florida or California. And I'm not sorry about this for the boys' sakes. In fact, I've been more worried about their relying too much on a fat inheritance. Without it, maybe they'll try harder to succeed, and along the way, feel better about themselves."

"I hadn't looked at it like that. Maybe Brad will quit wandering around the world, get a real job, and finally settle down with some nice girl."

Rose brushed a lock of hair away from Dan's forehead. "Honey, you look so tired. Why don't you take a nap before your shift."

"I am beat. I doubt if I can get to sleep after that bad news, but I'll try."

Rose watched Dan shuffle off, his head bent and his gait lacking that familiar bounce of confidence.

She looked around and saw that she was alone. The bartender had even disappeared. Lost in thought, she watched the lights come on all over town while calypso music drifted up from below.

"Good evening, Mrs. Good. Mind if I join you?"

Before she could answer, Officer Malone chose a chair next to her. A whiff of whiskey accompanied him.

"Good evening, Officer Malone. Of course I don't mind."

"Please call me Mike. I thought I'd find you here. Where's your husband?"

"Sleeping. He goes to work at midnight, and he's still adjusting to his work schedule."

"And how about you? Are you adjusting to life aboard a cruise ship?"

"It gets a little easier each day."

"I was sorry to hear about your loss. It must have been very disheartening."

"You know about that?"

"I was in the security office when that detective stopped by with the news. He was sure dreading to have to tell you."

After a minute, he continued, "Have you made any plans about what you'll do next?"

"Dan has a couple of ideas. Nothing definite."

He picked up Rose's empty glass. "Looks like red wine. I'll be right back."

Rose watched as he pulled some keys from his pocket to unlock the bar gate. He returned with a drink for himself and a glass of red wine.

"Officer Malone. You needn't do that."

"Please call me Mike."

He sipped his drink. "Rose, you are a beautiful woman and have a beautiful voice. How would you like to sing with the band in the dining room for the rest of your trip? Maybe even longer."

"Me? That would be wonderful, something I've always wanted to do. But doesn't the band already have a singer?"

"Yes, but she's a last-minute fill-in. Remember, I told you our regular singer had an emergency appendectomy just before we sailed? The fill-in usually works in the gift shop. She's not a bad singer, but then she's not a good one either. After what I heard out here on the deck the other night, I know you're terrific. You'd have good pay, more time off, and better quarters. What do you say?"

"Better quarters? Would Dan and I be able to have a cabin together?"

"No, I'm afraid not."

"What about the salon? Beverly needs my help."

"Don't bother yourself about that. I'll work something out."

"But I don't have anything suitable to wear."

"We have a treasure trove of evening clothes available. You can have your pick."

Rose remembered the dress she had admired a few days ago in the large closet near the laundry.

"When do I start?"

"Would tomorrow be too soon? You can rehearse with the band in the morning and be ready in time for the first dinner sitting. They have a large selection of music, so I'm sure you'll find songs you're comfortable with."

"Oh, Offi . . . Mike, I'm so excited. I don't know how I can thank you."

"I'm sure you'll think of something." Tipping his chair forward, he embraced Rose, planting a sloppy kiss on her mouth.

Surprised and disgusted, Rose pushed herself up and out of her chair, causing Malone to fall forward and land in a heap with his chair stuck to his rear end.

She stood looking down at him for a second, thinking how quickly her good news had turned sour. "Thanks for nothing, you conniving bastard!"

Chapter Thirty-Five

Officer Malone's curses followed her as Rose ran across the deck and pushed through the swinging door. "You'll be sorry for this, you ungrateful bitch! You hear me? You'll pay for this!"

She hurried through the empty cafeteria, and rather than wait for the elevator, took the stairs down to the crew deck and her cabin. Alisha wasn't there. She looked up and down the passageway, hoping to see a light under any door. *My God, isn't there anyone down here? He knows which cabin is mine. What if he follows me?*

Hearing the clanking of heavy footsteps coming down the metal stairs, Rose slipped into the cabin across the passageway from hers, crawled into the lower bunk, and pulled the blanket over her head.

She heard the door to her cabin open across the way. A few minutes later, loud talking and laughter echoed down the hallway from crewmembers exiting the elevator.

Relieved, she left the bunk and began smoothing the rumpled bedding. The overhead light flashed on and Rose turned to see a surprised young woman standing in the doorway, and beyond the woman, officer Malone exiting her cabin.

The irate woman began jabbering in a foreign tongue. As she slipped past her, Rose pointed across the passageway and with gestures tried to make it appear that she had just been confused.

When she turned on the light to her own cabin, Rose saw that mattresses and bedding had been pulled from both bunks to the floor, and closet and drawer contents strewn about. *That sick son of a bitch!*

Rose replaced things as best she could. As she struggled to lift her mattress up to the top bunk, Alisha appeared at her side to help. "What has happened in here?"

They shoved the mattress into place, and then Rose collapsed to the floor in tears. Alisha got to her knees and hugged her while Rose poured out her story.

As Alisha helped Rose to her feet, she said, "I have heard other stories about this man."

"Well, he needs to be reported," sobbed Rose. "Who else has had a similar experience with him?"

"I know of several, but they will not talk. They are too afraid of losing their jobs."

"Did he rape them?"

Alisha lowered her head and nodded. A tear rolled down her cheek.

"My God, Alisha. Did he rape *you*?"

"Please do not say anything! I *need* this job. Others depend on me. Please promise me you won't tell anyone."

Rose smoothed a strand of Alisha's long hair from her face. "I can't promise that, sweetie. There's no telling how many women that sicko has molested. He's using his position to prey on women who can't afford to fight back. Well, he finally chose one whose mission it will be to see that he gets what he deserves."

"What will you do?"

"I don't know yet, but I won't let him get away with this."

• • •

Thinking about the day's events, Rose tossed and turned in her bunk. Her thoughts were less about what lay ahead for her and Dan, than what she should do about Officer Malone. Could she trust Nigel? Or even the captain? She certainly wasn't going to tell Dan about what happened, at least not until they were off the ship. He might do something stupid out of anger.

She was still awake when the ship's engines roared to life at midnight. *Thank God tomorrow's Sunday, and I can sleep in.*

• • •

A rap on the door awakened Rose. She rolled over and peered down at Alisha's empty bunk. The door to the head was closed and the shower was running. Rose climbed down the ladder and ran her fingers through her hair before opening the door a crack to see an unfamiliar woman standing outside holding something in her arms. "Yes?"

"Are you Rosemary Good?"

"Who's asking?"

"My name is Henrietta Dulaney and I'm your new supervisor."

Rose threw open the door. "Has something happened to Beverly?"

"No, nothing's happened to Beverly. You've been reassigned. You and Alisha will be trading jobs. Is she here?"

Rose was speechless. Finally, she stammered, "Yes . . . she's in the shower. But I don't understand. *Why* are we trading jobs? It doesn't make sense."

"Missy, management doesn't have to make sense. We just need to do what we're told."

She stepped into the cabin and shoved the bundle she was carrying into Rose's arms. "Hurry up and get your uniform on. We have work to do."

Steam poured into the room as Alisha exited the shower wrapped in a towel. "Mrs. Dulaney! What are *you* doing here? Am I in trouble?"

Rose took the opportunity to slip into the head and use the toilet. *That Bastard is being true to his word. He said I'd pay. He's assigned me the most slavish job on the ship.*

When Rose emerged from the head, Alisha was crying. "I'm so sorry, Rose."

"Don't worry about it, Alisha. I only have a few more days onboard and this is your opportunity for a step up. Look, it's Sunday and you have the whole day off. Maybe you and Saud can get together."

Mrs. Dulaney looked askance at Alisha. "Saud? When have you had time to meet anyone?"

"You'll like Beverly, Alisha," Rose interrupted as she slipped into her new uniform, which was several sizes too big.

Mrs. Dulaney studied Rose. "From what Malone said, I thought you'd be a good-sized woman."

"How's that?" asked Rose.

"He said you was real full of yourself. But I can see he don't know beans. You can pick up some uniforms more your size during lunch break."

Rose cinched up the waist of the uniform as much as possible, pulled her hair back into a ponytail, and then leaned into the mirror to apply lipstick.

"You can forget about lookin' good where you're goin' gal. Come on. We've just got time for a little breakfast and then I've got to get you trained."

For Alisha's sake, Rose thought it best not to tell Mrs. Dulaney that training would not be necessary.

• • •

For the rest of the cruise, Rose worked twelve-hour days, and harder than she had ever worked in her life. She was lucky if she got to see Dan more than a few minutes every other day. He was perplexed about her job change and promised that he would speak to Officer Malone about it at the next opportunity, an opportunity that never came, since Malone purposely avoided both him and Rose.

On the first day of her new job cleaning heads, Rose was near the infirmary and stopped by to see how Larry was doing. She learned that due to his critical condition, he had been removed from the ship in Granada and flown by heliocoptor to the Jackson Memorial Hospital in Miami, where, although he was still comatose, he was put under guard. Rose suspected that not having trip insurance was a major factor in his hasty removal from the ship's infirmary.

The one advantage in her new job was that Rose's duties took her to areas of the ship that, as a crewmember, she would not be able to go otherwise. On her rounds one evening, she passed the room housing computers for the use of guests and found it empty. She slipped into the room, took a seat, and googled *Legal jurisdiction aboard a cruise ship*. She quickly learned that, especially in the case of a sexual predator, protection by the law on the high seas was almost nonexistent, especially if the ship was registered in a country other than the victim's. Rose then googled *Ocean Lady cruise ship*, and learned that the ship was registered in the U.S. and based in Miami. She wrote down the ship line's address and the name of its CEO and slipped the note into her pocket.

Chapter Thirty-Six

Passengers had departed the ship earlier in the day while the cleaning crews prepared it for Sunday's new batch of arrivals. Looking forward to finally leaving the ship tomorrow, Rose completed her last duty and took the service elevator down to the crew deck. She was surprised to see Nigel standing on the opposite side of the elevator door when it opened.

"Good evening, Mrs. Good. I've been waiting for you. Shall we have a seat in the cafeteria while I explain these papers to you?"

Rose wearily sat down and pushed her shoes off under the table. Nigel took a seat across from her. "You look tired, Mrs. Good. This will only take a minute." He laid some papers out before her and explained that since she and Dan had no passports, the papers were needed for them to reenter the United States. "You're lucky they were processed so quickly. Otherwise, you would have had to stay aboard for another cruise. Of course, you more than likely would have been paid this time. I'm sure the captain would consider that you and your husband had already worked off *this* voyage."

Rose picked up the papers. "Well, I certainly feel we have *more* than paid for our passage. I will be very thankful to leave this ship and all its heads behind."

"Ah, yes, it's a pity things didn't work out for you in the beauty salon."

"For your information, Nigel, things were working beautifully for me in the salon."

"Whatever you say, Mrs. Good. It was not your fault that you were put in a position where you had no previous training." Nigel stood to leave. "If I don't see you two again, say goodbye to your husband for me. I am so sorry about your loss and wish you both the best of luck."

"Thank you, Nigel. I haven't seen my husband in two days. Do you know where he is at the moment?"

"Why yes, he's at work. His final shift will be over around midnight. I imagine you two will meet up in the crew cafeteria in the morning before you depart. You can have one last meal on us."

On us? How generous. Dan and I have more than earned our keep!

• • •

After showering the next morning, Rose dressed in the clothes she wore when she had boarded the ship two weeks earlier. She stuffed the rest of her meager belongings into her large shoulder bag and then headed for the door. She took one last look at the cabin before pulling the door shut. *I am so not going to miss this place!*

Rose spotted Dan standing in the long line in the cafeteria, craning his neck looking for her. He grinned when he spotted her and called, "Go find us a table and I'll bring you your breakfast."

She was lucky to find an empty table in the noisy, crowded room. Dan soon joined her, carrying a tray heaping with breakfast burritos, pastires, sausages, freshly baked bread, and several kinds of fruit, plus coffee and juice. He sat down next to her and planted a big kiss on her cheek. "I've missed you, hon."

Rose grasped his hand and squeezed. "I've missed you, too. I never want to be without you again."

"Well, now, that's music to my ears."

Rose picked up a napkin off the tray. "Dan, why so much food? We can never eat all this."

"We don't have to eat it all now. You notice most of it is fruit and bread items, stuff that won't spoil quickly. I brought extra napkins, too, to wrap it in."

Rose picked up an apple and pear and wrapped them for her bag. "I don't feel one bit guilty about taking some with us, either," said Rose. "We put in a lot of work on this ship, and this is little enough to show for it."

Later, as they were leaving the cafeteria, Rose spotted Alisha and Saud at a far corner table. She tugged on Dan's arm. "There's my roommate and her new boyfriend. Let's go back so I can introduce you."

"Why don't you go on, Rose. I'm not in the mood to small talk with people I don't know and will never see again. I just want to get off this damned ship."

She handed him her heavy bag. "Okay. Wait for me by the elevator. I won't be long." Rose maneuvered her way through the crowded tables to them. "Hello, Alisha and Saud, I'm so glad I have the chance to say goodbye."

Alisha jumped up and hugged Rose. "Me too. You were already asleep when I came in last night, and were still sleeping when I left this morning. I was afraid I might not see you before you had to leave." Saud stood and pulled out a chair. "Please have a seat."

"I'm sorry, I can't stay. My husband's waiting for me."

"Before you leave, I must tell you something," said Alisha. She looked questionally at Saud. He smiled and nodded. "Saud and I are to be married."

Rose felt tears welling up. "Oh . . . I'm so happy for you both. When?"

"Soon," said Alisha. "Our parents promised us both to others when we were just children. We hate to go against their wishes, but we see how the rest of the world lives. We can be our own selves and follow our own hearts. And we have pledged our hearts to one another forever."

Rose took Alisha's hand and then reached for Saud's. "I hardly know what to say. I just know that when life offers you a chance at happiness, you are foolish not to take it."

"We owe our happiness to you," said Alisha. "If you had not taken my place at work that day, Saud and I might never have met."

Rose squeezed their hands. "Bless you both," she said before turning to leave.

With her eyes full of tears, Rose bumped into several tables as she made her way back through the crowded cafeteria. In the passageway, she found Dan impatiently pacing near the elevator.

"For cripes sake, what took you so . . . what the hell's wrong, Rose? Why are you crying?"

She reached into her bag and pulled out a tissue. She dabbed at her eyes and blew her nose. "I'll tell you later."

Rose and Dan joined the throng of staff and crew members exiting the ship for their day ashore, and then got in one of several lines going through customs, where their entry papers were processed. Dan was still carrying Rose's bag when they reached a second customs agent, a rather stern looking older man who instructed Dan to lay the bag on the counter to be searched. The agent immediately pulled oranges, apples, pears and bananas from the bag and, shaking his head, laid them on a counter behind him.

"Hey, what are you doing with that fruit?" asked Dan.

"Fresh fruits and vegetables are not allowed to enter," snapped the agent. He then removed bread and several pastries wrapped in paper napkins and laid them next to the bag. "You may keep the baked goods, however." The agent proceeded to pull a handful of Rose's underwear out of the bag. With his other hand, he pulled his glasses down his nose so that the glower he projected at Dan would have full effect.

"Those things aren't mine," said Dan.

"Oh?" said the agent. "Then what are they doing in your bag?"

"That happens to be *my* bag," said Rose, "And I'll thank you not to wave my panties around for everyone to see!"

The agent laid the underwear on the counter. "Oh. You two are together?" He shuffled through the rest of the bag's contents, replaced the clothing and pastries, and then closed the bag and shoved it across the counter to Rose. Looking at Dan he asked, "Where is the rest of your and your wife's luggage?"

"That's it," said Dan. "There is no more."

"Are you telling me the two of you went on a two-week cruise with no more than what the lady has in this one bag?"

"We lost the rest of it in a poker game with the ship's captain last night," said Dan. "Are we free to go now?"

The agent waved his hand in disgust. "Go!"

As they later made their way through the crowd toward the street, Dan stopped to fish through his pockets. He pulled out a few bills and counted them. "You got any money, Rose? I don't think I have enough for cab fare."

"I have a little saved up from tips. Hand me my bag."

"Rose! Dan!" came a shrill cry.

A taxi had just pulled into the street from the curb, and Margaret waved frantically out of the back window. "Over here!"

As Dan and Rose approached the taxi, Margaret yelled, "Get in!" and then proceeded to plop her large body toward her husband in order to make room in the backseat for Rose. The driver leaned across the front seat to open the passenger door for Dan. The honking from the line of taxis gathering behind theirs made conversation impossible until they had moved on a ways.

"Oh, I'm so glad I spotted you two," Margaret finally gushed. "We thought we might never see you again and we've been dying to hear if you found Larry. Right, Joe?"

Rose leaned forward to peer around Margaret, and extend her hand to the small man who appeared to be painfully smashed into the corner of the backseat. "Hello, Joe. Nice to see you again."

The plexiglass separating the front and back seat prevented Dan from offering his hand to the pair, but he waved, and his voice came over the speaker. "Hello again, folks."

"How did you two happen to be here?" asked Rose. "All the passengers were supposed to have left the ship yesterday."

"When I was packing at the hotel this morning, I discovered I had forgotten to retrieve my jewelry from the ship's purser," Margaret answered. "It was in the ship's safe. I'm so glad I discovered it before the ship set sail again."

Joe tapped on the plexiglass. "Our hotel is just a few blocks away and our flight doesn't leave until midafternoon. Can you come in and spend some time with us so we can catch up?"

"Better not," said Dan. "We've got to pick up our vehicle, and then we have some business to take care of."

"Well, then," said Margaret, "at least let us take you to your RV. Where did you leave it?"

"That would be great," said Dan. "The Miami Police Department is fairly close and shouldn't be too much out of your way."

"Police headquarters?" Margaret asked.

"Which is it?" yelled the driver.

"Police headquarters," yelled Joe, who then was suddenly smashed even more as the driver made a U-turn.

During the short trip to the police station, Dan and Rose filled the couple in on what had happened to Larry and Mitzy and the loss of their fortune. By the time the taxi stopped in front of the station, Margaret was blubbering. "Oh, you poor dears. What *are* you going to do?"

Rose hugged Margaret's arm. "Don't worry, we'll be fine."

I wish I could believe that, thought Rose.

"Why don't you come on back home to Salina, where you have friends who can help. You can stay with us till you get back on your feet. Right, Joe?"

Dan saved Joe's having to answer by opening the car door for Rose. As she slid out, she said, "It is so sweet of you to offer. If Larry lives, we'll probably have to go back for the trial. We'll see you then. Have a safe trip home, and thanks for the lift."

Dan and Rose stood on the sidewalk and waved until the taxi was out of sight. "That was a bit of luck," said Dan. "We were saved the cab fare."

When they entered the police station, Officer Dee Dean was at the front desk talking on the phone. She smiled when she saw them, and hurridly finished the phone conversation. "Well, if it's not the famous stowaways." She pulled a couple of newspapers out of a drawer and laid them on the desk. "I saved these for you."

Rose picked up the paper with Dan looking over her shoulder. "Oh, my heavens! We're on the front page of the *Miami Herald*. Ocean Lady Stowaways Caught."

"Where did they get our pictures?" asked Dan. "And how did they get a story on us?"

"Remember, because you didn't have passports, you had to be photographed when you first boarded the ship. We tried to find out how the newspaper got the information for this article and the one a few days ago . . . "

"There's another article?" asked Rose.

Dee handed her the second paper. "This one is about Mr. Near's near-fatal poisoning and that woman's disappearance."

"WHAT?" exclaimed Dan and Rose simultaneously. "He was *poisoned*?"

"Why, yes," answered Dee. "You didn't know?"

"No," answered Rose. "All we knew was that the same day he was found, he was flown to a hospital here in Miami. Is he still alive?"

Chapter Thirty-Seven

"Yes, he's still alive, but barely," answered Dee. "An officer from this precinct took him into custody at the airport and delivered him to the hospital. He's been under guard ever since."

"Has he regained consciousness yet?" asked Rose.

"He's been mumbling a lot, so he's still pretty much out of it."

"What happens to the bastard now?" asked Dan.

"He's being extradited back to Kansas. An extradition agent is coming in here tomorrow from Salina, Kansas to pick up the papers."

"So soon?" asked Rose. "Is he in any condition to travel?"

"He'd better be. The state's in a hurry to get rid of him," answered Dee. "Florida hospitals are going broke having to care for him and all the other indigents, mostly illegal aliens. Kansas has chartered a small plane for his transport and a nurse will accompany him, so he should be okay."

"Do you suppose we could see him?" asked Rose.

"See him?" bellowed Dan. "Why in the hell should we *see* him?"

"I just think we should," said Rose. "He doesn't have anyone now."

"And who the hell's to blame for that?"

"I'll be the one taking the agent to the hospital," said Dee. "If the captain says it's okay, you can accompany us."

Dan picked up the newspaper and read the first few paragraphs of the article. "It tells here about Mitzy being the alledged suspect in the poisoning, and about how the small plane she was on went down in a South American jungle. The Brazilian government sent out a search plane, but called the search off after a few days. No ground search is anticipated."

Dan read on, and then gave the paper an angry snap. "It even tells about our losing our life's savings, Rose! How the hell did they know about that?"

"The paper wouldn't divulge its sources," answered Dee. "Some member of the ship's staff must be a freelancing news reporter."

"Well, it burns me up that our business is spread all over the place like this," said Dan.

"It shouldn't," said Dee. "When you read the articles in depth, you'll see that you are put in a very sympathetic light."

Dan tossed the newspaper back on the desk. "Well I don't want sympathy! I'll bet the tongues have been wagging back in Salina."

"Speaking of the ship's staff," said Rose, "I need to file charges against one of them. How do I do that?"

"Oh? What kind of charges, and against whom?"

"The chief officer, Michael Malone."

"Because he had you cleaning heads?" asked Dan. "I doubt if . . . "

"Because he made a pass at me and raped my roommate," interrupted Rose. "And according to her, she wasn't the only one."

"WHAT?" yelled Dan. "When did this happen? Why didn't you tell me?"

Dee picked up a legal pad and pen. "Those are pretty serious charges. Let's go into the conference room. I want all the details."

Dan fidgeted and fumed while Dee took down Rose's story. At its conclusion, he asked through gritted teeth, "So what's going to be done with that son of a bitch?"

"It's a good thing the ship is sailing under the U.S. flag," answered Dee. "Otherwise, we wouldn't have jurisdiction. The first thing we'll do is notify the cruise line that charges have been filed against Malone. They may suspend him until further investigation."

"Well, let's hope they do," said Rose, "and as soon as possible."

Seemingly out of nowhere, a large black longhaired cat jumped into Rose's lap.

"Castro! Shame on you," scolded Dee. She got out of her chair to retrieve the cat.

"Oh, he's fine. I like cats. Can he stay?"

Dee smiled and sat back down. "If you don't mind, it's fine with me. He doesn't usually take to strangers like that."

Rose stroked the purring cat's head as the conversation continued. "If there's a trial, will I have to be here for it? We don't really know where we're going to be."

"Stay in touch. I'm pretty sure you'll have to give a deposition. I think I have all we need for right now. The captain will turn your statement over to a detective tomorrow, and he or she will get right on the case."

"But the ship sails at midnight tonight," said Dan.

"That *is* an impediment to the investigation," said Dee. "But at least the ship's captain and security officer will be notified of the charges, so they can keep an eye on Officer Malone.

Dee got up from her chair. "Any other questions?"

Dan reached down for the cat so that Rose could get up. "Yeah," he said, "Who belongs to the cat?"

Dee laughed. "He's the station mascot. A sweet little old man, Mr. Hayworth, used to live just around the corner and would stop in nearly every day when he and his cat went for a walk. Poor Mr. Hayworth had a stroke a year or so ago and had to go into a nursing home. Since everyone around here was pretty attached to the old man *and* the cat, he begged us to take in Castro. He's been pretty happy here, and we enjoy having him around."

"Is the old man Cuban?" asked Dan. "Is that why he named the cat Castro?"

Dee laughed again. "That's another story. The old man just called him Cat. The captain said the only way we could keep him was if we had him castrated. So after we did, some of the guys said he needed a fitting name and started calling him Castro."

As Dan was stroking the cat's neck, it let out a yeowl and squirmed, wanting to be let loose. "Whoa, big fellow." Dan sat back down to examine the unhappy feline. "Well, no wonder he yelled at me. He's got a big abscess on his neck."

"Really?" said Dee. She leaned down and lightly felt through the thick fur. "Oh, my. That's a pretty big lump. He's been off his feed the last few days, and seemed out of sorts. I guess this explains it. Looks like we'll have to take up a another collection for a vet bill."

"I can take care of this," said Dan. "It's a pretty simple procedure."

"Thanks, Dr. Good," said Dee. "But we'll have a veterinarian look after it."

"But I *am* a veterinarian."

"Oh?" said Dee. "I didn't realize. I thought you were a medical doctor. But where and how would you do the procedure?"

"Isn't our van in the impound yard out back?"

"Yes, but you won't have access to it until tomorrow. The yard is closed on Sunday and you'll have to get checked out and pay the storage fee."

"My medical supplies are in a bag in the van. Can I at least go get it?"

"No. The public isn't allowed out there. Maybe I can get it. What does your van look like?"

"It's blue, has Kansas license plates, and looks like it belongs in a junk yard. The black leather bag is on the floor behind the driver's seat."

"Why don't you two go on in the lounge and help yourselves to coffee. I'll have Officer Price cover for me while I go see what I can do. In the meantime, keep Castro in your sights. He's hard to find when he doesn't want to be found."

Castro followed them into the lounge. "Sit down, Rose," said Dan. "Maybe he'll jump up in your lap again. I'll get your coffee."

Rose sat down and patted her knee. "Come on, Castro, here's a nice warm lap for you." The cat took Rose up on her invitation and was soon curled up and napping peacefully.

Rose thoughtfully sipped her coffee. "Dan, how are we going to pay a two-week storage bill for our van? It's likely to cost several hundred dollars."

"Yeah, it'll probably max out our credit card. It will take time, but I'll find work to pay it off eventually. I just hate to have to pay the exorbitant interest. But right now, I'm worrying about where we're going to spend the night if they won't let us get to our van. I'd hate to have to add the cost of a hotel room to our debt."

Within a short time, Dee was back with Dan's medical bag. "Finding your van was easier than I thought it would be. Your description was right on. What kind of accident did you have in that thing?"

"No accident. That vehicle just represents a series of unfortunate events," said Dan.

Dee placed the bag on the table. "Well, here it is. Now what?"

"Get something we can put over this table top," said Dan. "I can operate right here."

"Right here?" asked Dee. "Some of the guys will be coming in here in an hour or so to eat their lunches. I don't think they'd like that idea."

"This will only take a few minutes, and I'll disinfect the table afterward. Would you rather I do it over there on the counter?"

"No, no. That's even worse." Dee opened a drawer and pulled out several dishtowels. "Will these do?"

"Perfect," said Dan. "Hand me a paper cup and that roll of paper towels."

Dan spread the dishtowels over the tabletop and laid out a razor, swabs, antiseptic, and a container of surgical instruments. He then soaked a paper towel in chloroform. "Turn your head, Rose, and try not to breathe any of these fumes." He held the towel next to the cat's nose. Castro's head jerked up, but then fell right back into Rose's lap. When Dan was sure the cat was fully anesthetized, he laid it on the table and shaved and washed the area around the abcess. He then washed his hands in the nearby sink. As he slipped on rubber gloves, he said, "This gets a little messy. You girls don't have to stay."

Both women leaned over the table to watch Dan as he deftly lanced the abcess and then drained its contents into the paper cup. While he was suturing the wound, he instructed Dee on how to take the stitches out in a few days. "All you need is a real small pair of scissors and some tweezers."

"I think I can handle that," said Dee. "Thanks so much for helping our kitty, Dr. Good."

After applying antibiotic ointment and a gauze bandage, Dan asked, "Now where shall we put the patient until he comes to?"

Back at the front desk, Dee fluffed up some paper towels in the bottom drawer, and Rose gently lowered Castro into it.

"So where are you headed from here?" asked Dee.

"I have no idea," answered Rose. "Until we can get our van back, we won't be going anywhere."

"I meant today. Like right now."

"Why, I don't know. We haven't planned that far ahead."

"Well, just go hang out in the break room. Sundays are slow, so there shouldn't be much traffic in there. You'll find some magazines and newspapers to occupy your time. I get off at three. I'd be glad to take you wherever you want to go."

For lunch, Dan and Rose helped themselves to an open jar of Cheese Whiz they found on the counter in the break room and made sandwiches from the bread they had brought from the ship. While they were eating, a couple of young officers appeared and withdrew sack lunches from the refrigerator at the other end of the room.

As they approached the table, one said, "Well, I'll be, if it isn't our heroine, Rosemary Good. Beat up any bad guys lately?" he laughed. "Has she been taking good care of you, Dan?"

The banter continued as the men ate their lunch, and Dan soon had had enough of the rehashing of events that had distinguished Rose to the local lawmen. He pushed himself back from the table. "I need some fresh air. Care to join me for a walk, Rose?"

After just one lap around the block, they returned to the break room, perspiring from the heat and humidity. The room was empty, so Dan stretched out on the couch for a nap while Rose worked the *Miami Herald's* crossword puzzle.

At precisely three o'clock, Dee entered the break room. "I've been thinking," she said. "My place is small, but I have a nice guest room that hardly ever gets used. Why don't you two just come home with me for the night?"

"Oh, we couldn't impose on you like that," said Rose.

Dan sat up and rubbed his eyes. "Why couldn't we?" he asked.

"Well, I do have an ulterior motive," said Dee, "so it will certainly not be an imposition. I have a couple of Pomeranians and the older one has almost stopped eating. If it's all right with you, Dan, I thought you could take a look at her."

"Be glad to."

Before they left, Dan instructed the new officer on duty on how to care for the recovering Castro.

Chapter Thirty-Eight

"Rise and shine, you two!" Dee yelled through the bedroom door. "Breakfast in forty minutes."

Showered and dressed, Rose and Dan sat down for breakfast at the table in Dee's small kitchen. "This looks scrumptious, Dee," said Rose. "Those biscuits look homemade. You shouldn't have gone to so much trouble."

Dee poured coffee for everyone. "Biscuits are my speciality, but I usually don't make them just for myself. So they're a treat for me, too."

Dee's Pomeranians were outside on the patio, their noses pressed against the sliding glass door.

Looking over at them, Dan asked, "So how's our patient this morning?"

"She's in a better mood than I've seen for days. Who would have ever guessed she had a bad tooth. No wonder she wouldn't eat."

"Just keep her on that canned dog food thinned with milk until her gum heals completely," said Dan.

• • •

They arrived at the police station at six o'clock. The extradition agent wasn't due to arrive until after nine.

"Do we have time to do whatever needs to be done about the van?" Dan asked.

"Certainly," answered Dee. "Come with me and I'll introduce you to Officer Salazar. He's in charge of the impounds."

While Dan went with Dee, Rose went to the break room, poured herself a cup of coffee and sat down at the table to read the morning paper, starting with the Help Wanted ads. After about an hour, Dan returned and sat down across from her with a big smile on his face. "Guess what. We didn't have to pay storage fees on the van."

"Really? How's that?"

"Because of you, and your heroics, Rose, the captain waived the $490 fee. He won't be in until ten o'clock, but I want to make it a point to thank him."

"That's wonderful!" said Rose.

"Here's some more good news. When the newspaper printed that story about us losing all our money, the department here took up a collection and paid the $110 towing fee."

"And here you thought they were just a bunch of jokers because they gave you a little ribbing."

"Ah, yeah, well, at least I fixed their damned cat for them. Speaking of which, have you seen him? Dee's been looking for him."

"He's snoring away, right here in my lap."

"Good. I want to change his bandage and apply some more ointment."

Rose continued going through the want ads while Dan took care of the cat, until one particular ad caught her attention. "Dan! How would you like to live in Orlando? Seaworld is advertising for a veteranarian."

"Treating dolphins and whales? That's a far cry from treating land animals. It would certainly be a challenge. What kind of salary are they offering?"

"The ad doesn't say. In our situation, how can we be choosy? I might even be able to get some kind of a job there. I bet it would be a fun place to work."

Dee appeared at the doorway. "I see you found Castro. How is he?"

"He's looking good," said Dan as he lowered the cat to the floor. The ungrateful animal trotted off toward the door in a huff, his tail flicking angrily. Dee reached down to pet him, but he darted away.

Rose laughed. "He evidently didn't appreciate having his nap interrupted."

"Well, I don't have time for him right now anyway," said Dee. "The extradition agent from Kansas is here. Let's get going."

Rose quickly folded the classifed section of the paper and stuck it in her purse.

Dee introduced the Goods to the agent Fred Conally as they walked through the station parking lot to a police car. He was a tall, bespecktacled man in his late fifties.

"Glad to meet you," Dan said as he stopped to offer his hand.

"You don't remember me, do you, Dr. Good?"

"You do seem rather familiar," said Dan.

"Remember the English Bulldog you operated on in your clinic about three years ago? The one that had been hit by a car? You had to amputate part of his left foreleg."

Dan thought for a minute. "Was the dog's name Ralph?"

"Yeah, that's him. I thought for sure he was a goner, but you pulled him through. I got him a prothsetic foot and he gets around pretty good. He doesn't do well burying bones, however."

When Rose and Dee reached the police car, Dee unlocked and opened the back door for Rose. "Over here, boys," she called to the two men who still stood in the middle of the parking lot talking. Dee then got into the driver's seat and turned on the engine.

Fred hung his arm over the front seat and talked to Dan and Rose all the way to the hospital. "You folks are famous back in home in Salina. You've been front-page news ever since you left town. Why, there was even a crowd at the airport to see me off this morning. Someone yelled, 'Bring the bastard back so we can string him up.' That prompted the Salina police chief to have a security team waiting for us when we land, and a motorcade to escort us from the airport to the hospital."

"Do you know Larry personally, Mr. Conally?" Rose asked.

"Not him, but I've had a few run-ins with his wife."

"You mean Charlotte?"

"Yeah, Charlotte Near. I hear they finally suspended her driver's license for driving under the influence. They ought to make the suspension permanent. I gave her at least three traffic tickets myself. My partner and I had to haul her in a couple of times and arrest her for public drunkenness, once at some bar, and another time at the Southgate Shopping Mall. And we weren't the only ones on the force that had dealings with her. She's a good-looking gal, but I'm afraid her beauty is only skin deep. Besides being a drunk, she's got a real mean streak."

"So you were on the force," said Dan.

"Yep. Thirty-six years. I started this extradition business when I retired, and have another couple of ex-cops working for me. It helps feed my golf habit, and I get to travel and meet interesting people, like you folks."

Dee pulled into a reserved parking spot near the hospital entrance. "We're here."

Inside, Dee said to Mr. Conally, "I'm going to escort the Goods to Mr. Near's room while you take care of the discharge papers. He's in room 417, in the east wing on the 4th floor."

Dee then led Dan and Rose through security.

As they silently rode up in the elevator, Rose wished she had never suggested seeing Larry. *If he's conscious, what am I going to say to him? Is Dan going to behave himself?*

An officer rose from the chair parked outside Larry's room. "Mornin,' Dee."

"Good morning, Ross. I'll bet you're glad to see the end of this duty. It must be boring."

"Not bad," he answered. "Nurse-watching can actually be pretty interesting."

Dee motioned to Dan and Rose, standing behind her. "This is Dr. and Mrs. Good and we're . . . "

"The Goods. I remember you folks. We met at the station a couple of weeks ago. Glad to see you again. But I must say I'm a bit surprised to see you *here*. Are you going to visit the prisoner?"

"Yes, they are," answered Dee. "How is he this morning?"

"The night shift said he came to yesterday evening and seemed fairly lucid. The doctor checked in on him a few minutes ago, and from what I could hear, he answered all the doctor's questions okay. Go on in. He's probably still awake."

"I'll have to accompany you," said Dee to Rose and Dan. "But I'll try to not be intrusive."

Larry's bed was raised so that he was in an almost sitting position. His head was rolled to one side, facing Rose, and his eyes were closed. She was shocked at the sight of him. The dark circles around his sunken eyes were in sharp contrast to his sagging, ashen-gray skin. A few wispy strands were all that was left of his once-thick crop of hair.

How could his appearance have changed so much in just a few days, wondered Rose.

They stood silently for a few minutes, Rose and Dan on one side of the bed, Dee on the other. Dee finally leaned toward Larry and softly said, "Mr. Near, are you awake? You have visitors."

Larry's eyes popped open and locked onto Rose. In them, Rose saw confusion slowly turn to recognition and then despair.

His hand made a feeble attempt toward her, but fell back upon the bed. "Rose," he rasped.

"Hello, Larry."

Larry's eyes then turned to Dan and he seemed surprised to see him there. He quickly turned away and put his shaking hands to his face. "Why are you here?"

"I don't rightly know," said Dan. "I don't think it was to wish you well."

Suddenly aware of Dee's presence, Larry turned toward her. "Mitzy? Oh . . . you're not Mitzy. Where is she?"

"Do you know why you're here?" asked Dee.

"Bad champagne. Mitzy drank some too. Oh, my God. Is she okay? Where is she?"

Beseechingly, Dee looked over at Rose and Dan.

"No one knows exactly *where* she is," said Rose.

Larry's head swiveled back toward her. "What do you mean?"

"You didn't drink bad champagne, you stupid bastard." said Dan. "Your redheaded floozy poisoned you. She meant to kill you."

The shock snapped Larry's head back into his pillows. His tear-filled eyes found Dan's.

"That hurts, doesn't it, fella?" asked Dan. "I know first hand *how much* it hurts. I had complete trust in you and loved you like a brother. You taught me what betrayal from someone you love and respect does to a person. It rips out your heart and puts a blight on your very soul."

Larry's hands covered his face and his entire body shook. "Can you ever forgive me?" he sobbed.

"I've thought about that a lot these last few weeks. What you did was not some spur of the moment vendetta brought on by something wrongful Rose or I did. How many days and weeks did you spend planning, and then carrying out your deceit, anyway?"

"It was Mitzy," sobbed Larry. "It was all her idea."

"Why, you sniveling coward. Fess up! She couldn't have done any of it without you. You haven't ruined just one life, you've ruined five, including your own. You ask forgiveness? Not from me, buddy. Not from me."

Rose grabbed Dan's arm, which was tense with rage. "That's enough, Dan, Let's go. Larry's suffering enough."

"Yeah, let's get the hell out of here," he answered.

At the door, Dan stopped and looked back at Larry. "The law's coming for you in a few minutes to take you home. Have a nice trip . . . to hell."

Back in the hallway, Rose leaned against the wall and sobbed. Dee put her arms around her and looked up at Dan. "You were awfully rough on a man in his condition."

"Actually, I thought I showed great restraint," said Dan. "I'm sorry I upset *you*, though, Rose."

A smiling Fred Conally strode up, followed by a male nurse pushing a guerney. He dropped the smile when he saw Rose's wet red eyes. "I assume the visit is over?"

"Yes," answered Dee. "We're leaving. This is Officer Ross Wiggins. He will take you, Larry, and the nurse to the airport."

• • •

They said their goodbyes and were soon heading north in their van on Highway 95. Rose rummaged around in the glove compartment until she found their cell phone. "I should have had this with me all along. The boys will be worried about not hearing from us. I just hope they haven't heard about our financial predicament."

"I don't know if you could have used it onboard the ship anyway," said Dan.

The phone battery was dead, so Rose plugged its cord into the van's lighter and tried calling. She had to leave a message on each phone. "Hi, sweetie, sorry we haven't called. We've been on a two-week Caribbean cruise and are on our way to Orlando. Give us a ring when you can."

"Uh oh," said Dan, "That little picture just came on the dashboard that means we need gas."

• • •

While Dan was at the gas pump, the cell phone rang and Rose picked it up. "Brad? Chess? That was quick."

"No, it's me, Monica."

"*Monica?* Why are you calling? Is Clyde all right?"

"Yes. He's fine. Where the hell have you two been? I've been trying to reach you for days."

"Judge Weaver knew how to contact us. Why didn't you ask him? And what do you want with us, anyway?"

"The judge is in South Africa and I haven't been able to reach him either. Something about downed lines. May I speak to Dan? I have a very important proposition for him."

I'll bet you do! thought Rose. "I doubt he'd be interested in any proposition from you, Monica, nor am I. Besides, Dan isn't available. He just went in the station to use the restroom."

"Well, then I'll tell *you.* I want Dan to take over the Ark and the foundation."

"*What?* Why?"

The judge and I are getting married and moving to South Africa. I can't leave until I find someone to take the reins here, and I can't think of a better man for the job than Dan."

"You and Judge Weaver are getting married? I can't believe it! And why South Africa?"

387

"I can hardly believe it myself. Vince's uncle owned a private game preserve and four-star lodge in the Karoo Heartlands. Vince loved to visit there and offered to take me several times, but I could never get away. Anyway, his uncle was a bachelor and Vince, his only living relative. He died about ten days ago and left everything to Vince. He's there now."

"This really surprises me, Monica, especially after the way you tried to snare Dan such a short time ago."

"Yes, I understand how it appears. I guess I'll always love Dan, but the time you two spent here pointed out to me how hopelessly pathetic my expectations have been. Vince and I have been good friends, and sometimes lovers, for years. When he told me he was moving halfway around the world, I was beside myself. I guess that's when I realized how much he means to me. He's always been there for me, and I just couldn't imagine life without him. So when I asked him to take me with him, he agreed. Because of the game preserve, I think my credentials with animals might have had some influence, but I don't really care. Neither of us wants to grow old alone, and I think we can have a good marriage."

"Judge Weaver seems like a very nice man. Quite handsome, too. And being friends is the best way to start a marriage. I'm happy for you, Monica, I really am."

"Then you'll let Dan take over the Ark?

"Monica, I don't make Dan's decisions for him. Here he comes now. You can ask him."

When Dan climbed into the driver's seat, Rose tried to hand him the phone, but he brushed it aside, saying, "I'm blocking the pump and there are people waiting."

While Dan drove looking for a parking place, Rose continued the conversation."He'll be with you . . . "

"I heard," said Monica. "I almost forgot to ask. Did you find Larry?"

"Don't you read the papers? Or watch TV?"

"I don't have time for such things."

"Yes, Larry's been found."

"He has? Did you get your money back?"

"It's a long, sad story, Monica, that I'll save for another time, but to answer your question, no, we didn't get it back, and we never will."

Dan turned off the ignition and reached for the phone. "This is Monica?"

During Dan and Monica's lengthy conversation, Rose's mind was awhirl. *I wouldn't mind living in that beautiful place as long as Monica is completely out of the picture. And it would be fun to help run it. I wouldn't even have to cook and clean. I enjoy teenagers and wouldn't mind being housemother to them. Plus, I think I'd be a good counselor and could help them stay on the right track. We should at least go back and check it all out. But what if it's just a ploy by Monica to get Dan back? If that's the case . . .*

Holding his hand over the phone's mouthpiece, Dan broke into Rose's thoughts. "What about it Rose? The Ark technically belongs to the foundation, but Monica says we'd have complete control over everything, just like we owned it. We'd have a small salary, and if we want, we can stay at the Ark the rest of our lives. The only condition in all of this is that we become Clyde's guardians and help him fulfill his dream of becoming a veterinarian. What do you say?"

"I'm not sure. What if . . . "

"Rose, we have to face facts. We have nothing, and nowhere to go. *Please.*"

"But what about the veterinarian job at Seaworld?"

"Rose, that's speculative. What Monica's offering is a sure thing, the best opportunity we're ever going to see. We have nothing to lose by accepting it."

Nothing to lose but maybe my husband. But I guess there's only one way to find out if her offer's for real.

Rose sighed. "Okay. We'll give it a try."

Dan reached over and gave Rose a big kiss before he returned to the phone.

"Monica? We can be there by day after tomorrow. Is that too soon? Great! See you then."

About the Author

Thousands of miles of travel in a converted van, sometimes with a trailerable sailboat in tow, and the numer-
ous characters and adventures met along the way, plus
the hardships faced by many during tough economic times,
provided the author inspiration for this book. S.C. Strange
is also an award-winning children's book author/illustrator,
under her married name, Sue C. Hughey. Her career encom-
passed both graphic arts and copywriting, and retirement
has allowed her to pursue her lifelong dream to write fiction.

Sue C. (Strange) Hughey was born in Oklahoma and
reared in Kansas. She was a Liberal Arts major at Wichita
University, where her father was an art professor. Her mother
was a poet and elementary school teacher in Wichita, where
Sue worked in the art departments at Boeing Aircraft and
two printing companies. After moving to Colorado with
her husband Harold (aka Hager) and two young sons, Sue
did freelance work for Denver-area art studios. She later
opened her own graphic arts studio, which evolved into a

mapping business, drafting maps for various U.S. Governmental agencies. During this time, Sue contracted with EPA to write and illustrate a booklet about the environment, which was distributed to millions of school children in the U.S. and Canada. She also researched, wrote, illustrated, and published a series of educational "map posters," which were highly successful in both the retail and school markets. The coin Sue designed for Colorado's Centennial, through an act of congress, became the first commemorative medallion ever minted in a U.S. mint (in Denver). She also designed Colorado's commemorative Bicentennial coin, produced by the Franklin Mint. She retired her business in 1996 and moved with her husband to Western Colorado, where they now reside.